I0679000

Blood Sea Tales
Book Four

Ash Walker

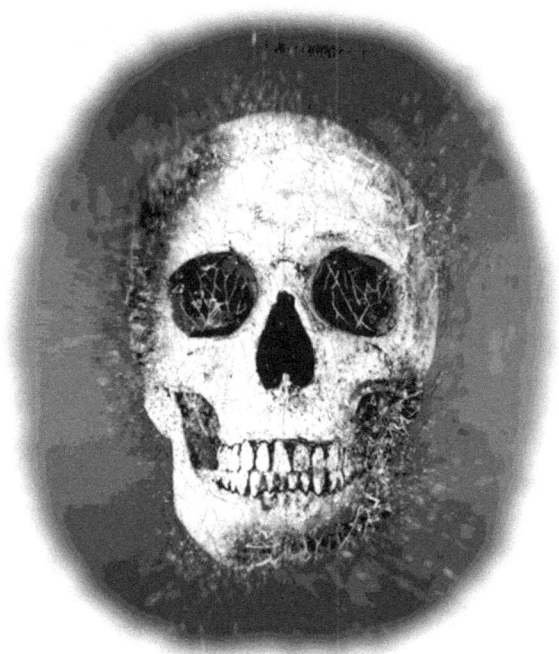

Chris A. Jackson

This is a work of fiction. Names, characters, places, and incidents are the products of the author's imagination. Any resemblances to actual persons, living or dead, events, or locales are coincidental.

Copyright © 2021 by Chris A. Jackson

All rights reserved. No part of this book may be reproduced or used in any manner without written permission of the copyright owner except for the use of quotations in a book review.

Published May 2021 by Jaxbooks Publishing

Cover design by Fiona Jayde

Interior art from Wikimedia used under creative commons licensing

Title page art from Pixibay by
Amir Boucenna

ISBN 978-1-939837-28-8 (paperback)
ISBN 978-1-939837-29-5 (ePub)
ISBN 978-1-939837-30-1 (Mobi)

jaxbooks.com

Acknowledgements

As always, thanks to my wife, Anne, for her help, patience,
and passion for the world we have created together.

Thanks to fashion photographer Cameron-James Wilson for
creating the digital model Shudu Gram, which inspired Hashi Severn.
To view this inspiring piece of art, go to
https://www.facebook.com/DigitalShudu/photos/a.183396392291
461/705427226755039/

A special thanks to those who have enjoyed the first three
volumes in this series.
Rest assured, the captain and crew of *Scourge* will return

This novel is dedicated to all of us who have lost loved ones to the
dreadful pandemic of 2020-2021.
May we have the courage to live on.

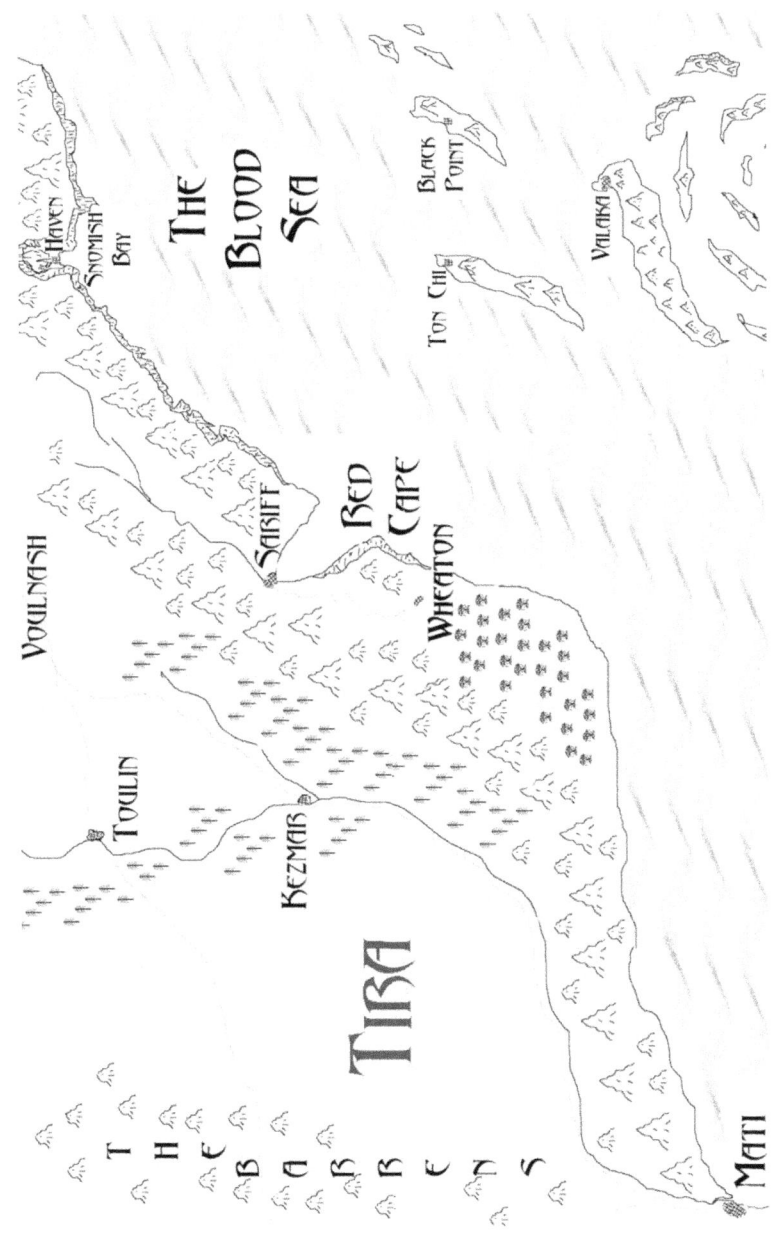

Chapter One
A Party to Remember

From the journal of Hashi Severn –

I've never been one to socialize. In fact, I may have crafted the practice of being alone into an art form. The dead are the only company I need.

May all the demons in the Nine Hells torment Teris Balshi for eternity, I cursed silently as my carriage pulled to a stop before the palace that pompous ass called home. We were one in a line of many, all but mine escorted by outriders. Peering out the window, I watched as the elaborate conveyances disgorged lords, ladies, and entourages in floods of fluff and finery. *Why would he throw a formal ball for Jhavika Keshmir? No one else got one when they joined the Council of Lords.*

Because he never tires of showing everyone how much money he has.

The comment didn't come from the grim wraith sitting beside me, my pale escort. He didn't speak unless I wanted him to, and certainly couldn't hear my thoughts. The voice was in my head. Only ever in my head.

My carriage rumbled forward. Several footmen waited to help guests disembark. Their eyes widened as they recognized my ebon carriage and four matching black horses. After a momentary hesitation, one summoned the courage to stride forward. His face a mask of propriety and calm, the servant opened the door and extended a white-gloved hand to help me down.

"Lady Severn."

I placed a hand in his, the contrast of my ebony skin against his ivory glove reminding me of the black and white of a chess board. *Chill of fear...just a touch,* I thought, and watched the blood drain from the man's face. Swallowing hard, his eyes twitched toward the bodice of my gown. I knew he wasn't eying my cleavage, but the enchanted dagger that rested there, cool obsidian and human bone against my skin—Soul Drinker, my constant companion, my comfort and my curse.

I stepped down and released the poor footman's hand, confident that he'd have a story to tell about me. Word of my mystique would spread.

He staggered back and gestured toward the foyer. "W...welcome."

I think you made him piss himself, Hashi.

A lady's got to maintain her reputation, I replied silently.

I tugged on the silver chain that led to the collar girding my escort's neck. The wraith stepped dutifully from the carriage, and the footman took another step back. Though I'd visited Balshi Keep many times, I'd never brought a wraith as my escort, and they're rather frightful to behold. He looked human, but bone-white and hairless, with obsidian-black teeth and black-on-black eyes. He'd *been* human once, but had tried to kill me, and there was only one consequence for that kind of behavior.

The hissing roar of the nearby waterfall filled my ears, and the very flagstones quaked beneath my feet. Shivering as the chill mist clung to my skin, I wondered how anyone could live with that relentless noise and damp. I strode up the stairs toward the foyer of Balshi's palace, head high, my wraith at my heels. From the corner of my eye, I spied an incongruous figure standing to one side of the lofty entrance.

That's Jhavika's pirate, Longbright.

Even though I pretended to ignore him, an image formed in my mind's eye—sharp, detailed, and outside from my line of sight—of the man watching me pass with an appraising eye. He struck me as both dangerous and interesting, every inch the pirate despite the finery he wore, from his scarred face to his flinty eyes, lean and hard, but attractive in an 'I'd just as soon gut you as look at you' sort of way.

We could have posed as 'don't fuck with me' bookends.

I wondered at his presence here. Captain Kevril Longbright was supposed to be out on the sea recruiting pirates into Haven's incipient privateer navy, a long-overdue step to secure the city's one vulnerability. If Jhavika had kept him in port merely to act as her escort tonight, she was being selfish. We needed him at sea, not attending balls.

Inside, I followed the directions of more footmen. My slinky gown swished against my legs as I climbed the sweeping stairway; I don't wear long dresses often and found the cool caress both pleasurable and distracting. Liveried guards stood at attention along a long hallway. *Lord Balshi's showing off his soldiery.*

Lambs for the slaughter, said the voice with cold humor.

Shut up, I growled mentally. *We're not slaughtering anyone tonight.*

*You always ruin my fun. It *is* a party, after all.*

I don't have much luck with parties.

*Relax. This one couldn't *possibly* go as poorly as the last one.*

Says the dead necromancer who's been to exactly one party in his entire existence.

I've been to hundreds of parties.

Ones that didn't involve human sacrifice?

That's just cruel, Hashi.

What can I say? I'm just a heartless bitch sometimes.

Sometimes? A chuckle rattled through my head like hail on a roof.

Shut up, old man, I thought without rancor as I brushed my fingers along the obsidian dagger at my breast. Ironically, and contrary to common belief, I *wasn't* a necromancer. All my power derived from Soul Drinker, or, rather, Saraknyal, the true necromancer whose soul resided within. I suppressed a smile. Saraknyal might be dead, but he still had a sense of humor...sort of.

Though Balshi's soldiery didn't impress me, the ballroom certainly did, and I had to keep myself from gaping. Big enough to serve as a dragon's lair, the soaring chamber gleamed in the light of innumerable glow crystals suspended by silver chandeliers. The radiance glinted off of soaring stained glass windows, and shimmering marble floors. The crowd of partygoers flitted about like tropical birds clad in rainbow plumage, chattering loudly, accepting offers of food and drink from an army of maids and footmen.

"Wine, Lady Severn?" A footman proffered a tray of crystal glasses.

"Please." I took one.

The footman evidently knew better than to offer one to my wraith escort, but merely bowed and said, "The guest of honor will be arriving soon. Lord Balshi would appreciate a round of polite applause."

"Of course he would." I showed him my teeth and sipped—the wine was quite good—before strolling further into the cavernous room. The crowd subtly shifted, trying to avoid the necromancer in the room without *seeming* to. That was fine with me; I wasn't much for small talk. Gazing around, my eyes sought out my fellow council members.

Nearby, Ursula Roque beamed, clutching the arm of a dashing young man who looked vaguely familiar. She spoke with Lord Malchi, and I saw the resemblance; Ursula's escort was his youngest son. *Forging alliances?* I wondered, then rejected the thought. The elder Malchi looked less than pleased at his son's choice of company, and Ursula was rubbing his nose in it. There was no love lost between the members of the Haven Council of Lords.

Roque's wearing that damned magical rapier, Saraknyal warned.

Really? I lowered my gaze to the sword at Ursula's hip. She regularly wore the weapon to council meetings, but I hadn't expected her to wear it here. The green scabbard and gleaming emerald on the pommel matched her outfit so perfectly that I'd barely noticed she was armed.

Beyond them, Lady Hatsu stood among her entourage, wearing a splendid kimono of red and gold. With her face painted like a kabuki doll, and the komei bodyguards' grim masks concealing their features, they displayed a dramatic tableau of Toki royalty.

I hate komei, Saraknyal groused.

You hate everything, old man. Enchanted weapons made Saraknyal nervous, and komei blades were legendary. Even necromancers weren't invincible.

Speaking of things I hate, Tori Blackbriar's wearing that gods-damned elf blade he favors. An image flashed into my mind of Tori on the other side of the room, kissing the hand of a fetching young woman on another man's arm. As usual, his libido superseded his good sense. He had a reputation with women.

I smiled wryly, despairing for the more gullible members of my sex. *Another broken heart in the making.* Emptying my wineglass, I signaled a footman for another. Balshi might be a pretentious ass, but he had good taste in wine. I sipped and relaxed a bit, surprising myself. Maybe this wouldn't be as bad as I'd anticipated. I looked around, scrutinizing the architecture. History and the unknown were passions of mine, and this palace was both. No one knew who had built it or why, for the city of Haven had originally been founded and built by gnomes, and this building wasn't gnomish in the slightest.

My roving gaze fell on Nahli Twince. The uncanny fae gave me a cordial nod, and I returned it.

*And don't even get me started on *her*. Fae magic is totally—*

Saraknyal, stop! I let annoyance tinge my thoughts. *This isn't a battlefield! Your paranoia—*

My paranoia keeps you alive!

I understand that, but if I have to be here, I'm at least going to try to enjoy myself. Unless there's an unsheathed enchanted blade or wizard casting a spell, just please keep quiet.

The sudden silence in my head seethed with resentment, but my attention was drawn away as the hall hushed. At the entry stood Jhavika and her pirate captain. Everyone moved away from the center aisle as if by some unspoken command, and the room erupted in polite applause. I handed my wineglass over to my silent escort and joined in. I had to admit they looked good together, sharp-eyed hawks, birds of a feather.

I recovered my wine as the applause subsided and finished it while our host regaled us with gratuitous platitudes and toasts to our newest council member. I caught a footman as the speech ended and took another glass of wine. I wasn't trying to impress anyone tonight, and Saraknyal could purge any toxin or intoxicant at a whim. Who knew necromancers didn't get hangovers?

The crowd milled about once again as servers circulated with trays of tidbits. I snagged a canapé, nibbled on it, and decided that Balshi's chef could use a few lessons. I decided to stick with the wine. As the crowd around Jhavika thinned, I deposited my empty glass on a wandering footman's tray and strolled forward. Paying my respects to the guest of honor wasn't optional, and I might as well get it over with.

"Congratulations again, Jhavika." I held out a hand to her, noting her slight reticence to take it. I'd shaken her hand once before, and she remembered. *Good.* "Your gown is quite fetching; gold is your color."

"And yours, Hashi, is quite...*revealing.* It suits you perfectly." She smiled sweetly.

I acknowledged her double entendre with a nod. "Thank you." I'd taken great pains in creating a gown that would enhance my mystique. The mildly enchanted silk—black as midnight, of course—not only hugged me like a second skin, but displayed my skeletal structure from all angles. I'd probably never get a chance to wear it again, given my avoidance of social functions, but damn, I looked good. I spotted Lord Balshi approaching, wished Jhavika well, and disengaged. I had no desire to talk to him.

Oh, and Jhavika's wearing her magical scourge.

No surprise there. As Jhavika turned to greet our host, I noted the scourge cunningly coiled at the bustle of her gown. She seemed to rarely go out without it, much like Tori with his elf blade, Roque with her rapier, and me with Soul Drinker. What a paranoid bunch we were.

Music from a string quartet filled the air, and the crowd shifted to the edges of the room as couples advanced onto the dance floor. I watched them for a while. The dance was nothing like those I remembered from my homeland of Mati—slow, serpentine undulations, graceful performance art. Rather, these dancers clung to one another and followed strict patterns and synchronized steps. Still, it was a pretty sight as they whirled and twirled in a continuum of color and motion. Charmed by the display, and more than a little mellowed by the wine, I found myself swaying slightly.

"They're beautiful, are they not?"

I started to find Nahli Twince and her two fox-masked escorts nearby. The fae always unnerved me a little, with her fathomless golden eyes and uncanny scrutiny.

"My mother was a dancer," I replied without thinking, immediately cursing myself for the slip. I may have been a historian, but my personal history was not one I willingly shared.

Nahli eyed me speculatively and nodded. "I imagine you take after her. You have a dancer's grace. Do you—"

"I don't dance." My retort was sharper than I'd intended. I don't talk about my mother or dancing; the pain of those memories is still too great, even after all these years.

Nahli ignored my impolite tone and turned to wave over a footman. Her gown, completely covered in white feathers, rustled with her movement. Her two escorts eyed me from behind their masks. They struck me as rather creepy, though I supposed the same could be said of my wraith. *To each her own.* We helped ourselves to fresh glasses of wine.

To dispel the awkward silence, I nodded toward the dance floor. "There's an odd couple."

"Lord Temuso and Captain Longbright." Nahli's head tilted slightly as she followed my gaze, watching as Temuso laughed and clutched the captain tight. "They seem very friendly."

"They do, and Jhavika seems not to like it." The guest of honor stood on the sidelines, red-faced and glaring daggers at her escort.

"Humans are strange." Nahli sounded puzzled rather than derisive.

"Are we?" I regarded her. I knew little about fae other than that they were inherently magical creatures and that their souls were of no use to necromancers. The Jungles of Nin were the fae homeland, or, at least, had been until the God-Emperor of Toki invaded in an attempt to harvest fae magic for his own. Nahli had fled to Haven to avoid capture. Thousands of others hadn't escaped. I'd often wondered if the god-emperor fed on magic as necromancers fed on human souls. "Do fae not play games of jealousy and possessiveness?"

"No, we don't. For people are not possessions." She looked at me, then shifted her gaze to my pale companion. "And souls are not playthings."

*No, they're *food!** Saraknyal snapped.

I'd wondered how long he would be able to hold his tongue. I understood his wrath with the fae's provocative insinuation, but I wasn't about to get into a discussion with Nahli about the morality of necromancy. Not here, and probably not ever. You'd think that a fae would have suffered enough prejudice not to pass it on. I'd done what I'd done to protect myself. If that damned me to the Nine Hells, I'd have a lot of company.

I smiled thinly and sipped my wine. As good as the drink was, I needed something stronger. I wondered if they had brandy, and looked around for a footman.

Hashi! Saraknyal bellowed, even as the crowd around me shifted.

Before I could react, a scene flashed into my mind: Jhavika, doubled over and staggering back from Longbright, a ruby-hilted dagger in his fist.

"What the *hell?*" I whirled to watch. Couples gasped and backed away from the pair, blocking some of my view.

He attacked her! Saraknyal said. *Tried to knife her in the gut. Her corset must be armored.*

The dagger's gem glistened like blood as Longbright advanced and slashed. Jhavika spun under his stroke and lashed out with the whip she wore at her back. Longbright blocked the stroke, the barbed lashes leaving lines of blood on his hand.

"Stop, Kevril!" Jhavika gasped.

To my shock, he did. For a moment, Longbright stood like a statue, his eyes wide with terror.

Hashi! There's magic afoot! Some kind of spell!

Beside me, Nahli gasped and backed away. The stunned dancers formed a circle around the dueling pair. Taller than most, I could see clearly, and Saraknyal's uncanny hearing rendered every word audible in my mind, despite the babble of the crowd.

Jhavika grinned in triumph. "Kevril Longbright, cut your own throat. Cut it to the bone!"

To my shock, Longbright raised the dagger toward his own throat. Then he flipped the blade and threw it at Jhavika's face. She dodged, but the weapon left a line of blood on her cheek.

"I'm *immune!*" the pirate growled. "And you're dead!"

Immune? I wondered, but my curiosity took a back seat to wonder as Longbright lunged to the attack. No one attempted to interfere. If Jhavika had somehow pissed off her escort, that was her problem.

"Vakna!" Jhavika cried out.

She's dead, Saraknyal predicted. *Her bodyguard's on the other side of the room.*

I agreed. I'm no warrior, but I've seen enough violence to recognize when someone's outmatched.

"Help me! He's gone mad. Friends, to my aid! Save me!"

Like that's going to happen. Jhavika apparently misunderstood the Council; the members were crime lords and exiles, after all, not friends.

Then Longbright grappled Jhavika's cat-o'-nine-tails, jerked her forward, and slashed right through her wrist, her severed hand still clinging to the haft of the scourge. Jhavika fell backward, and Longbright lunged in for the death stroke.

That's that. I thought it was over.

I was wrong.

My mouth fell open as Ursilla Roque and Getashi Temuso's crossed swords deflected Longbright's killing thrust. They all froze for an instant, and the looks of astonishment on the council members' faces struck me dumb.

Something's not right here, Saraknyal said, and I had to agree.

"Kill him!" Jhavika screamed, and her protectors lunged to the attack.

"Kevril! Run!" Temuso yelled, his features contorted in anguish even as he slashed at the captain.

He attacks Longbright, then tells him to run? *What the hell?*

Parrying masterfully, Longbright disengaged and dashed for the end of the hall. Guests dodged out of his way even as Balshi's guards closed in. I thought he was doomed, but he moved like a jaguar darting through a forest of steel. I could see how he'd survived so long as a pirate through the chaos of ship-borne battle. When he vaulted from Balshi's dais to smash through the stained-glass wall behind it, then leapt out into the night from the balcony rail, I had to bite back a bark of laughter.

Damn, he's good.

A hundred feet to the lake, Saraknyal observed. *I wonder if he'll survive the fall.*

Jhavika's screamed command silenced the cacophony of exclamations.

"All my allies, protect me! Brilla, your time is now! Take your place! The Queen of Haven commands her vassals to carry out their final orders! Strike down your lords and come to me!"

Queen of Haven? What the ever-loving fuck?

All Nine Hells broke loose.

Hashi! Images slammed into my mind's eye, fast and furious: blades, blood, death…

Beside me, Nahli clapped her hands and burst into the air as a huge white eagle, winging for the door. Her twin escorts, now revealed as actual fox-faced changelings, dashed and slashed behind her. The crowd of guests all fought their way toward the exit and escape. Some made it, many didn't.

And…I was alone. Well, not quite alone. My wraith stood impassively beside me, his black eyes scanning the area for threats, ready to defend me.

Now, this is my kind of party! Saraknyal quipped.

I gazed around at the blood-drenched marble floor strewn with bodies, felt the cool, misty breeze blowing in through the shattered stained-glass window. *What the hell just* happened?

Then my gaze fell on Jhavika. She stood clutching her severed wrist, surrounded by a cordon of steel. Though her features were contorted in pain, her eyes were fixed on me…on Soul Drinker.

Don't do it, I thought, *don't you dare*, but she evidently couldn't hear my thoughts.

"Vakna, kill Lady Severn and bring me Soul Drinker."

Shit just got serious, Saraknyal said.

I stared at Jhavika's mountainous bodyguard as he strode forth, and quirked a little smile of disbelief. *Really?* Jhavika Keshmir obviously didn't know who she was fucking with. With a flick of my hand, I released the chain restraining my wraith.

He stalked toward Vakna without the slightest hesitation, clawed fingers twitching in anticipation. Deflecting Vakna's first blow, the wraith lashed out to rip a handful of flesh from his opponent's face. Captain Vakna, however, proved much quicker than his size suggested, and spun to sweep my wraith's legs off at the knees. Black blood flooded across the white floor, but mere mortal wounds couldn't deter the immortal, and the wraith fought on, swiping and biting at the captain. Vakna's sword slashed away the attacks, reducing my undead warrior to twitching body parts.

That was my best wraith! I slipped Soul Drinker from its sheath, hoarfrost riming the bared blade as its power chilled my blood. *If he ruins this dress, I'm going to mount Jhavika's head on a plaque.*

Don't you think you should take this more seriously? Saraknyal warned.

Not unless there's something you're not telling me. I watched Vakna approach, my eyes fixed on his huge broadsword. *Should I be worried?*

About him? Not really. His sword is mere steel, but Roque and that komei pose serious threats.*

Then I guess I better make a good impression.

Vakna raised the sword for a cross-body slash, doubtless intending to slice me from shoulder to hip.

I lifted my empty hand as if to catch the razor-edged length of steel. *Dust to dust.* Necromantic energy flared as metal met flesh, aging the fine steel ten thousand years in an instant. Instead of blood, a cloud of rust puffed and settled to the floor.

Shock flashed across Jhavika's features.

Surprise, bitch!

Vakna stumbled, unbalanced by the sudden loss of his weapon, and I flicked out with Soul Drinker. The obsidian edge sliced through the shoulder of his dress tunic and the chainmail beneath as if the armor was paper. His flesh parted barely the depth of my fingernail, but it was enough.

Feed.

White mist trailed out of the wound and curled about Soul Drinker, dragged into the obsidian like indrawn smoke. Vakna wailed in terror and collapsed to his knees, his mouth gaping, his eyes fixed in horror as Saraknyal devoured his soul. Power surged through me as soul essence transformed into necromantic energy, a sensation both intoxicating and disturbing.

The trail of mist petered out. Though still upright, Vakna wasn't just dead; his soul had been consumed, gone, utterly and forever. No afterlife, no heaven, no hell...nothing.

Nothing but power.

Winter.

Vakna's skin color paled from gray to blue as the chill of all the dead souls in the deepest vault of Necrol froze him into a pillar of petrified flesh. I kicked it to the ground, shattering Vakna into a million pieces.

First impressions are so important...

Slaughter them all, Hashi, Saraknyal hissed in my mind. *Take their souls! Take this palace for your own! Take all of Haven!*

The suggestion was tempting—retribution for all those murdered tonight—but Saraknyal wasn't suggesting revenge; the necromancer was an addict, pure and simple, and his drug was human souls. I understood, the power was intoxicating, but oh the *price*. I fed him only enough to keep me safe. It was the only way I could live with myself.

We do this my way, old man. Arching an eyebrow, I pointed Soul Drinker straight at the deranged woman who sought to be Queen of Haven and said, "Do not vex me, Jhavika."

Behind me, from the dais, Brilla Balshi cried out shrill and hysterical. "Say the word, my love, and I'll have the witch riddled with arrows!"

"My love?" Well that's interesting.

Jhavika glanced in Brilla's direction, and I could almost see the gears in her mind turning, calculating, analyzing. If she didn't take my warning to heart, things would get ugly very quickly. *Do the math, Jhavika. You can't win.*

Looking back at me with an indifferent expression, Jhavika said, "No. Let her go. I have no need of her."

No need of me? I smiled coldly at Jhavika and was rewarded with a quick spasm of fear in her eyes.

Fear...such a valuable weapon.

Turning my back on her, I passed by my dismembered wraith. I couldn't just leave him in pieces like that. I allowed Saraknyal to feed upon its mangled soul, a pitiful meal after Vakna's robust essence. The twitching corpse stilled, the pale flesh darkening.

I strode from the ballroom as if I hadn't a care in the world, as if I hadn't just destroyed a man's soul. As if my entire life hadn't just turned upside down...again.

Chapter Two
Ashes to Ashes

The secret to life is a good pair of boots.

I glanced back over my shoulder at the mountain pass I'd just traversed, stamping my feet to shed the snow that lingered on the well-worn leather. Three days through ice and across scree, yet my feet remained warm, dry, and unblistered. I'd paid a pretty penny for the boots back in Mati, the city-state of my birth, but I considered that a good investment.

Turning back, I gazed south across the vast grasslands of the former Empire of Tinaros. It had once been a rich and powerful nation, its modest villages, thriving cities, and vast plantations home to millions of citizens. Now I was likely the only human being within its borders. The current residents of this land loathed humans and didn't usually allow them access. But I'd been here before, and we had an understanding.

At least I hoped we did.

Don't start second guessing yourself, Hashi! I adjusted my pack straps and trekked on downhill at an easy pace until I reached the tree line. The uneven footing forced me to focus, drowning out my nagging conscience.

Upon reaching the scraggly pines, I shrugged off my pack. The sun still shone high, but it would be too dangerous to continue without permission. I cleared a patch of ground, arranged a circle of stones, and collected dead wood for a fire, picking out some pieces still wet enough to send up smoke. I lit it the tinder and blew gently on it until small flames caught, then fed it until it burned hot enough to add the wet wood. Smoke rose into the sky above the scrubby trees. The locals preferred the lowlands to the wooded foothills, but my fire wouldn't go unnoticed. They watched the passes constantly, and never failed to meet intruders.

Snapping open my blanket and settling it on the ground, I laid out my gear: bow and quiver—more for defense than hunting, though I'd only seen mountain goats and deer over the pass, not any of the stealthy mountain cats—two hunting knives, tools, compass, rope, waxed map case, thin cord for setting snares, and climbing gear. These items, though essential to my survival, I knew wouldn't interest my hosts. Even so, I didn't want to give them any reason to deny my entry. Foremost I meticulously positioned my trade goods, payment for the privilege of being allowed to plunder this country.

Well, plunder wasn't really the word for it. Acquiring historical artifacts was how I preferred to think of my trade. The wealthy patriarchs of Mati loved to bedeck their homes in shiny antiquities and fancy themselves scholarly. I put food in my mouth and a roof over my head by providing said antiquities. Sometimes I cringed at selling a piece when the buyer didn't appreciate the history behind it, but in the end, this was my job. Ancient civilizations and their artifacts fascinated me, and I'd spent a good deal of the last ten years reading history—my one true indulgence. Hence the draw of Tinaros, an empire of ruins virtually untouched by human hands for the last half millennia. The vanquishers of this land didn't care for the trinkets hidden beneath the stones of fallen cities. In fact, they were happy to have me take them away. The fewer remnants of humans left in their land, the better, as far as they were concerned.

Consequently, when my mentor Gunyan found reference to a likely trove in the far reaches of Tinaros, I was eager to be off, despite the hardships of such a long and arduous journey. I'd probably spend a month on this single excursion, but the potential payoff could be worth a fortune.

The thought sent chills of anticipation up my spine that had nothing to do with the biting breeze blowing off the mountain peaks. I sat and fed my fire, staring into the flames, focusing on my pending inspection to keep my mind from wandering down dangerous paths.

I heard my expected visitors long before I saw them. They weren't trying to be quiet, and weren't particularly stealthy in the first place. The troop shuffled around the scrubby trees, bobbing up and down as they scrutinized me. I kept my hands out and open and my mouth shut.

The roo are startling to behold at first, even humorous with their bounding gaits and curious countenances, but thinking of them as slightly comical aboriginal herbivores is a deadly mistake. Just because someone's a vegetarian doesn't mean they're a pacifist. The roo are intelligent, fast, deadly warriors—faster than horses in open country, and far more agile—and wield potent magic.

After about half an hour scrutinizing me, they suddenly erupted in a ululating cry and charged from all sides, bounding fifteen feet at a single hop. They stopped barely ten feet away, lance tips pointed at me, boomerangs and bolas poised, their small eyes wide, watching me for any move.

I sat perfectly still.

Finally, one of them jostled to the fore. I could tell he was male by the lack of an abdominal pouch, and that he was their leader by his ornamentation and paint. Though his hands were empty, weapons hung from the two woven-grass baldrics that crossed over his chest. He looked me over, then at the array of items lying on the blanket. Finally, he bobbed his head and sat back on his tail, a relaxed posture that settled the entire troop.

"Ash Walker, you come again to take away things from the land."

It wasn't a question, but I knew the proper response and enough of their language to give it. My research into the roo and respect for their culture were undoubtedly why they allowed me passage upon their lands. Ash Walker was the name they had bestowed upon me during my first visit, when they found me sifting through the ashes of a ruin. It seemed appropriate in more ways than one.

"With the permission of the roo, yes, and to leave the land as I found it."

The roo believe that the land is sacred, a living thing greater than the creatures that live upon it. I'm not convinced they're wrong. The former human denizens of Tinaros certainly learned not to tell them so.

"And what do you offer for this privilege?"

"Anything I have here." I swept a hand over the blanket, emphasizing those items I knew they coveted. "The black stone of the islands, glass for ornaments, colors for your paints, and seeds of the fire plants."

As one, the roo leaned closer to admire the offerings. The obsidian they knapped into weapons and tools. The glass would make beads or amulets, and the dyes would paint their fur. Most highly prized, though, were the seeds. The roo don't practice agriculture exactly, but they sow the seeds of preferred plants about the landscape. They love hot peppers, and I'd brought a number of varieties.

The leader grunted and poked a few of the items. "No fire water?"

"No." I'd learned my lesson about bringing them alcohol. They get aggressive when intoxicated, and a drunken roo is a threat to life and limb.

He grunted again, then bobbed his head. "How long will you walk the land, and where will you go?"

"I'll walk for one face of the moon. Let me show you where." I delved my case and withdrew a small-scale map of Tinaros. I traced a river with a finger. "I'll travel to the great water path, then cross here where it's shallow, and climb into the high mountains to ruins here." I tapped a symbol labeled 'Tawkh Keep' in my own language. Gunyan's research suggested that it had been the home of a powerful ruler, and rich people had all the best stuff.

The roo blinked at the map. "Bad place."

"Yes." All remaining ruins of men were deemed bad places by the roo. "If I find things there, I'll take them away, back to the lands of men so they will no longer poison this land."

He grunted and motioned two others forward, both females with large abdominal pouches. One pouch contained a joey, which poked its head out to look at me, big ears flapping. The two females gathered up the proffered trade goods and stuffed them into their pouches. Immediately, the joey ducked down to rummage through the trinkets.

"You will only take away the works of humans," the leader commanded. "You will take plants and animals only for your own

17

food. You will leave nothing behind. You will build no walls, dig no holes, burn no living wood or grass. We will watch you. We will inspect all that you take with you when you go."

"Yes," I agreed, bobbing my head.

"If you speak false, you will die, Ash Walker."

"Yes, if I speak false, I will die."

The leader grunted, bobbed his head, and ululated that piercing cry once again. In a cloud of dust, the troop bounded off downhill, their musky scent lingering on the breeze. I smothered my fire and packed up my things. The meeting couldn't have gone better, and I was eager to be on my way. I'd filled my waterskins in the pass, and wouldn't find more until I reached the river.

As I reached easier ground and warmer temperatures, I paused to doff my warmer clothes and donned a light linen shirt and short pants. Turing to the southeast, I focused on the distant peaks of the Iron Wall Mountains and started walking.

One. Two. Three. I counted my steps more to keep my mind occupied than to calculate my progress. My idle mind would quickly spiral into dark places.

Step by step, with a tight leash on my thoughts and my sight focused straight ahead, I strode toward my destination and whatever treasures awaited me.

With long legs and muscles as hard as oak, I set a steady pace, eating salty jerky and trail bread without stopping. *1700 steps per mile, 120 steps per minute, 7200 steps per hour, just over four miles per hour.* I'd walked a lot over the last few years, over some of the roughest terrain surrounding Mati. The hot, dry air fairly sucked the moisture from my flesh, but I drank sparingly from my waterskin. My body would reach an equilibrium, sweating only as much as I needed to keep from baking alive.

I walked on as the sky darkened from blue to cobalt slashed with crimson. Not too far ahead I spotted ruins, and quickened my pace. I dare not walk in the dark. I might step into a prairie dog burrow, and the jackals that hunted the grasslands in packs might try for larger prey if injured. I doubted anything would bother me during the night, but I'd sleep with my back to a wall if I could, and a knife in my hand nonetheless. As if in communion with my thoughts, a jackal yowled in the twilight.

I reached the ruined plantation house before night fully enclosed the landscape. There wasn't a lot left of the place, just a foundation of cut stone and a few timbers charred to ashes and rotted away. I camped in the corner of two collapsed walls, starting a fire from dead grass and scraps of wood. While I waited for a small pot of water to heat for tea, I delved my pack for the one item I'd hidden from the roo, a glow crystal. It's a simple device that can barely be categorized as magical, but invaluable to my investigations of historic ruins, smaller and much easier to carry than torches. I tapped it twice with a fingernail, and said, "Moonlight." It flared to a low pearly glow, and I set out exploring.

I looked for the well and found it, but it was filled in, undoubtedly by the roo. They viewed such thing as injuries to the land. I sighed in disappointment. The roo had not only exterminated every human in the empire of Tinaros, but had largely dismantled every structure that marred the land.

Proceeding with care to avoid hidden cellars or pits, I poked around with the toe of my boot, not expecting to find anything worthwhile. I dredged up a few pot shards and rusted metal tools, nothing of value. Amidst a pile of loose refuse, however, my light glinted upon a white porcelain bowl that seemed largely intact. Crouching down to examine it, I turned the bowl over. It was, in fact, a human skull. A small skull. A child's skull. I put it back exactly as I'd found it, rubbing my hand on my pant leg.

Bounded on three sides by mountains and on the fourth by the sea, the nation of Tinaros had been insular from the start. Early settlers had quickly built towns and cities, spread intensive agriculture, irrigated the grasslands, mined the mountains, and dammed the river. Unfortunately for the Tinarans, what they considered the expansion of civilization, the roo considered a profane injury to the earth. The Tinarans' greatest mistake, however, was in underestimating the roo.

The roo are mild-mannered herbivores, social and gregarious among themselves. They're loving parents, artists, stewards of the land, and story tellers. They have no writing, their long, intricate history passed from generation to generation by word of mouth. A few non-roo have attempted to unwind the tapestry of roo stories to determine fact from fiction, but none have thus far succeeded. I once read a frustrated account by one historian; "Roo history," he'd complained, "depends on which roo you talk to."

So, since history is written by the winners and the roo don't write, much remains unknown about the genocidal war they waged against the Tinarans. The few Tinaran survivors told stories of massacres, plantation-consuming fires, and weapons empowered by earth magic that toppled buildings. Those who sought refuge in the open were slaughtered. Afterwards, entire cities had been torn apart, stone by stone, and returned to the earth.

I settled down by my fire for a meager dinner, sipping tea and eating hard cheese and trail bread, staring up at the stars and listening to the night sounds. I took off my boots and rubbed my feet. Although physically tired, I wasn't yet sleepy. I hadn't brought anything to read, for I couldn't afford the added weight. I peered out into the night. Not one light shone, not one voice spoke in this land devoid of human life.

I contemplated the child's skull I'd found, someone's son or daughter. Had they been happy here? Had their parents loved them, held them, promised that everything would be all right as the roo set fire to their home? Had their mother told them that she loved them even as they burned?

Mothers are supposed to love their children, aren't they?

For a moment I pictured my own mother: tall and graceful, beautiful...disgruntled, resentful, and hateful. I closed my eyes and began trembling, my limbs shuddering uncontrollably, my teeth chattering, but not from the cold. Evenings were always the worst for me, with nothing to do but think, remember, despair...

Curling into a ball, my mind cast about frantically for something—anything—to latch onto and banish the wrenching memories. I clenched my eyes tight against the hot tears that stung my eyes. I couldn't afford them. I had two more days to the river, and I'd run out of water if I wasn't careful. If that happened, another archeologist would probably find my bones lying in a ruin somewhere.

I didn't even know who the tears were for: the child who had died here five hundred years ago, or the one whose mother wished she'd never been born.

My premonition nearly came true; I'd run out of water by the time I found the river. My throat sore, my skin dry, and my tongue scratchy from lack of moisture, I was sucking on a pebble when I mounted a low rise and spied the line of lush green. Laughing aloud—and nearly swallowing my pebble—I rushed forth. I dropped my pack at the shore, kicking off my boots and stripping out of my sweaty clothes before plunging into the cool, clear water. I languished for a while, drinking my fill and letting the water flow over my skin. When my fingers began to wrinkle and I started to shiver, I waded out and flopped down onto a soft bed of vegetation to bask in the sun, my dark skin soaking up the heat.

On impulse, I decided to take the rest of the day here to relax and recuperate.

I washed my clothes, fished, and scavenged the brushy shrubs that grew along the river bank for berries. My early dinner consisted of fresh fish, trail bread slathered with crushed berries, and cup after cup of wonderful, cool water. I whiled away the afternoon catching fish and drying them over a small fire to bolster my provisions.

The next day I forded the river and hiked southwest, paralleling the shore far enough to avoid anything that might come down from the mountains to drink. I saw antelope aplenty, and many small predators. I heard the roar of a mountain cat, but never saw any, though I spotted prints. They undoubtedly knew I was there.

For four days I followed the watercourse, regularly consulting my maps and drawings, hoping that the old texts were accurate. On the fifth day, I held up one of my sketches and grinned triumph; the contours of the mountainous horizon to the northwest matched the inked lines on the parchment.

I filled my waterskins until they were near bursting, drank as much water as I could, and set out in a precise northwesterly direction, excited to finally be in the final stretch. I had enough water and dried fish for six days, maybe seven. If I was lucky, I'd find a tributary or snow to replenish my water, and snare small game.

"Give me ten days," I pleaded to no particular god. If I could find the ruins of Tawkh Keep in three days, and make it back to the river in the same time, I'd have four glorious days to delve its secrets.

If the roo haven't reduced the keep to rubble. That dread taunted me, but I exiled it from my mind. Gunyan's research seemed solid, an account several decades old by an explorer who risked crossing the mountains from Fornice. We'd wracked our brains wondering why someone would build a keep way up in the mountains, far from the centers of population, trade, and government.

I honestly didn't care. Call me a grave robber if you like, but the dead have no need of money, and I did. One really good find was all I needed. The plutocracy of Mati had taught me that there are only two types of people: those who have money, and those who don't. Those who have it make the rules, and those who don't follow the rules. Money meant safety, security, and comfort. They also say that money can't buy you love, but I'd like to test that theory.

"One good find."

It became my mantra as I strode on, the words keeping time with my footsteps. One good find would change my life.

Chapter Three
Complications

From the journal of Hashi Severn –

Why are people never satisfied with what they have? Give someone a comfortable living, and they'll want a fortune. Give them a house, and they'll want a castle. Give them a city, and they'll want a kingdom. All I want is to be left alone.

The courtyard of Balshi's palace seethed in chaos. Carriages sped away into the night, retainers scrabbling to mount skittish horses, fights breaking out with Balshi guards. I managed to reach my own carriage without being run down.

Boarding quickly, I commanded the driver, "Bromish! Ash Keep, at once!"

"Yes, mistress!" With a crack of the whip, the coach lurched into motion.

Flinging myself onto the seat, I muttered what I'd been wondering since I left the ballroom. "What the hell just happened?"

Jhavika Keshmir lost her hand and her enchanted scourge, showed everyone how many very dedicated friends she has, tried to stage a coup, and attempted to kill you, Saraknyal said in my head. *Weren't you paying attention?*

Sarcasm doesn't become you. I glanced out the window to ensure that we weren't being followed by an army. *A gods-damned coup!* The delicate balance of power in Haven had just been thrown into a meat grinder, and I had to make some sense of it. *How did things get so fucking complicated?*

Well, first you developed an unhealthy fascination with history...

"Oh, shut the hell up, old man. I don't need your bullshit tonight. You've been fed, now be quiet for a few minutes, please."

Temper, temper, he chided before falling silent.

I realized my fist was still clutching the blade, the tingling power of soul essence igniting my nerve endings. I sheathed the weapon and forced a deep, calming breath.

It didn't help.

"How many?" The question had been whirling around my mind for the last half mile, and finally escaped.

How many what?

"How many council members were killed?" The quick images in the midst of all the chaos hadn't really registered.

Four. And if you can believe it, they were all murdered by their own retainers. Balshi's throat was slit by his sister. One of Lady Hatsu's komei decapitated his comrade, then cut her down. Fa-Chen and Blinth Tinworthy were spitted by their own guards.

"How did she *do* it?" I whispered. Jhavika was a low-level player in Haven, admitted to the Council only because of her nautical background and plan for establishing a navy to protect the city. "How could she control so many allies?"

Control? I don't know if that's the right term, exactly.

"It *is* the right term. You saw Roque and Temuso's faces when they saved her life. Like their minds had no idea what their bodies were doing."

Ahhh…

Ahhh what? What are you thinking?

Remember when she lashed Captain Longbright with that cat-o'-nine-tails?

Yes, of course.

I told you there was magic afoot.

Well, yes, it's a magical weapon.

No, like an enchantment being cast! A powerful one!

A spell? She lashes people, and the scourge casts a spell?

Just like you wield me and I cast spells. Yes.

Are you telling me that thing's a soul blade?

*No, my dear. Or at least, I don't think so. Many magical weapons cast spells when they strike. Usually pain, paralysis, or injury. But this one...I don't know."

Control! I suddenly realized. *Jhavika commanded Longbright to cut his throat!*

But he didn't.

No, but she expected *him to. He said he was immune. Immune to what? It* has *to be that scourge of hers. Nothing else makes sense!*

But he took it from her, Saraknyal reminded me. *How could she still control anyone if he took the means by which she controlled them?*

I don't know, but when she told her allies to murder their lords, they did, and she didn't have the scourge then. A gods-damned komei, Saraknyal. They're oath-bound to defend their charges.

They are. That's telling indeed. Their oaths are inviolate.

Until Jhavika violated them, I thought. *Roque, Temuso, Matesh, and Brilla Balshi all came to her aid. They must all be under her enchantment.* I stiffened when I considered the ramifications. *This is bad...*

Saraknyal's thoughts obviously ran along the same lines. *If she controls the council members, then she likely controls their houses, so that makes five for her, including her own.*

And Balshi's is the most powerful by far. Four dead council members, four enslaved by Jhavika, leaving five intact houses...if we're lucky. And potentially facing a magical weapon that could enslave us all. My breath hissed out between clenched teeth. *We are so fucked.*

We? Saraknyal's laughter chilled my blood. *I'm dead, my dear, and therefore unfuckable.*

Until Jhavika has her komei murder me and takes you. Or worse, gets that scourge back and lashes me with it. The thought of that kind of slavery made my blood run even colder.

There is that.

Maybe I should have killed her. That might have broken the spell.

You would have had to kill a komei and several lords to get to her, at least a couple of them with enchanted blades. You're lucky she didn't call your bluff. But that's in the past, my dear. We need to decide what to do now.*

I don't think she'll bide her time too long. She'll consolidate her forces and try to kill the other council members.

She'll be after Captain Longbright first. She may have many under her control, but I think we can safely assume that, without her scourge, she can't enslave any more. If he manages to sail out of Haven before she can kill him, she'll have to rely on a finite force that could potentially be whittled down.

"She'll go after him!" I agreed. "Though she doesn't have any ships."

She won't need ships if she can catch Longbright before he sets sail.

He had a point. If the scourge was indeed the source of Jhavika's power, she'd want it back at all costs. "She'll send soldiers to the quay. Keep him from reaching his ship, and she's won."

Unless someone else finds him first.

I nodded. "The enemy of my enemy…" Thumping hard on the roof of the carriage, I yelled, "Bromish! To the quay, as quick as you can manage!"

"Mistress! That's right through the center of the city, and we have no escort! We'll be mobbed!"

"Just do it!" I drew Soul Drinker and carefully slit the seam of my dress to my hip, then opened the coach door and clambered up to the driver's seat.

*Hashi! What the *hell* are you doing?*

Being proactive! I'd hated to ruin my dress, but though I might be invulnerable to weapons, falling off a moving carriage onto a cobblestone street could break my fool neck, and I had to be able to move.

Bromish started and stared at me like I'd grown horns and a tail. "Mistress!"

"Drive for the waterfront. I promise you, nobody will bother us."

He looked at the naked blade in my hand, then my naked leg, swallowed hard, and said, "Yes, mistress!" He hauled on the reins, and we careened around a corner, downhill into the morass of Haven.

Driving into that fetid mire of human suffering brought back a lot of memories, most bad. I hadn't always been rich and powerful. I'd lived down here once, and thanked all the gods that I'd gotten out.

The dregs of Haven saw a coach with no outriders and responded predictably. We were past the first mob before they could react. Others heard their shouts and catcalls and ventured out of their holes onto the street ahead of us. They hefted makeshift weapons: boards and bricks, a few knives, even a battered sword. One man started to swing a weighted net woven from rope over his head, aiming for my galloping horses.

Now, Saraknyal. Chill their blood for me.

Don't be so melodramatic, my dear.

Shut up and do it!

Magic swelled in me, and mirth bubbled from my chest. My throat stung as an icy torrent of terror rushed up, and a voice not my own burst forth in a peal of unearthly laughter, high-pitched and horrible. The sound of it saturated the night, drowning out every other sound, drenching the very air with its essence. *Fear...* The coach lamps fluttered and died, torches and lights in the buildings winked out, and the converging rabble quailed, dodging out of our way, shrinking back into the holes from whence they came, their confidence shattered.

The carriage lurched forward, and I had to clutch the seat to keep from falling off. Beside me, Bromish cowered in terror, his hands quaking on the reins while the horses tossed their heads and bolted across the cobbles, panicked.

In my zeal, I'd forgotten the horses and my driver. The fear spell couldn't be targeted. If the team blundered into a building, my brilliant plan would likely get us all killed. I rested a hand on Bromish's shoulder. "Steady on! Don't run us into a wall!"

"Yes, mistress!" Spittle flew from his lips, but I felt his trembling ease.

Bromish settled quickly. He knew I wasn't a monster, unlike those we left behind us curled fetal in the gutters, mired in their own shit and piss, terrified out of their minds. More shapes moved in ahead of us, and I let out another peal of icy mirth. They shrank back, and we thundered past untouched.

You have such a lovely voice, my dear. Music to my ears.

You don't have ears, old man.

You wound me, Hashi.

You're dead and quite beyond wounding. I gripped the blade and scanned the darkness ahead. Thankfully, the street remained relatively straight and clear, and our team seemed to have regained their wits. They were used to my presence, and less affected by the induced terror of my laugh than most horses would have been. Still, two of them had emptied their bowels.

The street widened and became slightly cleaner. We were nearing the waterfront.

"Easy now." I patted Bromish's shoulder. "Don't run us into the bay."

"Yes, mistress."

The wide quay opened up before us, and Bromish turned the coach, hauling back on the reins and calling to the horses. The team tossed their heads, but eased to a stop, lathered and heaving. I stood and scanned the long, stone waterfront.

No coaches, no boats, no people...no Captain Longbright. *Maybe we beat him here,* but I dismissed the thought. He'd obviously planned his attempt on Jhavika, and so would have planned an escape, likely have a boat waiting. *Where the hell...*

Cries from out on the water drew my attention to the bay. Lamps were lit on every moored ship, but one sported more lights than the others, illuminating sailors rushing along the deck and throughout the rigging. The clatter of a capstan and roaring calls of, "Topcrew aloft! Secure that boat! Tops'ls and tris'ls, you swabs!" gave me all the information I needed.

"That's got to be *Scourge*," I said.

And they wouldn't be setting sail without their captain, Saraknyal surmised. *He must have gotten here just before we did. He's a resourceful one.*

And tough as a keg of nails if he swam Mirror Lake, then ran through the city without getting cut to ribbons. I thought of the man I'd seen dancing with Temuso and wondered once again at his motives for trying to murder Jhavika. *But why in the Nine Hells did he do it? By all accounts, they'd been business partners for years.*

I believe that's what they call a falling out. Saraknyal chuckled and added, *Only he didn't fall, he jumped.*

I cringed at the abysmal joke. *That's what she gets for trusting anyone, I suppose.*

Or that's what he gets for trusting her, Saraknyal amended.

Valid point, I acceded. Who knew what had precipitated this evening's events.

"Pardon me, mistress, but what in all Nine Hells happened at that party?" Poor Bromish looked up at me in wide-eyed puzzlement. "Feller flew from a window, then everyone came runnin' out. Big bloody bird flew out the front door!"

"Jhavika Keshmir staged a coup." I pointed to the ship as sails unfurled. "That pirate started the whole damned thing."

And if he hadn't, Jhavika's machinations would have continued in secret.

"You're right about that," I mused.

"Mistress?" Bromish blinked up at me.

"Never mind, Bromish. Back to the keep. Sorry for the detour."

"Yes, mistress." He lashed the reins and urged our team around a corner into a dark street. "Might need that magic of yours again to get us safe home, though."

"Of course." I sat back down, mentally asking Saraknyal to lend me his magic once more.

*Of course, my dear, but you know, if you'd just allowed me to take a few more souls at that party, I'd have power enough for *real* defense, not the mere frightening of children.*

Shut up, I snapped mentally. *You fed tonight, be content with that.*

I shuddered at the lingering sensation of Vakna's soul surging through me. Saraknyal's disregard for the souls he consumed disgusted me, but I had to own up to the truth; I was his accomplice. I fed him to keep myself safe, destroyed souls to save my own. Gripping Soul Drinker hard as if to strangle the necromancer, I both cursed and blessed the day I found him.

Chapter Four
Delving Death

Who the hell *builds a keep halfway up a gods-damned mountain?*

I stopped and bent over, hands on knees, gasping for breath in the thin air, my legs numb from days of climbing. The first day after leaving the river had been an easy trek across the grasslands. The second day, the foothills steepened, and I made camp in high scrub forest. Since dawn I'd been trudging and scrabbling up the steep slope toward my goal, praying that the traveler's account of this misplaced keep was accurate.

Once again, I wore layers of clothes to ward off the biting wind that blew unceasingly across the rocky ground. I'd left the tree line far below. It seemed an impossible place to construct a keep. Dwarves built strongholds in such places, but from the inside out, generally from the remnants of mines. But dwarves also ate fungus, so I counted them as verifiably insane anyway.

As my heaving breaths eased, I straightened and shrugged my shoulders to loosen the muscles beneath my pack, squinting up at the sheer cliffs and the tangle of stone that was Tawkh Keep. I'd never seen anything like it. The structure resembled a haphazard jumble of gray stone jammed into the cleft of the mountainside with no apparent architectural or aesthetic sensibilities. I'd expected minarets or battlements, crenellations or bastions, but it sported none of those. There were a few high windows, but no arrow slits or defensive elements at all. The outer wall was uneven, as if great blocks of stone were simply stacked randomly at odd angles. Whoever had designed it must not have cared a whit for visual appeal, and hired a thousand gnomes addicted to black lotus to build it without supervision.

This didn't bode well. If the keep's lord hadn't had an aesthetic bone in their body, they probably wouldn't have left behind rooms full of treasure for me to loot. *If I came all this way and wasted a month of my life for nothing, I'll tear this place down myself.*

Crouching at an ice-crusted drift to scoop snow into my waterskins, I noted one other curious detail; despite its haphazard construction, the keep appeared undamaged. There were no signs of siege, assault, or the typical cracked stonework that bespoke of earth magic wielded by the roo.

"Bad place," the roo troop leader had said. Maybe they hadn't come here at all. *Too far up the mountains, or some other reason?* I wondered.

But I'd come all this way; there was no point in leaving without investigating.

A single main gate pierced the outer wall, partially obstructed by a portcullis that five hundred years had reduced to a rusted ruin. No crest identified who live here, who ruled this barren mountainside. *Curious indeed.* I'd seen a lot of ruins, and the one thing common to them all was some form of identification, a reflection of the ego that had created them.

Who the hell were you? I wondered.

Pulling out my glow crystal and tapping it on—"Lamplight."—I edged between the rusted ends of the old portcullis and into the dark.

The tunnel was tall enough for me to walk without stooping, so it wasn't gnomish, and no self-respecting dwarf would have constructed stonework like this. The passage looked like something a child might have made from blocks, the walls uneven, the way randomly twisted. Only the floor was smooth.

There were no defensive arrow slits or channels for burning oil, but that didn't discount the chance for traps or decayed stonework to give way, so I proceeded slowly. This wasn't my first delve into an abandoned mountain stronghold, but it was certainly the strangest.

The passage continued for perhaps sixty feet before opening into a vaulted chamber with many exits. Actually, 'vaulted' was too grand a term for the tiers of stone blocks stacked at all angles, each overhanging the one below until they finally met overhead. I didn't understand even *how* something like this could be built, let alone why.

The chamber was about a hundred feet across with seven exiting tunnels, each as oddly crooked as the one I'd just traversed. Some led upward, some down, and some continued flat into the darkness. They were spaced randomly, and no two looked alike or possessed any lintel or archway. The chamber itself sported no columns, no engravings, no bas-relief depictions of lords or ladies. Not even any brackets for torches, tapestries, or glow crystals. Nothing but a blank confusion of gray stone.

"Well, this is creepy." My words died without an echo.

Marking the exit with a piece of chalk—Gunyan had trained me to be methodical in my searches, and I certainly didn't want to get lost in this rabbit warren—I took the first passage to the left. It sloped downward, the floor cut with random gouges to provide better footing. The worked stone walls devolved to living rock gouged at incongruous angles.

This place is carved right into the mountain.

The way twisted and branched; I marked my path and bore continuously left. Down, down, down, the air became slightly warmer, the décor unchanging. Finally, the tunnel simply ended.

For a moment, I thought the way was blocked with a wall of black stone, but my light didn't glint off anything. Then I realized that there was no stone, nothing, just a completely open space ahead, right and left, up and down.

"What the hell?" This time, my words echoed faintly. I inched forward, raising my light high. Stopping when I stood a foot from the edge—I couldn't make myself go any farther—I squinted into the darkness to no avail. I couldn't see the far wall, and had no way to tell if the cavern was natural, the result of some cataclysm, or hewn out of the mountain. I tapped my glow crystal twice and said, "Daylight."

The light intensified, and I shaded my eyes. The far wall stood some hundred yards away, a blank barrier that looked to have been clawed out of the stone. There were no signs that a bridge had once traversed this void, nor any exit on the other side. I leaned forward, holding my stone out over the empty space, and peered up. The ceiling looming high overhead also looked randomly cut from the living rock, save for a few spots where pieces might have fallen away. Perhaps this had been the quarry that provided the stone for the keep's construction.

Not trusting the edge, I lay flat, inched forward, and peered over into the blackness below.

There, in the depths, I saw...and understood.

Bones.

Perhaps fifty yards below, my light illuminated a mountain of bones, surely the remains of thousands of corpses. Squinting, I tried to discern details. The round skulls I assumed to be humans or dwarves, and the larger sloped skulls with jutting jaws could have been ogres. Numerous elongated roo skulls grinned up at me as well.

"Shit!" Lowering my head, I ran my free hand over my close-cropped hair in sudden realization. This scale of death could only mean one thing. "A gods-damned necromancer."

Necromancy was banned in virtually every civilized nation of the world. Wars had been fought to eradicate the practice for the simple reason that necromancers didn't just kill people, they consumed them. Not their flesh, but their very souls. Dabbling in such vile magic warranted summary execution.

Not so in Tinaros. Tinaran governing philosophy had disallowed no discipline of scholarship, magic, or engineering. Necromancy flourished. In fact, some historians argued that the roo had committed genocide in Tinaros not solely because they didn't like agriculture or mining or buildings of cut stone, but because the rulers allowed necromancers to defile the land with their profane magic.

Now the roo's 'bad place' comment made more sense. Too bad Gunyan's research hadn't discovered this little detail; it would have saved me a long and probably unprofitable trip. If the keep's appearance and this pit of bones were any indications, this necromancer had been more interested in their craft than wealth, comfort, or aesthetics.

"Well, damn."

I edged back from the drop and dimmed my glow crystal to moonlight. Lying there waiting for my eyes to adjust, I thought furiously about what to do. Should I even explore the rest of the keep? Aesthetically pleasing or not, necromancers wielded potent magic, which could mean valuable artifacts. However, if I bumbled into a trap, I could end up dead, or worse, undead. But as the cold stone chilled my back, my frustration mellowed to reluctant acceptance of my circumstance. Yes, necromancers were soul-devouring fiends, but they were human, and humans liked stuff. And not *all* magic was abhorrent. A few benign enchanted trinkets might at least make this trip profitable.

"Well, it's not like you've got anything better to do for the next few days, Hashi." I rose to my feet and worked my way back to the last branching passage. Scrawling an X on the wall, I turned down the next tunnel to continue my methodical exploration.

By the end of my second day of exploration, I'd found two more disposal pits, vast barred cells littered with bones, forges, and coal-fired rending pots large enough for me to lay down inside. I didn't, of course, for I had a good idea what had been rendered in those cauldrons. I did, however, fill a bag with coal to keep me warm at night. While I searched, I also wondered why the keep had been abandoned. If the stories were to be believed, necromancers didn't die of old age, a benefit of their consumption of souls. Had this necromancer seen the genocide coming and fled? If so, it had been premature, since the roo apparently hadn't even come near this place.

But speculation could only sustain my interest for so long, and by now I'd tired of the cold stone, austere rooms with blank walls, workshops where unimaginable horrors must have occurred, and the ever-present musk of ancient death. So, when I found an iron door inlaid with bronze scrollwork, I had to blink to make sure I wasn't hallucinating.

"Hello. What are you?"

I examined the door carefully without touching it. The tarnished green metalwork looked like simple adornment—the swirls and spikes didn't blur in my vision like magical script, anyway—but it was the first I'd seen. I reminded myself that I was in a mage's keep, and I pulled on a pair of gloves. Probably not the best deterrent to being blasted by magic, but it was all I had. I tried the latch, but it wouldn't move; locked or welded in place by corrosion, I had no way to know. It did have an actual keyhole. Too bad I hadn't found any keys.

"You're not keeping me out that easily." Rummaging through my pack, I recovered a hammer and cold chisel.

First, I gave the latch a few love taps. That didn't help. *Okay, we'll do this the hard way.*

Applying the chisel, I knocked rust and corroded bronze from the keyhole, then the bolt of the latch. When I had reduced the lock to scrap, and the door still didn't open, I swore and attacked the hinges. Removing the pins accomplished nothing, so I swore some more, gritted my teeth, and worked my chisel all the way around the portal's edge, driving it deep into the rock to break the door free. I felt the slightest shift and attacked with renewed vigor.

Suddenly, the door fell outward and nearly squashed me flat.

"Fuuuck..." I hissed through gritted teeth, staring down at the two-inch-thick slab of iron lying a finger-width from the toes of my boots. I'd broken my own first rule: be careful. I wouldn't make it far with two crushed feet, and I didn't want my bones to join those of the thousands of others who had perished here.

"Don't screw around, Hashi."

Putting my tools away, I peered beyond the fallen door and realized that the light suffusing the room wasn't from my glow crystal. There were actual windows here. Edging into the room, I leaned against the stone sill and breathed deep of the cool, fresh air—intoxicating after the dry, stifling atmosphere that pervaded the rest of the keep—and squinted out at the twilit landscape. From this high vantage the view out over the foothills to the grasslands was nothing less than spectacular. Perhaps this necromancer had harbored a splinter of appreciation for beauty in their soul after all.

"Back to work." I surveyed the room, felt a grin stretch my face.

Tables, desks, tools, shelves of moldering books, pots, pens, alchemical equipment, and a rusted coal brazier filled the space. Someone had worked here. Someone alive. Long gone, by the thick layer of dust, but everything was laid out as if ready for someone's return.

"Well, whoever you were, you didn't just move out. Nobody leaves their favorite pen and books behind."

With exquisite care, and mumbling "Necromancer, necromancer..." as a cautionary reminder, I used a pair of bamboo chopsticks to inspect nooks, crannies, and poke through things. I examined everything in minute detail, stowing a few items—an ornate pen, an ink well, a pair of calipers, engraving tools, and a cut piece of quartz—in my pack. The books had succumbed to rot, mold, damp, and time. A pity; books always fetched a good price.

Another door opened into a spartan living area—no ornamentation, no knickknacks, no gold-plated busts or marble likenesses, no tapestries to adorn or alleviate the chill of the stone walls—only more bookshelves full of moldy pages and another coal brazier. The bed consisted of a stone slab with the remnants of some kind of cloth-covered mattress, but it was all too rotted away to tell what it had looked like. I found it strange that, with all this rot and decay, I'd seen no signs of vermin, either recent or in the past, no rodents' nests in the mattress or insect holes in the books. Maybe some subtle magic kept them at bay, probably not an unreasonable precaution when you live in a keep full of dead things.

Four etched-granite bookends went into my pack; they were heavy, but I could always dump them if I found something better. Squatting down, I ran my fingers over the perfectly square edges of the bed's base. Unlike the haphazard construction throughout the rest of the keep, it had been crafted with skill and care. *And hidden compartments?* I speculated hopefully. *Come on, give me something...*

Skimming across the face of the stone, my fingertips encountered a hair-thin crack. *Hello! Careful now, Hashi!*

Increasing the light of my glow crystal, I discerned the outline of a drawer, about three feet wide and several inches high. Unfortunately, I could find no latches, hinges, or knobs to open the thing. I checked all around the rest of the bed's base, but this was the only compartment. I tried pushing and prying with the tip of a knife, but got nowhere.

"Fine, then." Realizing the risk of resorting to force, I delved my pack for my hammer, the one with a ball on one side and a flat face on the other. Stone might never rust or decay, but it was brittle.

I drew my arm back to swing...and stopped.

"Necromancer..." Heeding my self-reminder and wary of some ugly surprise, I shifted to one side and struck the center of the drawer hard.

The smooth stone fractured on the first hit, a thin crack from top to bottom. I struck again a few inches from the previous impact, and another crack formed. A piece as wide as my hand fell out. I shone my light inside. I wasn't about to stick my hand in there, even with a glove on, but I had a short pry bar in my pack. I hooked the crook into the hole and pulled. Damned if the drawer didn't slide out with only a slight resistance. My grin stretched in anticipation, then drooped as I beheld layer upon layer of moldering robes and other garments too long decayed to tell what they were. I stirred around with my pry bar, but found nothing interesting.

"Really?" I seethed. "Not even a belt buckle?"

Disgruntled, I turned my attention to the similarly constructed block-like tables to either side of the bed. If the bed had a drawer, maybe these did, too.

Indeed, the first one did possess another featureless drawer. Prying and pushing did nothing, so I resorted to the hammer once again. The drawer yielded sheaves of rotten parchment marked with ancient Betwani script, the language of the dead Tinaran civilization. I could read Betwani, but could make out only a few, faded words. These might be correspondence, orders, or shopping lists for all I knew. Regardless, they crumbled in my grasp, so I'd never know. Searching beneath them yielded nothing. The second bedside table revealed orderly piles of rotted clothing, silk, by the look of them. Then the tip of my pry bar clinked on something metal beneath the remnants.

Trading the pry bar for a small brush, I whisked the rotted silk aside like so much ash to reveal the backside of a small hand mirror, the first personal grooming item I'd seen. I caught my breath as the light gleamed on the gold frame and handle deeply inlaid with striking designs and symbols. *This* would be worth a pretty penny. I retrieved a pair of pliers and picked it up by the handle, gingerly turned it around to look at the glass...then promptly dropped it with a gasp of shock, my heart hammering in my chest.

The face staring back at me wasn't mine.

Instead of a young woman with ebony skin and close-cropped hair, the glass revealed a middle-aged, light-skinned man with a hawkish nose and high cheekbones.

"Gods and devils!" I staggered back a step as the man's image also mouthed the oath.

Squinting at the device from a safe distance, I could now see nothing in the glass but a reflection of the ceiling. *Magic, surely, but what kind?* Had the necromancer enchanted a mirror with the image of a father, brother, son, or lover? Its lips had moved, so could it speak?

"Can you hear me?"

I received no reply.

I inched forward to peer down at the mirror, ready to jerk back. The man's salt and pepper hair edged up into my view. I leaned a little farther, and brown eyes with wrinkled corners stared out of the glass at me. I blinked, and the eyes blinked back at me.

What the...

I closed one eye, and the image closed the corresponding eye. I opened it, and it opened. A shiver raced up my spine, and my scalp prickled. Gritting my teeth, I leaned forward until the entire face came into view. I twitched my nose, stuck out my tongue, grimaced, and the image contorted likewise.

"Who are you?" I asked, and the man's lips moved exactly as mine had. I raised a hand to touch my face, and the man's hand, the fingertips ink-stained, nails bitten short, touched his own face. The reflection in the mirror was me...but not me. *The necromancer?* I wondered.

Tentatively, I reached out a hand to touch the mirror, and the man's hand imitated my motion. My fingertips felt only glass, however, not his fingertips. It was a mirror, but it displayed someone else's features. I wondered, perversely, what I would see if I stripped naked, but decided I'd rather not.

"Why?" I wondered aloud. Picking it up again by the handle, I turned it over a few times, eying the reflections of the walls and floor. They remained the same, moldering books and all. Only when I looked into the mirror was the reflection altered. "Why would a necromancer want to look at himself like this?"

The answer suddenly seemed obvious: *Because he didn't like the way he actually looked?*

I peered into the eyes in the mirror. Was this vanity?

Whatever it was, someone would pay for such an oddity, so I wrapped it in a cloth, stuffed it in my pack, and continued my search. The sleeping chamber had two other doors, both stone with bronze hinges. One opened easily to reveal a water closet. Even necromancers had to take a dump occasionally, I supposed. The other door resisted my efforts, but yielded after a few encouraging love taps with the hammer on the hinges.

The room beyond wasn't large, the walls unadorned stone, nothing of interest...except for the huge stone block resting smack in the middle. About eight feet long, three high, and three wide, it bore elaborately crafted inscriptions around the edge, the gold inlay glittering in my light. The room was, undeniably, a crypt, the stone box a sarcophagus.

"Paydirt," I said with a grin.

This was it, the find I'd been hoping for. So many cultures lavished their dead with treasures to be enjoyed in the afterlife that it was rare to discover an unplundered tomb. The sealed door I'd chiseled out of its frame told me no one had beat me to this one. I was the first to enter this room since the lord of the keep had been laid to rest.

Maybe necromancers do *die of old age...* The thought disconcerted me, for every book I'd read on the subject said they didn't. But here lay one's sarcophagus. My light no longer seemed to illuminate the room as much as cast forbidding shadows. I shivered, but told myself it was the oncoming night dropping the temperature.

"Stop it, Hashi! Get back to work." I wasn't a frightened little girl anymore.

The obvious question now was, did I really want to crack open the coffin of a necromancer?

"Hell, no," was my unequivocal answer. But so far I had only the mirror and a few trinkets to show for my efforts on this expedition.

In my experience, life consisted of doing a lot of things you didn't want to do, so I stepped into the room and shone my light upon the inscriptions around the edge of the sarcophagus. The characters were Betwani, which I could translate easily enough. There were no details of the necromancer's life, date of birth, or even a name, only a date and a most curious passage.

"Within I reside for all time. I have no recourse, and refuse to answer Mortas' summons. The gods I have cheated of their prize. Eternity is mine."

What the hell is that supposed to mean?

I gingerly touched the lid with a gloved hand, then removed my glove and ran my fingers lightly over the stone. I felt nothing unusual, despite the legend that necromancy chills the blood. Then again, most legends were nonsense espoused by story tellers. I was a historian who preferred fact to fiction. Still, I hesitated.

"Come on, Hashi, it's just a corpse. You've dealt with corpses before."

I dropped my pack and held my glow crystal in my teeth to light my work, then took up my pry bar, fitted the edge in the seam beneath the lettering, and smacked it with the hammer. The seam was filled with a tar-like substance, a barrier against moisture, but nothing solid. The tip of my pry bar wedged in easily, and I put my weight on it. The lid lifted an inch. Wooden wedges from my pack kept the crack open, and I worked my way around. This wasn't my first dance with the dead.

When I had the seal free, I flipped my pry bar around, fitted the blade of the crook under the lip, braced myself, and pried. The lid lifted with a puff of ancient, rancid air. Trying not to breathe it in, I slid another wedge under the edge of the lid where it slid down the inner wall of the outer box. Again, I worked my way around. When I had the entire lid suspended by six wooden wedges, I moved to the long side nearest the exit—I may be a fool, but I'm not a complete idiot—placed the heels of my palms against the lid, braced my back straight, and heaved with my legs.

Two hundred pounds of stone tilted up and slid off the far edge
of the sarcophagus, crashing to the floor with an impact that shook
the room and echoed around the small crypt. I drew a sharp breath
as my light glinted off of staring eyes, and nearly swallowed my glow
crystal. I spat the stone into my hand and coughed a laugh as I
realized that the eyes were painted upon the inner coffin, cunningly
wrought in the likeness of the man I'd seen in the hand mirror.

I wondered at the custom of layered coffins. Did people
honestly think a grave robber would go to all the trouble of lifting
the outer lid of a sarcophagus, only to stop when they found the
inner coffin carved or molded to reflect the inhabitant's likeness? I
certainly never had.

There were no possessions or canopic jars tucked into the space
between the inner and outer containers, so I simply applied my pry
bar and heaved. The stone lid came up with some resistance and a
puff of dust from the long-decayed corpse within. It weighed half
what the outer one had, so I just grabbed one end and heaved it up
until the foot slid off and it wedged there. Raising my glow crystal
again, I peered inside. Instead of another coffin—I'd read accounts
of kings having as many as seven within one another—I beheld the
desiccated remains of a man.

"Not looking so good these days, are you?" I mused, praying to
all the gods I knew that he wouldn't answer.

He didn't.

To my dismay, it became immediately apparent that this man
had been a minimalist. He wore no elaborate funerary mask or fancy
clothing, no golden torc or crown, no rings or jewelry, and held no
scepter or staff. His skin was black with age and long past decaying,
his hands clutched together at his breast. He wore a simple robe of
ebony cloth that seemed to have resisted the years remarkably well,
but nothing else. Not even shoes.

"Well, damn!"

I sighed and started to turn away in defeat when the light from
my crystal glinted off of something clutched in the dead man's
hands. I peered closely and saw polished bone. Eying the object
between the desiccated fingers, I recognized the pommel of a dagger,

the blade of which had been thrust into the corpse's chest, seemingly by his own hands.

"Suicide?"

It made a sick kind of sense. According to the date on the sarcophagus, the necromancer had been entombed during the roo genocidal war nearly five centuries ago. How ironic that this man had apparently killed himself to avoid death by roo hands, only to have the roo not even assault his keep.

I probed the dead fingers with my pry bar, and they came away from the dagger's hilt easily. I'm a lot of things, but squeamish isn't one of them, and I'd been handling human remains for a decade. With his dead digits pried free, I had a much better view. The haft of the dagger looked to be crafted from a single bone—human, probably, given that this was a necromancer—wrapped in black leather that looked disturbingly like the corpse's own leathery flesh, and a short crosspiece knapped from black stone, perhaps obsidian. It stood up from his chest like a monolith.

Musing on the situation, I realized that my suicide theory didn't make sense given the inscription on the sarcophagus.

"I refuse to answer Mortas' summons," I recited.

Of course, a necromancer would worship the god of death, but to refuse the Deathless One's summons? Suicide or no, when the necromancer died, his soul would be relegated to Mortas. And, given the atrocities ascribed to necromancers, that soul would certainly be condemned to an eternity of torment in Necrol, Mortas' domain.

So, what kind of necromancer thinks to cheat Mortas by jamming an obsidian dagger in his own chest?

A rhetorical question, but the answer was plain enough: this one had. A part of me wanted to jerk the blade out of his chest to see if he'd come back to life, while another part of me worried that he might do just that. I tapped on the pommel of the dagger with my crowbar, considering. If he *did* come back to life, I could just jam the knife right back where I found it. If he didn't, then maybe there was something special about this dagger. Perhaps it was enchanted to act as a necromancer does, utterly consuming a soul so that nothing remained to be claimed or judged. *Cheated the gods... Oblivion instead of endless torment?*

Only one way to find out.

I traded my pry bar for a sturdy pair of pliers, gripped the leather-wrapped hilt of the dagger, and jerked. A deadly length of obsidian scraped out from between ancient bones.

Nothing happened. The dead necromancer remained dead, and the dagger remained firmly gripped in my pliers. *Well, that's good.*

"Daylight," I said, tapping my glow crystal. Holding the blade close to the light, I turned it one way and the other. It had been beautifully shaped, surely. Not smooth and polished, but knapped from a raw piece of obsidian, the edge uneven yet perfectly uniform. Knapping is an art form, the shape of the blade conforming to the grain of the stone. One mistake spoils the symmetry. This expertly crafted blade gleamed darkly, each rounded fracture distinct, rendering the edge slightly serrated and keener than any razor.

"Come on, what's special here, Hashi?" I asked myself, for there had to be something. This weapon killed a necromancer, not an easy thing, if the legends were true.

The necromancer Azrael was destroyed by an elf blade, an inherently magical weapon. I sure as hell wasn't a mage, so I had no idea if this dagger was enchanted.

I placed it on the floor and knelt, rummaging through my pack for my magnifying lens. With my glow crystal shining right on the blade and my lens focused, I could see there was more to the weapon than simple stone, leather, and bone. Beneath my lens, tiny characters swam upon the surface of the blade. They moved under my gaze, denying my eyes the ability to focus upon them.

"Magic." I swallowed hard, my mouth suddenly dry. "But what *kind* of magic?"

I sat back on my heels and glared at the thing. Tired and hungry, I was in no condition to investigate the dagger's secrets. I'd take it back to my camp and have a closer look in the morning. I also decided to leave on the morrow, having little doubt that I'd found everything of value here.

"You better be worth it!" I picked the blade up again with my pliers, wrapped it in a rag, and put it in my pack. I needed to sleep on this.

Of course, I couldn't sleep. Lying out on the mountainside with a coal fire burning merrily to keep me warm, and a million stars twinkling overhead, I couldn't help wondering what this strange magical dagger could be. I knew myself well enough to realize that my obsessive mind wouldn't let it go, but I needed sleep if I intended to trek back down the mountain in the morning.

"To hell with it."

I sat up and wrapped my blanket around my shoulders. Donning gloves, I pulled the obsidian blade from my pack, unfolded the wrappings, and, using pliers, lay it on the rag. The ruddy light of my fire gleamed like blood on the blade. *No blood*, I realized. The obsidian was utterly clean, shiny enough to reflect light. *How did he stab himself without drawing blood?* Another puzzle I couldn't unravel, and honestly didn't know if I wanted to.

Gritting my teeth, I touched the pommel of the dagger with one gloved finger. Other than my own singing nerves, I felt nothing. But then, what did magic feel like? A tingle, a shock, a chill?

Still, I had to be careful.

I retrieved a hunting knife and whetstone from my pack, honing the fine steel until the edge shaved the hairs off the back of my arm. *This is stupid*, I argued with myself as I doffed my left glove, but my insatiable curiosity wouldn't be stilled until I discovered what this weapon was. Holding my bared hand above the enchanted dagger, I rested the keen edge of the hunting knife against the inside of the second knuckle on my left little finger. If I felt a curse start to take hold of me and couldn't pull away, I'd sever my finger.

One might think these precautions excessive, but history—real history, not fanciful legend—is rife with tales of cursed magical weapons.

Taking a deep breath, I told myself, *Just do it!* and touched the obsidian dagger with my sacrificial finger.

Well, aren't we a cautious one.

I jerked away, slicing my finger in my haste. My heart hammered in my chest as I looked frantically around, but I knew no one was there. The voice had sounded in my head. I sucked on the cut I'd inflicted and remembered the face in the mirror.

"Who are you?" I whispered.

There was no reply. Lurching to my feet, I paced around my camp, my gaze fixed on the obsidian dagger as if it might fly up and stab me. What had happened? The blade had felt like ice, but that could have simply been the cold of the mountain air. I'd felt no obvious magic, no compulsion or shock. I also felt no desire to return to the blade or pick it up. In fact, I felt like wrapping the thing up, taking it back into the keep, and jamming it right back where I'd found it.

But that voice…

Enchanted weapons that spoke to their wielders were not unheard of, but they were rarer than dragon eggs and much more valuable. Soul blades, they were called, a willing union of a mortal's soul and a weapon crafted specifically to accept it. And they were powerful.

"But whose soul?" The obvious answer was the necromancer's, but I couldn't be sure.

I sat back down, placed the edge of my hunting knife back under the bloodied knuckle of my finger, gritted my teeth against the pending chill, and touched the obsidian blade again. "Can you hear me?"

Yes, even when you're not touching me. You talk to yourself a lot, Hashi.

Furiously resisting the impulse to pull away again, I narrowed my eyes at the thing. Not only a talking blade, but a snide one. "Who are you?"

My name is Saraknyal. I was the lord of the keep you've been exploring. My, but you made a lot of noise. Thank you, by the way, for pulling me out of there. I was bored out of my skull, so to speak.

So it is *the necromancer*, I thought.

Precisely, he answered, shocking me so that I almost cut myself again.

I swallowed my panic. "You can read my mind?"

No, the voice assured me, *but I can hear your subvocalized thoughts. You know, when you talk to yourself, but silently? And only when you're touching me.*

I pulled my finger away. I didn't trust this mysterious voice in the slightest. I had to think about this.

Sucking on my cut finger and wrapping my blanket around my shoulders to banish a chill that had little to do with the cool mountain air, I stared at the obsidian blade.

No wonder he was bored, I thought, *locked away for five hundred years. It's a wonder he's still sane.* Then I considered, *Maybe he isn't.* But he hadn't *sounded* insane. Hell, he'd even thanked me. Actually, conversing with a necromantic soul blade about which I knew nothing didn't seem like a sane thing for *me* to be doing. But my insatiable curiosity got the better of me.

I leaned forward and touched the blade again. "You're a soul blade, aren't you?"

You're astute, Hashi.

"And the mirror? Is that you, too?"

Of course. Who else would it be?

"It's a little odd to put an image of yourself in a mirror when you can just look in a mundane mirror."

Grant an old man a little vanity. My younger self was quite good-looking. My mirror allowed me to remember those days. The centuries weren't exactly kind to my mortal flesh.

"I thought necromancers were immortal."

A myth spread by people who know little of necromancy. We're not immortal, but we do utilize soul energy to prolong our lives. The roo denied me access to that resource when they slaughtered the people of Tinaros.

"Couldn't you...um...utilize roo souls?" My own question horrified me. Why was I conversing with a necromancer about consuming souls?

No. Roo souls are totally inadequate for my needs. The roo destroyed my way of life as utterly as they destroyed the Tinaran empire. I bound my soul to this blade to cheat death. By the way, just how long have I been interred?

"Almost five hundred years, if the date on your sarcophagus is accurate."

Five hundred years, he mused. *Well, it feels good to be out and about again, thanks to you, Hashi. I think we could work well together.*

"*Together?*" I choked a scornful laugh. "Why the *hell* would I pair up with a gods-damned necromancer?"

Answer me this: why are you here, Hashi? What draws you to these ancient ruins?

"I'm a dealer in antiquities," I confessed. "A historian."

*A seeker of treasure and knowledge. You've found both, for I have the knowledge of centuries, and I'm *certainly* a treasure.*

"Ha!" I scoffed. "Knowledgeable, perhaps, but a *treasure?*"

*Yes, a *treasure*, Hashi,* Saraknyal assured me. *I can give you the things all mortals want: power, riches...*

"At what cost?" I demanded, not that I considered for a second taking him up on the offer. "Human souls?"

Dwarves, ogres, or gnomes will do, too, if you're squeamish about humans.

"That's disgusting! I think the world would be better off if I destroyed you." I reached into my pack and pulled out my largest hammer. Holding the hilt against a rock, the blade braced against another, I raised the tool and swung.

Wait, Hashi! You can't—

The blow struck true, right at the juncture of the blade and haft, but my hammer rebounded from the impact, sending a jolt up my arm. The rock the blade had rested upon was chipped, but the dagger remained unblemished.

*As I was saying, you *can't* destroy me. Nothing you have can touch me.*

"Okay, then I'll just leave you." I recalled the discard pit and considered how appropriate it would be for the necromancer to lay forever amongst the bones of his victims.

Listen to me, Hashi," Saraknyal pleaded, his tone low and intense. *I understand if you don't want to use me for yourself. So just sell me to some rich collector! You'll make a *fortune*! You can live like a princess, and they'll have a soul blade to sit on their mantle.*

"You're trying to trick me."

No, I'm not! I'd simply rather spend forever in a glass case looking out at the world than back in my sarcophagus.

I cocked my head. Apparently he'd told the truth about not reading my thoughts, if he believed that I intended to put him back in his crypt, and not toss him into the refuse pit. Good to know. But I couldn't listen to him anymore. I needed to think this through. Without another word, I rewrapped the dagger and stuffed the vile thing back into my pack.

As much as I hated to admit it, Saraknyal was right about one thing: the right collector would pay a fortune for such an artifact. Gunyan had sold other items that were supposedly cursed and dangerous. In fact, some Mati princes seemed to revel in possessing and displaying powerful and dangerous relics. Gunyan would know who to sell this thing to, and we'd both be rich. Or I could throw the thing in a pit and walked away empty-handed.

I piled coal on my fire, lay back on the rocky ground, and stared up at the stars. My options sucked, but that was nothing new.

Chapter Five
Home and Hearth

From the journal of Hashi Severn –

Power... I've never wanted it. Others strive for dominion over others, for riches and armies. All I ever wanted was comfort and safety...and perhaps a really good library. I have achieved that, or at least I thought I had. May the gods damn Jhavika for screwing that up.

The drive back to Ash Keep proved uneventful, except for one more gang of thugs that I sent scrabbling back into their holes with a peal of fearful laughter.

You really should have let me take the wretches' souls, Hashi! Saraknyal urged. *War's brewing! We'll need all the power we can get if Jhavika comes calling with an army.*

No. He had a point, but I was in no mood. *We've destroyed enough souls tonight.*

My carriage clattered around one more corner, and my home loomed tall above the cobbled street, its façade dark and foreboding...rather like mine. High walls of black granite topped with spiked crenellations served as a first line of defense against the riffraff of Haven. We clattered under the portcullis of the main gate and stopped in the courtyard. My arrival, hours earlier than expected, created a stir.

I stepped down as my stablemaster hurried over, the napkin still tucked into his collar evidence of a disturbed dinner. "Sorry about the mess, Ralik. We had to make a detour through the city."

"Shite to the hocks, they are, mistress, but it'll wash off." Ralik grabbed the traces and led the team away, muttering under his breath.

"Shades! Secure the gate and postern door."

"Yes, mistress!" My shades, ebon-skinned and red-eyed, hurried to comply. Not particularly bright, though they could follow complex commands, their unremitting rage and hunger constituted my second line of defense against anyone insane or determined enough to make it over the wall.

Metal clanged as the portcullis dropped. If, or rather *when* Jhavika chose to deal with the surviving council members, she'd find Ash Keep a hard nut to crack. I waved over the captain of my guard, my only remaining wraith. Silently, I cursed Jhavika once again for my escort's loss. Far more cognizant creatures than shades, wraiths were complex and difficult to create. Not to mention that the process made me nauseous.

"Mistress?" The wraith's voice sounded like someone dragging a brick over rough stone.

"Secure the keep. Jhavika Keshmir tried to stage a coup and killed several council members. We could be facing war. I'll be in my chambers. Call for me if anything happens."

"At once, mistress!"

I breathed deep and strode for the main entrance. My butler awaited me there. He'd been with me for many years and served with utter devotion. Loyalty like that couldn't be bought or frightened into anyone, and I'd need that loyalty right now.

"Joss, organize the household staff. Nobody goes out until further notice. Anyone acting strangely is to be brought to me." I only employed about a dozen servants. They were sworn to secrecy and knew what it meant to betray me, but they were free to leave any time they liked. Few ever had. I kept them safe and saw to their needs, even allowing their families to live in the keep. I considered them loyal, but the control that Jhavika exerted over so many at the party disconcerted me. I had no idea if she might have enchanted any of my people.

"Strangely, mistress?"

"Anything unusual. We may have a spy in our midst." Too bad Saraknyal hadn't been able to detect that particular magic. It would have made things simpler.

"At once, mistress!" As Joss hurried off as fast as his club foot would allow, however, I had a horrible thought.

What about my shades, Saraknyal? Do you think any could be enchanted by Jhavika? I sent them out as messengers all the time, and it would have been easy for her to lash one with the scourge.

I don't think so. Their minds—or what's left of their minds—are utterly bound to you. A wraith, maybe yes, but you've only the one left, and it hasn't turned on you, so I think we can discount that.

Good to know. I had only a score of shades, and couldn't afford to lose any. Granted, they were each worth a hundred common soldiers, but they'd be spread thin if it came to war.

Another thought struck me before Joss exited the entry hall. "Joss, also send word to Bryce and any of Waymar's people in the city, too." The former operated an antique shop for me and ran my spy network. Waymar had been my smuggler for years, sailing his small, nimble ships throughout the Blood Sea and beyond, buying and selling antiquities at my behest. "Jhavika Keshmir's staging a coup, and I need to know what's happening and where. Have Waymar's people watch the harbor and report to me in the morning."

Joss' eyes widened at the mention of a coup. "Yes, mistress!"

I marched across the entry hall under the cold stone gazes of the eight Toki sculptures standing on plinths to either side. The statues—several centuries old and salvaged from a sunken ship outside of Hyko harbor—depicted long-dead komei generals. Their traditional grim masks suited my mood perfectly.

I started up the stairs, my mind still spinning with the night's events. *What have I missed?* I asked Saraknyal.

Nothing I can think of, unless you want to storm Fa-Chen's keep before Jhavika takes control of his house and ships to send them after Longbright. If you choose to do that, I might suggest you change clothes first, though the alterations you made to your gown are quite fetching.

"Not tonight. I've got to think this through." Jhavika clearly tried to kill every council member she didn't have control over. She'd failed, but with the soldiers of several houses now at her command, she had Haven by the balls. Three flights up, another shade stood at the door to my chambers. "Report to the outer wall. The keep's on lockdown."

"Yes, mistress." He strode off without a question.

I stepped inside my chambers, closed the door behind me, and leaned back against the solid wood, only now allowing myself to tremble in reaction to the evening's events. Years had passed since death had stalked me so closely. It wasn't the thought of death that upset me so, but the afterlife. Each soul I'd destroyed would count against me when I faced Demia's judgement. I'd long ago extracted a promise from Saraknyal to consume my soul upon my death, to grant me oblivion rather than an eternity of torment. But I wasn't ready for oblivion yet.

"I need a drink." I tossed Soul Drinker onto my desk and stalked to the bedroom, peeling out of my dress on the way. I resolved to have it mended. I'm not really vain, but I looked good in it, and I didn't have many dresses.

I kicked off my sandals and scanties and pulled my favorite robe from my armoire. Cinching the tie tight, I strode back out into the sitting room—really more of an office—poured a brandy, and headed for my balcony. I opened the glass door and stepped out. I sipped as I stared out at the city, willing the tension to ebb away. *You're safe here, Hashi. Relax.*

Careful, my dear. Jhavika could have sent assassins.

I doubt it, unless she's got assassins who can fly. I peered over the edge, seventy feet of sheer granite fit so closely a razor wouldn't slip between the stones, suddenly uncertain. A couple of hours ago I hadn't thought that anyone could stage a coup against the Council. So many thoroughly enslaved to Jhavika's magic. *She sent Vakna after me, and he couldn't refuse. He had to know he was risking his soul. No one should have to die like that.*

He was trying to murder *you, Hashi. What were you* supposed *to do?*

"I wasn't talking to you." I tilted my snifter and cleared my throat. Sometimes, having Saraknyal hear my every subvocalized thought wore on my nerves.

Seriously, you need to grow a spine and go on the offensive! Four of the Council are dead! There'll be a power vacuum. You need to fill it!

I glared at the dagger lying on my desk. "What part of 'I wasn't talking to you' don't you understand?"

You know I'm right, Hashi. You just don't want to do what it takes.

"Fuck you, old man." I stalked over to my desk, put down my brandy, and snatched up the dagger. The cold power smoldering within chilled my blood, power that had saved my life, but damned my soul. "I'm tired of listening to you tonight."

I opened the lid of the lead-lined box on the corner of my desk and dropped the dagger in.

Hashi! Wait! You need—

I slammed the lid, cutting him off. Sometimes I needed to be alone in my mind, and the box was the only way to shut him up. Picking up my brandy again, I strode back out onto my balcony. To hell with worrying about assassins; I needed to breathe.

The breeze fluttered my robe. Lightning lit the sky far to the northeast, a summer squall. Monsoon season was upon us once again, but I didn't mind. I preferred the muggy trade winds to the chill of the Dragon's Breath that occasionally howled out of the mountains.

Unfortunately, the breeze also blew the stench of the streets up to my balcony. I'd chosen to live in Haven not because of its attractions—it had few—but because I'd had no other choice. Necromancers were shunned by every civilized nation, leaving this festering heap of lawlessness as my only refuge. I'd built a good life here, a profitable business that kept me comfortable, kept my people safe and content. Now, in one evening, everything I'd worked to achieve had been put at risk. All because of the ambition of Jhavika Keshmir.

"I should have fucking killed her." I knocked back my brandy and expelled a gusty sigh. I had to think, decide what to do, how best to respond to Jhavika's declaration of war.

War...

As a historian, I'd read many books about war. There were lessons to be learned from the past, mistakes made that could be avoided in the future, strategies and philosophies that had been proven on battlefields all over the world.

The first rule of war was to know your enemy. I needed information. I knew precious little about Jhavika beyond what she'd shown us at the couple of council meetings she'd attended. She was formerly a pirate, currently a business woman, and no longer allied with Longbright, considering tonight's fiasco, but with who knew how many enchanted allies at her beck and call. When Waymar and Bryce reported tomorrow morning, I'd have a better picture of what Jhavika was doing.

The second rule of war was deception. I'd already deceived Jhavika into thinking I was invulnerable. My performance tonight might deter her for a while, but I'd seen the avarice in her eyes when she gazed at Soul Drinker. She'd try again. Also, she'd seen my wraith defeated. My undead minions weren't invincible.

The third rule of war was power. I rubbed my face in frustration as I pondered how little power I actually possessed. A score of undead warriors, a few spies, three small smuggling ships, and my necromancer reputation wouldn't keep Jhavika and her armies at bay for long. If I'd listened to Saraknyal, I'd have created an army of undead, but the cost of that endeavor was far beyond what I was willing to pay.

I need allies.

The other surviving council members were probably holed up in their keeps just as I was, with stout walls and sturdy soldiers between themselves and the world. Unfortunately, that would only play into Jhavika's hands. She'd pick us off one by one with overwhelming forces. Alone, we'd all succumb. Only together might get through this.

The dreaded necromancer of Haven would have to ask for help.

Chapter Six
Civilization

It took only a little more than two days to reach the river again, an easier downhill trek. My pack was heavier with the trinkets I'd scavenged at the keep. The rag-wrapped soul blade I'd tucked into the very bottom where I wouldn't inadvertently touch it. I couldn't in good conscience leave it behind; I'd come to collect valuable artifacts, and the soul blade was the most valuable thing I'd ever found, worth a fortune. Surely Gunyan could find a buyer for it.

As before, I quickly shed my clothes and plunged into the cool water, washing myself clean of dust, sweat, and the lingering miasma of death from the keep. Refreshed, I took up my bow and a fishing arrow and waded back out. In minutes, I had a fat trout roasting over a driftwood fire on the shore. I rinsed my hands, climbed back up the bank, and lay on warm stones, arms out, head thrown back, eyes closed, to allow the sun to dry my body.

You really are a striking young woman, Hashi.

I jerked like I'd been struck by lightning. Snatching up my discarded shirt and struggling to pull it on, I glared at my pack. "How am I hearing you?" I wasn't touching the blade, and it was wrapped and stowed away. I grabbed my pants and nearly fell trying to pull them up my wet legs. "And for that matter, how can you see me through the pack?"

You can hear me because I've had time to study your soul, Hashi. Souls sing like tuning forks, each one has a different pitch and harmonic. Once I learned yours, I attuned my thoughts to match it and...here we are. His laughter turned my stomach. *And cloth is no barrier to my senses, my dear. What's the fun in crafting a soul blade to sequester your soul without giving it some magical abilities? So, that shirt you're wearing isn't really accomplishing much.*

"You're a disgusting pervert!" I pulled clean clothes from my pack and turned my back to change. Even so, I felt like something slimy was crawling up my spine. "Don't *ever* ogle me like that!"

Let me assure you, my dear, I have no interest in ogling you. I've not given a whit for the opposite sex for more than seven centuries, even when I was still alive. I gave all that up for my art.

"Your *art?*" I snorted a derisive laugh as I fastened the last buttons of my shirt and cinched my belt tight, for all the good the garments apparently did me. "The *art* of destroying souls for power?"

Ah, yes, revile me for what I've done in the quest for power. His disembodied voice fairly dripped sarcasm. *How do you think that fish's soul felt when you plucked it out of the river and jammed a knife in its gut?*

"Fish don't have souls." I whirled away to gather more wood for my fire. "And I'm not discussing this with you."

Why not? Who better to discuss the philosophy of the soul with than someone who devoted his life to understanding and utilizing the power sequestered within them? Besides, who else do you have to talk to?

"No one, and that's how I like it. Now shut up, or I'll find some way to dispose of you where nobody will *ever* find you."

Very well. I meant no offense. Saraknyal fell silent and, thankfully, stayed that way.

Only three days later, when I was fording the shallows at the same spot I had before, did he break his silence.

There's a mountain cat in the foliage to your left, Hashi.

I froze, still knee deep in the river. "Where?"

In the middle of the bushes there. If you touch me, I can show you.

"Oh, *hell* no!" I muttered. Scanning the bushes, I saw nothing. For all I knew, this was a ruse to get me to touch the blade again. But was I willing to bet my life that he was lying? I couldn't string my bow in the water, so I slowly reached down to pick up a stone. I shouted loud and threw it, immediately reaching for another. Before I could snag a second stone, the bushes rustled, and a blur of beige shot away, gone in an instant.

It's gone, Hashi. You frightened it away.

"Thanks for the warning." I splashed out of the stream and put my hands on my knees, willing my heart to stop pounding.

You're welcome.

Straightening, I strung my bow as a precaution and set about filling my waterskins in preparation for my trek across the arid grasslands. I'd already stocked up on dried fish, and there was still plenty of daylight.

I struggled not to ask, but I had to know the answer to one question. "Why...why did you warn me?"

Why wouldn't I? He seemed startled by the question. *You rescued me from an eternity of boredom, Hashi. The least I could do is prevent you from being eaten alive.*

I snorted a laugh of realization. "And if I was eaten alive, you'd spend eternity at the bottom of a river." I fitted the cap of my last waterskin and returned to my pack.

True, but that's still a step up from the inside of a coffin.

I thought about that as I shouldered my burdens. "You couldn't see through the lid of your sarcophagus?"

No.

"That was pretty stupid." I adjusted straps, cinched my boot laces and started off to the east. "Why not just wrap yourself in cloth instead?"

I thought to keep scavengers from finding me. The roo, especially.

I chuckled coldly. "Well, you're in trouble, then, because they'll inspect everything I've got before they let me leave."

They know you're here?

"Of course they know I'm here. They don't mind me taking away human artifacts so long as I don't defile the land."

How considerate of them. His voice dripped derision.

"You don't like the roo much."

They annihilated my entire civilization, Hashi.

"You mean they took away your herd of *cattle*!" I spat.

What do you think you know of Tinaros?

The question surprised me, since I'd already told him I was a historian. "*Think* I know? I *know* they didn't abolish necromancy.

Their economy was bolstered by undead slave labor. The roo rose up and exterminated them, either for their defilement of the land or their profane practice of necromancy."

A convenient history prejudiced against the study of necromancy.

"*Enlighten* me, then. How is the practice of destroying souls a noble pursuit?"

Very well. Tinaros had strict laws governing everything, including the practice of necromancy. Anyone convicted of a violent crime—murder, the unwarranted consumption of a soul, rape, assault, armed theft, or child abuse—was given the option of either being put to death or having their soul consumed.

I stopped short, grimacing. "Tell another lie, why don't you? Who in their right mind would chose the latter?"

Consider the afterlife, Hashi. When you die, your soul is judged by Demia, then sent to the realm of whichever god she deems appropriate. Evil deeds in life warrant dire consequences after death. Would you willingly endure an eternity of torment in the Nine Hells, have your soul riven with endless pain, then forged together with other tormented souls into the spirit of a demon? Or would you chose painless oblivion?

Gods and devils... I hadn't thought of it that way. I walked on in silence for some time, trying to imagine a nation governed by such laws.

You must think what to do if the roo try to take me away, Hashi.

His non sequitur comment took me off guard. "I already have; I let them take you."

Even if they find some way to destroy me?

I smiled grimly. "*Especially* if they have some way to destroy you." I'd already tried and failed, after all.

That's very cold of you.

"This from a *necromancer*?" I barked a laugh and walked on.

Why do you do that?

Saraknyal's question startled me out of my reverie as I trekked over the seemingly endless sea of arid grassland. "Do what?"

You've counted more than fifteen thousand steps since breakfast. And when you're not counting, you're calculating or reciting or doing some other rote task. It's driving me crazy.

I hadn't realized that he could hear me doing my mental exercises; they were second nature after so long. "None of your business."

Come on, Hashi. You do it for a reason. Talking to me has got to be better than counting every step you take.

I didn't want to have a conversation with him, but I had no other way to shut him up. "They're mental exercises to...help pass the time."

They don't work, he grumbled. *They make time stretch out so tediously that I'm actually thinking fondly of my sarcophagus.*

"And your prattling's making me wish I'd left you there," I countered.

It's deeper than that. You're troubled about something.

"I'm not troubled by anything but you. Now shut up."

No. What has gone so wrong in your short life that you can't even let your mind wander?

I coughed a bitter laugh to hide my shock that he'd hit so close to the truth. "Nothing, and you're the last person I'd pour my heart out to anyway. Now shut up."

If you don't tell me what troubles you, I'll sing every bawdy sea chanty I know.

"You do, and I'll bury you right here and walk away."

And return to Mati with nothing to show for your month-long trek through the desolation of Tinaros? I think not.

I walked on in silence.

Oh, way down south in Mati town, where the girls are tall and their skin is brown, I fell I love with a dark-eyed beauty, who loved to watch me—

"My mother hated me, all right!" I screeched, immediately ashamed that I'd allowed him to provoke me.

Saraknyal fell silent and I walked along for some time until my thoughts began spinning down familiar paths. I started mentally counting my steps in base five to distract myself.

I'm sorry, Hashi. I didn't mean to pry.

"*Fuck* you. Of *course* you meant to pry. You're provoking me for your own entertainment!"

I wasn't.

I refused to reply and resumed my count, but my memories had been stirred like the ashes of a bonfire, and the embers of resentment glowed hot. My mother...beautiful, graceful, a dancer. She started dancing for a few silvers at inns and clubs, but soon worked her way up to festivals and special occasions hosted by the wealthy. Her popularity grew until she caught the eye of one of the many princes of Mati. He wooed her, offered to make her his fifth wife, but she became pregnant before they wed. He cast her away like a used rag, denying the child was his. Denying that *I* was his.

The grasslands blurred before me, and I blinked to prevent the tears from falling.

Unable to earn money by dancing with a swelling belly, my mother sought out a merchant who had previously begged her for her hand. They were wed, but after I was born, he refused to allow her to dance again, despite her desperate desire to return to the stage. She blamed me.

My mother's face rose in my mind, her lips twisted in scorn.

I recalled sneaking in to spy on her dancing alone in the courtyard when my stepfather wasn't home. I practiced until my feet ached, thinking that if I could dance like her, she would love me. When I finally danced for her, her admonishing screams echoed off the courtyard walls.

My stepfather ignored me—the get of my mother's first lover—until I began to grow up. Then he paid too much attention to me, tried to get me alone. I was only thirteen, but wise enough to know what would happen if I stayed in that house.

A low vibration through the soles of my boots jolted me out of my misery. I stopped and shaded my eyes, squinting into the distance. A dust plume smudged the horizon.

"There they are."

*There *who* are?*

"The roo." I dropped my pack, unwound my shirt from my head—I'd given up on modesty in front of Saraknyal—and put it on.

You can't let them take me away, Hashi! They're superstitious primitives! They'll destroy me!

"I can't stop them." I was torn. If they did take the dagger, it would be a weight off of my shoulders. However, it also meant that I'd return to Mati with nothing.

I stood with my hands outspread and empty as the roo circled me once before closing in. With their lances poised, they halted, and their leader hopped forward.

"Ash Walker. You leave our land now?"

"Yes." I couldn't tell if they were the same troop I'd encountered before, but they obviously knew me.

"Show us what you want to take with you."

"Yes." I slowly emptied my pack, laying everything out for inspection. I placed the mirror glass-side down, unsure of how they'd react to the necromancer's visage. Lastly, making sure not to touch it, I unwrapped the soul blade.

"Few items." The roo leader squinted down at the pieces.

"Yes. There wasn't much there but bones."

He grunted and nodded, then pointed to the obsidian dagger. "Where did you find that?"

"In a grave, thrust into the chest of the lord of the keep." I thought about it, and added, "He was a necromancer."

*What are you *doing?**

I ignored Saraknyal.

The roo troop murmured and twitched their tails. "And this stone knife killed him?"

"Yes." It was true enough. "There's magic in it. Bad magic. I don't think you want it here."

The leader shuffled back a step and motioned another forward. Swirling patterns of vivid blue dye adorned her fur, and carved splinters of bone pierced her ears, nose, and the lip of her pouch. A shaman, I supposed.

She hopped closer and squinted down at the blade, then bobbed her head. "Death magic!"

The others murmured again, their hands hard on their weapons.

"You're brave to have handled this thing, and strong to have survived doing so, Ash Walker." The leader sounded strangely appreciative.

"I was very careful."

"What will you do with it?"

"Take it to the city of my people, where powerful men will keep it safe." That was true, too, for whoever I sold it to would undoubtedly keep it under lock and key. Probably in a nice glass case where other rich people could stare at it and shiver in awe.

He grunted and nodded, and the shaman bobbed her head as well. "We thank you for taking this thing away, Ash Walker. Here." He handed over a large gourd. "Water to help you over the mountains."

I took it, surprised. The roo might tolerate humans, but they rarely helped them. I sketched a grateful bow. "Thank you."

He grunted and bobbed his head, then warbled a cry that sent the entire troop bounding away in a cloud of dust. They were out of sight before Saraknyal broke the silence.

Thank you, Hashi.

"I didn't do anything." I started putting things back in my pack.

You didn't tell them about me.

I finished packing in silence, then pulled the plug from the gourd and gulped down several mouthfuls. With the extra water, I'd make the pass easily. Shrugging into my pack, I started off.

*He was right, too, you know. You *are* brave and strong.*

I snorted in disgust. "Just shut up."

Yes, oh strong and brave one.

I growled at his sarcasm and kept walking.

I rode into Mati four days later. The pass had been remarkably clear. I picked up my horse in the little foothills village where I'd left him—the roo don't like horses, which was why I'd walked in Tinaros—and made good time along the roads to the city. Saraknyal initiated conversation a few times, but finally desisted when I refused to respond.

The city hadn't miraculously changed in a month. Caravans of rich Tiran merchants entered ahead of me, robed in silks and satins and sitting atop their wagons while their guards, clad in mail and helms, watched everyone with hawk eyes. Along the sides of the road, beggars and half-naked children huddled in the shade with wooden bowls, pleading for alms or food. The haves and have-nots.

Nudging my horse forward, I endured the inspection of the city guards at the gate. They scrutinized me more closely than my pack, nudging each other with leering smiles. I knew better than to protest; I didn't feel like being strip-searched. Half an hour later, I gave my horse over to the stable where I'd rented him and walked the four blocks to my home.

The ill-named *Antiques Extraordinaire* was, in fact, just another trinket shop, extraordinary to no one but me. Its owner had given me a purpose and a home, and I'd be forever grateful to him. I opened the door, ducked under the jingling bells, and grinned at Gunyan as he looked up from behind the counter.

"Hashi girl!" He levered himself up from his stool and staggered, a grimace of pain creasing his wizened features. Gunyan was old, and his joints plagued him ceaselessly, but his mind was sharper than any knight's sword. "Good to see you back! How'd it go?"

"Interestingly." A glance around the cluttered showroom confirmed that there were no customers. I flipped the sign in the window to 'closed' and threw the bolt on the door. "Come in the back and I'll let you pour me a brandy while we look over my finds."

"Of course, of course!" Gunyan tottered through the bead curtain into the back room, his posture bent. I followed at his speed.

After two years living on the street, I'd found Gunyan's shop and asked for work. He'd looked me over and asked me right back if I was serious or just another flighty street urchin who was going to steal from him or turn to whoring in a month. I promised him I'd never steal, so long as he fed me, and told him that I left home to avoid that kind of abuse, so why would I spread my legs to strangers. He offered to take me on for a year, and if I performed up to his standards, he'd teach me more. At the time, I hadn't known there was much to learn about dealing in old junk. By the end of that first year, I was hooked.

First he set me to cleaning up his trinkets. Intrinsic to that task, he taught me to spot forgeries and recognize an item's true value. When I asked what some strange engravings meant, Gunyan taught me different scripts and symbols, how to read hieratic and hieroglyphics, dwarvish and Betwani, dead languages and runes. When I mastered these with astonishing ease, he introduced me to the glory of books. When I wasn't brushing or chipping or polishing, I was reading about lost cultures, faraway lands, and vanished religions. History became my passion.

After that first year, Gunyan took me on as his legal apprentice. When I turned eighteen, he advanced me to journeyman. When I turned twenty, he wrote me into his will as his sole heir. He had nobody else to leave the shop to. Learning the trade became my life. I had a dry place to sleep, safety, comfort, food, and a profession I loved. I began collecting for him, tramping into the wilderness to unearth antiquities to sell in the shop or auction off. I also, for the first time in my life, had a friend. Though our relationship remained professional, I owed him more than I could ever repay.

But Gunyan was dying.

As I followed him into the back room—larger than the showroom by double, and festooned with hundreds of pieces being refurbished and an entire library of books—Saraknyal asked, *What's his malady?*

The bone-wasting disease. Now be quiet. I don't want you speaking to me now.

While Gunyan poured me a brandy, I put my pack on the table he always kept clear for looking at new items, and tried to calm my nerves, wondering how he would react to the soul blade. Whatever he decided to do with it, I would agree.

He hitched himself up on a stool and grinned, his old eyes twinkling in anticipation. "So, show me, Hashi girl."

"Well..." I sipped my brandy and began my tale slowly, knowing he'd want every detail. "...the first thing I discovered is that the account we read about Tawkh Keep left out one pertinent detail." I pulled items from my bag one at a time, first the pen and inkwell, then the calipers and other tools I'd found, then the mirror. "The lord of the keep was a necromancer."

"Ah, well, we always knew that *could* be the case." He fingered the tools, squinting at them dubiously, then arched his eyebrows appreciatively. "The hand mirror will bring a—" He caught his breath as he looked into the glass. "Gods and devils!"

"That's what I said." I demonstrated how the thing worked, that it moved like a reflection but displayed the necromancer's face. "I...think he made this so he could look at his younger self."

*You *know* I did,* Saraknyal said.

I ignored the comment.

Gunyan continued to fiddle with the mirror. "True or not, it'll make a great story. 'Necromancer abandons his keep, leaving behind only a reflection of his former self.' I like it!"

"Well...the thing is...the necromancer *didn't* abandon his keep. I found him."

"You *did?*" Gunyan's eyes widened, and he put down the mirror to keep from dropping it.

"Yes. Entombed in a sarcophagus, with this thrust into his chest." I withdrew the wrapped dagger from my pack, set it on the table, and unfolded the rag. "Clutched in the necromancer's own hands."

His mouth fell open. "Suicide?"

"I thought that at first." I told him of the inscriptions on the sarcophagus, then retrieved my magnifier and glow crystal to show him the tiny script engraved on the blade, how it blurred and moved. "But I was wrong." I put the magnifier down. It was time for the whole truth. "It's a soul blade, Gunyan. The necromancer's in there. His name is Saraknyal. He spoke to me."

And he's right here listening to you. You're being rude, you know!

Shut up!

"He...did?" Gunyan looked from me to the blade, then back. "Are you okay?"

"I'm fine. In fact, he won't shut up, and he's got a snide streak. He can hear and see us, so keep that in mind. He can't, however, really *do* anything."

65

I never told you that. I can do plenty, given the adequate resources.

I knew what resources he was talking about, and wasn't about to give him that.

"And the roo let you take this away?" Gunyan asked.

"They seemed *thankful* that I was taking it away." I quaffed brandy and cleared my throat. "I know what you're thinking, Gunyan, and I thought the same. It's a vile thing. I even tried to destroy it when I first discovered what it was."

"How?"

"With a hammer." I shrugged.

My ears are still ringing from that, Saraknyal said. *Or would be, if I had ears.*

I ignored him. "It didn't even scratch it. So, it was either bring it back, or dump it into a pit for some future archeologist to find and come back empty-handed."

"No, no, you did the right thing bringing it back, but we have to be careful with this." Gunyan stretched one gnarled hand toward the blade, then pulled it back. "Mati has laws against necromancy."

"But this *isn't* necromancy, it's an imprisoned necromancer." I finished my brandy and cocked an eyebrow at him. "And soul blades are worth a fortune."

"Yes, but this is...different. A weapon with a *necromancer* in it..." He rubbed his whiskers with one gnarled old hand and his eyes narrowed. "I need to think about this, Hashi girl. I might be able to arrange an auction with the right people, collectors who like dangerous artifacts."

"I thought you might know someone. If not, I guess we could throw it into the sea."

You really think giving me to the merfolk would work out well for you?

Damn, if Saraknyal didn't have a point. Merfolk had good reasons to hate land folk, and probably wouldn't have qualms about using him against us.

"Oh, there are plenty who would want it, but we've got to be careful how we present this." He blinked and smiled at me. "Get cleaned up and have a rest. You're trail weary. I'll put out some feelers and set something up."

"Good." I stood and grinned at him, relieved at his acceptance of my discovery. "I knew you'd know what to do."

"Yes, well, wrap it up again and put it away somewhere. It's giving me the shivers." He waved a hand at the blade.

"It does that." I wrapped up the dagger and took it to a cabinet.

Not intentionally, Saraknyal said. *You can leave me out. It's not like I can walk away, you know.*

You can if someone steals you. I opened a drawer and dropped the blade inside. *Sleep tight.*

You know I don't sleep. Besides, if you go too far, we can't talk.

Really! That's a bonus! I walked away, relieved to have him out of my head. I had an appointment with a bath, a meal, and at least one more brandy.

Chapter Seven
Fear and Avarice

From the journal of Hashi Severn –

While there is peace in solitude, there is strength in numbers. I've learned how to protect myself from betrayal and earn loyalty. Trust is something else entirely. Trusting anyone implicitly is, in my opinion, the biggest mistake anyone can make. It's never worked for me, at least.

After a restless night fighting off nightmares of Jhavika attacking me with her cat-o'-nine-tails, I rose early. As I finished breakfast, a knock sounded on my chamber door.

"Come in." I downed the last of my tea as Joss entered.

"Kopi Marin here to see you, mistress."

"Good!" I stood as he ushered the woman in. Kopi was one of Glosh Waymar's captains. Her little cutter, *Cat's Eye*, was in port. "Tea or blackbrew, Kopi?"

"No, thank you, mistress." She touched her brow with a knuckle in the nautical fashion. "I been up all night. Any more blackbrew and my head'll rupture."

"What news, then?" I gestured to a chair and took another.

"The harbor was like a kicked hornet's nest all night. Jhavika Keshmir and some other lords commandeered six of Fa-Chen's ships and sailed in company with *Golden Harlot* about six hours ago."

"Seven ships?" I gaped at Kopi.

Jhavika sailed after Longbright herself? That's insane! Saraknyal had been quiet all morning, but nothing good lasts forever. He had a point, though.

"And Keshmir sailed away herself?"

"Aye, and a grim sight it was. She took *Tiger Lily* as her flagship after hangin' four of her officers from the yardarms." Kopi handed me a sheet of parchment scrawled with her observations.

I perused it quickly. "I don't see Lord Temuso's name here."

"Nope. Didn't see Temuso's crest anywheres."

I shook my head in consternation. *Would Jhavika have left Temuso in command of her forces here? Why not send him after Scourge with the others while she takes the city?*

Temuso told Longbright to escape. I doubt she'd trust him that much.

Then where is he?

In Jhavika's dungeon, maybe?

I didn't like the loose end. "Thank you, Kopi. Go get some sleep, but keep an eye on the harbor for me. Trouble's brewing."

"Oh, aye!" She stood with a wry grin. "Trouble's already done boiled right over the lip of the pot, mistress."

"That it has. Be careful."

She knuckled her brow again and left, but Joss came back in before the door closed.

"Note from Bryce for you, mistress." He handed it over.

"Thank you. I'll be sending messages soon, Joss, so send up a shade." I'd commanded my shades to obey my butler years ago to make my life easier.

"Yes, mistress."

I cracked the note, and my anxiety rose with every word. In the night, Fa-Chen's heir, Que-Chen, had been evacuated from his keep by a sizable force of soldiers, but Bryce didn't know where the boy had been taken.

Jhavika took hold of Fa-Chen's house for his ships.

I nodded and continued reading. "And the rumor around town is that Longbright murdered five lords, then fled the city. Who was the fifth?"

Keshmir must have murdered someone else. I told you she'd send assassins.

I scribbled a note to Bryce to stay safe, but keep his eyes and ears sharp to any news. I handed it to the shade Joss had sent. It shuffled out as a maid delivered my accustomed second pot of tea along with yet another letter.

"From Lord Blackbriar, mistress," she informed me with a fleeting smile.

"Tori? What the..." I cracked the seal and read Tori's flowing hand.

Lady Severn,

I trust this this note finds you in good health. After the shocking events of last evening, I was relieved, at least, to learn that you left Lord Balshi's keep alive. To my knowledge, Lord Malchi, Lady Twince, Lady Brickhammer, myself, and you were the only council members not under Jhavika's sway to survive.

I've learned many things this night, and have sent missives to those lords I've listed requesting that we meet on neutral ground. There is a club I know that is reasonably safe, *Last Chance*, on the rooftop floor on the corner of Wrought Iron Avenue and Crown Street. The proprietor, Vill Shance, is discreet and willing to host a meeting for a modest sum, which I've already paid. I am requesting that we meet at midday today. Please send your response promptly.

Best wishes for your continued good health and welfare,

Lord Tori Blackbriar

I knew of the club, but had never been there. I found its name ironically apt, since it might indeed be our last chance.

It could be a trap, Saraknyal warned.

Could be, but I doubt it. That's Tori's signature. I sipped tea and considered. *We're going. In the off chance that this is some kind of deception,*

I'll send copies of my reply to the other lords, too. I dashed off a note and rang the bell for Joss.

At least you're being careful, but I still think you should—

I know what you think I should do, but I'm not going to act alone. Jhavika just sailed away with half of the Council. The rest of us have to act together before she returns.

Fine, but you don't play well with others, Hashi.

Then I'll have to learn fast, won't I?

Joss arrived, breathing hard from the stairs. "Yes, mistress?"

I held out the letter. "Draft four copies of this and address them to Nahli Twince, Reginald Malchi, Tori Blackbriar, and Ingrid Brickhammer. After I sign them, I want them delivered as fast as possible. Send four shades, and have them get replies."

"Right away, mistress." He hurried out.

I rose to pace my office. My balcony didn't have a view of the harbor, but I could see the sea just over the hilltop. Retrieving a telescope from a shelf, I scanned the blue horizon. *Not a ship in sight. Good. At least Jhavika isn't returning yet.*

Jhavika's a fool to go after that pirate herself.

But she's not a fool, I reminded him. *She probably doesn't trust anyone else to do it right. She's got the air of a control freak.*

And you're a fool to trust the other council members.

"You know me better than that, Saraknyal. Now shut up and let me think."

Two hours later, I got my replies. All the council members had received invitations from Tori, and would attend precisely at noon. *Now all I have to decide is what to wear.* I went to my clothes press and opened the doors.

Maybe...black? Saraknyal suggested with a snide chuckle.

"Oh, shut up." I surveyed my selection of apparel and frowned. "Okay, so maybe I'm in a wardrobe rut."

You need to get out more, my dear.

"No..." I picked out a pair of black leather pants and comfortable boots. "I really don't."

Last Chance was a high-end gambling club. I don't gamble, except with my soul, and I do that every day. The club catered to anyone with money, and the proprietress was no stranger to entertaining members of the Council. Never, however, so many at once, and never one accompanied by undead.

Vill Shance met me at the door with her arms folded and a defiant expression. An islander with a touch of Mati blood, she was an attractive woman, with lustrous black hair, skin slightly lighter than mine, full lips, strong features, and smoldering dark eyes.

"Not those two." She nodded to the two grim shades behind me. "Not in my club."

I narrowed my eyes and smiled without humor. "I *promise* they won't touch anything."

"I don't care. They're not coming inside." Her jaw clenched.

How exactly does she think she'll stop you from bringing them in? Saraknyal chided.

I saw no reason to make a scene or an enemy. I shrugged and sighed. "Your club, your rules." I ordered my shades to stand beside the door, then strode past the proprietress, who bowed slightly as she waved me in.

Inside, tables for cards, dice, and other games of supposed chance were arranged around two bars and stage. I wondered what kind of acts they had. As Saraknyal often reminded me, I didn't get out much. I spotted no customers, wait staff, pit bosses, or bartenders. Evidently, Tori had arranged for the entire club to be ours for privacy's sake.

The other council members were already seated around a large card table, drinks and trays of tidbits arrayed before them. Their own body guards had been allowed, of course, but I didn't care. Eschewing my own escort made me look invulnerable, not defenseless. Few of my peers looked well rested. I couldn't blame them; neither was I.

"Lady Severn." Tori stood politely and flashed a dazzling smile.

The man made me uneasy. He always looked as if he'd just stepped out of a salon, his hair a mass of golden waves, moustache and goatee perfectly groomed. A deep purple doublet hugged his torso, and one hand rested on the hilt of his dueling sword. He bowed shortly, and I returned a nod as I took the only empty seat. He seemed unduly cheerful considering the events of the previous night.

"Good to see you still breathin', Hashi." Ingrid Brickhammer smiled grimly. She wore chainmail and a long-handled war hammer at her hip. Her two escorts were similarly armed and armored.

"Good to *be* breathing. Seems like I'm the last to arrive. Brandy, please," I said as Vill raised a questioning eyebrow.

"Don't worry. We weren't talking about you." Tori Blackbriar sat and sipped a glass of light wine, suave and relaxed as usual. One would never know that he'd skewered his lovely escort through the heart last night when she tried to knife him.

"Actually, we *were*," Reginald Malchi countered, his eyes flinty on me. "You were the only council member Jhavika didn't try to murder. Why exactly *is* that, Lady Severn?"

I returned his glare. "She *did* try to murder me, Lord Malchi. If you'd stayed a moment longer, you'd have witnessed the attempt. Jhavika tried to take Soul Drinker from me. The captain of her guard paid the price for her stupidity."

"That *was* foolish of her," Tori acceded.

"Gods-damned Jhavika," Ingrid grumbled menacingly. "You all heard her. Bloody Queen of Haven is her aim, and she nearly got it!"

"An unexpected typhoon is upon us," Tori said. "We need to share resources if we hope to weather this storm."

"Indeed," Malchi agreed with a hard set to his jaw. He looked bulky beneath his dress jacket, shirt, and ruffled ascot tie; armor, no doubt. "We were lucky to get out alive."

"Lucky?" Nahli Twince cast her pupiless golden gaze upon us all one at a time, unnerving on a good day, downright creepy in this situation. Her light silk gown ruffled as if a breeze blew through the room, one that touched only her. At her shoulders, her escorts stood like a pair of beautiful bookends, perhaps the same changelings from the party, though they currently looked entirely human.
"Determined, skilled, and resourceful, yes, but *luck* had little to do with our survival."

"Aye to that," Ingrid growled. "And I had more trouble waitin' for me at home. Seems Jhavika had her fingers in my pot."

"Mine as well," Malchi agreed. "Five of my people...men I *trusted*. My eldest son was injured by one of them after I told my household what happened. I never thought it possible."

"It's magic." I accepted a snifter from Vill and swirled it under my nose, waiting until she'd gone to continue. She took a position on the far side of the room, attentive but well out of ear shot. "She's controlling people with magic."

"Yes," Nahli agreed. "The spell is subtle and insidious."

"Before we go there, may I suggest we all share information?" Tori cut in. "I'll start. The heirs of the houses whose lords were murdered last night, except for Balshi's, of course, were abducted by Jhavika or her allies and taken to her keep. Also, Lord Temuso didn't survive the party."

Well, that answers what happened to him, anyway, Saraknyal said.

"What?" Malchi glared around the table, then fixed his eyes upon me again. "Did *you* kill him, Hashi?"

"No, I didn't!" I found the news as surprising as the others. "He was alive and at Jhavika's side when I left."

"I wish you'd have killed *Jhavika*," Ingrid grumbled.

"I didn't have the opportunity." I turned back to Blackbriar. "What of Temuso's house?"

"From what I can gather, it's utterly dissolved. He had no heir. I'm currently looking for his people, but they've made themselves scarce. Apparently, when his carriage came back without him, they all packed up and vanished. His keep's completely empty. I'm making discreet inquiries today at his former places of business."

"That's incredible!" Malchi stared at Tori slack-jawed. "How could they know..."

"He must have prepared for his own death," Nahli suggested. "He danced with Captain Longbright, then told him to run after the attack. Perhaps he knew something, maybe even that he was controlled by Jhavika's magic."

Quite a supposition, Saraknyal scoffed, but I didn't share his scorn.

Temuso's laughter as they danced had seemed as genuine as the terror in his eyes when Jhavika commanded him to defend her. Not confusion, like Roque exhibited, but sheer horror. He'd known exactly what was going on...and it terrified him.

"What else?" Tori asked, eyeing us all. "I know you all have spies."

"Not as good as *yours*, evidently," Malchi said with a snort.

"Jhavika sailed out of Haven with seven ships in the small hours of the morning." Only Nahli showed no surprise, but then, she rarely showed any emotion at all. "She commandeered six of Fa-Chen's ships. She took *Tiger Lily* herself, while Roque, Brilla Balshi, and Matesh commanded three others. I don't know who captained the other two. Captain Tan on *Golden Harlot* sailed in company. The fleet didn't readily give over to Jhavika; there were summary executions aboard *Tiger Lily* before they sailed."

"I can confirm this," Nahli said. "Four officers hung from the yardarms of one ship when they sailed out of the harbor."

Tori shook his head, Malchi looked shocked, and Ingrid grumbled under her breath in dwarvish.

I delved a pocket and dropped a slip of paper on the table. "That's a list of the ships she took. They sailed with sizable contingents of soldiers aboard each."

"She's got no shortage of soldiers from her allies, as well as from Fa-Chen, Lady Hatsu, and Blinth Tinworthy's houses." Tori downed his wine and waved for another glass. "Tinworthy and Fa-Chen soldiers are helping defend Jhavika's keep, and all the others are buttoned up tighter than a highlander's codpiece."

I stifled a snort and resisted the urge to ask Tori how exactly he knew how tight a highlander's codpiece was buttoned. I didn't know why, but I always felt like laughing when Tori cracked wise. That bothered me.

"They can't be too heavily defended if Jhavika took sizable forces to sea," Malchi surmised. "Why in the names of all the gods would she go after Longbright herself? She stages a successful coup, then sails away? That's bizarre."

"Longbright maimed her and took her scourge," Nahli said, relieving me from saying it.

"Her *scourge*? You mean that cat-o'-nine-tails she wears?" Ingrid asked.

75

"It's enchanted," I added. "It *might* be how she's controlling people, but I can't figure out how the magic works. Even though Longbright took it from her, she still retains control."

Malchi frowned dubiously. "How do you know she's using *magic* to control them? Maybe it's just a conspiracy."

"No, Hashi is correct," Nahli confirmed. "And that's why Jhavika won't rest until she gets the scourge back. She's understandably angry, but her actions aren't balanced. I believe the magic may be affecting *her* as well."

"But she lashed Longbright with that thing. If that's how she casts this spell, why wasn't he ensorcelled?" Malchi looked to Nahli, then me.

"I did feel some type of magic when she struck him, but he evidently resisted the compulsion." Nahli shrugged.

Don't tell them what you heard him say, Hashi. You don't want to reveal too much.

I waved a hand. "I think we're digressing from the real point here. If Jhavika's holding the heirs of the assassinated council members hostage, she controls seven Council votes."

Ingrid Brickhammer shook her head. "Votes don't mean squat. If this is war, it's all about soldiers, and right now she's got more soldiers, spies, and assassins at her disposal than the five of us combined."

"But most of them are at sea," Tori said with a cocked eyebrow.

Be careful of Blackbriar, Saraknyal warned in my mind. *I don't like the way he's looking at you, and he's wearing that elf blade.*

I glanced over at Tori. His half-lidded gaze seemed amused or secretive, but his hand was nowhere near his sword.

"We've got to tip the balance before Jhavika gets back with the bulk of her forces." Malchi waved to Vill, and she brought a bottle to the table to refill his glass and Ingrid's.

"Easier said than done," Ingrid muttered. "Jhavika's keep's a fortress, and she's dropped that flyin' bridge to the fourth floor. There's only one way in: the front door. The other keeps are no easier."

"You have floorplans?" I asked. Ingrid employed most of the stoneworkers in Haven. In fact, she'd remodeled Ash Keep for me.

She nodded. "I do, and let me tell you, it was built for defense."

"There's one more thing," Tori interjected. "Jhavika's spread rumors that Captain Longbright attacked Lord Balshi's party and tried to murder the entire Council. She's cast herself as the avenging hero."

"That surprises you?" I cocked an eyebrow at him. "History's written by the winners."

"She hasn't won yet, but these rumors are just misdirection." Nahli ran a slender finger along the rim of her wineglass, producing a musical note. "Smoke and mirrors to cover her own actions."

"The *point* is," Malchi looked annoyed at having lost control of the conversation, "with Jhavika gone, there's no real Council *left* in Haven but *us*. We need to decide what to do."

Lay waste to her soldiers, create an army of shades, and welcome Jhavika back properly when she returns, Saraknyal suggested.

That plan would probably work, but I didn't want to pay the price.

"And we have to act sooner rather than later," Ingrid said. "There's no way to know how long Jhavika will be gone, but I don't think Captain Longbright stands much of a chance."

"Don't sell him short." I shot her a feral smile. "I'd have bet long odds that he wouldn't escape that party, but he did."

"Some of the best moves I've ever seen," Tori agreed. "And he's evidently a fox at sea."

"That's true enough," Malchi agreed. "He took one of my ships last year without a single casualty on either side. He's not a maniac, but he *is* a sly one."

"He might sail for open sea," Tori suggested.

Nahli shook her head. "I don't think so. The Blood Sea is his hunting ground. The fox doesn't venture into the open when the hounds are at bay. He goes to ground."

"We have to decide what to do *here* before Jhavika returns!" Malchi insisted.

Chris A. Jackson

"Well, assaulting Jhavika's or her allies' keeps is a non-starter," Ingrid stated flatly. "We don't have siege engines, and it'd cost too many lives. We need a plan that makes us stronger and her weaker, not the opposite."

And you won't take my suggestion, Saraknyal grumbled.

You're not helping! I downed my brandy and waved to Vill Shance for a refill. It was going to be a long meeting.

Chapter Eight
The Price of Souls

I wore my best to the auction, a long crimson dress with snug sleeves and a modest neckline. Still, I felt like a beggar compared to the potential buyers in their silks, satins, and gold embroidery. Gunyan had gathered together four princes and a merchant who was currently courting one of the king's nieces, a prince in the making. The haves were schooling like sharks with blood in the water.

Maybe I shouldn't have worn red.

Gunyan had rented a room at a posh inn for the auction. This wouldn't be the first one I'd run—Gunyan rarely left the shop anymore due to his malady—and I enjoyed wrangling rich people out of their money. An attendant served wine while I took my place behind a low table, upon which I placed an ornate mahogany box, the soul blade inside. The potential buyers took their seats, smiling and chatting, several eying me. I couldn't tell if they were leering or just anticipating the auction. Their escorts—bodyguards, wizards, even a few experts in ancient artifacts—watched me with blank expressions.

Once all were settled, I rapped the table with my knuckles, smiled graciously, and curtsied appropriately. "Highnesses, gentlemen, thank you for coming. On behalf of my master, Gunyan Merico, I welcome you." I knew their names, of course, but I'd not be using them. It wasn't appropriate for a commoner to address a prince by name. I wondered if their mistresses and wives called them 'Highness' in the throes of passion. "Today, I'll be auctioning a rare piece indeed, an artifact recovered from the lost empire of Tinaros. An artifact not only beautiful, but magical and unique in all the world."

Two of the princes smirked, but the other two looked interested, and the merchant fairly salivated.

They're a pompous bunch, aren't they? Saraknyal said, though I'd not yet opened the box. Evidently, he could see through the thin wood as well as he could cloth.

Don't talk to me. I have to pay attention. "The artifact was recovered from Tawkh Keep, at the edge of the Ironwall Mountains. A dreadful place once ruled by a foul necromancer by the name of Saraknyal."

That got their attention, and the smirks melted like snow on a hot skillet.

Foul? That's not very nice, Hashi.

Shut up!

"A necromancer?" One prince, a gray-beard by the name of Kefichi, scowled profoundly.

"Yes, Highness, but fear not. The necromancer is quite dead." I smiled sweetly and opened the lid to the box. "And this is the implement that took his life."

I lifted the blade out of the box by the handle, touching it with fingertips only. Still, its chill ran up my arm like a static shock. I suppressed a shudder of revulsion as the buyers' eyes widened. Two of them even made "Oooo," sounds, clearly intrigued.

"Took his life?" The younger prince named Waffo looked skeptical. "How do you know this?"

"Because, Highness, I discovered the necromancer's resting place, with this dagger thrust into his heart by his own hands."

The merchant sat on the edge of his seat, but Waffo's skepticism devolved to a scowl, and Kefichi muttered something beneath his breath. It seemed to me like an act to throw off their rival buyers, façades to feign disinterest.

"Upon Saraknyal's sarcophagus, carved into the very stone within which he was entombed, and inlaid with gold, I found the necromancer's epitaph. 'Within I reside for all time. I have no recourse, and refuse to answer Mortas' summons. The gods I have cheated of their prize. Eternity is mine.'"

"And you say that the blade is enchanted?" Kefichi asked.

I nodded. "Please, Highness, have your learned companion verify this."

Kefichi nodded to a short man who stood at his shoulder. The fellow bowed, stepped around his lord up to the table, and lifted a small locket from a fold of his robe.

Don't let him touch me with that thing! Saraknyal said, a tremor in his voice like I'd never heard before.

I thought it best to comply. "Please don't touch the blade, sir." I smiled at him and held very still.

"Of course not." He flicked the locket with a fingernail and mumbled something. His eyes widened, and he stepped back. Turning to Kefichi, he said, "Profoundly enchanted, Highness."

I smiled to the room. "You see?"

"But what does the inscription *mean*?" demanded another prince by the name of Hiatha. "'Cheated the gods of their prize'?"

"Ah, that's but a hint at what makes this piece truly unique," I teased.

The buyers all looked from one to another, as did their escorts. No one was smirking or looking bored now.

Saraknyal interrupted with an ominous warning. *Don't tell them, Hashi. They're frightened. They won't react well to finding a necromancer in their company.*

They'll find out eventually, and if I don't tell them the truth, I'll be arrested for fraud. I held the dagger higher, displayed it to best advantage. "You see, my lords, this blade was crafted by Saraknyal himself to sequester his soul upon his death. It's a soul blade, and the necromancer resides within."

"What?" Waffo lurched to his feet.

"Preposterous!" Hiatha proclaimed.

"You bring a necromancer into Mati?" Kefichi stood and glared at me. "Foolish girl!"

I told you, Saraknyal said.

My smile faltered for a moment before I regained my composure. "My lords, please let me assure you, Saraknyal is quite impotent."

I'm really not, he chided, but I continued.

"He's imprisoned within, incapable of wielding any magic whatsoever."

I could, if you gave me the soul of that pompous ass, Hashi.

"This is an abomination!" Kefichi bellowed, pointing a finger at me, his beard bristling. "This witless girl has brought evil into our city!"

"It is *contained*, Your Highness." I dropped the blade into the box and closed the lid to prove my claim. "It's harmless!"

"Until it consumes our *souls*!" he raged. "It's likely already enchanted this girl!"

The merchant and two of the princes backed away and fled the room, while Waffo and Kefichi's retainers stepped between their lords and me.

"The authorities will hear of this, Miss Severn, and your master will answer to the king's justice!" Waffo whirled for the door.

"I've broken no laws, Your Highnesses!"

"You're ensorcelled by a necromancer!" Kefichi raged, following Waffo out.

The door slammed, leaving me standing there slack-jawed, the poor attendant backed against a wall, his face a mask of terror.

When I'm right, I'm right, Saraknyal quipped. *I might suggest vacating the premises before the city guard arrives.*

"Shit!" I scooped up the box and headed for the door.

As in deep, and you're in it, he agreed. *You really should listen to me, Hashi. I do have some experience with people who fear me.*

Fine! I'm listening! How do I get them to listen to me? I lengthened my stride as I exited the inn and started for home.

You can't. You've lied to them already. I'm not impotent and I can exert my powers. All I need is a little soul energy. If you hope to survive this, you'll have to defend yourself. If you take me in your hand and allow me to feed, they won't be able to harm you.

I'm not destroying a human soul to save myself, you foul creature! I just need to convince them that you're not a threat!

But I am a threat. They're right.

Well, then that you're a contained threat, and that I'm not ensorcelled.

How do you know you're not?

82

Because I'm going to throw you in the fucking sea! I changed direction toward the waterfront. They'd be looking for me at Gunyan's shop. If I got rid of the blade first, they'd have no physical evidence that I'd done anything wrong, just accusations.

At least take me out of this box! Saraknyal pleaded. *They'll be looking for a woman carrying a mahogany box, and I'll be better able to warn you if they spot you.*

Fine! I ducked into an alley, pulled the dagger out of the box, and dropped the container. Slipping the blade through the sash of my dress, I folded the material to conceal it. When I reached the waterfront, I could pull it free and throw it quickly. Without the dagger, I could claim I'd made it all up to try to defraud the buyers. I'd spend some time in prison, but at least they wouldn't hang me. Maybe...

I almost made it.

Two blocks from the waterfront, Saraknyal warned me that city guards were closing in. *I can hear the clanking of their armor, Hashi. You have to take me in hand and defend yourself.*

No! I'm not letting you destroy someone's soul!

Even at the risk of your own life?

I'd rather risk my life than my soul! I changed course through an alley and emerged from the other end to spot a squad of soldiers half a block away, headed for the waterfront. I spun on my heel and tried to walk at a measured pace.

Hashi! Another troop's coming around the—

"There! In the fancy dress!" A guard pointed at me from a block ahead, half a dozen more rounding the corner behind him. He raised a whistle to his lips and blew hard, the shrill note echoing off the inns and warehouses.

I turned and ran, ducking back through the alley.

Use me, Hashi! It's your only hope!

"No!" My dress dragged at my legs, slowing me, but I refused to let my hand reach for the blade tucked under my belt. If I touched it, I'd be tempted to use it.

By the time I reached the end of the alley, soldiers had filled it behind me. I dashed into the street right into another squad answering the call of the whistle. I darted left, but my long legs got tangled in my dress. I stumbled, but didn't quite fall. Shouts rang out behind, then something hit my legs, and I sprawled to the cobbles.

I skinned both palms and couldn't get up. A bolo had pinned my dress to my legs.

Draw me! Cut yourself free!

I kicked to free myself, but something came down between my shoulders, and my chin struck a cobble. I tasted blood, and my head swam.

"You're under arrest on suspicion of necromancy!" The guard's knee crushed the breath out of me, and his iron grip closed on first one wrist, then the other.

"Here! Use this!"

Something cinched around my wrists and tightened down hard, thin cord or wire.

"Wait!" I finally managed through bloody teeth. I'd bitten my lip, but my senses had returned. "I'm not a necro—"

"Gag her, before she casts a spell!"

Someone wrenched my head back so hard that my mouth came open, and they stuffed something in. Before I could spit it out, a rope pulled tight around the back of my neck, wedging the gag deep into my throat. I coughed and struggled to breathe.

"Bind her legs and get her up!"

They expertly wrapped up my legs and lifted me by my arms, wrenching both shoulders in the process. A full score of soldiers surrounded me, some with weapons drawn. They held me tight while an officer examined me.

"That's the one, all right, but I don't see any dagger."

"Something under her skirt there," the one holding my right arm said. "Felt it when I had her arms pinned." He reached down and tugged at my dress. "Yeah, it's right here."

"Don't touch it!" the officer warned. "It's got her ensorcelled, and it'll do the same to you!"

I screamed through the gag that I wasn't ensorcelled, but it did no good. *I* couldn't even understand me.

I'm so sorry, my dear, but I warned you.

Shut up! I raged, fighting to free my hands, but the bindings cut into my wrists.

84

They've bound your wrists with silver wire, Hashi. I can't break it, even if I had the power, which I don't.

Not that I could get away even if my bonds suddenly vanished. They'd take me to prison, and eventually someone would take the dagger from me. Then, maybe, they'd give me a chance to speak.

"To Kopshi Square! Prince Kefichi said he'd be there. His wizard said he knew how to take care of a necromancer."

The square? They carried out public executions at the square. I struggled as they dragged me along, unable to walk properly with my legs bound. My feet dragged over the cobbles. I screamed through the gag to no avail. By the time we reached Kopshi Square, the toes of my shoes had worn through, my feet were badly bruised, and my shoulders felt like they were coming out of the sockets.

When I saw what Prince Kefichi's wizard had prepared, however, I struggled with new vigor. Driftwood had been piled around a square post. The man who had confirmed the dagger was magical poured oil from a skin onto the wood. A crowd milled about the edges of the square.

"There's the witch!" Prince Kefichi pointed at me, backing away as the guards dragged me thrashing forward. "Good work! She still has the cursed thing?"

"Yes, Highness. It's there at her belt." The guardsman pointed at my hip.

"Good! We'll end this menace permanently!"

Idiot, Saraknyal scoffed. *Fire won't hurt me in the slightest.*

But I'll die screaming! I thrashed and tried to kick, but all it earned me was a fist in my stomach. I could barely breathe to begin with, and now I might puke. If I did, I'd choke to death. Better than burning, but not by much.

They hauled me onto the pile of wood and slammed my back against the post. Rope encircled me, drawn cruelly tight and hampering my breathing even further. The world turned gray at the edges, but I didn't quite lose consciousness. When they released me, I sagged against the ropes.

Shouts and cries rang out from the crowd, vile epithets and curses. The princes had evidently worked them up, telling them I was ensorcelled by a necromancer. Kefichi's wizard poured a trail of oil away from the wood, and the crowd went still.

"For the crime of necromancy, freely admitted and verified by four princes of the blood, we consign this blasphemer to the flames!" Kefichi raised one hand, and I managed to stand up enough to relieve the pressure on my ribs. He looked at me and grinned in triumph. "May the gods have mercy on her soul!"

Maybe he's not an idiot, Saraknyal commented. *The wizard must know fire won't harm a soul blade. They'll pick me up from the ashes and claim victory, then take possession without paying a single coin. You watch.*

I'll be dead, you piece of shit!

Well, yes. I'm sorry about that, but I did warn you.

I tried to reach the ropes with my bound hands, but the knots were behind the post. I wrenched and pulled, my wrists now slick with blood from the bindings. *Help me, Saraknyal! I don't want to die like this!*

As you so astutely noted, I have no power. Not without at least some soul essence to work with.

"Light it!" Kefichi commanded, and the wizard pointed at the trail of oil. Sparks spat from his finger, and the oil ignited. Flames trailed toward my waiting pyre.

I chewed at the gag, wrenched my arms until I felt blood trickling down my fingers. "Help me!" I screamed into the gag, kicking at the wood piled at my feet.

The flames reached the pile, and the oil-soaked wood ignited. *Saraknyal! Help me. Don't let me die like this!*

I need soul essence to help you, my dear. I'm sorry.

Take mine! Flames licked at my feet, the heat building. Agony blossomed and radiated up my legs. I screamed again into the rag. *Destroy my soul! I can't die like this!*

Your soul?

Yes! Destroy me! Please! The hem of my dress smoldered.

Hashi, you must touch the dagger! I can help you if you can touch me and give me consent!

Please! I wrenched my wrists to reach the dagger, twisting my body as my feet blistered. Digging my fingers into the folded cloth, I pulled the soul blade an inch closer. *Destroy me!*

*I don't need to consume all of your soul, Hashi, just a portion. Give me a part of yourself that you loathe, a part of your soul that you would be better off without, and I'll teach these ignorant swine what *real* power is! But you must give me consent!*

A part of my soul? Even in agony, straining to reach the dagger's pommel, I considered what part of myself I would willingly destroy. The answer came easily: the part of my soul that had only ever brought me pain. The part of my soul that my own mother had tormented. My fingertip brushed the bone pommel of the dagger. *I give you consent! Take my loneliness! Take my desire for companionship. Take my need for love!*

Very well.

I felt it then, the necromancer's essence worming into the ethereal substance of Hashi Severn, winnowing through my soul like a miner sifting through sand for gold. I shivered despite the flames blistering my feet. As my dress ignited, an inner heat seared through me as a piece of my soul flared, then quenched...gone.

Yes... Saraknyal crowed in ecstasy. *Thank you, Hashi. Now, laugh for me, and think 'chill of fear'.*

How the hell can I laugh with the gag in my mouth?! I raged silently, but it suddenly wasn't there, only a few bits of moldering cloth easily spat out. The ropes around me puffed into dust, the cords on my legs gone. Only my wrists remained bound.

But I was on fire.

Look at their faces and laugh, Hashi! Teach them fear!

Through my agony, I took in the self-righteous victory painting my prosecutors' faces, the bloodlust of the amassed crowd, the stoic resolve of the soldiers, and I laughed a peal of terrible mirth in a voice utterly not my own. *Chill of fear!*

The flames withered and died, and the crowd reeled back in terror. The wood shifted, and I pitched forward, landing on blistered feet. The now-silent crowd stared at me in shock, the princes' eyes wide, the wizard's mouth gaping. Soldiers hesitantly reached for swords and raised crossbows.

Free me, Hashi! Use the blade to cut the wire on your wrists!

I strained again, and hooked two blood-slicked fingers around the haft of the soul blade. Its power chilled me to the bone, blunting my pain. I pulled it free, awkwardly reversed my grip, and brought the blade down between my wrists.

It cut the silver wire like butter.

The sight of my bloody hands suddenly free must have snapped the guards out of their terror. Half a dozen crossbows cracked.

I thought I was dead, but the bolts puffed into rust and splinters the instant they touched me.

Dust to dust, Saraknyal whispered in my mind.

I gaped down at my burned and riddled dress, but other than some blisters, my flesh was untouched. My shock, and the looks of horror on the faces of my would-be executioners, brought another peal of laughter from my throat.

"Cut her down!" Kefichi screamed, backing away. "Kill her, or we're all doomed!"

Oh, they're doomed all right. Now use me, Hashi. Take your vengeance for this injustice, for your pain, for the shreds of your sacrificed soul! Let me feed and teach them terror!

My head swimming with smoke and agony, and my nerves singing with the chill of Saraknyal's power, his words lit a fire within me. They'd unjustly tried to murder me, these powerful men who wouldn't listen. They deserved to be taught a lesson that all of Mati would remember.

Two soldiers charged with swords raised, their eyes under the lips of their helms wide with fear, but their jaws set in determination.

Fear not their blades! Pierce their flesh and allow me to feed!

I raised a warding hand despite Saraknyal's assurance—a lifetime of self-preserving instinct is not so easily abandoned—but true to his word, the first blade vanished into a cloud of rust as it touched me. The soldier staggered with his unspent momentum, and I buried the soul blade in his gut. *Feed!*

Saraknyal fed.

Ice water surged through my veins, arcane power swelling a hundredfold, tingling across my every nerve. I gasped with the rush.

YES! Saraknyal bellowed. *Now the other!*

I stared for a moment into the man's dead, soulless eyes before he crumpled like a puppet with its strings cut. A moment too long. I cringed as the second solder's blade fell, but it fared no better, dissolving as it sliced through the high collar of my dress. I slashed desperately, and the blade cut through chainmail, flesh, and bone. His severed arm fell away, hot blood spraying me, his scream dying as a pearly white mist trailed from his flesh, swirling around the obsidian blade before sinking into its surface. The man fell, another soulless husk, as his soul's energy flooded into me.

Lightning crackled in the wizard's hands, and he threw it at me like a javelin.

"To earth!" I shouted, realizing that Saraknyal had lent me the words.

The spear of electricity crackled along my skin, then down into the cobblestones at my feet. I stared down at my smoldering dress in amazement, unsure how I still lived.

*Raise them, Hashi. The dead are yours to command!"

"Arise!" Again, the word formed in my head, and there was power in it. I felt a slight drain in the seething energy that filled me, and the two corpses stiffened and stood. Horrorstruck, I stared at them for a moment, then turned my gaze on the wizard who had tried to murder me. My remorse melted away. *You should have listened to me.* I pointed the soul blade at him. "Kill him."

The dead shambled forth at my command toward the terrified wizard. He turned and ran. I wondered if they'd catch him.

"Nothing will touch her!" Kefichi screamed, turning to flee.

The rest of the crowd had already fled the square in a screaming stampede. The soldiers, however, stood their ground. Another flight of crossbow bolts disintegrated, and an officer charged me with a war hammer. The weapon puffed into rust as it met my outstretched fingers, and I slashed out to nick his wrist with the soul blade. Again, a pearly mist trailed after the blade and was drawn in like the smoke of a pipe being inhaled. An intoxicating rush, the energy swelled within me. The officer stiffened, and I animated his corpse before he even fell.

"Defend me," I ordered it, and the soldiers stared as their dead commander drew a dagger and faced them.

Behind you!

I whirled in time to catch the fist of a soldier on my cheekbone. The blow knocked me sprawling, my ears ringing and stars exploding behind my eyes. Thankfully, I retained a grip on the dagger.

"Mob her!" the lucky soldier bellowed. "She's not invulnerable!"

When he reached down to grab the neck of my dress, I stabbed him in the arm. He gasped once as Saraknyal devoured his soul, and collapsed, but he'd made his point. I could be hurt.

Even as I raised the man who had struck me, twenty soldiers charged, fists clenched and ready. They'd learned. I lurched up, but I had nowhere to run.

Use my eyes, my senses! Defend yourself!

Everything leapt to crystal clarity in my mind's eye: every sound, every scent, every image all around me. For a moment it staggered me, but I oriented myself, turning my back to my two undead defenders and bracing myself.

I was no warrior, but I knew how to use a knife; living on the street teaches you a few things. I also knew how men fought, how they relied on their strength to overpower a weaker foe. But that didn't matter here; all I needed to do was nick them with the soul blade.

The first soldier to attack thrust his sword through one zombie's chest. The blade stuck. My guardian gripped the soldier's hand on the hilt, yanked him closer, and stabbed him in the throat. The others didn't fare much better, and those who dared to attack me, far worse. The soul blade met their flailing fists and sliced through their armor like paper. Three of my assailants fed Saraknyal before they even knew what had happened. Every one filled me with energy until I felt I might burst.

Fear, Hashi! Break their confidence!

I released a cackling peal of icy mirth, staggering my foes. Two more fell before they recovered, and each rose again as my ally. In seconds, seven more zombies faced a diminishing force of soldiers whose courage had been shattered by Saraknyal's magic.

They faltered, hesitated, and broke.

As they ran, I took stock of myself; bruised and battered, my feet blistered, and my wrists bleeding, but I was alive. The blade in my hand fairly howled with power.

More! Saraknyal raged in my mind. *Hunt them down! Command your minions to drag those pompous princes back here for me to feast upon!*

I heaved a breath and looked around. Empty husks of men encircled me, ready for my commands. In that instant, I realized what I had done. I had destroyed human souls, the very thing I'd condemned Saraknyal for.

I was damned.

"Oh, gods..." The strength left my legs, and I collapsed to hands and knees. My breakfast made a hasty exit out of my mouth, followed by a bout of retching.

Hashi?

Shut up. I spat and fought for control. Failing, I retched again. *I'm damned... I'm lost...*

Oh, quit whining!

Fuck you! This is your fault!

It is not my fault. I warned you, and you didn't listen. I saved your life!

At the cost of my soul.

Oh, your poor soul! Sarcasm dripped from every word. *Grow a fucking spine why don't you! I've tasted your soul, and there's nothing special about it! The souls you took today were intent on sending yours to Hell, so get over it!*

I thought about that for a heartbeat, then retched again. Bile burned my throat.

Are you done? he asked as I wiped my mouth with my sleeve.

"Fuck you." I spat, hawked, and spat again.

I'm quite beyond carnal desires, my dear, but if you'd like to employ the haft of my blade as a sexual aid, I'm sure—

I snatched up the fallen dagger and threw it as hard as I could. Unfortunately, its trajectory met with one of my undead minions, piercing its skull to the hilt.

Feel better?

"I hate you," I hissed through gritted teeth.

You've got a lot of company. Now get me out of here and let's get to work.

I sat back on my heels. "What makes you think for a second that I'll ever touch you again?"

Because burning at the stake is far worse, and I'm your only way out of this city. Unless, of course, you choose to take the souls of every man, woman, and child in this wretched cesspool and assume the throne. He paused, his amusement palpable. *That could be fun, too.*

I nearly puked again.

There is, however, one more thing you may want to consider.

What? I heaved a breath, forcing my stomach to settle.

Gunyan.

Realization struck me like a charging bull. The princes knew where I lived, knew Gunyan. Whether they thought I would go there or not, they'd come down on him like a ton of bricks.

"Shit!" I heaved myself up, paused to wrench Saraknyal's soul blade from the zombie's skull, and ran for home.

Got any plan for how to get out of Mati? Saraknyal asked as I ran.

"None. Now shut the fuck up!" My feet were killing me, and my wrists felt like they were on fire.

*Of course. Because doing things *your* way has gone so swimmingly well.*

I gritted my teeth and ran.

I burst through the door of *Antiques Extraordinaire*. Gunyan looked up from behind the counter, his eyes widening at my state. "Hashi? What in the name of—"

"We're in trouble!" I slammed the door, threw the bolt, and dashed for the back room.

"What happened to you?" He tottered after me, but by the time he made it through the beaded curtain, I was upstairs.

"They called me a necromancer and tried to burn me at the stake in Kopshi Square!" I barged into my room and tore off the shreds of my burned and tattered dress. My feet were blistered, my wrists lacerated, and I ached all over, but I had no time. "We've got to get out of Mati!" I pulled on a shirt and pants, gritting my teeth as the material raked over my blisters.

"What? Hashi, you're not making sense!"

"They said the soul blade had ensorcelled me, and accused me of necromancy!" I sat and struggled into socks and my good boots, biting back tears. "They wouldn't listen to me. They arrested me, tied me to a post, and tried to burn me alive!"

"Gods and devils, Hashi girl! How did you get away?"

"The...blade." I damned myself with my confession. "I used it."

"Oh, no!" Gunyan's words, brittle with horror, barely reached me from where he stood at the bottom of the steps. "No, Hashi girl!"

"Saraknyal...helped me," I struggled to explain. I stood and winced, but my feet felt better in my boots. Hesitating but a second, I snatched up the soul blade, its power chilling my flesh and humming across my nerves until I slipped it through my belt. "He saved my life, but..."

"But what, girl?" Gunyan asked.

But I'm damned to Hell for destroying souls. I couldn't say it.

"They tried to kill me, Gunyan." I grabbed up my old pack and hurried down the stairs. "I had to fight back. I'm afraid I...killed some people. Soldiers."

"With the soul blade?" Gunyan gaped at me as I brushed past him.

"Yes. It's *powerful*, Gunyan." I started stuffing anything of value that I could find into my bag. We would need money. "They won't believe me if I tell them I'm not ensorcelled by it. We've got to get out of here. Pack up whatever you can think of and get ready!"

"Hashi!" His gnarled hand closed on my arm, and I turned to face him. "I can't travel. Not like this." He gestured to his knobby, twisted legs. "Not fast enough to get away. You should go alone, and quickly. They'll come here looking for you."

I stared at him blankly. "But they'll take you!"

"Maybe, but I'm just an old man, Hashi. I'm no threat to anyone. I'll tell them you ran away and took that cursed thing with you." He gestured to the dagger at my belt. "I'm sorry, Hashi."

"Sorry? Why?" I blinked at him, confused. "I'm the one who dug this fucking thing up. You didn't do anything!"

*Technically, you didn't dig me up, and he *did* arrange the auction,* Saraknyal said.

"Shut up!" I clenched my fists and closed my eyes. *Just leave me the hell alone!*

"What? Hashi, what's going on? You're not making sense." Gunyan took a step back from me.

I hated the fear on his face. "It's Saraknyal," I said. "He won't shut up, and I... I had to *use* the blade, Gunyan, the magic. I...I think I'm doomed."

"Doomed? What do you mean?"

"It's horrible! It...I had to fight and it...took their *souls*!" I gasped a breath at the admission, closing my eyes against the tears. "I'm lost, Gunyan. I'm doomed to Hell."

"Oh, nonsense!" His bone-thin arms encircled me, and he pulled me in as tightly as he could, the first time in nine years that he embraced me. "Stop it. You're not doomed to anything. It was that damned necromancer that did it, Hashi girl. You aren't a necromancer any more than I am."

*True, but *I* am, and the authorities won't argue the fine points. You need to get a move on!*

For once, Saraknyal's suggestion made sense.

I pushed Gunyan to arm's length. "We've got to go, Gunyan. Please. Come with me."

"I *can't*, Hashi! You know I can't. I can barely hobble across the shop. You need to go. Quickly now!" He turned to a cabinet. "Here. I've got some money stashed away. You should take it. They'll watch the harbor, but you can buy a horse and ride north. They won't chase you into Tira."

Tira? The kingdom of Sofro lies to the north. The kingdom of Tira is hundreds of leagues northeast!

Shut up! Sofro hasn't been a kingdom for two centuries. Tira's an empire.

You really need to catch me up on current events.

"Here!" Gunyan shoved a leather pouch into my hands. "Go, Hashi!"

"Gunyan, I—"

Glass shattered in the front room.

Too late, Saraknyal quipped, and I would have throttled him if he'd had a neck.

I hurried to peer through the beaded curtain and found the showroom in flames. Someone had thrown a flask of burning oil through the window. Shouts rang out from the street, bellowed orders, even one scream. Flaming arrows followed, thunking into the wall near me, flames licking at the wood. The shop didn't have another door, abutting other buildings on three sides. They were going to burn an entire city block to get me.

Don't these morons ever *learn?*

"Evidently not." I put a hand on the dagger's hilt and laughed. The flames died, and the raised voices outside quieted. I whirled toward the back room. "Gunyan, they're trying to burn the shop. They're not going to ask questions. You *have* to come with me!" I stuffed the money into my pack and shouldered it.

His dark face went ashen with terror. "Burn the shop? That's *insane!*"

"It's *fear*. Fear of me. Now come on!" I grabbed his arm and pulled him with me. "Just stay behind me!"

"But they'll shoot you!" He tugged back, but his frailty couldn't match my panic.

"Don't worry. I've got this." I gripped the soul blade's hilt with my other hand and drew it from my belt. The bone-shaking chill carried with it a horrible feeling of power, invulnerability, even Saraknyal's insatiable hunger. I let go of Gunyan's arm to throw the door bolt. "They don't know much about necromancers."

As soon as I pulled open the door, crossbows cracked in a ragged volley. Fear must have ruined their aim, for only about half struck me and puffed into dust. Several others buzzed past close enough for me to feel the breeze or sunk into the door frame. Soldiers lined the street, while bystanders cowered behind them, wide-eyed.

I glared and laughed again, sending them shrinking back in terror.

"Come on, Gunyan. I—" I reached back, but he wasn't there. Turning, I found him lying on the floor.

One of the crossbow bolts that had narrowly missed me had found him. He clutched the shaft in bloody hands, his eyes wide with surprise.

"Gunyan!" I collapsed beside him.

"Hashi...girl..." His eyes fluttered.

I gripped the shaft of the bolt. *Saraknyal, can you destroy the bolt?*

Yes, but it won't help him. The damage is done. I can't heal him.

Do it!

Very well.

The arrow puffed into dust, and bright blood pulsed from the wound. Gunyan gasped, then coughed, blood flecking his lips.

"Hashi! I'm...sorry..."

"Hush, Gunyan. I'm going to—"

He gasped again, his eyes widening, and the life faded from his gaze. The only human being I'd cared about in the entire world, and I'd killed him. A horrific sob tore from my throat. I felt as if a part of me died with him, as if Saraknyal had consumed another shred of my soul. Perhaps I should have told him to do exactly that, to destroy me utterly. It seemed a simple escape.

Hashi! Look out!

I turned as the soldier hurled a fist at me. The blow caught me on the temple, but glancingly. I lashed out with the dagger—*feed*—and Saraknyal did the rest. My assailant dropped like a steer in a slaughterhouse. Other soldiers edged closer, their fists clenched.

I lurched up to face them. "Are you *insane?*" I screamed. "Do you *want* your souls destroyed?"

That gave them pause. Soldiers faced death regularly, but this was different. Maybe I could prevent an all-out slaughter.

"I'm leaving Mati!" I pointed the soul blade at them, power crackling in my hand, frosty mist trailing from the blade. "Try to stop me, and you'll perish!"

"Charge her!" an officer commanded from behind the first rank.

They charged.

Scream and give them winter! Saraknyal ordered.

I didn't know what to expect, but complied. My own solutions had resulted in Gunyan's death and the damning of my soul. What else did I have to lose? I gulped a ragged breath and screamed.

Winter.

Frost billowed from my mouth like an icy hurricane. The blast caught three soldiers in the fore and froze them solid. Their momentum sent them toppling forward, and blue flesh shattered into shards of ice at my feet.

The rest of them stopped, some of them frostbitten, gaping at me and their fallen companions.

"I...am...*leaving!*" I raged through clenched teeth.

"Attack!" the officer bellowed again, but his soldiers were having none of it. They backed away from me in horror. I couldn't blame them.

I pointed my blade at the officer and bared my teeth. "Why don't *you* lead them in the charge?"

He glared at me and stumbled back a step.

"Wise choice." I turned and dashed off, jamming the soul blade through my belt. I cursed the day I found it. I cursed myself for bringing it back with me, for thinking I could sell it for a fortune. I cursed my damned soul, my cowardice that had led me down this path. If I'd burned to death in the square, Gunyan would still be alive.

So, tell me why there's an empire to the north instead of the kingdom of Sofro.

Shut the hell up or so help me, I'll throw you in the sewer!

Fine, but may I make a suggestion for your own survival?

Yes.

Gunyan was right, you need a horse.

I knew he was right, but I wasn't thinking straight. If I tried to walk out of the city, the princes would send an army to stand in my way. That wouldn't stop me, not with the Saraknyal's powers at my command, but I didn't want more destroyed souls on my conscience. I turned at the next corner, heading for the same hostler where I'd rented my mount before. With Gunyan's money, there would be no arguments.

Gunyan... My heart wrenched in my chest. His death dragged at my soul, ripping tears from my eyes that burned like fire.

Thankfully, Saraknyal remained silent.

Chapter Nine
A Timely Response

From the journal of Hashi Severn –

I've found that sometimes doing something quickly is better than taking the time to figure out the careful approach. Those who hesitate are quite often lost to history.

Gods, I hate meetings, I thought as I gazed around the table at my quibbling colleagues. I waved to Vill Shance for another brandy.

"The heirs that Jhavika kidnapped are the key to our maintaining control of Haven, and they're all sitting in one spot," Malchi insisted. "If we free them, they owe us, and we'll have eight houses on our side. That *might* be enough to face Jhavika's combined forces."

"It's not," Ingrid grumbled. "Not with Balshi's house on her side."

I did the math in my head and silently agreed with Ingrid.

You could offer to thin them out a little, Saraknyal suggested.

I knew just what he meant by "thin out", and hoped it wouldn't come to that. But regardless of which actions we took, there was one point that needed emphasizing.

"Whatever we decide to do, we have to move quickly. If we hesitate or get into a squabbling match, Jhavika will return with her scourge and her slave-army, and we're *all* either dead or enslaved." I tapped my fingers impatiently on the table. "Doing something quickly and decisively is better than sitting on our asses trying to figure out the best response."

"I agree," Nahli said.

"But what *is* that quick and decisive action?" Tori arched an eyebrow at me. "Can you use your necromantic powers to breach Jhavika's main gate?"

We could, you know. Jhavika's soldiers would be lined up like game pieces, ready for us to knock down. It doesn't get any better than that!

Two hundred soldiers charging in one mass might challenge even you, old man.

Maybe...

Crafting my words so as not to hint at my limitations, I said, "It depends on what you mean by 'breach'. I can destroy a metal gate or portcullis, but they won't let me just walk into the keep unchallenged. I'd rather not face a few *hundred* soldiers with nothing but a dagger."

Ingrid Brickhammer looked contemplative. "What about that time when you—"

"No." I shook my head emphatically. "These troops *can't* stand down. Not if they're under Jhavika's control like the others we've seen. They'll fight to the death. That's too much even for me to face."

"Aye," Ingrid agreed reluctantly. "Well, for my part, I've got crews workin' on the old harbor siege engines. Once they're back in condition we can throw two-hundred-pound stone balls at any ship in the harbor or trying to come through the pass from Snomish Bay. We can also coat them with coal tar and set them alight. Jhavika comes sailing back, we give her a proper welcome."

"A good idea," Malchi agreed. "And I can arm what few ships I have in port. Hashi, one of your smugglers is in port, too, yes?"

"Yes, but she's not a warship, and her crew aren't soldiers."

"No, but they could scout the coast, range out to sea and watch for Jhavika's ships," Tori suggested. "That, along with arming Reginald's ships and Ingrid finishing with the shore batteries, will give us a good first line of defense."

"Okay, I'll tell my smugglers to keep a seaward watch." I hoped Marin had gotten some sleep.

"But what about the heirs?" Malchi insisted. "They're the key to shifting the balance of power."

"Even if Hashi could destroy their front gate, a frontal assault would be too costly," Tori said.

"Then a stealthy approach seems warranted," Nahli suggested. She turned to Ingrid. "You say that you have floorplans, correct? There are balconies."

"Yes, but—"

"Then I can get *into* Jhavika's keep, but I can't get the heirs *out*. At least not the way I got in. But with help..."

Tori turned to me. "There you go, Hashi. If Nahli can sneak you in, you can deal with small groups of soldiers or guards as you make your way through the keep. No need to face them all at once."

"What?" I sputtered, imagining the carnage. "Why don't *you* go? You're the swordsman! Find the heirs and get them out through a window or something."

He smiled and caressed the hilt of his sword. "I may be a swordsman, but I can't face such an onslaught. You can."

I seethed inside, because I knew he was right.

And we bolster Haven's defenses with an army of undead! Saraknyal added with delight.

Shut. Up.

Nahli's fathomless eyes fixed upon me. "I did not mean to be accompanied by a *necromancer*." She pronounced the word like a curse, which it was.

"I'm with Twince!" Malchi exclaimed. "What's to stop her from turning everyone in that keep into undead and taking over the entire city?"

I glared at him. "If that was my intention, don't you think I'd have *done* it already? If you don't trust me, then why don't *you* go?"

"Please. Let's all cool down." Tori patted the air with his hands in a calming gesture. "Hashi, you know that you're the only one of us who can prevail over such a force. We've all heard the stories."

I sighed inwardly. It was true that I'd spent years cultivating a wicked reputation. Now that reputation had come back to bite me.

You're just being squeamish, my dear, Saraknyal said. *Transforming Jhavika's troops into your own will make you stronger and her weaker. It's the logical path. And if you can rescue the heirs... It's a win-win.*

He was right, damn him. If Jhavika returned and we hadn't strengthened our position by allying with the three houses currently being held hostage, it would be a rout. By taking Jhavika's keep, we could even those odds, reduce the bloodshed and the chance of ending up her slaves. *The lesser of two evils…*

"All right, I'll do this, but I'll do it *my* way." I turned to Nahli. "Get me in secretly, and I'll take her forces from the rear. I can bolster my own force before all Nine Hells break loose." I waved Vill Shance over again. "Just leave the bottle, please."

Nahli narrowed her eyes at me, but said nothing.

Vill put the bottle down on the table with a scowl and whirled away.

Malchi cleared his throat. "So, can you promise us that you won't wipe out every living thing in that keep and raise an army of undead?"

"Dear gods, just stop!" I slapped my palm down onto the table in frustration and glared. "Get it through your head; I don't kill people indiscriminately. Anyone who doesn't try to kill me or interfere with getting the three heirs out will live."

Tori arched an eyebrow at me, a strange expression on his features. "I never thought I'd meet a necromancer so reticent to practice their craft."

"But you'll *still* command an army of undead," Malchi insisted stubbornly.

"An army?" I shrugged. "Probably not. It depends on how forcefully the soldiers defend the keep."

*More would be better, Hashi. Especially if you have to face Jhavika and *her* army.*

I sighed. "Unfortunately, the only way to achieve *your* goal of making us stronger and Jhavika weaker is to convert some of her soldiers into mine. If you don't want me to do it…"

"She's absolutely correct," Tori said with a nod of affirmation. "And it *was* our idea, not hers. I trust Hashi a *hell* of a lot more than Jhavika Keshmir, I tell you that!"

"So do I," Nahli added, though her lips were pursed. "I may not approve of her *methods*, but I agree that this is the best strategy for prevailing over Jhavika."

"I vote we do it," Ingrid said.

Malchi made a sour face, but finally nodded. "Very well, I agree."

Shit! I had half hoped that they'd vote it down and relieve me of the burden, but no such luck. Frankly, it needed to be done, and I was the only one to do it.

"But I have one stipulation." Malchi looked from face to face warily. "The heirs are to be taken to three separate locations until we find out if it's safe to return them to their own keeps."

"I'm fine with that," I agreed with a shrug. "Choose amongst yourselves who's going to take them, because I'm not."

Not eager for the pitter patter of little feet? Saraknyal's sense of humor left much to be desired.

"I propose that one go to Tori, one to Ingrid, and one to Reginald." Nahli made a dismissive gesture. "A child would find my home...disconcerting."

"Fine, then we all agree." Tori flashed a grin. "Now we just have to figure out the details, and you know what they say about *those*."

"Aye, devils reside there." Ingrid lifted her glass. "Here's to the devils! Maybe they'll be kinder if we toast them."

I barked a laugh and raised my snifter.

"I'll have coaches waiting outside Jhavika's front gate to whisk the heirs away to safety." Tori promised. "Just get them down to the courtyard, and we'll take over."

"Okay," I said, "but I need some information from those of you who discovered Jhavika's spies in your households. What might I expect from her soldiers?"

"Well, I can tell you one thing." Ingrid sipped her whiskey, her gray eyes flinty. "There's no talkin' to them, no changin' their minds, and no stoppin' them but with force. None of the ones in my keep survived."

"I had a similar experience," Malchi agreed. "They refused to surrender. The one we subdued fought his restraints to the point of...self-mutilation. I ordered him put down."

I tried to wash the lump in my throat down with another sip of brandy. This is what I'd be facing in Jhavika's keep. Fear wouldn't keep them at bay. "Okay, let's get this over with."

"Excellent!" Tori turned to Nahli. "How soon can we proceed?"

"I'll need time to prepare." Nahli pursed her lips in thought. "I hadn't thought to bring someone else in with me. Three days, perhaps. This will *not* be easy."

"Three *days?*" Malchi looked stricken. "Jhavika could be back any moment! We can't—"

"What you can't do is rush magic, Lord Malchi." There was no derision in Nahli's tone, but a clear statement of fact. "This will be a delicate enchantment."

"Why?" I asked warily. "How are you going to get us in?"

"The same way I escaped Lord Balshi's party." She smiled at me, and I felt a little ill. "You remember, I'm sure."

"I remember you changing into a bloody great bird," Ingrid said.

"Wait! You mean you're going to change *me* into a..." I swallowed hard.

Don't let her do it, Hashi! She'll transform you into a slug and leave you like that!

Shut up! You're not helping! I didn't need Saraknyal telling me how dangerous this would be.

"For me, the ability's innate, but I'll have to...graft my ability to you. The form you take will be of your choosing, Hashi. Fear not."

Easy for her to say, Saraknyal grumbled.

"Pardon me, but how do I know you'll change me back? You've amply expressed your opinion of necromancers."

"Because, as Tori said, we *need* you." She nodded to Tori, then me. "You'll just have to trust me, as I will trust you to do as *you've* promised."

I downed my brandy. *Trust... Why does it always boil down to trust?*

Because life's not fair, and death is worse.

"So, it's decided then." Malchi started ticking things off on his fingers. "I'll arm what ships I have in port. Hashi will send her smugglers scouting for Jhavika's fleet. Ingrid will see to the shore batteries. Nahli will prepare her magic. And... I'm sorry, Tori, what exactly will *you* be doing again?"

"I'll prepare transport for the heirs, and send out my spies to gather information and counter Jhavika's propaganda campaign." He grinned and raised his glass. "To our success!"

We all raised our glasses in toast, and I tossed back the last of my brandy.

"Three days, then." Ingrid stood. "Everyone keep in touch."

I stood. "I'll let you know if my smugglers see any ship within ten miles of the city. Nahli, contact me when you're ready. I'd suggest we do this at night."

"I agree. Two nights from tonight, I should be ready." She rose and flowed out of the room.

Blackbriar's going to chat up Vill Shance. Saraknyal sounded amused. *He certainly has a way with women.*

I watched Tori and Vill through Saraknyal's perception. I couldn't hear them, but she smiled and laughed at something he said. He shook her hand, then brought it up to kiss. If her skin hadn't been so dark, I would have sworn she'd blushed.

He certainly does. I wondered idly what Tori's way with women really was. *There's more to that man than meets the eye.*

He doesn't fear you, Hashi. He would make a good wraith.

Shut up. I've got enough on my mind. I strode out and collected my bodyguards. *If we go into Jhavika's keep, there'll be souls destroyed.*

I never will understand why you're so squeamish about that. I say you're doing them a favor. No one in Haven is a saint, Hashi. They're all going to share the same fate in the afterlife.

Jhavika's soldiers are ensorcelled, not evil, Saraknyal. For all you know, they could *be saints.*

I doubt it, and they won't be suffering, regardless. Oblivion is...well, simply nothing.

Oblivion... I supposed I would find out when the time came.

Chapter Ten
No Safe Harbor

Mati is a big city, so a woman on a horse, even if her shirt is riddled with holes, doesn't draw much attention. I bought the same sturdy gelding I'd ridden only a few days ago, a saddle, saddlebags, and some fodder for my mount, and rode out of the city at a hasty but careful pace. Word spread about the incident in the square, but few specifics. Rumors of a necromancer running rampant through the city and hordes of undead slaughtering people bore no relation to a young woman on horseback heading out on a trip. The guards at the northern gate barely glanced at me as I rode through.

Well, that was less difficult than I thought it would be.

Saraknyal's constant vigilance had made my escape easier, but I wasn't going to thank him. Yes, he'd saved my life, but I now regretted the decision. It had cost me more than I'd reckoned.

So, now will you tell me why there's an empire north of Mati instead of the Kingdom of Sofro?

I almost laughed at the irony. *Actually, you'd probably appreciate the story. It involves a necromancer coming back from the dead.*

Really?

No, I'm making shit up just to entertain you.

Droll, Hashi, but I'm serious. I'd like to know what's transpired in the last half millennia. All I've had to entertain myself is the inside of a coffin and my own moldering corpse. I could write a treatise on the decomposition of the human body, but the geopolitical situation has rather left me in the dust. Besides, conversation will pass the time, and you've got nothing better to do.

Yes, I do. I need to think of what to do, where to go. I steered my horse off the road to avoid a tangle of two caravans passing in opposite directions. The road north was always busy, which might slow me down, but also served to conceal me among other travelers. *I'm going to reach a fork in this road in a few hours, and I need to decide which direction to take.*

Well, if I knew the lay of the land and what our options were, perhaps we could discuss it.

Damn if he didn't have another point. Just because I despised him didn't mean Saraknyal wasn't intelligent. *Fine. Listen, then, to the history of the Necromancer War.*

Saraknyal knew the name of Azrael, and asked a lot of questions I couldn't answer. History didn't tell how the necromancer had risen from the grave to possess a young sorceress, only that the kingdoms of Tira and Sofro had been at war, and that the former had been losing. Then, in the midst of their war, the two kingdoms faced a common foe, an undead one. They allied forces and finally destroyed the necromancer. The great walled citadel of Nolshir, Sofro's capital, had been razed, and the sovereigns of both kingdoms perished in the final conflict. The resulting empire of Tira was born from the ashes.

"Tira is rich in lands, and prosperous," I finished. "Mati's the empire's only easy avenue to sea trade."

That explains why Mati is so rich, but why are you hesitant to make a home in Tira?

Because of you, I grumbled beneath my breath.

Me? He seemed honestly surprised. *I don't understand.*

After nearly being destroyed by a necromancer, you think they don't have strict laws against the practice?

Oh, well, if you're careful, they won't know about me, er...us, will they?

Word will spread by courier. The prosperity of Mati and Tira are intertwined. Mati will warn them about me...you...us.

Well, that does present a problem, then. I'd recommend staying off the beaten track.

Right now, the beaten track is all we have. The question is, do we head northwest at the fork toward Nolshir, or northeast into the forest?

You said Nolshir was destroyed.

They rebuilt it. It's a major city, but Tiravore's the capital of the empire.

Well, I vote for the forest. We should cross the river.

I glanced to my right. The forest rose green and thick on the far side of the river that paralleled the road. The Tir River was deep and broad, and I considered once again throwing the soul blade away. Surely, nobody would ever find it buried in the silt of a riverbed. Without it, I could make my way to Tira and find work. I had valuable skills, and could eventually set up my own shop. However, word would spread, and my name and description would eventually reach Tiravore. I wondered if the emperor would bother seeking proof of my guilt or simply have me executed. Without Saraknyal, I would be at their mercy.

We can't ford the river here.

How far until we can cross?

I don't know. I think there are bridges at Kezmar.

I would recommend haste, then. We must stay ahead of any couriers from Mati.

Good advice. I urged my horse to the best pace I thought prudent. At the fork, we bore to the northeast, and the caravan traffic diminished by half. The river supplied abundant water, and I let my mount rest and drink every hour or so. We passed through tiny villages that were little more than waypoints for caravans, and I bought food and supplies for camping. As we climbed to the higher plateau, the nights would be colder.

Gods, I hate the cold...

Oh, I should have mentioned; if you keep a hand on me, you won't feel the cold.

"What?" I glanced down at the obsidian blade, suspecting some ulterior motive. "How?"

What part of 'I'm magical' don't you understand?

I temporized. *What I mean is, the magic has to come from somewhere. How much will keeping me warm cost you?*

Oh, a pittance. I'm quite energized at the moment, though that last spell did cost a bit.

The icy breath one?

Yes, that one. It's called 'Breath of Winter.' It can also be cast through touch. Anyway, I can keep you warm for weeks without needing to feed again.

Weeks... The trip might take more than weeks. *I'm not going to let you destroy more souls just so I can sleep warmly at night.*

Suit yourself. Saraknyal sounded insulted by my refusal.

I rode on for the remainder of the day in blissful silence. As night fell, I found a clearing under an oak tree near the riverside and set up a quick camp. Deadfall provided a tidy fire, and my horse seemed happy munching the verdant grass along the riverside. I ate trail bread and dried meat, and drank tea. The weather was mild, and I was far enough off the road that I felt I wouldn't be found by any passing soldiers. Still, thoughts of being attacked while I slept kept me awake until I was nodding with weariness.

Don't worry, Hashi. I'll watch for you and wake you if anyone approaches. You don't have to touch the blade. Remember, I have a vested interest in keeping you safe. You needn't worry.

"Said every man who ever tried to convince a woman to sleep with him."

I'm not a man. Not anymore.

"And I don't trust you."

Is it me you don't trust, or yourself?

"What?"

I'm not forcing you into anything, Hashi. You could have thrown me away anytime you wanted. You don't trust yourself to accept my help because you think you'll become addicted to it or something. So it's yourself you don't trust, not me.

"Shut up, old man." Once again, he was right. But every time I used the dagger, I was indirectly consuming someone's soul. Just the thought of it made me sick. When would the temptation be too great to use the dagger simply for my own comfort?

He fell silent, and I lay back to stare up at the stars. They were beautiful, and it was peaceful here beside the river, with the murmur of water and occasional splash of a fish. My fire burned low, and my eyes drooped. Then, in that moment, I jolted awake with a shocking realization: my mind was quiet. Every night of my life, lying down to go to sleep had tormented me with memories and yearnings, but...not now. I wasn't lonely. I felt no longing for companionship, for someone to hold me, for the love I'd never been given as a child. That part of me was gone.

Not just gone, but devoured...sacrificed to save my life.

I didn't know whether to thank Saraknyal or curse him. Instead, I rolled over, placed the dagger carefully near my hand, and went to sleep.

Pushing my poor horse as hard as I dared, I made the town of Kezmar in five more very long days, and seemed to have beaten the news from Mati. At least nobody stopped me at the town gate to ask about necromancers. The Tir River forked here. A bridge spanned the west fork where the trade road crossed into town, then continued along the western shore of the river to Voulnash, some three days to the northeast. Unfortunately, there was no bridge across the east fork toward the forest. I certainly didn't want to head further into Tira, which was where the trade road would take me. I spent some of Gunyan's money on a room at a small inn with a stable, and the innkeeper told me of a fordable spot on the east branch just upstream of town. The next morning, I sought an outfitter recommended by the innkeeper and bought supplies, warmer clothing, and, blessedly, maps. After some quick study, I formulated a plan.

"Sariff." I tapped the map and traced a line with my finger.

What's so special about Sariff?

"It's not in Tira, for one thing, and the kingdom is pretty much isolated except for sea trade. I doubt Mati will send a warning there about me, though rumors might make it that far."

But the mountains...

"There are passes, though it'll be rough going. I'll have to get rid of my horse."

Or eat it.

I wondered if he was trying to be funny or not, then dismissed it and continued with my plans. I had good boots, a sturdy pack, saddle bags to hold my additional gear, and the soul blade to keep me safe. My blistered feet were still sore, but healing well. I sold my horse and saddle, bought a good bow and arrows, and set out before midday. I found the ford of the eastern tributary before sunset. Doffing my boots and pants, I waded across. The water was shallow, swift, and icy, meltwater from the mountains. I twisted an ankle on a rock, but made the eastern shore easily. There, as night fell, I built a fire, fished, and ate well. Again, I stared up at the stars in peaceful silence, blissfully unconcerned with my solitude.

A blessing or a curse? I wondered.

What?

"You," I said, irked at the invasion of my thoughts. If I was going to keep Saraknyal around, I had to learn not to talk to myself, even silently. "I still don't know what to do with you. You saved my life, but you damned me to Hell."

At your request, he reminded me.

"Consent from a woman who's burning alive isn't exactly *consent*, Saraknyal."

Fine. Next time I'll let you be burned alive.

"Too late for that. I'm doomed to Hell now. You can't doom me again. That ship has sailed."

Then you'll just have to trust me, I guess.

"No, I really don't." I'd been thinking about this a lot. "We need to come to an understanding."

Meaning you've decided to keep me?

"At least until I know I'm safe, yes."

You need me, Hashi, he said coldly.

"I really *don't*. I can get over the mountains by myself, and make a home in Sariff without your help or protection. If you don't agree to do as I say, I'll find a secluded spot and bury you. Someone might find you, but not if I bury you deep or drop you down a crevasse on a mountain."

I'm not your slave, Hashi. If we're going to continue this relationship, it has to be a partnership.

"No, it *doesn't*." I said it without the slightest rancor. "You saved my life, and I appreciate that. But you've also been telling me what to do."

Because you have no idea what skills I possess!

I continued as if he hadn't spoken. "And I've been so naïve and panicked that I've just accepted it. But no more. I'll learn from you, I'll listen to your wisdom, but you have no say in my actions. *I* decide when you exert your magic through me, and what that magic will do. I'll take suggestions, but I make the calls."

Forgive me, Hashi, but your decisions to date have not yielded favorable results.

"Maybe, but they're *my* mistakes to make. Nothing you say is going to change my mind. I'm in charge."

Hashi, I have no control over your actions, so this entire conversation is moot. Do as you please. I'll keep you alive as best I can.

"Good." I settled down, placed the dagger between me and my fire, and closed my eyes. "Good night."

Silence, and I wondered if he was sulking. Honestly, I didn't care. I had greater concerns on my mind, like surviving a trek over unknown mountains. It wasn't like I had much of a choice, however. As Saraknyal had said, my decisions to date hadn't yielded many viable options.

Hashi, you're freezing.

"Shut up!" I growled between clenched teeth. My jaws hurt, but clenching kept my teeth from chattering. Wiping the blown snow from my eyes, I scanned the rocky snowscape. Snow cats prowled these high mountain passes, camouflaged against the blinding white landscape until they pounced on unwary prey. "Am I being stalked?"

No, but you're in danger of freezing to death, and an eternity buried in a glacier would be even more boring than my sarcophagus. Take me in hand and I can keep you warm.

A sharp retort died on my half-frozen lips, and I exhaled a plume of exasperated breath. Saraknyal was right; I'd never survive the frigid air and icy winds of the high mountains without his help. Girding my nerves and swallowing my pride, I fumbled off one glove and grasped the haft of the blade at my belt.

I expected a flood of warmth. What I got was the odd cessation of my ability to feel cold. I wasn't warm, but I wasn't cold either. My shivering subsided, and my fingers moved without the ache of impending frostbite. Feeling returned to my near-frozen feet. A disturbing sensation shadowed my relief, however, a subtle hum that permeated my entire body. Saraknyal's magic. I tried to ignore it, concentrating instead on my goal, the mountain pass still thousands of feet above me.

Just until I reach someplace warm. I lashed the soul blade to my forearm under my clothes to keep from dropping it, freeing my hands.

Even though I felt no cold, the trip was far from easy. The wind and snow pushed me back and dragged at my legs. My waterskin froze solid, forcing me to eat snow. I couldn't start a fire, so I chewed cold jerky and trail bread. When darkness fell, I dropped down where I stood, utterly exhausted, and immediately fell asleep. I woke to daylight filtering through the snow that had fallen or blown over me during the night, thrashed out of my burrow, and trudged on. Crossing the mountains took four days rather than the two I had estimated. Maybe I missed the pass I'd intended to traverse, for my map was sketchy at best. Without Saraknyal, I'd have perished.

The downhill side was faster, but more treacherous. Twice I fell and tumbled, rising bruised but alive. At midday, I reached the tree line. A full hour before the sun slipped behind the peaks, the snow petered out. Overwhelmed with joy at my survival, I stopped early and built a huge fire. I unlashed the blade and dropped it beside my pack.

You're not out of the woods yet, literally or figuratively, Saraknyal warned. *You should keep me in your hand tonight.*

"Shut up." I would sleep better without the hum of magic thrilling along my bones. That night, I ate hot food, drank about a gallon of tea, and slept until morning without Saraknyal's magic electrifying my every nerve.

Trekking east and constantly downhill, temperatures rose steadily until I'd doffed all but a shirt and short pants. Foliage shifted from temperate to more tropical than I was used to, and my progress slowed. Saraknyal began pointing out snakes, and I cut a walking stick to fend them off. I found a road two days later, and consulted my map. To the north lay the city of Sariff, and to the south, the farming town of Wheaton. I turned north and lengthened my stride.

Sariff surprised me only in its many similarities to Mati: rich neighborhoods, poor districts, a busy waterfront, shops, restaurants, a few haves and many have-nots. Saraknyal had questions about the kingdom, so I told him what I knew of its history.

Sariff was commonly described as violent and isolationist, but prosperous and largely orderly. The Jaguar King ruled with absolute power, but his reign wasn't directly hereditary; his son didn't inherit the throne. Upon the king's death, his five nearest female relatives would name the next Jaguar King, perform the rites—also violent and secretive—and crown him. Consequently, the female relatives of the king wielded enormous power, which set off its own struggle for supremacy as distant relatives often assassinated closer relatives to the king. The system offered stability and an incredibly competitive courtship of those five female relatives. Great games and contests were arranged to prove the suitors' skills, bravery, and determination. Many died, but that risk was their choice.

Fortunately, in the city of Sariff, I didn't stand out overmuch. The local women were stockier and more muscular than I, but many were dark-skinned with close-cropped hair, so few people gave me a second glance. The sea trade also brought people from distant lands, so the populace was fairly diverse. Sariff shared a common language with Mati and the rest of the Blood Sea region, so communication wasn't an issue.

I found an inn, took a room, and had a long, hot bath. The inn's washroom wasn't private, but they did change the water out between bathers. I languished, ordering more heated water twice. Finally clean, dry, and comfortable, I took stock of my situation. I had enough money for a month's lodging if I wasn't choosy, though it would severely deplete my funds. My first order of business would be a permanent residence, and my second, gainful employment.

The next day I found a flat near a market and a well, paid for a month in advance, and moved in. Then I started looking for work. I took Saraknyal with me, of course, keeping the blade hidden in a leather sheath hooked to my belt on the inside of my waistband. He didn't comment about literally being in my pants, thank the gods.

I sought out junk shops, pawn shops, and antiquities dealers. The first I stepped into brought a pang of guilt and loss with the memory of Gunyan. He'd been a mentor, a teacher, and a friend. I used everything I'd learned from him as I perused shop after shop and sold the few trinkets I'd brought with me. This not only gave me money, but allowed me to market my skills to the proprietors. When I told the owner of a shop with the unlikely name of *Antique Relics* that much of her stock was forgeries, she threatened to have me arrested.

"You're welcome to try, but I've committed no crime," I told her. "And I'm actually doing you a favor."

"Favor!" She glared at me with sharp, dark eyes framed by wrinkled skin. "You tell lies about my wares and call it a favor?"

"I'm not lying, and I'm only telling *you*, so yes, I think I *am* doing you a favor. You should know that whoever sold you this junk is cheating you." I then proceeded to show her exactly how I knew the items in question were cheap knockoffs.

Her glare softened somewhat, but she still looked at me with suspicion. "Where did you learn this?"

"My former mentor taught me. He passed away, and I came here for a fresh start." It wasn't really a lie. "In fact, I'm looking for work, if you're interested."

Her eyes widened, then narrowed. "Come back tomorrow. I have to ask some questions about you."

I agreed, told her where I was staying, and walked out as if I didn't care. She wasn't going to ask about me, but about the antiques I'd told her were forgeries. She might even set the authorities on the dealer who sold them to her. That night, I went to bed with several more potential job opportunities, as well as a tidy pile of gold in my pouch. The next day, I returned to *Antique Relics* and the proprietor offered me a job.

"On a trial basis at first," she warned.

"And what will I be doing for you?" I asked.

"For the first few days, just going through my inventory. I want you to look for forgeries and give me your best estimates of values. I'm...cleaning house a bit after I confirmed that you were right about those pieces." She tried to smile, but it looked like her face didn't usually make that expression.

I nodded amiably, and we haggled for my wages. I shook her hand and introduced myself as Hashi Smythe. She told me her name was Bethilla, and tried to smile again.

That afternoon I spent quiet hours going through her inventory. I identified some more forgeries, but also some very nice pieces that would bring in a good price. By the end of the week, Bethilla allowed me to interact with the customers. After a few profitable sales, she gave me a full-fledged smile, and my own stool at the counter. I began to feel comfortable with my new life.

What a mistake that was.

Less than a week later, I woke to screams from the street outside my flat.

"What the hell?" I lurched out of bed, dashed to the window, and looked out. The street was too dark to see much, but I picked out a few figures, indistinct in the gloom. I frowned; this was supposed to be a safe neighborhood, not a place where screams were common. "Saraknyal, can you see?"

Not from here.

I hurried to the bedside table, snatched up the dagger, and returned to the window. Wrenching it open, I thrust out the sheathed blade. "Show me!"

The dark street leapt to crystal clarity in my mind. Across the way, a man stood backed against a wall, his face contorted in terror. Five figures stumbled down the middle of the street. He was dressed like a streetwalker, and for a moment I thought he was being accosted by a bunch of drunks. But they weren't attacking him. In fact, they ignored him completely.

Then I saw what they were, and the bottom fell out of my stomach. "Oh, *hell* no!" The shambling figures were clearly dead, bones showing through blackened flesh, abdomens empty beneath protruding rib cages. One walked on the stump of a missing foot.

Well, well, aren't they persistent! I never thought they'd make it over the mountains.

"Wait! Those can't be..."

*Yours. Yes, they are. Those guards who attempted to arrest you in Mati."

"Shit!" I dropped to the floor and pressed my back against the wall beneath the window, my mind spinning. "What the hell are they doing here?"

What did you expect them to do? They're your servants, Hashi. You commanded them to defend you. They'll follow you and do your bidding until they rot away to nothing.

"Well, get the hell *rid* of them!"

Why? He sounded incredulous. *Zombies might not smell nice, but they're formidable protectors. They could—*

Because the authorities will start looking for a necromancer, you idiot! I slammed the window shut and glared down at the dagger in my hand. *Why didn't you tell me they'd follow?*

I honestly didn't think of it, Hashi. I'm sorry.

"Well, do something! Can't you...well...banish them?"

All I can do is unanimate them, I'm afraid. They'll drop where they stand.

Which is right outside my door! I bit my lip and cursed. "Do it! Do it right now! They may have come into the city after dark, and that trollop is the only one who saw them."

Very well. Just look at them and think the word 'begone.'

I crouched and opened the window, thrust the dagger out, and found my undead minions still approaching my door. The terrified streetwalker had fled. I fixed the zombies in my mind's eye and thought, *Begone!*

They fell into heaps of rotting meat.

I slammed the window and cowered in the dark flat, clutching the blade and cursing every curse I knew.

All they'll find is four long-dead corpses and one hysterical prostitute. Saraknyal assured me. *They won't take his account seriously, and even if they do, they won't know to look for you.*

"You're delusional," I replied between clenched teeth. "Undead are unheard-of! They'll look for the source, a necromancer, and I'm new here. They'll suspect me."

You're being paranoid. Just go on with your life like nothing's happened, act surprised and appalled like everyone else, and claim ignorance. It's not like you've got a big red N tattooed on your forehead!

I cursed him again, long and inventively. "Okay, but from now on, no more zombies. They'll only cause me trouble."

Whatever you say, Hashi. I don't want trouble any more than you do, but I'm afraid I'm not...acquainted with local customs. In Tinaros, nobody would have thought twice about a few zombies walking down a street. They're not dangerous unless they're attacked or someone tries to restrain them.

They're disgusting abominations, Saraknyal!

*Well, of course, they are! So are most kings, queens, emperors, and tyrants, but you don't see everyone screaming and cowering when *they* walk by!*

You actually do, in some nations. The God-Emperor of Toki, for instance.

*Toki's emperor is a *god*? Really?*

I forgot, sometimes, how out of touch Saraknyal was with the world. *Probably not really, but he might as well be. He wields more magic than most gods, and apparently has no qualms about liquefying anyone who doesn't pay proper obeisance. So, people do actually cower before him.*

Interesting.

His inquisitive tone gave me chills.

I didn't sleep the rest of the night. There were some noises outside, but I kept my window closed and my light out. When I emerged from my flat, there were no corpses lying on the street, so someone must have cleaned them up. I went to my job as usual.

By midday, the city was abuzz with rumors. Corpses had been found, long dead, and there were accounts that they'd been animate. Another was found on the southern road, legless and crawling, clearly undead. The king's Jaguar Warriors reduced it to mulch and burned the remains. Murmurs of necromancy could be heard at every tea house and pub.

I went about my business, daring to hope that nothing would come of this.

Chapter Eleven
Lessons in Trust

From the journal of Hashi Severn –

Why does it always come down to trusting people? There are levels of trust, and I generally subscribe only to those with the least risk. In this endeavor, however, I must give up my very humanity into another's hands. I swear to all the gods and devils that I will piss on that fae's shoes if she betrays me.

There were few preparations for me to make for our assault on Jhavika's keep, so for two days I fretted, paced, worried, studied the floorplans Ingrid Brickhammer had provided, and bugged the living hell out of my people. Bryce's spies watched Jhavika's keep, as well as those of her allies and the kidnapped heirs, but all remained buttoned up tight. Kopi sailed search patterns just over the horizon, watching for Jhavika's ships.

Too little to do meant too much time to think about the souls I would destroy taking that keep. And try as I might to convince myself that it would be self-defense if they attacked first, I knew the enchantment allowed them no choice.

A necessary evil...

Finally Nahli's note arrived, summoning me to her home at sunset. I dressed in black the exact hue of my skin: snug pants, soft-soled boots, and a shirt of brushed silk, no bright metal or shiny buttons to gleam and make me a target. Soul Drinker rode against my forearm, obsidian cool against my skin, ready to draw. I half expected to feel the blade trembling in anticipation of the night's pending events.

You can't hold back tonight, Hashi, Saraknyal warned as my coach neared Nahli's keep. *Jhavika's forces won't yield. Her compulsion won't let them.*

We only destroy as many as are necessary.

Of course, Hashi. Any who can flee, we allow to leave. Those who don't, however...

His eagerness nauseated me.

We pulled to a stop and I got out. I waved off the four shades perched upon the coach as they started to climb down. "Go with Bromish. Protect him and stand guard at the keep."

I watched the carriage rumble out of sight, then approached the ornate postern door and knocked. I snatched my tingling hand away, for the polished bronze filigree adorning the portal fairly pulsed with magic.

I'm not comfortable with this fae magic, Hashi. What happens to me during the transformation?

I hadn't thought of that, I considered in sudden panic. Without Soul Drinker, I was nothing—a fact that Saraknyal never ceased to remind me of. *I'll ask.*

The postern door opened to reveal a narrow-faced man in a pastel tunic, an ornate sword at his hip. With a nod and a smile, he stepped aside and waved me in.

"Welcome, Lady Severn."

I stepped past him into a narrow, arched hallway lined with more bronze filigree. The magic felt like static on my skin, raising goosebumps. I shivered.

The man secured the door and beckoned me to accompany him, his movements as fluid as a dancer's. "This way, if you please."

He didn't look fae, but they often chose to mask their appearance. Avoiding prejudice, I assumed. At the far end of the corridor, he worked a latch on another door and swung it wide. I followed him through...and into the depths of a primeval forest.

Holy mother of...well...trees! Saraknyal exclaimed.

I gaped in agreement. I'd expected gardens—several treetops were visible above the keep walls from outside—but this seemed impossible. I could barely discern the door I'd just passed through, so dense was the foliage. Trees soared into the sky, far higher than the walls; birds and bats flew in chaotic patterns; fireflies lit the air. Tiny winged humans soared in games of chase and catch. *Sprites*, I realized. Even stranger fae peered at me from the dense cover: diminutive men with grasshopper legs, women with fawn faces and drooping ears. A human-sized woman wearing little more than a gossamer shift floated past on hummingbird wings, a sublime smile on her ethereal features as she inspected me. The very air pulsed with life.

This is amazing! An irresistible smile curved my lips. *The trees are higher than the tower!*

*The trees *are* the tower, Hashi."

I looked up and realized he was right. There was no inner keep, only more soaring trees, their branches full of fae. *How...how did we not know this was here?*

Fae magic, Saraknyal grumbled. *The damned creatures fart rainbows, you know!*

I like rainbows.

"This way, if you please, milady." My escort beckoned, and I followed, trying to keep my mouth from hanging open.

The ground felt springy beneath my feet, the scents of flowers filling the air. I swore I could taste the magic on my tongue as I drew breath, and my skin prickled with it. More fae peered out of the lush growth as I passed, whispering to one another, pointing at me and gesturing, laughing musically. A woman sporting deer antlers and dressed in only a few leaves scowled at me from around the bole of a massive oak. From atop a mossy boulder, a satyr leered at me as he fondled his engorged manhood, his eyebrows wagging suggestively. I tried not to stare, but probably failed.

I can see why Twince didn't want to host any of the heirs.

It doesn't seem quite appropriate for children, does it? It hardly seemed appropriate for adults, but who was I to judge? Fae weren't human and didn't possess human mores or inhibitions. Life for fae was one long, impetuous romp. Secretly, I envied their carefree existence. I might not long for companionship, but *gods* it looked like fun.

"Here, milady." We stopped at the trunk of a massive poplar, and my escort placed a hand against it. The rough bark parted with a groan, and warm light spilled out over us. "Lady Twince awaits you within."

"Thank you." Girding my nerves, I stepped through.

The interior proved much larger than the tree's girth—more fae magic, I assumed—comfortably appointed in pale wood furniture that looked grown rather than crafted, with nooks and couches upholstered in pastel-hued silk and cotton. I couldn't find a light source, but light there was. In fact, there wasn't a shadow to be found in the entire room.

A stairway curved up to one side, and upon it stood Nahli Twince. "Good evening, Hashi." She smiled at me, a genuinely warm expression like I'd never seen on her face before. She wore a translucent gown of pastel green that accentuated her form.

I swallowed hard and deliberately looked her in the eyes. "I *hope* it will be."

"Yes." Her smile faltered. "I fear we face dire deeds this night, but there is nothing to do but confront them." She gestured up the stairs. "Come with me, please."

I ascended the stairs behind her. "This…" I waved a hand toward our surroundings, "isn't what I expected."

"Life rarely is." She smiled over her shoulder at me.

She's freaking me out with that too-friendly smile.

I had to agree with Saraknyal; this wasn't the Nahli I knew. "You're different here, aren't you? Different than you are outside, I mean."

"Yes. My heart's lighter here, with the magic of my homeland coursing through me. You feel it, too, don't you?"

"Yes, like the static right before lightning strikes."

She laughed. "There will be no lightning here, Hashi. I promise."

We ascended past several floors, and I glimpsed fae of several shapes, sizes, and sexes lounging on low divans and pillows. They smiled and whispered as we climbed past. Finally the stairs ended in a vast room without furnishings that spread the width of the entire tree. A graceful ceiling arched overhead, and four balconies faced north, south, east, and west, each gabled by beautiful latticework entwined with ivy. Through the apertures I saw Haven, but realized that I could no longer *smell* it.

"The air's fresher here," I said gratefully.

"Everything here is as I will it to be." Nahli flowed to the center of the room as if her feet didn't touch the floor. I followed, then stopped abruptly. The floor and arched ceiling were worked, or perhaps *grown*, in intricate patterns that moved in my vision. I felt a little sick with the motion.

This is an arcane focus, Saraknyal said.

"This is where you'll cast the spell?" I asked.

Nahli shrugged, her gown undulating with the simple motion. "It's not a spell in the conventional sense, Hashi. Not like you're used to. I'm going to graft my ability to change form onto you for the duration of our flight."

"So, I'll have control of the transformation?"

"Not the duration. Only the form you choose. You'll revert to your natural state when we no longer touch."

*Ask her about what happens to *me*!*

"And my things, my clothes, and...Soul Drinker, they'll transform with me?"

"Not exactly, but they'll be there when you revert." She shrugged again, and I couldn't help but watch the way the gown moved over her skin. I wondered if it was a gown at all. "This will be taxing for me, Hashi. I must warn you that I'll only be able to do this for you once tonight."

"So you said. There's only one way out. Through Jhavika's army." My hand reflexively reached under my sleeve to touch Soul Drinker. *You ready for this, old man?*

*Absolutely not. I'm not keen on being *not exactly* transformed.*

Neither am I. I nodded to Nahli. "I'm ready if you are."

She smiled again and held out a hand. "Then take my hand and think of an animal you've known."

*Shit! I *knew* there'd be touching involved. I don't like this!*

Too late to back out now. I put my hand in hers. It was very warm. "An animal I've *known*?"

"Yes, a beloved pet or companion. Something small enough for me to carry in my arms."

I thought back. We'd owned a small black cat when I was a girl. It was intended to keep vermin at bay, but I had loved to stroke its silky fur. "Okay, got it. We had a cat."

"Perfect. Now close your eyes and concentrate on that creature."

I closed my eyes and thought of the furry little cat in my lap, stroking its fur, listening to it purr...

Light flared around me, and everything...*shifted,* and by everything, I mean me. My body melted, reshaped, twisting and bending. There was no pain, just disorientation and a prickly discomfort. I opened my eyes and stared at myself in shock. Fur sprouted over my skin, a tail popped out of the base of my spine, my hands formed into paws, my nails now claws. Even more startling than the physical changes were my senses: the light was brighter, the scratch of my feet upon the floor louder, scents sharper.

I looked up to Nahli, but a great black eagle towered over me, vast wings extended. One taloned foot clutched my foreleg. A yowl escaped my throat as the other clawed foot reached for me. The talons didn't pierce my flesh, but cradled me gently about my midsection. Then, with one billowing beat of her wings, we swooped out and over Haven.

I yowled in terror.

Twinkling lamps lit the cityscape below, rivaling the stars above. My sharper senses and high vantage transformed the foul city into a thing of beauty. Even the rank odors seemed different: interesting, informative, each one distinct. My fear transformed to awe.

Saraknyal? Are you here? Are you seeing this?

He didn't reply, which troubled me deeply. If Nahli's magic had somehow separated his soul from the blade, he would go to Hell, and I'd be in deep trouble. If Saraknyal was truly gone, I'd be going into Jhavika's keep with absolutely no way to defend myself.

I hope you're still with me, old man.

Twisting my head around—delighted with my feline flexibility— I gazed back at Nahli's keep. The place looked much like it had from the street, stone walls with a few trees peeking out above, absolutely no hint of a fae-thronged jungle. A good disguise. Twisting again, I spotted Ash Keep, its familiar ebony bulk rising from amongst its lower neighbors, and, of course, Balshi's castle like a beacon on the highlands beside the lake. A few other buildings I recognized, but the bird's eye perspective rendered much of the view foreign. I hoped Nahli knew where we were going.

We swooped low over rooftops and the furled awnings of markets and eateries. There were lights and people out and about down there, ignorant of us flying overhead.

Banking hard, Nahli curved around a lofty keep: Jhavika's. My keen feline eyes picked out soldiers on the outer wall and front courtyard, most human, but some gnomes. None of them noticed us. We swooped over a walled garden toward a high balcony, and Nahli billowed her wings. When my dangling paws were only a few feet from the stone platform, she let me go.

I transformed as I fell, landing heavily on hands and knees. My senses reverted to my own, and I drew a deep, calming breath. *Saraknyal? Are you there?*

Yes. That was...disorienting.

Wings flapped, and I looked up to find the eagle that was Nahli Twince perched on the balcony railing. I stood. "I'm good, Nahli. Are you—"

She shifted before my eyes, disconcerting to watch. She no longer wore the pastel green gown, but a close-fitted garment of shimmering black cloth. She also no longer smiled, and her golden eyes narrowed at me. "You are not what you seem. I felt something...some*one* with you."

Uh-oh.

There was no denying it now. "You felt Soul Drinker, Nahli. He's—"

"A soul blade." She shivered. "I presumed as much, but...Hashi, how can you *stand* the thing?"

Tell her it's easier than being transformed into a fucking cat! Saraknyal snapped.

"He takes some getting used to, but that's my problem, not yours." I drew the blade and turned for the door into the keep. There was no sense in delaying. "Thanks for the ride. Now if you—"

"I'm staying with you," Nahli said.

I turned to face her, furious at this sudden change in plan. "I don't need a chaperone!"

"You saw the number of soldiers below, and there are undoubtedly more within the keep. Rescuing the heirs is essential, and two will have a better chance of success than one, no?" One slim eyebrow arched.

A fae at your back in a fight? Don't go there, Hashi!

I felt the same, and narrowed my eyes at her. "And I don't need the distraction of looking after you. Can you even fight?"

In a blink, a massive black tiger stood before me, perhaps ten feet long from nose to tail, its huge head as high as my stomach. It—she—yawned, displaying impressive fangs. Deadly claws scraped the stone underfoot as Nahli kneaded the parapet with her front paws. She blinked at me once, slowly, then reverted to her normal self.

"Is that form sufficient for battle?" she asked.

Damn, that would *help!*

But just think how easily a creature like that could take you down, Saraknyal warned.

Good point. I could defend myself against blades and arrows, but not teeth and claws. "I prefer to work alone."

"And the *Council* prefers that I accompany you."

*Ahhh, so *that's* it.*

"Really? After that whole discussion the other day, they still don't trust me to do this without raising an army and taking over the city? Why not tell me earlier?"

Nahli shrugged, her mien neutral.

Because you would've backed out. She waited until you had no choice.

I looked over the parapet at the long drop to the ground. Saraknyal was right; the only way out now was through Jhavika's army. I reined in my anger and stabbed a finger toward Nahli. "All right, you can tag along, but I'm doing this *my* way. Now, where are we?"

"Jhavika's chambers." Nahli said, unperturbed by my ire. "It's the only place I knew for certain would be vacant." Then, without another word, she transformed once again into the tiger.

"Uh...can you understand me when you're like that?"

Nahli responded by rubbing her nose and whiskers against my hip, a rumble resonating in her chest.

"I'll take that as a yes." I gripped the latch—*Dust to dust*—and the lock corroded to powder. Pulling it open, I stepped inside a vast bedchamber, luxurious, but with far too much gold and frippery for my taste. Silently crossing to the inside door, I touched it with the tip of Soul Drinker, hoping that the wood was thin enough for Saraknyal to see through. *Anything out there?*

A lavishly appointed sitting room with a huge desk, bookshelves, and two doors. No people.

I tried the latch and it opened. Recalling the floorplans, I identified the far room as an adjoining bath, and the door to the left as an exit to the hallway. As I strode across the soft rug, I took a moment to lust after the contents of Jhavika's bookshelves, and this probably wasn't even her full library. The tiger padded silently behind me. I checked the bath—empty—then pressed the tip of Soul Drinker to the hall door.

The hallway's lit with glow crystals, and there's one guard beside the door.

Guarding an empty room?

Job security, I guess. You don't want him to sound an alarm.

Really? Forcing my nerves to calm, I relayed the information to Nahli. "I'll take care of him. You watch my back. I'm immune to swords and arrows, you're not. We'll keep it quiet as long as we can, though someone's bound to raise an alarm eventually."

She growled softly, her expressive eyes narrowing and long tail lashing.

Saraknyal, do you have enough energy to make a shade? I asked.

No.

Okay, then. I drew a deep breath and let it out slowly. *Just don't think about it, Hashi. Necessary evils...*

I disintegrated the door latch, yanked it open, and stabbed the guard before he could draw breath to scream. *Feed.* The moment Soul Drinker pierced his flesh, he gasped, convulsed, and crumpled. As power coursed through me, I animated the corpse. *One more soul obliterated by my hand.*

Whiner, Saraknyal chided. *You need to focus, Hashi! If you fold, you're going to die, and one of Jhavika's people is going to pick me up. Consider how *that* will go.*

Saraknyal was right.

I addressed my new minion. "Draw your sword. Follow me. Defend me."

The zombie drew his weapon and waited. I turned to Nahli. "We do this floor first, then work our way down. If we find soldiers guarding a room, we investigate." We were on the fourth floor now, but according to the floorplans, there wasn't much in the higher levels. I started down the hallway, and my zombie shambled along with me.

Now *do you have enough for a shade?*

Barely. Don't skimp on me, Hashi. The last thing you want is for me to run out of energy.

That was true; my life and more depended upon Saraknyal's magic. I needed to maintain a delicate balance between merely killing soldiers and actually destroying souls for energy to cast spells or make shades. As insane as it sounded, the more shades I made, the more souls I would save.

We proceeded carefully, door to door, hall by hall, my soft boots whisking along carpeted floors, Nahli padding silently behind. I edged Saraknyal around corners and pressed him against closed doors, using his magical sight to best advantage. The keep was quite a lot bigger than mine, and I caught myself inspecting Jhavika's possessions. Not many true antiques, and the décor wasn't to my taste, but she had some nice things. Finally, as we approached yet another corner, Nahli's low growl brought me up short.

I glanced back. Her ears lay flat against her head, eyes fixed on the corner, tail twitching.

She senses something.

Then her senses are sharper than mine.

By my reckoning, we'd cleared one half of the fourth floor, with the opposite wing still unexplored. I edged Soul Drinker's tip beyond the corner. *Show me.* The view of the hallway opened in my mind. Two guards stood at the head of a wide staircase, maybe fifty feet away.

Damn! Fifty feet would give them too much time to scream for help.

I held up two fingers to Nahli and made a patting motion for her to stay put, then whispered to my zombie, "Kill one, hold the other." That was about as complex an order as zombies could manage.

It strode around the corner, and I edged Soul Drinker out to observe. The guards would know this man, allowing my minion to get close without raising an alarm. The zombie only made about five steps before they noticed it.

"Yanci? What are you doing away from your post?" The guard sounded baffled rather than suspicious. "What's with the sword?"

"Put the sword away, Yanci!" the other barked, drawing his own blade.

"Something's not right, Berk," said the second man as he also drew his weapon. "He's—" My zombie thrust his sword at the nearer guard, but he parried easily. Zombies aren't very dexterous. "Shit! Yanci, stop!"

"Fuck this!" The first man lunged and ran the zombie through. This allowed my minion to grasp his wrist and hold him tight. The guard screamed.

That's not good.

"Fuck!" I hissed, and dashed around the corner.

The second soldier buried his sword in the zombie's chest, then fell with a gurgling cry as my minion's blade slashed his throat. I arrived as the surviving guard buried a dagger in the zombie's neck, only to have that hand also clamped in an iron grip.

I stepped up, grasped the man's terrified face in one hand, and said, "Look at me!"

He did and froze, his mouth gaping in a silent scream.

I fixed his eyes with mine, breathed in his soul, and thought, *Shade.*

Saraknyal did the rest.

The man's soul twisted and changed, melting and reforming into an essence of only hunger, rage, and obedience. It took only a second, but my stomach clenched as the horror coalesced within me. It had been years since I'd made a shade, and I'd forgotten how truly abhorrent it felt.

129

Before the man's body died, I exhaled the defiled soul back into it. His flesh darkened to black, eyes shifting hue to blood red, teeth shattering to jagged shards.

There was a compulsion on him, Hashi. It was broken when you took his soul. You don't want to make a wraith from any of these ones. Since they retain a portion of their soul, I don't think it would break Jhavika's spell.

Right. The last thing I wanted was a wraith under Jhavika's control running loose. I swallowed my revulsion and released my new shade, then raised the dead man as a zombie. "Take your weapons. Defend me."

The two pulled their swords from my first zombie and all three formed up.

A growl sounded behind me. My shade immediately turned to Nahli and raised its weapon, but her attention was focused down the corridor to the opposite wing, not on me.

"Stop!" I commanded. "Not her. She's an ally. Only attack Jhavika's soldiers, and only those who try to harm us. Is that clear?"

"Yes, mistress," the shade growled, its jagged teeth bared.

Someone's coming, Saraknyal warned.

Great. I turned just as three more guards clattered around the corner, weapons in hand. They skidded to a stop when they saw us, their eyes wide. Frankly, the sight of us would have stopped me, too.

My minions started forward, but I called out, "Wait!"

Wait? For what, a passing hackney? Kill them, Hashi!

Shut up! I leveled Soul Drinker at the trio and said, "We're here for the heirs of the murdered council members. Hand them over and you survive. Oppose us, and I feast on your souls."

That ought to do the trick. I'm sure they'll hand the tykes right over.

I hate it when he's sarcastic.

"To arms!" one of the three bellowed, and they all charged us.

Told you, Saraknyal snarked.

I also hate it when he's right. *I had to try.*

I laughed fear. They didn't slow, but did look utterly terrified. *No surrender... Damn you, Jhavika!* I gritted my teeth and dashed forth with my minions.

I've learned some knife fighting in the decades I've wielded Soul Drinker, developing my own unorthodox style. I inherited my mother's grace as well as her looks, and it's served me well. Ignoring the soldiers' weapons, I concentrated on getting Soul Drinker into my first opponent's flesh. His soul tore away, and its energy surged through me. I raised his corpse and immediately reached out to grasp the next soldier. Stabbed in the stomach by a shade, she was doubled over her wound. I jerked her up and pulled her face close to mine.

"Look at me."

She did, and it was over in seconds. My original shade had torn out the last soldier's throat with its teeth. I'd gained another shade and two more zombies from the exchange. I sported nothing worse than a slashed shirt and gut-wrenching nausea.

Two souls destroyed, two changed, and two freed. I kept a tally in my mind. I'd save as many souls as I could, but that ratio would probably hold throughout the night.

A resonant roar shook the hallway, and I whirled to find Nahli bristling at the top of the wide staircase. Metal clattered and shouts of alarm rose from below. More soldiers were coming.

"With me! Quickly!" I dashed back to face the onslaught. Four soldiers charged up the stairs, weapons in hand and murder in their eyes. I laughed a peal of terror, but these, too, didn't hesitate. *More of Jhavika's slaves.* Two pissed themselves, but all four leapt to the attack.

I gritted my teeth and allowed Soul Drinker to feed.

Chapter Twelve
The Scent of Death

In the days following the arrival of the zombies in Sariff, I walked around on tenterhooks. Rumors spread like wildfire through the city. Yet another animate corpse had been spotted by a farmer some leagues from the southern road. It was evidently almost limbless, but still struggling to squirm along toward the city. Soldiers had been sent, but instead of destroying this one, they'd captured it with nets and put it in a cage to bring back.

I worked at *Antique Relics* and tried to ignore the buzz of news, but dread niggled my mind like a dirge I couldn't banish. *Why in the names of all the devils in all Nine Hells would they bring that thing back to the city?* I finally asked Saraknyal. We'd barely spoken since the night the zombies had arrived, but my temper had cooled, and I needed his advice.

To analyze, probably. He sounded as worried as I felt.

Why? What do they hope to find? I continued brushing the thin layer of powdery oxidation from an antique Toki bronze figurine, a meticulous task that would have been soothing if I hadn't been in a state of near panic.

Me, I'm afraid.

His words stopped me cold. *How can they hope to do that?*

*Magic is like a fingerprint, my dear, specific to its owner. There are no other necromancers in Sariff, or at least I don't *think* there are. If the king has a competent wizard, they may be able to work out a means to locate me.*

I dropped the figurine onto my work bench. *Shit!* If they found the soul blade, they'd find me. No one would believe I wasn't the source of the necromancy, and even if they did, I'd be condemned by association. There was only one thing I could do.

I strode from the workroom to the front of the shop and headed for the door. "I've got to go out for a bit, Bethilla."

"Where? What's wrong?" The woman was sharp, and must have heard something in my voice. She knew I was upset.

"Nothing's wrong. I just forgot something. I'll be back soon."

"Well, don't be long! I'm not paying you to—"

The door closed, cutting off her tirade.

Where are you going, Hashi?

I didn't answer, but turned for the waterfront. I had no choice, and I wasn't about to discuss it with Saraknyal. I had to get rid of this thing; it had already cursed my soul to Hell, and now it was drawing the attention of more people who would burn me at the stake. The memory of the flames licking at my feet hastened my steps.

You're not going toward your flat, Hashi. If you intend to leave the city, you'll need your things.

Again, I didn't answer, but kept on my course. The bustling streets seemed to be closing in on me, people staring, cringing away. They weren't, of course, but memories of Mati and Kopshi Square had ignited my paranoia.

You're heading toward the waterfront, Hashi.

I didn't answer.

Throwing me away won't help you.

He wasn't reading my mind, but it didn't take a lot to figure out what I intended. *Yes, it will. Once you're gone, they'll have no connection to me.* The zombies were found on my street, but there was no way they could link their appearance to me specifically. They might suspect me, since I was new in town, but there'd be no evidence.

Yes they will, Hashi.

"What?" I stopped so quickly that a man bumped into me from behind. He apologized and strode on, glancing back curiously. I'd spoken aloud without realizing it. I sidled off to the side of the street, pretending interest in a shop's display. *What do you mean?*

I mean, if you throw me away, and the king does have a wizard capable of tracking me down, they'll find me.

So?

So, my dear, eventually someone will touch me, and when they do, I'll tell them of you.

Terror knotted my guts. "You fucker!"

A passing woman stared at me, and I realized I'd spoken aloud again. I cursed under my breath and strode off in a different direction.

Yes, well, call me what you will, but I've grown accustomed to you, Hashi. I'd rather you keep me and we flee this city together.

I don't care what you want!

That much is obvious.

Why would you do that to me? Why out me to them? What does it matter to you? You're dead!

As I said, I've grown accustomed to you. I'd rather spend my years riding on your hip, out in public, experiencing the world, than locked away in a tomb, buried at sea, or, if they can figure out a way, destroyed utterly.

You really are a piece of work, Saraknyal.

Yes, I am, but I didn't survive nearly a millennium by being kind or soft-hearted. Take me and flee the city, or you burn at the stake like you did in Mati, only without me to quench the flames this time. Those are your choices.

His emotionless pragmatism ignited my fury. *Heartless bastard!* I redirected my steps toward my flat. *I hate you with every fiber of my being, Saraknyal.*

Well, thanks to me, you have rather fewer fibers than you started out with. Let's not get into a situation where the rest of it gets sent to Hell.

I seethed and lengthened my stride. Thanks to the necromancer, I now only had one choice: get my things and flee. But how? Horse or ship? I didn't want to wait for a ship to sail, but a sea voyage would be easier and give me more options. The Blood Sea sported a number of small independent city-states. I could take the first ship available, so long as it wasn't headed back to Mati or into the Empire of Toki. A small trader would be the best choice. If I was lucky, I'd find one ready to leave port soon.

But my luck wasn't running so well. When I turned onto my street, I found it full of soldiers.

I staggered to a stop, my mind spinning. *How the hell...? Why come here?*

They're searching, Hashi! Saraknyal sounded nervous. *They had to start somewhere. I would suggest you leave the vicinity quickly without drawing attention.*

But I need my things! I had my money pouch with me, of course, but little more. I wore a light shirt and airy skirt I'd bought for work, hardly adequate travel wear. I wore sandals, not my good boots, and my pack and bow were in my flat with all of my camping supplies. *I can't leave with nothing but the clothes on my back!*

*You should be more concerned with the *skin* on your back, my dear!* Saraknyal's nervousness had edged toward panic. *They're using magic! That man in the red coat! Look!*

I slipped a finger between the buttons of my shirt to touch the soul blade, and the scene sharpened in my mind. Soldiers looked nervously up at the buildings and two other men—one wearing a gray robe, the other a red-beaded jacket and gaudy pantaloons— stood with heads down. Then Red Jacket turned, one of his hands extended out flat, palm up. Above his palm floated a red teardrop gem, a garnet or ruby. That gem twitched and turned...toward me.

Go! Now!

I spun and walked off, trying not to look like I was fleeing for my life. Behind me, through Saraknyal's perception, I saw the red-coated wizard point, and every eye on the street looked my direction. I turned a corner out of their view, and ran.

Shit! Shit! Shit! Did they fix on me or just the direction?

Just the direction, I think, but... They're following.

Damn you to Hell, Saraknyal! I turned another corner, my flat sandals skidding on the cobbles.

Water under the bridge, my dear. I don't think a ship is an option any longer. You should probably try to procure a horse, at least, and maybe some pants and better shoes.

I don't have time to go shopping! I got my bearings and headed north, reducing my pace to a long-legged walk. Running was drawing too much attention.

*I wasn't suggesting you *buy* them, just *get* them.*

You want me to steal clothes and a horse?

*They're going to burn you at the stake for necromancy, Hashi. I don't think a *theft* charge is going to worsen your sentence.*

He had a point.

I strode on, and spotted a cobbler's shop. Ducking in, I greeted the shoemaker with a smile and a friendly, "Hello! I'm looking for a pair of hiking boots, and I'm in a bit of a rush. My employer doesn't want me gone long, you see."

"Well, have a seat then, miss." He smiled at me and stood from the bench where he was nailing a new sole onto a pair of dress boots. "I'll just take some measurements. I'm sure I can have something for you in a week or so."

"I'm afraid I need them now." I sat and eyed the door nervously. "Immediately would be good."

"Oh, I'm sure I can't—"

"I'll take whatever you have that will fit. Please! I'll pay you handsomely!" I jingled my pouch in emphasis.

His eyes widened appreciatively. "I'll see what I have. Just let me measure you."

"Thank you!"

Knifing him would have been faster, Saraknyal said.

And leave me looking through dozens of pairs of shoes for one that fits?

Oh, well, valid point.

Your answer to everything is knifing people!

Well, I am a knife, so...

I cursed under my breath while the cobbler measured my feet, then went into a back room to rifle through his wares. He came back with a dusty pair of boots that looked ready to fall apart.

"I was going to rebuild the soles on these, but got distracted. They should last you a while, but they're a little stiff." He looked chagrinned. "And they don't really match your attire."

I pulled one on. It was slightly large, and the leather was cracked and hard. "Do you have any socks, and maybe some oil?"

"Oh, surely."

"Name your price."

"Um, ten silver?" They were worth maybe four, but I didn't have time to haggle.

I pulled a gold crown from my pouch and handed it over. "For the socks and oil, too. I'll wear them!"

"My, but you *are* in a hurry!" He pocketed the gold and retrieved a pair of woolen socks and a tin of oil from a drawer. "Here you are."

"Thank you!" I yanked on the socks, stuffed my feet in the boots, jerked the laces tight, and started for the door. "You can keep the sandals!"

"Well, thank you, miss! Have a nice—"

Hashi! The door!

The door opened, the aperture blocked by a red-coated man with a blood-red gem hovering over his palm. A number of soldiers flanked him. His pale eyes fixed upon me and widened, and his mouth opened.

I stuffed a hand through the buttons of my shirt and tore the soul blade free. I had no choice. Only one thing would stop them. I screamed, and winter tore from my throat, blasting through the doorway.

The icy torrent froze the wizard solid. The gem dropped into his palm then fell to the floor, and its owner toppled like a fallen statue, shattering into pieces of blue petrified flesh. The two nearest soldiers were also frozen, and the others badly frostbitten. They reeled back, shouting curses, arms raised to shield their eyes. Those farther behind drew swords and raised crossbows.

I whirled toward the terrified cobbler. "Back door!"

He stumbled back, pointing hysterically at a door to another room, his finger trembling.

"Sorry for the trouble." As I dashed for the door, crossbow bolts zipped through the front. Two struck me and puffed into dust.

I wrenched open the door, lurched through, and slammed it behind me. The back room was crammed with shelves full of shoes and supplies. I pulled two of the shelves down behind me to slow pursuit, and yanked open the back door. An alley. I turned north and ran.

Good job killing the wizard. They won't be able to track you.

I had no choice. Now shut up and keep watching and listening. I turned a corner to throw off pursuit, and turned north again at the next. *I need a horse!*

There was a stable at the south entrance to the city when we came in. Maybe there's one to the north.

Maybe? I tucked the dagger through my belt, keeping one hand on it, and lengthened my stride in an attempt to out-distance the soldiers who would be fanning out and working their way north. They knew what I looked like now, and would undoubtedly ask passersby if they'd spotted me. Tall, dark women in torn shirts, breezy skirts, and old boots, running for their lives aren't a common sight anywhere. They'd be on my trail in minutes.

Also, you might consider taking another soul. That spell nearly drained me.

You're lying. I could feel his power thrilling up my arm.

I'm not. If you try to use that one again, you won't like the results.

I stand forewarned. Now keep watch!

I am keeping watch. Multitasking isn't hard when you've got no arms or legs to keep track of. His acerbic humor did nothing for my mood.

Sariff is a big city, but I made the northern gate in about a quarter hour with no further incidents. I had no way to know how quickly the alarm might be approaching, but right now, the guards at the gate didn't look like they'd been alerted to a rampaging necromancer. I untucked my shirt to hide the dagger and approached at a relaxed pace. The soldiers stationed there eyed me professionally, and one raised a hand.

"Hold on there, miss. You look like you've been accosted." He nodded to my torn and sweaty shirt. "Where are you headed in such a hurry?"

"I *was* accosted!" I snapped, latching onto an idea. "I barely got out of there alive! I work at a pub, you see, and one of the patrons tried to...well..." I tried to look frightened. It wasn't hard. "The barman just laughed, so I ran, but the man followed me. I bought these stupid boots because I lost one of my shoes! I need a horse! I need to get out of here before he finds me."

"Now, miss, don't you worry. You're safe here with us. So, what place was this, and who was this man?" From a belt pouch, he fished a notebook and a short bit of pencil.

"I'm *not* safe! He said he was powerful, that he had friends in the palace!" I edged away from him. "I just want to get away from here. Please."

Two more guards stepped from the gatehouse to join their comrades. Four soldiers now, two blocking my way.

You're going to have to kill them, Hashi, Saraknyal said.

No! I gritted my teeth.

Coward, he growled. *Remember the flames, Hashi! They'll burn you!*

Shut up! I edged another half-step away from the soldiers.

"If he accosted you, we need his description so we can question him, miss," the first guard explained.

I cursed myself for making up the story. Of course, they'd want the man's side, the powerful man who had friends in the palace.

"No." I stepped back from them, sideways in the gate, the thick city wall against my back. "I'm leaving the city." I reached under my shirt and gripped the dagger, but didn't draw it. "Now just let me go, or I promise you, you'll regret it."

"Miss, take your hand out from there!" All four reached for their swords. "We won't hurt you. We just want to get to the bottom of this."

I drew a breath and laughed. *Fear!*

The four soldiers staggered back, and I dashed through the gate and ran for it.

I had ten yards on them before they shook off the fear enough to even react, and gained another twenty before they started to follow. Armed and armored, they'd never catch me. Unfortunately, they first yelled out to the guards stationed atop the wall.

"Stop her!"

The only way they could stop me was shoot me, which they did. Evidently, if you run from the authorities in Sariff, you're guilty. When their bolts puffed into dust, however, they realized something was amiss. I ran for everything I was worth, dashing into the tangle of buildings clustered outside the city. There were stockyards, sheep pens, tanneries, a slaughterhouse, and—*Gods of Light shine on me!*—a hostler.

I vaulted the four-rail fence and grabbed the rope halter of the first mare that didn't shy away. The hostler shouted out, but I smiled and waved.

"How much for this fine mare?" There were a number of bridles hanging over the fence, so I snatched one up. "And this bridle." I didn't have enough money for a saddle or the time to rig one.

"Vive golden crowns, lady, but why you jump my vence?" His highlander accent was almost too thick to understand. "You look like someone chasing you."

"Someone *is*, and you stand to profit by it!" I tore the pouch from my belt, poured out four gold and a bunch of silver, and tossed it to him. "I hate haggling! Now open the gate, or you'll probably be arrested for aiding a criminal!"

He juggled the shower of gold and silver and hastened to open the gate.

I vaulted to the mare's back, hauled her around by her rope bridle, and kicked her smartly. She responded calmly, for which I was grateful, and cantered out of the corral. I pointed her north and coaxed her into a gallop. She seemed reluctant, but so was I. Riding at a gallop without a saddle was a new experience for me, both jolting and alarming. I gripped tight with my legs and grabbed a handful of mane to keep myself aboard. Shouts rang out behind me, but I didn't look back. If they didn't shoot my horse out from under me, I'd make it.

Please, please, please... I don't know if my pleas found the ear of a sympathetic god or not, but the shouts dwindled and my horse wasn't killed. I began to breathe easier.

Nicely done, Hashi, Saraknyal complimented, and it sounded sincere.

"Thank you." I meant it. I'd escaped without destroying one human soul. "No more zombies, though. At least none permanent. If those things hadn't followed me, I would have been fine."

Yes, I know, and I'm truly sorry. I just didn't think... Saraknyal sighed mentally. *You must understand, Hashi, I've only lived in a culture where necromancy was legal and...well...approved of.*

We need to work on that. I still hadn't forgiven him for threatening to betray me, but screaming at him would be pointless. I needed his protection now more than ever. I pushed the mare as hard as I dared, and ventured off the road at the first opportunity.

So, where are we going, and don't you think you should find some supplies? I might be able to keep you warm, but I can't fill your belly.

"I don't see any shops out here, idiot!" He was, however, right. I needed some basic things: a flint and steel, tinder box, cord for snares, a hatchet for wood... And *pants* would be nice. The mare's backbone was leaving a permanent imprint on my backside. But if I ventured into a town or village, I'd probably find that word of the events in the city had preceded me. The Jaguar King was renowned for the swiftness and lethality of his response to any threat.

That brought up the greater concern. "They'll come after me, Saraknyal."

No doubt, but they shouldn't be much of a threat. Lambs to the slaughter, my dear.

"You don't know about the Jaguar Warriors, do you?"

The what?

"I thought not." I kicked my poor mare a little harder. She didn't like the rough country, and the farther we got from the road, the rougher it got. "The Jaguar Warriors are...well..." I really didn't know how to describe all that I'd read about them. "When it comes to jungle warfare, they're the most deadly warriors in the world. They're trained to it from birth, inured to pain, fear, and fatigue. They have one purpose in life: to serve the Jaguar King. If he tells them to find me, they will."

Then let them.

I recoiled at his comment, and a tree limb almost took off my head. "What?"

Let them find you. Set a trap and take them down. You know you can, you're just being squeamish again.

"And you just want to feed again, don't you?"

Well, yes, but that's beside the point.

"No, it's not. You're addicted to the power taking souls gives you, Saraknyal. You don't think clearly when you start lusting for your next meal."

I'm thinking perfectly clearly.

"Said every man who was blinded by alcohol, drugs, sex, or gold!" I spat.

*Oh, and the judgment of *women* is *never* clouded by those things? Spare me!*

His acerbic reply caught me off guard. "Okay, fine. It's not about gender, it's about *addiction*. You crave nothing more than the rush you get from taking a soul. Admit it!"

Well, since none of those other things you mentioned offer any satisfaction to me whatsoever, then yes, I admit that the power given me by consuming a soul is my one remaining indulgence. Go ahead and judge me for that weakness.

"Hell, yes, I'll judge you for that!" I retorted. "It's worse than any of those other things, because it comes at the cost of a *soul!* How do you not *get* that?"

*And what *is* a soul, Hashi Severn? Why is it so precious? What makes it so special?*

"It's everything a person is! What *could* be more precious?"

Or more painful? he countered. *The part of your soul that I took was causing you pain. It's gone. Every soul harbors its own anguish. I take it away, and the pain is gone. What's so terrible about that?*

"You make it sound like amputating an infected limb!" I accused.

That's quite a good analogy, actually. When it's gone, there is no more pain.

"When it's gone, there's no more *anything!* No more joy, no more love, no more beauty..."

And when was the last time your soul gave you any joy, love, or beauty?

His words cut me more deeply than any ever had, even those from my mother. Truth be told, I couldn't remember when I'd last felt *any* of those things.

Then I did.

"Northeast of Mati," I said. "Just lying there at night gazing at the stars. They were beautiful."

Yes, he conceded, then added, *and who was there with you?*

I didn't answer, *refused* to answer, because I knew.

I was there with you, Hashi. I felt the joy in your soul with the simple beauty of the stars. Even though you didn't know I was, I shared it with you.

The thought of him spying on me like that felt like a violation. "I *hate* you," I seethed.

*Get...in...fucking...*line*, Hashi Severn!*

I'd never heard such vehemence from him, and it startled me.

*I've had more people hate me than you will ever know in your entire *life*!* he screamed into my mind. *You know how many fucks I give for that?*

I knew the answer.

ZERO!

Though his rage frightened me, I knew he really couldn't hurt me. Instead, I wondered what had made him like this, so bitter, so vengeful.

The answer was simple: someone had hurt him. Like my mother had done to me, someone had damaged Saraknyal, warped and molded him into an emotional cripple. But there our paths had diverged. Whereas I had withdrawn into my pain, shielding myself from everyone in fear of them hurting me, Saraknyal lashed out, feeding on the souls of others, taking their power for his own. The thought that I could become like him—especially if I blindly took his counsel—turned my stomach. But at the same time, I pitied him.

"I'm sorry," I said, not knowing exactly what I was sorry for.

What? He sounded taken aback. *Sorry for what?*

"Sorry that you think as you do. I'm sorry your life turned you into this...thing."

*Thing? I'm a *person*, Hashi!*

"You were once," I said. "I don't know what you are now."

To that, he had no answer.

Chapter Thirteen
The Reaping of Souls

From the journal of Hashi Severn –

What is good? What is evil? Where is the line between the two? Demia, Keeper of the Slain, judges all souls. I wonder how I'll be judged. *If* I'll be judged. Perhaps, when my time comes, I'll have Saraknyal consume me.

The fight on the stairway escalated to a pitched battle. Two more soldiers charged from our rear. Nahli took the first down with her jaws clamped on his neck. I screamed for my shades to help her, and the second man collapsed with a sword through his chest.

On the stairs, I had my hands full, but weapons dissolved to dust and splinters, and blood spattered the burnished marble. When the last soldier fell, I had gained another shade and three more zombies. Before I could breathe a sigh of relief, however, more of Jhavika's guards thundered up behind the fallen. I laughed, and terror blanched their faces, but it didn't stay their advance.

Wave after wave charged us as we slashed our way down the stairs. Each one I tried to dissuade, laughing terror and raising bloodied corpses, but they just kept coming.

In short, I laid waste to Jhavika's forces. There was no other way to describe it. Every encounter whittled down her army and added to my own. I hoarded energy and screamed winter when they attacked in groups too large to handle. My zombies were slashed and torn, but fought on. My shades ripped and stabbed at anything with a heartbeat.

But still, they kept coming.

The soldiers conscripted from other houses retreated in the face of my terror-filled laughter. Not so for Jhavika's enchanted slaves, screaming their horror from spittle-flecked lips until they died or I drank in their souls and transformed them into abominations.

Nahli stayed close behind me, growling when threats approached. Saraknyal...well, he was in his glory, reveling in the slaughter. I tried to stay focused and alive, and forged forward; there'd be time later for remorse.

Floor after floor we descended, leaving nothing behind us but blood and a few body parts, too occupied with our foes to search the outlying wings for the heirs. We occasionally encountered noncombatants: terrified concubines, maids, footmen, and others. They were panicked, unarmed, and didn't fight. I commanded four of my new shades to hold them in a banquet hall, and not eat them.

When we reached the ground floor, Jhavika's remaining slaves threw everything they had left at us, but by then I had about thirty shades and twice as many zombies. Soul Drinker hummed with power as I froze and slashed our attackers, laughing like a maniac to scare off those who could flee. By the time we charged into the courtyard amidst a hail of crossbow bolts from the outer wall, my forces had doubled.

The end was inexorable. Soldiers hurled themselves against my wall of undead flesh, unable to relent. I screamed frustration as they charged and died, cursing Jhavika for every wasted life and lost soul. How many perished, I'd lost count.

Finally, it was over. I stood in the courtyard surrounded by more than a hundred zombies and perhaps sixty shades, my clothes in tatters from arrows and blades, my flesh untouched but for a few bruises. I glanced around. The darkness hid much of the slaughter, but intermittent lantern light illuminated more than I wanted to see. I had destroyed more souls in this one night than I had in all my years past. I was beyond all hope of redemption.

Nahli cowered just inside the keep's entry hall. In fae form once again, her anguished expression betrayed her horror.

I'm surprised she hasn't just taken wing, I thought scornfully.

She's here to watch you, Saraknyal reminded.

I turned my back to the fae and heaved an exhausted sigh, wiping tears and blood from my face. I dared not show her how much this had devastated me. *Later... Later, when nobody can see.*

"Zombies, go there." I pointed to the farthest corner of the courtyard, and my shambling army complied, crowding tight against the high outer wall. "Begone!"

They collapsed as one, my marionette army with their strings cut.

I turned to my shades and split them into two unequal groups. "You, man the gates and walls. Nobody comes in and nobody goes out unless I say so. If you find anyone alive, escort them to the feasting hall. If they offer resistance, kill them. The rest of you, stay with me. And none of you eats anything or anyone!"

I watched the shades set about following my commands, and had a sudden sick revelation. They'd merely exchanged one form of enslavement for another. In the thrall of my death magic, they were unable to disobey, unable to relent...exactly as they had been under Jhavika's enchantment. The irony almost made me puke.

"Hashi," Nahli said as she approached. "The Council will—"

"I don't give a *fuck* what the Council thinks! I've *done* their dirty work!"

Nahli took a step back from me, her pupiless eyes widening.

I felt immediately guilty and realized I still held Soul Drinker in my hand. I tore away my tattered sleeve and sheathed the blade. "We're not finished yet. We still need to find the heirs. Maybe the servants will tell us where they are." I whirled and strode for the banquet hall.

"And maybe they won't." She fell into step beside me, clearly uncomfortable with the night's events, the riven souls, my undead army, and me. "I don't know how you stand this, Hashi. I'm glad you're on our side, but..."

"But I disgust you." I could hear it in her voice, usually so calm and emotionless. "I disgust myself, Nahli. You *know* I didn't want to do this."

"There is hope for you, then," she said.

I stopped suddenly and whirled to face her. "Don't you *dare* judge me unless you're ready to step up and do the job yourself." Still bristling, I spun and stalked away.

Don't alienate her, Hashi, Saraknyal warned.

I don't really care if she doesn't like me.

I like you, he said.

Yeah, well, your opinion is biased.

True.

We entered the feasting hall. About fifty of Jhavika's servants cowered at the tables, most in nightclothes. I raked them with my gaze, but couldn't pick out anyone seemingly senior. "We came for the prisoners. Where are they?"

"Prisoners?" An older man in a frilled nightshirt and robe stepped to the fore, his gray hair disheveled, his brow wrinkled in confusion. "What prisoners?"

"The heirs to houses Chen, Tinworthy, and Hatsu."

"Oh! They are Lady Keshmir's *guests*, not her prisoners."

I stepped up to the man. "Where are they?"

"In the guest wing, on the fifth floor."

Well, so much for assuming there was nothing of interest upstairs, I silently grumbled.

Would you really have rather found them first and dragged them along during our battle?

There was that. "Are they under guard?"

"Yes, for their protection. You must understand, our mistress brought them here to keep them *safe*. After that pirate attack at Lord Balshi's party—"

"Don't bother. I was there. I saw what happened, and we know you're being controlled by magic."

"*Controlled?*" His face went blank. "I'm sure I don't know what you mean."

"They've undoubtedly been commanded never to mention it," Nahli said.

"Of course." I sighed and looked them over again. "What's your name?"

"Lewin. I'm Lady Keshmir's sage." He bowed shortly. "You must be Lady Severn and Lady Twince of the Council of Lords. I'd welcome you to my mistress' home, but under the circumstances..."

"Can anyone tell the guards assigned to the heirs to stand down and surrender?"

"I'm...afraid only Lady Keshmir has the authority."

I turned to Nahli. "Can you think of any way to subdue the guards without killing them?" I was sick to death of death.

She blinked at me, and, for once, I saw surprise on her face. "I... No. I have no way to circumvent Jhavika's control or render them helpless without getting far too close, which would undoubtedly provoke an attack."

I nodded and turned back to the sage. "How many guards on each heir?"

"Two each, as well as one personal attendant."

"Okay." I surveyed the motley group. "Stay here! You'll be safe as long as you don't try to escape or hurt anyone." Ordering half of my force to watch them, I turned to Nahli. "Do you want to come with me or talk to these folk?"

"I'll come with you to help secure the heirs, but..." She turned to Lewin. "Have the guards been ordered to kill the heirs rather than allow them to be taken?"

Good question, Saraknyal acceded.

The sage looked shocked. "Oh, no! Only to keep them safe."

"Good." Nahli nodded to me. "Let's go."

We found them easily enough, one floor above where we'd come in. The guards had evidently been commanded not to leave their posts, and now faced us with drawn weapons. I tried to talk them out of resistance, but it was pointless. In the end, I had my shades murder them. There was no point to sacrificing more souls.

Spoil sport, Saraknyal chided.

Shut up.

We broke into the first room to find a teenaged boy cowering in the corner, an attendant kneeling beside him, offering a tray of sweets. Fa-Chen's son, Que-Chen, was terrified of us, and I couldn't blame him. What was left of my clothes were stiff with blood and two shades stood at my shoulders. I assured him we were to rescue him, not murder him, but that didn't seem to help. Nahli coaxed him to his feet with a calming touch. The second room yielded Hatsu's niece, Mah. Perhaps eleven years old, she just stared at us with wide, dark eyes, her formal kimono incongruously identical to the doll she clutched tight. She followed us out without a word.

I gestured to the last door. "Smash it down," I commanded my shades. They did, and I stepped inside.

"Thank the Trickster, it's about gods-damned time!" A tiny gnomish boy confronted me with arms akimbo, and I almost burst into laughter at the look on his face. Barely two feet tall, his doll-like eyes wide with a curious combination of dismay and impatience. "You've got to get me out of here! Lady Keshmir's a fool! She doesn't know what she's done!"

"Vinchi Tinworthy, I presume? Son of Blinth Tinworthy?" I gave him a polite nod.

"Of course! But you don't understand! It's about the—"

"Don't worry. We're getting you out." I ushered him into the hallway and asked Nahli, "Take them out, would you? I'm going to explore the rest of the keep."

The fae looked intently at me. "The Council will want to—"

"With all due respect to the *Council*," I bristled, "*I'm* the one who took this keep, so I'm going to explore it!"

She did help you, Hashi, Saraknyal reminded me.

"We can split the spoils, since I couldn't have gotten in without you. Anything that involves Jhavika's plans will go to the Council." I wasn't in the mood to argue. I commanded my shades, "Escort Lady Twince and the heirs out of the keep's main gate and protect them until they are safely away. Lord Blackbriar should have transport outside by now. Nahli, our job's done here as soon as you get the heirs to their temporary guardians."

Surprisingly unperturbed at my tirade, Nahli gave me one last long, scrutinous look, then nodded once. "Very well. Come along, young lords and lady."

"You don't *understand!*" the little gnome insisted. "Lady Keshmir ordered the mine foremen to command *all* the miners to defend our keep! They've left the mines untended! We're in trouble! All of us!"

Frankly, I couldn't have cared less about a bunch of miners at that moment. "We'll discuss it with the other council members in the morning, Lord Tinworthy." I waved them away, and Nahli ushered them downstairs.

I searched Jhavika's keep from top to bottom, starting at the highest tower and delving the deepest dungeon. I found the exercise oddly therapeutic; my methodical search held at bay the horrors I'd committed this night. I felt as if I was exploring an ancient ruin...back when my life was simple.

I went through Jhavika's personal chambers carefully. She had a lot of beautiful clothes, though none that would fit me; some lovely jewelry, which I stuffed into my pockets; an amazing array of maps; and some interesting books. I perused the subjects: tactics, strategy, warfare, the politics of every city-state and nation east of the Ironwall Mountains.

Not much light reading.

She's got the library of someone obsessed with conquest, Saraknyal pointed out.

Maybe she had her eyes on more than Haven, I surmised.

Rifling through Jhavika's desk, I discovered lists of her own forces, spies, and slaves. *Excellent!* I leaned back in her chair and examined the names of those she'd enchanted, praying that I would find none of my own people. I didn't. It also didn't seem a very long list, maybe a few hundred names, and most were her own soldiers. I tucked the most important-looking documents into a leather satchel, slung it over my shoulder, and continued my search. One floor below I found Jhavika's library, and my mouth fell open. A treasure trove of books. I ran my fingers lovingly over the bindings, breathed deep of the scent of leather and parchment.

Very nice! Saraknyal said.

"These I'll be taking as part of my share of the spoils."

A girl can't have too many books, after all.

I chuckled and forced myself to continue my exploration.

In the lowest reaches of the keep, besides impressive wine cellars and stocks of foodstuffs, I found a clean and well-lit dungeon. There were perhaps two dozen cells, half of them occupied. The prisoners spoke to me freely, evidently awaiting enslavement. Five of them had simply been kidnapped off the street. The others were a couple of barmaids, one slim young man who worked in a brothel, a blacksmith, and a number of laborers. I freed them all and hustled them up to the great hall to be held with the others.

There, I addressed the entire group.

"I know what you've all been told to believe, and I probably can't change what you're thinking, but here's the truth: Your mistress staged a coup against the Council of Lords and had several of them murdered. She tried to have *me* murdered. That didn't work out for her." They looked confused and worried; no wonder, since I'd just slaughtered Jhavika's entire household guard. "We're going to keep you here under guard. You can move about the keep as you wish, see to your duties and care for yourselves, but you can't leave. If you try, my shades will restrain you. The Council will be by to speak with you. If you have any questions, feel free to ask."

"Can we go?" asked one of the men I'd pulled from the dungeon. "We ain't part of this and don't want to be."

"*No* one is leaving," I reiterated, "until we talk with everyone. Anything else?"

There were no other questions.

Exhaustion settled over me like a leaden blanket. It had been a long, horrible night. All I wanted was a bath, a brandy, and my bed.

I took my shades out to the courtyard and gave them instructions. "Guard the keep; nobody goes in or out without my permission. Don't harm anyone inside the keep. Send word to Ash Keep if anything or anyone tries to keep you from the tasks I've just assigned you."

I surveyed the courtyard and cringed at the pile of slain soldiers that littered one corner. *I should deal with that.*

Do it tomorrow, Hashi. You're exhausted. They're not going anywhere.

Gods, I hope they don't. I commanded my shades, "Strip the dead of anything valuable. I'll dispose of them in the morning."

"Yes, mistress."

I looked up; the faintest hint of the coming dawn lit the eastern sky. No wonder I was tired. With an escort of four shades, I left the keep through the postern door.

Outside, to my surprise, waited a coach with a mounted escort.

"Hashi! How are you?" Tori Blackbriar stepped lightly down from the conveyance, dressed, as always, as if he might be attending a ball, blazing smile intact.

*What's *he* doing here?* Saraknyal asked.

"What are you doing here?" I echoed, eying him suspiciously. "Where are the heirs?"

"Safe, as we agreed. Nahli said you intended to search the keep, so I thought I'd stay and see how you fared." His eyes roved over my slashed clothing. "No trouble?"

I stared at him in disbelief. "You waited half the night to see how I *fared?* Nahli could have told you."

"Oh, she did. I just wanted to ensure that you were all right."

"Or maybe ensure that I didn't pillage the keep before the rest of you got a chance?" I challenged him. I'd ride a succubus to Hell before I told him about the jewelry in my pockets.

Tori waved a dismissive hand. "You've earned whatever you found, Hashi. You've turned the tide against Jhavika. We owe you our gratitude and more."

Is there a point to his babbling?

I shrugged, trying to relieve the knots in the muscles of my shoulders and neck. "It's been a long night, Tori. I'm going home."

He held up a hand. "That's another reason I waited. The streets aren't safe, and walking is tiresome. You've been through hell, Hashi. Let me give you a ride."

*Inside the *coach* with him? Don't do it, Hashi!* Saraknyal protested.

"I like to walk. It clears my head." I forced a cold smile. "And I'm *perfectly* safe."

"As you wish." Tori gave me a courtly bow and a smile, then climbed aboard his carriage and waved through the open window. "We're meeting at Lord Malchi's keep at noon."

"Very well." His coach and escort clattered off.

What's up with him?

I don't know, I admitted, *but he's starting to give me the creeps.*

Says the woman walking down a dark street in a lawless city with four shades on her heels.

Yes, well, Tori gives me a different type of creeps. He's always been polite at council meetings, but lately he's been over the top. He's just so gods-damned friendly! What the hell does he want from me?

What does Tori Blackbriar want from all women? Their heels drumming his backside!

Don't be disgusting, I thought, but I lacked the energy to put any emotion into it.

Chapter Fourteen
Survival

Half a day of hard riding through the increasingly rough terrain of northern Sariff taught me two things: the jungle was going to be a problem for my mount, and I would have killed for a saddle.

My mare picked her way cautiously through the thick and tangling undergrowth, tree roots that lurked under fallen leaves, and the increasingly treacherous footing. She stumbled more than once, and I feared she'd break a leg. Sweat drenched us both. The air was stifling, and a million varieties of biting insects seemed intent on sucking us dry.

Needless to say, our pace slowed drastically. When the light started to fail—not that much sunlight could pierce the heavy canopy of trees and vines overhead anyway—I searched for someplace to camp, but found only heavy foliage in all directions. My head drooped despairingly. Not long ago, I'd believed that I'd found my new home. Now I was on the run in the jungle with no water, no food, no bedroll, and no way to make a fire.

There! Saraknyal said. *A clearing.*

Through the gloom ahead, I spotted a void in the jungle and urged my mare toward it. A tree with a bole as thick as I was tall had fallen and torn a dozen more down with it. Grass and other plants that didn't grow in the constant shade of the jungle had proliferated in the open space, stretching toward the precious sunlight. I spotted papaya trees and laughed.

"Thank...the Gods...of Light!" I heaved between labored breaths as I slid off my mount's back.

Do you really think the gods felled this tree for you, Hashi?

Saraknyal had been largely silent through the afternoon. Our angry exchange earlier had opened wounds for both of us, and given me a lot to think about. I felt that, perhaps, I understood the necromancer a little better. I wasn't sure if that was a good thing or not.

"Are you absolutely sure they *didn't?*" I tied my mare's reins to a branch and shoved my way through the undergrowth to the nearest papaya tree.

Not absolutely sure, but I think it egotistical to think that they did.

"Just covering all possibilities." I reached the tree and gazed up. Two of the lowest fruits were ripe, the higher ones green, but all well out of my reach. Several overripe fruits lay scattered around the tree, broken open by the fall and crawling with ants. The air was sickly sweet with the scent of their rotting flesh. "If they did fell the tree for me, and I didn't thank them, that would make me ungrateful. If they didn't fell it, no harm done in thanking them anyway." I stepped around the ants, wary of their stings, and drew the only tool I had.

You're a very careful person, Hashi.

"Am I?" I clenched the wrapped hilt of the obsidian blade between my teeth, made sure the trunk of the tree wasn't also crawling with ants, and started to shinny up.

Why not simply cut the tree down? he asked.

Because that would kill it, and I don't kill things if I don't have to.

How noble of you.

Gods, I was sick of his sarcasm.

I reached the lowest fruit, snatched the blade from my teeth, and cut the stems of the two ripe papayas. They thumped to the grassy ground, and I slid down. One had cracked open, but the other was intact, and neither had hit a swarm of ants. I scooped them up and returned to my horse. She stood placidly cropping the tough grass, her coat matted with sweat. I had no cloth to wipe her down with, and no water for myself, let alone her, but the grass and fruit should provide some moisture. I cut the broken papaya into quarters, scooped out the seeds, and ate one piece in greedy, sweet gulps, juice dripping off my chin. The flesh was soft and moist, quenching both my thirst and hunger. I ate a second quarter, and then fed the other two to my mare. She chomped them happily, then nosed the uncut fruit.

"No, you don't. That's breakfast." I picked up the fruit and put it out of her reach, then looked around for a place to sleep where I wouldn't be visited by crawling insects or snakes.

The massive tree had fallen some years ago, but its branches still sported leaves. I led my mount to the tree's crown and tied her to a branch. With little trouble, I found a nook in the branches that I could recline in. It wasn't exactly comfortable, but at least it wasn't on the ground. The bark of the tree was smooth, and my perch wide enough to support me without the fear of toppling off. I had no blanket, but the night promised to be warm. If it didn't rain, I'd be fine.

If you keep a hand on me, I can keep the mosquitos at bay, Saraknyal said.

"Huh. Handy that." The thought of using soul energy as insect repellant repulsed me, but I'd never get any sleep being attacked by bugs, so I reclined with one hand resting on the dagger's hilt. I lay there for a long time staring up at the patch of exposed sky, listening to the drone of buzzing insects, chirping frogs, and bats, exhausted, stressed, and depressed. I'd had the perfect place, and it had all evaporated like water in the desert.

Have you decided where to go?

"Not many options. To the west is Tira. To the east mountains run right down to the sea. To the north are the Jungles of Nin."

*Not the Jungles of Nin. They're full of fae. I *hate* fae!*

I cocked my head. "Why do you hate them?"

Because they're the essence of magic, and therefore a threat to me. They also hate necromancy even more than humans. Besides, I can't use their souls.

"Like you can't use roo souls?"

Correct. Find somewhere else.

"No *map*." I gritted my teeth against the surge of temper. Getting angry wouldn't help. "I'm working from memory here."

But I have a flawless memory, and I perused your maps. What would you like to know?

I rolled my eyes. "Why didn't you say that in the first place?"

You didn't ask. What about Haven?

"Haven? What haven?"

*A city to the northeast, on the coast of the Blood Sea. In *my* day, it was called Rinkletwine. Do you know why they changed the name?*

"Haven!" I exclaimed, my memory duly jogged. "It *used* to be gnomish, but they abandoned it about four hundred years ago. No one knows why. It was resettled about a century ago by a bunch of pirates and warlords. It's reputed to be...not a very safe place."

The name 'Haven' seems to suggest otherwise.

"Yeah, well, I think they meant a haven for criminals and exiles."

Sounds perfect, but there are mountains to be crossed.

"I'll need supplies."

There must be villages and farms to the north.

"I suppose, but word's going to spread quickly about me, and I don't have much money left."

Sell your horse. You won't get over the mountains with it anyway.

"Maybe I can trade her to a farmer for some things."

Or eat the horse and take what you need. It's not like anyone can hurt you.

"I'm not going to steal from poor farmers, Saraknyal."

Suit yourself, but one look at you and anyone will know you're on the run.

Another valid point. I yawned. "I'll think about it in the morning."

I closed my eyes, listening to the jungle, smelling the thick scents of rotting vegetation and the papaya I'd eaten. I tried to ignore my thirst. My belly was full, and unless I was eaten by a jungle cat in the night, I'd survived the day. I'd put a solid fifty miles between me and the city of Sariff, enough to outpace any pursuit. Or so I thought as I slipped into sleep.

Hashi! Wake up! Trouble!

I rolled off my perch before I was even fully awake, hitting the ground hard on hands and knees and barking a shin on a branch. Stifling a cry, I blinked away tears and gripped the soul blade's hilt as if my life depended upon it, which it undoubtedly did. *What?*

Your horse scented something it doesn't like. I don't know what it is.

I peered over the log into the dark jungle. Despite Saraknyal's perception illuminating everything, I couldn't see any threat, but he was right about my mare. She was stomping and tugging at her tether. Something was wrong. I turned a slow circle.

Probably a big ca—

Something shot out of the darkness straight at my face. I didn't even have time to gasp before the arrow disintegrated and my eyes were full of dust. I dropped, spat, and rolled under the log I'd been sleeping on, blinking in a vain attempt to clear my eyes. *What the hell? Can you see anything?*

Yes. Use my sight, Hashi.

I rolled up to hands and knees and fought not to wipe my eyes. I didn't need eyes; I could see through Saraknyal.

Two—no, three figures resolved in the jungle, bows drawn, faces painted to mimic the foliage, black tattoos on their dark skin.

Jaguar Warriors! Shit!

There are at least two more.

I rose to my feet and laughed fear into the night.

Nothing happened. They didn't move, didn't quail with terror—hell, they didn't even look startled. *Saraknyal? What...*

The spell worked! I don't know why it didn't affect them.

Of course! Jaguar Warriors didn't feel fear. It had been trained out of them from birth. I was in trouble.

Arrows whistled out of the night at me, but they puffed into dust. I backed against the tree and shouted, "You can't hurt me! Go now, and you'll survive!"

The warriors charged out of the brush, four from the front and two more behind, swords drawn, faces blank.

I guess threats don't work either.

The winter spell? I had about two seconds.

I don't have the energy for it!

Well, fuck!

With my back to the tree, I thought only two or three could get to me at once, but I was wrong. As three slashed at me from the front, another leapt up onto the log above me to thrust his sword down. I forced myself to ignore the blades—*Don't fail me now, Saraknyal*—and they puffed into clouds of rust. I slashed at the man's

157

legs above me, but he jumped, and I missed. These Jaguar Warriors were inhumanly quick.

The three in front of me now attacked with their fists. I intercepted one swing with the soul blade. The man stiffened, and power chilled up my arm as Saraknyal fed. The second man's fist landed a glancing blow to my temple. My ears rang and my knees folded. As I crashed to the ground, I screamed winter, freezing their legs. The two warriors fell, but still thrashed at me with their arms, immune to fear and pain. I slashed and caught another on the wrist. Power flooded into me.

Then an arm snaked around my throat, and a hand pressed against the side of my head. Hard muscles tensed, and pain lanced up my neck. I couldn't breathe, but I feared my neck would snap before I suffocated. I stabbed wildly, and the dagger connected. The arm went limp and fell away from my neck.

Struggling to my feet, I gasped for breath and looked around, but the others had vanished. *Where are they?*

Three dead. The one in front of you is unconscious. One more behind the log with a bow, and another near your horse.

I raised the three corpses with a thought. The zombies lurched up, one on stumps of frozen legs, and faced the jungle to defend me.

"Go!" I screamed into the night. "I don't want to destroy you! Tell your king I'm leaving his land!"

An arrow struck the zombie that had so recently tried to snap my neck, but it remained stock still. The other warrior whistled a shrill note, then leapt up onto my horse's back. She shied, but he grabbed her reins and slashed her tether. As he whirled the horse around, the one with the bow jumped up behind him. By the time I opened my mouth to curse, they'd disappeared into the foliage.

They're gone, Hashi.

Gone or just hiding? They were very good at blending into the jungle.

Gone. I can still hear your horse, and it's running away from us.

I collapsed to my knees and swore under my breath, rubbing my tender neck. I tried to blink the grit from my eyes, but it stung like blazes. "Are any of them carrying a waterskin?"

Yes, they all are.

Collecting the waterskin from the body in front of me, I put the soul blade down long enough to rinse the crud from my eyes and mouth. Without Saraknyal's help, I couldn't see very well, but I could at least open my eyes. The three Jaguar Warrior zombies stood defensively around me, facing outward, daggers in hand. Curious about these renowned warriors, I circled them, scrutinizing every detail. Given that two had fled, I might very well have to face more.

Each carried a canvas pack on his back and a straight, double-edged short sword with crescent guards in a sheath beneath. These were obviously backup blades, since the ones they attacked me with were disintegrated. Clothed in padded leather armor, each also carried a plethora of gear: light rope, pouches containing tinder and flint, matches, bandages, gloves, and bags of preserved food. I smiled; I may have lost my horse, but I'd gained everything I needed to survive in the wilds.

"Fair trade," I said, then turned to the unconscious man. "I suppose you want me to feed him to you."

I have another idea, if you're willing. You could use a guardian, and these Jaguar Warriors are skilled, and more importantly, fearless.

"What do you mean, a guardian?" I gestured toward the zombies. "I don't want any more of these, and plan to banish them as soon as—"

No, not another zombie. This fellow's still alive, you see, and his fearlessness would make him a perfect wraith.

"A *wraith*?" I knew what wraiths were—the legends, anyway—humans twisted by magic into half-dead monsters, the most fell warriors of the necromancer. I picked up the soul blade and peered down at the unconscious man. "But his legs are frozen solid. He can't walk."

*That won't matter to a wraith, my dear. Wraiths are immune to pain, cold, poison, and barely notice fire and physical attacks. They're also intelligent, tireless, and retain the skills of their former lives. He'll still be a Jaguar Warrior, Hashi, but he'll be *yours*.*

"How do you make a wraith?" I asked, wary of Saraknyal's motives.

It's a laborious process, but well worth the effort. I strip away everything from his soul that we don't need.

"Like you did to mine?"

Not exactly. This is more...invasive, and without the subject's consent, of course.

"But he'll still be alive?"

Technically, yes, but...changed. More importantly, unlike zombies, he'll pass for human.

I was torn. If I was going to Haven, I'd need money, and good swords and armor would be worth a tidy sum. However, I couldn't could carry it all myself. An extra pair of hands would be invaluable, but there was no way I was going to take along zombies. And having a Jaguar Warrior at my side in a lawless city like Haven wasn't the worst idea Saraknyal had ever had.

Not as bad as consuming someone's soul, I reasoned. "And why does fearlessness make him perfect?"

Because fear is the single barrier to creating a wraith. If the subject fears you, the process won't work. Usually you supplant the fear with another strong emotion, say avarice, lust, or hatred. These fellows, however, showed no fear whatsoever, even after you slaughtered three of them. They didn't flee because they were afraid. They simply saw that their chances for victory were next to nil, and decided to withdraw.

"Okay." I knelt next to the unconscious man. "How does this work?"

Just open his eyes and look into them, then say, 'Look into my soul.' I'll do the rest.

I shivered. "On second thought, I don't like the sound of this."

I'm trying to help you, Hashi. Saraknyal sounded a little exasperated. *You only have three choices here: let him die, let me take his soul, or make him a wraith. He did try to murder you, after all.*

"True, but he was only following orders."

From your description of these Jaguar Warriors, that all they do. He's little more than a wraith already.

I grimaced, undecided. I could use help getting over the mountains. And Haven...

160

You really can't do better than a wraith, my dear. They last indefinitely, and are near-human in appearance. If you're going to walk into a den of thieves, warlords, and cutthroats, you need something like that at your side.

It all sounded very convincing.

"Okay, let's do this." I moved before I changed my mind again. Kneeling beside him, I leaned forward, opened the unconscious man's eyes—they were dark and bloodshot—looked into them, and said, "Look into my soul."

Power stirred in the soul blade, chilling my veins. Gazing into the Jaguar Warrior's eyes, I felt as if I *could* actually see into his soul. Something deep within him roused, stirred, and rose up. The power coursing through me latched onto the warrior's essence and, like claws rending flesh, tore it to shreds.

The man gasped a breath and screamed.

I tried to break the connection between my eyes and his, but couldn't look away. I was the bridge between the necromancer and his victim, the conduit for his foul magic.

Shhhh, be still, Saraknyal cooed through me into the man's soul. *Let it go. You don't need it. It's not important. Let it go...*

The tatters of the warrior's soul floated up through me and into Saraknyal, leaving a core of something that wasn't quiet whole, wasn't quite human.

Surely I was damning myself again. This seemed even worse than destroying a soul; we were profaning it beyond recognition. And I'd condoned it for my own benefit, allowed Saraknyal to use me. Was I becoming something abhorrent, something evil? Was I becoming someone who *should* be burned at the stake?

Let it go, I told myself, echoing Saraknyal's words. *I've only done what I had to do to survive. Anyone would have, faced with what I've been through. They tried to murder me.*

That's right, Hashi. You only did what you had to do to survive.

Deep down, though, I knew it was a lie. I'd damned myself, and I was digging myself deeper with every new atrocity. *Let it go...*

Strange, I couldn't tell any longer if it was Saraknyal saying it...or me.

Chapter Fifteen
The Gnomish Secret

From the journal of Hashi Severn –

I never thought to see fear in Nahli Twince's fathomless eyes, but there it was. Fear of me. Well, maybe that's not a bad thing. Only Tori Blackbriar shows no fear when he looks at me, and I don't know why. Is he a fool or does he know something I don't?

I arrived back at Ash Keep in a dark mood, the weight of the atrocities I'd committed heavy on my mind. I told my people that all went well. A huge copper tub was already waiting in my room, bless them. Splattered head to toe with blood, I was physically fine save for a few bruises. It seemed impossible that I'd wreaked such slaughter and remained untouched.

Necromancer... I truly lived up to that name this night. *How many...*

Do you really want an accurate count or are you just moping again?

Shut up, old man. I can't handle your shit right now.

I put Soul Drinker in the lead-lined box, soaked in the tub, and sipped brandy, letting warm water and good liquor ease my nerves, trying to erase images of so many terrified faces. Jhavika's soldiers had known what they were fighting, that they didn't have a chance, that they risked not only their lives, but their very souls. But they'd had no a choice.

Gods damn you to all Nine Hells, Jhavika Keshmir. How many? Two hundred? Three hundred? I reached for the bottle and poured myself another brandy. *I did what I had to do*, I told myself. *I saved as many as I could.*

The cold logic didn't help. I doubted the ghosts of those I'd slain rather than consumed would thank me. Tears tracked down my cheeks to drip into my tepid bath, but I didn't know if I was crying for the souls of those I'd destroyed, or my own.

Rising from the water, I dried myself, donned my favorite robe, poured more brandy, sat in my favorite chair, and stared out at the festering cesspool of Haven.

...what I had to do...

If Jhavika retrieved that damned scourge and returned with five hundred or a thousand slaves, what then? Wade through them as I had last night? The other houses didn't have enough troops to oppose her. Every victory would make her stronger, and those who opposed her weaker.

I laughed sourly as I considered the irony. Who was the lesser evil? The one who enslaved others in pursuit of conquest, or the one who destroyed them to save her own skin? At least Jhavika's slaves still possessed their souls.

I watched the sunrise, unmoved by the beauty and unable to sleep. I drank and obsessed until mid-morning, then freed Saraknyal from his box, had him banish my intoxication—yes, I was pretty much wrecked—forced myself to eat breakfast, and ordered my carriage readied. I had work to do before I joined the other lords at Malchi's keep.

I regretted eating breakfast as soon as I stepped through the postern door into Jhavika's courtyard. The stench nearly folded my knees. Choking back bile, I waved over one of my shades.

"Open the gate. I'm taking the slain out of here. When the courtyard's clear, close the gate again and clean up the mess."

"Yes, mistress." The big gate groaned open, the portcullis squealing up its iron tracks.

Facing the mound of decomposing flesh that had been Jhavika's household guard, I gripped Soul Drinker and said, "Arise."

They did. It wasn't pretty.

"Follow me," I ordered, and strode through the open gates to my carriage.

Bromish looked dubiously at the shuffling crowd of zombies. "Where to, mistress?"

"The northeastern promontory, and drive slowly. I don't want any to straggle." I boarded and closed the door.

We proceeded through Haven at a walk, skirting the periphery to avoid the most heavily populated areas. Unsurprisingly, the gangs and cutthroats didn't bother us. Uphill we drove to the headland that girded the harbor. We passed by the lighthouse and massive shore batteries where Ingrid's people labored to complete their repairs. The ancient gnomish catapults were in pieces, all of their windings and mechanisms being refurbished; I hoped the work would be done by the time Jhavika returned. The workers stopped and stared at my shambling escort, muttering amongst themselves and making warding signs.

Word's going to spread about this.

*Look at it this way: nobody will *ever* mess with you after this.*

Said every necromancer who ever burned at the stake.

He didn't reply.

Bromish pulled up where the road ended at the promontory, and I got out. A low line of clouds to the east promised rain, summer squalls that would lash Haven by midday. *Good*, I thought. *Maybe it'll wash away the filth...at least for a while.*

I wondered idly if standing in the rain would wash away my sins.

The wind was already kicking up as I staggered toward the precipice. Incoming swells boomed against the base of the cliff some two hundred feet below, the ground trembling beneath my boots. Out to sea, gray sheets of rain slanted down from towering dark clouds. Thunder rumbled and lightning flashed, an apt accompaniment to my black mood.

"Go!" I commanded my undead victims, pointing out to sea.

They shambled off the cliff without pause, plummeting into the surf below. When the last had toppled over the precipice, I peered over the edge at the carnage, still thrashing even as the waves pounded them against the rocks.

"Begone!" I screamed, and the thrashing stopped.

The scavengers of the sea would feed well, and Haven would be spared the stench of their decomposition.

I gauged the time of day as I boarded my carriage. "Lord Malchi's keep, Bromish. We're due at midday." I leaned back and closed my eyes, but even that darkness couldn't hide unbidden visions of corpses thrashing in the surf.

"Yes, mistress." Bromish flicked the reins and directed us back down the hill into Haven.

You should stop by Jhavika's keep and pick up an escort, Saraknyal suggested.

"No. I don't want to frighten the heirs. They've been through enough."

And if the Council concludes that last night's performance proves that you're too powerful, and decides to put an end to you?

"Then they'll put an end to me." I considered that prospect for a moment, and shrugged. Right now, I couldn't bring myself to care. "But I don't think they will. We're not done."

*And when they *are* done? Do you think they'll continue to tolerate your presence?*

"*If* we manage to deal with Jhavika and her minions, we'll see, won't we?"

I'd never been to Malchi's estate. I found it formidable, but as pretentious as the man himself. The original stonework had been refurbished in an overly ornate style that clashed with the underlying architecture. *Like ribbons and bows on a bullock*, I thought.

Thunder rumbled overhead.

The gate, a lofty affair with gold-painted iron reinforcements, opened readily at my driver's hail, and we rolled into the inner court before the rain hit. Blackbriar and Brickhammer's coaches were already there, but not Nahli's. I wondered if she would attend or choose to shun me after witnessing the atrocities of last night.

I stepped down and started toward the door, then had a thought and turned back to my coach. "Bromish," I said in a low voice, "do me a favor and mingle with the other drivers and stable hands. I'd like to know what rumors are spreading about me."

He smiled and nodded. "Of course, mistress."

The two guards at the door to the keep snapped to attention as I approached, and the attending butler bowed and waved a hand inward. Everyone always seemed so much more polite when I didn't have an undead escort. "Lady Severn. This way, if you please."

I followed him down an ornate corridor, as gaudy and ostentatious as the exterior. And incongruously empty. Several families of the Malchi clan lived here: three sons, a daughter, their spouses, and numerous grandchildren. I neither saw nor heard any of them, but then, perhaps they'd thought it prudent to keep the youngsters clear of the visiting necromancer.

The butler waved me into a small banquet hall where the council members all sat around a table. I started to find Nahli Twince there, too. I opened my mouth to ask where her carriage was, then realized that, having revealed her ability to shape-shift at will to the other council members, she'd probably just flown in.

"Good morning, Hashi!" Tori grinned as he stood and bowed.

How does he always look so dapper? He was up all night!

If we turned him into a shade, he'd never need sleep again.

Shut up.

Ingrid gave me a polite nod, but Nahli's attention seemed to be elsewhere, and Malchi outright scowled at me.

What crawled up his butt and died? Saraknyal grumbled.

"Morning, everyone." I took a seat and asked for tea from a hovering footman. "Problem, Lord Malchi?"

"More than one, actually," he growled.

"Reg has a burr in his saddle about your little procession through the city this mornin'." Ingrid lifted a cup in toast as the servant poured my tea. "What was that about anyway?"

"Disposing of the dead," I said, sipping. "I couldn't very well leave them to rot in Jhavika's keep."

"Why not?" Malchi demanded.

I thought for a moment he was being sarcastic, but he seemed serious. Slowly, as if talking to a child, I said, "Because there are still living *people* there, and rotting flesh breeds pestilence. We need information from Jhavika's retainers, which we won't get if they all perish from fever."

"Fine, but you must understand how that looked to everyone else."

Like a parade in honor of Mortas? Saraknyal quipped.

"No, I don't. How did it look to you?"

"Like a show of force." Malchi's eyes narrowed. "And you left an army of shades guarding Jhavika's keep like it's your own personal prize."

"Jhavika's keep is not my prize, though I *will* be taking my pick of spoils as payment for my efforts last night, as I'm sure Nahli and Tori have already told you. And if sixty is an army, then yes, I did. They're keeping the retainers safe and won't let them wander off." Exhausted and depressed, I was in no mood for this. "This was the *Council's* idea, remember? You wanted the heirs safe; they're safe. You wanted Jhavika's forces neutralized; they're neutralized. You wanted the noncombatants held for questioning; they're held. What's the fucking problem?"

"No problems with the accomplishments themselves, Hashi, it's *how* you accomplished them that's got our knickers in a twist." Ingrid poured blackbrew into her cup and fixed me with an even stare. "We knew it wasn't going to be pretty, but trooping a hundred zombies through the city..."

I stood, bristling with anger. "It wasn't a parade, it was *waste* disposal! Would you would have preferred I brought them *here?*" I emphasized my last words with a hard slap to the table.

Three of the four lords stiffened in their seats, and bodyguards shifted. Tori was the only one who didn't look defensive, merely cocking an eyebrow in something like amusement.

Now, Hashi, don't do anything rash.

Saraknyal counseling restraint brought me up short. I dragged a breath into my lungs. "I gave you *exactly* what you asked for. If you don't like my *methods*, perhaps I should just leave."

"Leave?" Tori's amused look vanished. "Leave the Council...or *Haven?*"

"Both. Why not? It's become *obvious* that I've outlasted my welcome. When Jhavika comes back with two *thousand* enslaved soldiers, and you have fuck-all to fight them, give her my regards." I turned for the door.

"Hashi, wait!" Tori's chair screeched across the floor, and he dashed to head me off.

Reflexively, I clenched Soul Drinker, but Tori's hand wasn't anywhere near his sword. In fact, both were up and empty as he faced me.

"You're taking this personally, and you shouldn't." He sounded sincere, but for once I'd wiped that ingratiating smile off his face. He lowered his voice. "They're *scared*, Hashi! Give them a little break, and maybe some assurance that they're not next on your list for conquest."

"I don't have a *list!*" I said it loudly enough to be heard by everyone and turned to face the table. "If I did, you'd all be shades already."

"That's not *exactly* reassuring," Tori said, but his smile was back.

"Hashi, *please*." Nahli stood, finally looking at me. "Resume your seat with us. Whether we approve of your methods or not, you're an invaluable member of this council."

"Because I do your *dirty* work for you, slaughter innocent soldiers who can't surrender when you don't have the *stomach!*" My voice broke on the last, and I hated myself for it.

Shit, Hashi, why don't you just spit on the floor! Calm down!

"We all have our strengths," Nahli countered.

"Except for me." Tori buffed his nails on his breast with a sideways grin. "I just look good and crack wise."

I had to stifle a smirk despite myself.

"Tori has his spy network, Malchi his ships, Ingrid her craftspeople, and I have my magic." Nahli gestured to a chair. "Your powers make us uncomfortable, just like mine made *you* uncomfortable in my home. Please sit."

I recalled my discomfort in her keep, and nodded. "Fine." I strode back to the table. "But cut the bullshit. I wasn't *threatening* anyone by disposing of the dead." I sat and looked Malchi in the eye. "What else is bothering you besides *me*, then?"

His scowl remained undiminished. "The Tinworthy tyke keeps going on and on about the mines and some dread horror. He says Jhavika ordered the foremen to shut down the mine to fortify the guards, and that that has caused some...problems."

"Problems?" I remembered the little gnome was upset, but hadn't really been listening at the time. "What sort of problems?"

"He wouldn't go into detail." Malchi simply shrugged. "Said he needed to speak to the entire Council."

"I think we should hear this from young Lord Tinworthy," Nahli suggested. "All three heirs, in fact. They've been told what happened at the party. We need to hear their sides of recent events."

"I agree," Tori said. "And we should stop thinking of them as *tykes*. They're the heads of their houses now, and they're frightened."

"Are you sure they're not ensorcelled?" I asked.

"Positive," Nahli assured me. "I felt the enchantment when I touched some of Jhavika's retainers last night. Its aura is subtle, but detectable, and completely absent from the heirs."

"Well, that's bloody handy!" Ingrid said.

"Indeed," Malchi agreed, waving a footman to retrieve the heirs.

The three entered and took seats at the table, gravitating toward the lords who had taken them in. Que-Chen looked more composed than he had last night, though he eyed me warily as he took a seat beside Tori Blackbriar. I wondered what his father had told him about me. Mah Hatsu looked like the porcelain-faced doll she still clutched, garbed in silk and ready to shatter as she settled in next to Ingrid. Tiny Vinchi Tinworthy looked upset and put out as he took his seat beside Lord Malchi. It didn't help that he could barely see over the table until a footman provided a booster for the lad's chair.

"First, let me welcome you three to the Council of Lords, and assure you that you're safe." Malchi waved his footmen forward to lay out platters of tidbits and assorted beverages. "You've been through a lot, we understand, and we'd like to hear your accounts. We'll try to get you back to your houses as soon as—"

"No," Mah Hatsu interrupted, her eyes wide. "Don't do that, please. Something's...wrong with them."

"She's right!" Vinchi Tinworthy agreed. "Key people in my house are being controlled somehow by Lady Keshmir. We were dragged from our homes by trusted members of our own households and delivered to her like baggage!"

Que-Chen nodded in agreement.

"Very well, we'll keep you safe in our own keeps, then, until this is resolved." Malchi turned to Vinchi Tinworthy. "Now, Vinchi, please tell the rest of the Council what you told me last night."

"Thank you, Lord Malchi." The tiny gnome looked around the table. "Lady Keshmir has made a grave error that has likely doomed all of Haven."

"A bigger error than trying to have us all killed?" Tori quipped.

"Yes. Much bigger." Vinchi's determined mien wavered, and he looked uncomfortably around the table. "I don't... I maybe shouldn't tell you all of this. I took an oath to never reveal the secret, but..."

*Oooo, secrets! I *like* secrets!*

Hush, old man. Still, the young gnome's pronouncement piqued my curiosity.

"Please, young lord," Nahli assured him. "We cannot help if we don't know what's wrong."

"Right." The young gnome cleared his throat. "You all know that Haven used to be the gnomish city of Rinkletwine, right? And that it was abandoned for years, right? Well, that happened because the miners found something, a stone, that...caused death."

"What?" Ingrid's eyes widened.

*Caused death? Now, *that's* interesting!*

I ignored Saraknyal and asked, "Caused death *how?*"

"Let me explain." He cleared his throat again and took a sip of tea. "Do any of you know the legend of the Cornerstones?"

"Yes, I've heard it." Ingrid's usually ruddy features had gone pale.

I'd read of it, too, a legend from half the world away. "Four foci of elemental energy, weren't they?"

Vinci nodded. "Yes, exactly. Foci of earth, air, fire, and water; conduits to the elemental spheres."

"But they were lost." Ingrid looked perplexed. "Hundreds of years ago, the Cornerstones were lost."

"Yes, but...what they found here was *another* stone. One connected to *another* elemental sphere."

"What others are there besides the four elements?" Malchi asked.

"Life and death," Nahli answered, her face blank. "The gnomes found a conduit to the Void? The sphere of death?"

"Yes," Vinchi confirmed, nodding vigorously. "And it...consumed them. Those who weren't killed outright fled the mines and abandoned the city."

*Void essence... We're in trouble, Hashi! Void essence consumes *everything*! Even *me*!*

My heart skipped a beat. *As if the Jhavika debacle wasn't enough...*

170

"But *someone* must have dealt with it." Tori looked confused. "I mean, we're *here*, right?"

"Yes, the gnomes returned and contained the stone. I don't know exactly how, but I *do* know that about a third of our miners work constantly to *keep* it contained." His big eyes swept the table. "Then Lady Keshmir pulled all the miners out of the mines to take up arms."

"But they would have known!" Ingrid interjected. "They'd have to have known they'd kill us all, *everyone*, if they didn't keep it contained!"

Vinchi looked at her and shook his head. "You don't understand gnomes. We follow the orders of our elders, superiors, and lords. I don't doubt the miners put up a fuss, but when it came down to brass tacks, they'd do as they were told."

"Gnomish society is very structured that way," Tori agreed. "The question is, what do we do?"

There's no stopping this thing, Hashi. We should just leave, sail away.

"Flee," I said aloud, fighting the urge to get up and do exactly that. If *Saraknyal* was scared... "What else can we do?"

"The gnomes contained it before. They should be able to do so again, no?" Tori cocked that eyebrow at me again, and I considered shaving it off with Soul Drinker.

"I don't understand this Death Stone thing," Que-Chen said, obviously not as quick of wit as his father had been.

"There is balance in all things, young lord," Nahli explained. "There are six elemental spheres, not four. The Cornerstones were the conduits the gods used to channel the elements in the creation of the world. Earth opposes air, fire opposes water, and life—*positive* energy—opposes death—negative energy. The Void is the elemental sphere of negative energy. Apparently this stone emits Void essence into our world, where it consumes all other forms of energy. This includes life energy, or," she then looked to me, "as Lady Severn understands it, soul essence."

Bullshit, Saraknyal spat. *Souls are *not* simply positive energy.*

"Souls are more than simply positive energy, but the analogy's close enough. Suffice to say that this Cornerstone puts out energy

171

that will not only kill us, but consume our souls." I turned to Vinchi. "And you don't know how your people contained this thing to begin with?"

"No. I'm sorry, but I don't. As the heir, I was told of the *existence* of the Death Stone, but not the details of how it's contained. That would have come when I was older." His lower lip trembled. "My father didn't expect I'd inherit so soon."

"Who does know?" Ingrid asked gently.

Vinchi shrugged. "Any number of my father's senior people, I guess. Master Geoil, his loremaster, certainly, and probably the four senior foremen of the mines. But I heard that one of the foremen was killed, and I think the other three are spelled by Lady Keshmir. They command the miners."

"None of the lesser officials or servants?" Malchi asked.

"Maybe. I don't know." Vinchi shrugged again. "My father has...*had* a number of learned people in his service. I don't know what's happened to them."

"We've *got* to get into Tinworthy Keep," Ingrid grumbled. "Someone there *not* enslaved by Jhavika should be able to help us deal with this in the same way the gnomes did before."

"Logical, but first we must somehow neutralize those whom Jhavika *has* enslaved," Nahli said.

Every eye turned to me.

My stomach lurched. "No. I'm not breaking into Tinworthy Keep and slaughtering gnomes! The way they follow orders, those in charge would command them to attack me, and I'd have no option but to wade through them!" I heaved a breath, clenching down on my frazzled nerves. "Not happening!"

"I second that," Tori said. "Hashi bore the burden of last night's action on our behalf; we can't ask her to assume sole responsibility for retaking Tinworthy Keep, too."

I looked sharply at Tori, surprised to have him back me up, but grateful for any kind of support.

What's his agenda? Saraknyal asked suspiciously.

"So, if gnomes follow orders, have *him* give the orders." Mah Hatsu pointed at Vinchi. "*He's* their lord, isn't he?"

"The lass has a point," Ingrid said with a smile, patting the girl's shoulder with one massive hand.

"Will they follow your orders?" Malchi asked dubiously. "I mean, you're heir, but..."

"Legally, I became Lord Tinworthy the instant my father was killed." Vinchi sat up stock straight, pushing his meager height to its maximum.

I wrinkled my forehead. "And you're *how* old?"

"Forty-two." The gnome gestured toward Que-Chen. "Not quite his age in human terms, I guess. I know I'm young. I'd have a regent to guide me until I learn all my duties, but I'm still the rightful lord of House Tinworthy."

"All we have to do is get them to listen," Tori stated matter-of-factly.

"But trying to get into Tinworthy Keep will only get us shot full of arrows," Vinchi countered. "One of the soldiers stationed at Lady Keshmir's keep told me that the miners had been ordered to keep everyone out. If the foremen have been enchanted by Lady Keshmir, I doubt they'll recognize my authority. We wouldn't even be able to get close."

Again, everyone looked at me.

I leaned back in my chair and folded my arms defiantly across my chest. "I told you, I'm not breaking in and slaughtering anyone. Not even Jhavika's slaves."

"But you shouldn't have to!" Tori winked at me. "All you need to do is stand and prevent young Lord Tinworthy here from being shot full of arrows."

I glared at him, but refrained from telling him to fuck himself. There were children present.

"I don't understand," Que-Chen said. "How can she do that?"

"The same way she took Lady Keshmir's keep and saved your arse, lad." Ingrid pulled a dagger and threw it at me.

I didn't even dodge, but closed my eyes to keep the dust out of them. After the cloud settled, I fingered the hole in my shirt and glared at her. "You owe me a shirt."

"Oh! Well, *that's* handy!" Que-Chen said nervously.

I regarded the others and considered their unspoken request, then sighed. "All right." I looked to Vinchi Tinworthy. "I *can* keep you safe."

Be careful what you promise, Saraknyal warned.

He was right, and the memory of Gunyan's death smote my heart. "Well, *reasonably* safe. I'll do my best, that's all I can offer."

"*None* of us are safe while the Death Stone is untended, Lady Severn." Vinchi's face took on years that he didn't yet possess, and he nodded. "I accept your offer of protection."

"I'll go with you." Tori grinned and rolled his shoulders. "I'm not without skills, and I can be *quite* persuasive."

"That's what all the young ladies in Haven say, anyway," Ingrid said with a bark of laughter.

Que-Chen blushed furiously. He was staying with Tori, and I wondered how much he'd heard about Lord Blackbriar's exploits.

Don't trust him to watch your back, Hashi. He'll plant that elf blade in it.

Though I doubted Tori would murder me out of hand, I shook my head. "I can't protect both of you."

He just smiled at me. "I can protect myself. I just can't protect myself *and* Lord Tinworthy, which is why your presence is necessary."

I ground my teeth, but decided not to fight it. If Tori wanted to get himself killed, that was his choice. "Fine, but not today. Frankly, I'm exhausted and short tempered. Tomorrow morning I'll discuss strategy with Tori and Vinchi, and we'll try to talk sense to the foremen." I looked to the little gnome. "Are you okay with that?"

"Yes, Lady Severn. The stone's deep within the mine. If they've sealed the mine, it's probably safe for a time."

"Good!" Malchi looked honestly pleased for the first time that morning. "Que-Chen, you and I will talk to the captains of your ships still in port. If any of Jhavika's...slaves are in command, they won't listen, but if they're not, seeing their new lord in person should fortify their allegiance to your house."

Que-Chen looked a little pale, but nodded. "I'll speak to them."

"What about your house, Lady Hatsu?" Ingrid asked the girl.

She shook her head emphatically. "Let them rot! My own governess delivered me to Keshmir's keep under guard. There's no talking to them."

That seemed both harsh and well-reasoned coming from an eleven-year-old girl, and my estimation of her climbed a notch.

"Might I suggest Reginald and I trade guests?" Tori nodded to Que-Chen and Vinchi. "Since I'll be going with Hashi and Vinchi tomorrow, and Lord Malchi will be trying to talk reason to Que-Chen's captains, it seems only reasonable. Saves a lot of riding about town."

"Fine with me," Malchi agreed.

"Tomorrow then." I started to stand, but Tori interrupted.

"Good! Come by my estate tomorrow for breakfast, Hashi, and we'll talk over our plan." He flashed me that grin again. "Unless you'd prefer we come to your keep."

"No, I'll come to yours." Not once had I entertained a guest at Ash Keep, and I wasn't about to start now.

Not a great idea, Hashi. You're not being careful enough about him.

I have no choice. We all need to work together now or we're all screwed.

"Excellent!" Tori stood and swept an elegant bow to the table. "I'll take my leave, then. Lord Tinworthy, if you'd come with me, I'll leave Lord Que-Chen in Lord Malchi's capable hands." He barked a laugh. "All these lords and ladies! I feel like I'm back at court!"

I spun on my heel and marched for the door. Unfortunately, Tori matched my steps and flashed that insufferable grin.

"Any preferences for breakfast?"

"No." I eyed him, considered a snide comment, then let it go. "I'm sorry, Tori, but I'm exhausted. After last night...well, I didn't sleep."

"I know *just* the thing to help with insomnia." He waggled his brows lasciviously.

I stopped cold and narrowed my eyes at him.

He looked surprised at my ire. "What?"

"I'm not one of your *conquests*, Lord Blackbriar. Leave off."

His eyebrows arched. "Very well, Lady Severn. My apologies if my offer was unwelcome." He gave me a short, respectful bow, his face expressionless. "On the morrow, then."

"Sure." I turned and strode for my carriage.

Bromish waited dutifully, opening the door for me before clambering up to the driver's seat. The brief squall had relented, and the air felt fresher for it. When we were halfway home, I opened the speaking hatch and asked, "What news from the other groomsmen?"

"Nothing much, other than they're all scared spitless of you. They asked me if I was under your spell, or if you'd taken part of my soul to keep me loyal."

"And what did you tell them?"

"That I weren't under no spell as far as I knew. Told 'em you might be scary as hell, but workin' for you was, as far as I could say, the safest job in Haven." He cackled. "Took them all aback, it did."

"Well done." I shut the hatch and leaned back, closing my eyes. Keeping people afraid of me had kept me safe for decades, but spreading the word that I wasn't a homicidal maniac had a real purpose. *Like keeping me from being tied to a post and having a fire lit under my feet...*

*Let them try *that* again,* Saraknyal hissed.

I rubbed my eyes and begged to be left alone. "Let's not, shall we?"

Chapter Sixteen
Unsafe Haven

The morning after the attack by the Jaguar Warriors, I packed up absolutely everything I could and prepared to trek east toward the mountains. The going would be easier out of the jungle-clogged low country. I ate some of the preserved food the warriors carried, as well as my papaya. The only thing I missed was my morning tea.

I donned a padded leather hauberk over my shirt and a pair of sturdy pants, though they didn't fit very well, the legs too short and the waist too wide. My skirt I cut into strips to shield my arms and neck from thorns, and a wider swatch to use as a scarf to cover my face and head when we ventured to higher altitudes. A sword rode at my hip, and a bow and a quiver full of arrows over my shoulder. None of the warriors' boots fit me, but they were solid and well made, so I strapped them to a makeshift pack with the rest of the supplies and equipment. My pale wraith bore the heavy pack with little difficulty and no complaint. I avoided looking at him, knowing my complicity in making him an undead horror. His skin was now the hue of tea with too much milk instead of the deep teak it had been the night before. The whites of his eyes were deep gray, as were his teeth. He looked very *wrong*, but Saraknyal assured me that this was normal.

Normal... Never had I thought that walking through the jungle with a wraith at my command would be anything close to normal.

Do they eat? I asked Saraknyal, saving my breath for walking.

After a fashion, but they don't require much sustenance.

What do you mean, 'after a fashion'?

They'll consume just about anything; rotten meat, insects, small animals... You didn't notice the few bites that were missing from the corpses this morning?

177

I swallowed hard and tried to not puke. *No, I didn't notice. What else can he do?*

A fully mature wraith can breathe killing frost, but to a lesser degree than the winter spell I cast through you, and not very often. Their blood is poisonous, too, in case you want to envenom your arrows. He'll follow complex commands, and can answer simple questions, but don't expect leaps of analytical reasoning.

Okay. And you said they're immune to cold?

Yes. Completely. You're thinking of the pass over the mountains?

Yeah. As far as I know, there isn't a pass. We'll have a serious climb.

Well, you needn't fear the cold, and the wraith can break trail. You'll be fine.

I also don't know exactly where to try to cross. If we miss Haven, we're screwed.

If I remember correctly from the map, you should continue northeast until you reach the headwaters of the river, then turn east. From the crest, you should be able to see the cliffs of the bay and alter your course appropriately.

Thanks. Too bad Jaguar Warriors don't carry compasses.

Interesting, that. You may want to ask your wraith how they tell direction.

I did, and damned if I didn't get an answer.

"Time, sun, and stars."

"How do you keep track of time?" None of them had carried a timepiece of any kind.

"A mental count from sunrise and sunset."

I stopped and stared at him. "You're kidding me. You count seconds every day?"

"Yes." He pointed at the sun through the high canopy. "It is three hours, twenty-two minutes, twelve seconds past sunrise. That is east-southeast. East, north, west, south." He pointed in each direction in turn.

"Well, I'll be damned." I realized the irony of that declaration and clenched my jaw. I was already damned. "Head east-northeast until the jungle thins."

"Yes, mistress." He led the way, and I followed, trusting him to choose the best path.

I told you he'd be useful, Saraknyal said.

Yes, you did. I wasn't about to thank him.

We walked for days. The going was rough, but we encountered no more Jaguar Warriors. There was plenty of small game, which I shot for meat, picking fruit to supplement my food supply. I built fires at night, and my wraith sat sleeplessly to tend them and keep watch while I rested.

Every evening I continued the wraith's transformation. If Saraknyal had told me that it was such a drawn-out affair, I probably would have refused. I feared the necromancer was getting to know me too well. So, night after night, I held the warrior's gaze while Saraknyal meticulously shredded what remained of the man's soul. He paled further, and his luxurious black hair fell out in clumps. His eyes and teeth darkened to the hue of polished onyx. His voice became gravelly, like he'd gargled broken glass. It revolted me, what I was doing to this man, but I had no choice. I wanted to survive.

The jungle thinned as we climbed, making our way easier. Game was less plentiful, but we spotted a few high plantations growing blackbrew and cocoa. I snatched a few ripe cocoa pods and sucked the sweet pulp from the seeds as we trekked into the foothills.

The air chilled with the increasing altitude, and I slept with the soul blade in my hand to keep from shivering. Six days into our passage, a truly tremendous mountain range hove out of the horizon to the north. Far downhill to the west, I could still make out the river by the color of the trees, though it was much smaller now. *Two more days,* I gauged, *then we'll turn east.*

*Then the *real* fun begins.*

I looked to the mountains and cringed. Even this close to the equator, the peaks of the coastal range were snow-capped, looming sharp and white into the clear blue sky. They called them the Dragon's Teeth, and I thought the name apt.

I must be fucking crazy.

Not at all, my dear. You're just determined to survive. It's quite an admirable quality, you know.

Don't flatter me, Saraknyal. If I die on a mountain top, you're going to end up frozen in a glacier for ten thousand years. Your efforts to keep me alive are self-centered, not altruistic.

True, but I do have your best interests at heart.

If you had a heart, I quipped.

Well, there is that.

Two days later, we turned east.

My legs were used to hardship, but I discovered new levels of fatigue. We camped at the tree line for a night, and I relished the warmth of a fire, probably my last for several days. I shot a hare and cooked it over the flames, knowing I would need strength. My wraith ate the offal and bones, chewing them up and swallowing the splinters.

As soon as the pearly dawn light was sufficient to see, I instructed my wraith to lead the way, picking out the easiest trail and the lowest pass through the peaks. We climbed past patches of snow-streaked rock and lichen, inadequately clothed for the biting cold, but neither of us felt it, the wraith because it was undead, and me because of Saraknyal strapped against the bare skin of my forearm.

The first night we huddled in the lee of a boulder field, and I slept on our packs. Exhaustion made it feel like a feather bed. My wraith stood watch, tireless and vigilant.

The following day, we encountered snow in deep drifts. My wraith broke trail, and I followed, head wrapped in my old skirt with a slit for my eyes. Concentrating on placing one foot in front of the other, pressing down on my knees with my hands at every step, I called regular stops to catch my breath in the thin air. Plagued by headaches and nausea, I sipped water from the skin I kept inside my clothes to prevent it from freezing. The whole world seemed to be reduced to blue sky, white snow, and a never-ending climb. Without Saraknyal's magic and the wraith's labor, I would have died there. Then, quite suddenly, the incline leveled out. I called a halt and squinted into the wind-blown frost.

The view took my breath away.

Mountain peaks jutted toward the sky all around us, but to the east and far, far below, I spied the sea. To the northeast, I picked out the cliffs of Snomish Bay. We still had mountains to traverse, but lower than our current ear-popping altitude. I called my wraith over and pointed.

"There!" I could barely hear myself over the howling wind. "There lies Haven! Pick the easiest and safest path you can!"

"Yes, mistress." The pale creature trudged off, breaking through chest-high drifts.

I followed. After the long climb, my legs didn't know what to do with the descending slope. I slipped and fell, and laughed at my own clumsiness.

What's funny? Saraknyal probably though I had a brain hemorrhage from the altitude.

"It's all downhill from here on, old man! That's what's funny!" I got up and trudged on, a wide grin splitting my face. Maybe the thin air was affecting me, but our goal was in sight, and it lifted my heart.

"What a fucking cesspool!" I lifted my makeshift scarf back up over my nose and mouth, but it did little to stifle the stench of open sewers wafting up on the sea breeze.

From my perch beside a boulder well above the city, I surveyed my new home. Haven looked only slightly better than it smelled, blocky stone buildings jumbled together, crowding the slopes up from the ship-specked harbor. Every piece of land was either built upon, cultivated, or quarried, sometimes sporting layers of structures. Even the roofs were fodder for construction, topped with everything from ramshackle sheds to full-blown marketplaces. Bridges spanned the rooftops in a complex pattern to rival any spider's web. Interspersed among the lower buildings, several walled keeps loomed. A few outlying estates also clung to the hillsides, and even one full-fledged palace set on the high promontory beside a thundering waterfall.

I frowned, underwhelmed by my first impression. "What in the names of all the demons in the Nine Hells possessed people to live here?"

You said it was lawless, so probably the same reasons that drove you here. Running from the gallows.

Safe assumption. We worked our way downhill to the outskirts of town. The buildings were blocky and squat—typical gnomish design—but many renovated to accommodate tall folk. I ventured cautiously into the narrow streets. It quickly became evident that the good life was lived on high. Laughter and music filtered down from above. People in fine clothing strolled the bridges that spanned the streets at multiple levels. Some spans were stone, and others rope with wood slats, but all served to keep the haves above the have-nots.

No joy filtered down to street level. Even in the middle of the day there were few people about, and those were bedraggled and wary. Dressed in rags and clutching makeshift weapons in filthy hands, they stared at me hungrily. I didn't look much better, which probably saved me from being attacked outright for the gear we carried. Then again, it could have been the armor and weapons we wore that made the scavengers think twice. At my command, my wraith brandished a naked sword in one hand. I'd settled my impromptu scarf over his head to hide his newly grotesque features. Even the unlawful might have standards when it came to the undead.

We need to find a place to stay, I told Saraknyal. I hadn't seen an inn or boarding house yet. Most doors were boarded or bricked shut, and no signboards or placards advertised lodgings. *Tell me if you spot anything.*

Nothing but vagabonds and shit so far, he grumbled.

Perhaps I'd find inns and shops on the higher levels, but first I'd have to find some stairs. Looking up, I spied a woman emptying a chamber pot out a window and narrowly dodged out of the way. I wrinkled my nose and walked in the middle of the street, through that was no cleaner. The further we penetrated into Haven, the filthier it got, and the hungrier and more feral the faces peering at us from shadowed alcoves and alleys.

"Head toward the waterfront," I told my wraith. If there was one place we would find inns and pubs, it would be the waterfront.

"Yes, mistress." He looked up at the sky, gauging the direction, and we turned a corner.

I glimpsed a ship's mast between the buildings ahead, but halfway down the block four grimy figures stepped into our way. They carried weapons—clubs and rusty knives—and, unlike most of the destitute squatters we'd seen so far, appeared to be hale and determined.

The welcoming committee? Saraknyal quipped.

"This here's *our* street," said a woman with a feral grin. She was small, her hair tangled and her face filthy, but her teeth shone incongruously white. She was obviously in charge. "You're trespassin'."

"Fine." I started to backtrack, but four more people emerged from hiding behind us.

"Too late for that, missy. Time to pay the penalty." She chuckled and stepped toward us, followed closely by the others.

My wraith growled and brandished his sword. I held up a hand, "Wait! You really don't want to do that," I warned the woman.

"Why not? Eight against two, you don't stand a chance." Her grin stiffened, and I wondered if she might be covering fear with bravado. "You hand over that pack and your shiny swords, I let you keep your clothes. You don't, we leave you dead in the street for the rats to gnaw."

I laughed fear. Several of the would-be attackers wavered, but they didn't flee. A hardness settled in the woman's eyes. Anger. She didn't like being laughed at. Need, I guessed, sometimes superseded fear.

"Take them!" she snapped.

"Cover my back!" I commanded my wraith, and it immediately turned to defend me from behind.

Two wild-eyed men charged me, and I barely had time to get the soul blade from its sheath before a nail-studded club swung at my head. I closed my eyes to keep the dust from blinding me, observing everything through Saraknyal's senses.

As the club dissolved, I lashed out with the dagger to rake the man's forearm. Saraknyal fed, and the man dropped. Behind me, my wraith parried a knife stroke and thrust out a bare hand, black nails like claws piercing his opponent under the ribs. The man screamed and thrashed as he was lifted and flung aside like a ragdoll, leaving a handful of eviscerated organs in the wraith's grasp.

My second opponent's dagger puffed into rust as he thrust at me, but I didn't slash back.

"Stop!" I snapped, glaring at the woman who had ordered the attack. The others hesitated, looking between their leader and me, apparently daunted by our seeming invulnerability. "*Now* do you believe me when I say you do *NOT* want to fuck with me?" I was really sick of people not heeding my warnings.

Kill them all, Hashi! They deserve it!

I ignored Saraknyal.

"Okay, okay!" The woman backed up, and her people with her. "You're a badass. Got that. But you walk through Haven carryin' a pack full of gear people could use, you're just askin' to get took."

"And you figured *you* were the ones to do the taking."

"Only *one* rule in Haven: the strong take, and the weak die. Just didn't know how strong you were." She squinted at me then, her eyes flicking between me and my wraith. "You're new here, ain't ya?"

"Yes." I slipped the soul blade back in its sheath.

"What's *he*, then?" She pointed past me to my pale companion, and I turned. The scarf had fallen off his head to reveal his unnatural features. As if that wasn't enough, he was eating the dripping viscera clutched in his hand. The others stared aghast at the gore between his gnashing black teeth, but their leader just swallowed hard, her eyes narrowed, calculating. "I thought albino, but he ain't even human, is he?"

"He's a wraith." I looked back to the woman, hiding my own disgust. "*My* wraith."

*You shouldn't have told them that! Get it through your head, Hashi: people don't *like* necromancers!*

He was right, but the woman's face reflected something other than terror. Avarice...for the power I wielded, for my invulnerability.

Like me, these people were survivors; they did what they had to do to stay alive. Then another thought came to me.

"You know Haven," I said to her. "Where can I find someplace to stay?"

The woman looked surprised, then thoughtful. "Yeah, we know Haven." She glanced to her companions—a pathetic bunch, now that I took a good look, skinny and pale, their eyes dull with desperation and need—then back to me. "Tell you what, you stick with us, and we'll help you out." She pointed to my wraith. "With that thing along, and that shit you pulled with that dagger, we'll carve out a neighborhood, maybe even a whole city block."

"Carve out? What do you mean?"

"I mean, take it over from whatever gang's runnin' it. Get a protection racket goin'." She shrugged. "People here don't care about nothin' but keepin' safe and fillin' their bellies. If we offer to help them with that, keep the other gangs off 'em, they'll pay us."

Don't trust them, Hashi! They'll stab you in the back at the first opportunity!

Trust them? You think I'm stupid?

I didn't say that, but you're better off alone!

No, I'm not. Not here. I need someone who knows this place.

Don't say I didn't warn you when they try to murder you.

I won't. I nodded to the woman. "What's your name?"

"Miras."

"Okay, Miras. I'm Hashi. We'll work together for a while, but I want to make one thing clear to you and all your people."

She bristled a little, but nodded. "Okay, let's hear it."

"You doublecross me..." I raked them all with a glare. "If *any* of you doublecross me, *this* will be your end." I raised the two corpses with a thought, and Miras' gang stumbled back.

"Gods and devils!" one man muttered, making a warding sign.

"Not devils, just magic. *My* magic." I glared at them all again. "So, are we clear? You cross me, and I consume your soul. Got it?"

"Sure!"

"No worries!"

"We ain't stupid!"

185

I nodded in satisfaction at the fearful chorus, and banished the corpses.

"Good. Now take this." I unclipped the short sword from my hip and held it out to Miras.

She took it, slipped the fine blade an inch from the scabbard, and her eyes widened. "Sweet!"

"There are two more swords and four daggers in that pack, and three bows." I turned to my wraith, trying not to grimace at his gore-smeared face. "Wipe the blood off your face and distribute the spare weapons."

"Yes, mistress." He did, and I was satisfied to see the others still nervous about him. They were nervous about me, too.

Good.

"Now, Miras, let's find someplace to stay, and maybe get some food. I just walked over those fucking mountains," I hooked a thumb at the looming peaks, "and I'm starving."

Her jaw dropped. "No way! You climbed over the *Dragon's Teeth?*"

"Yes." I grinned at her. "Go ahead and call me a liar."

"Never!" She laughed. "Just follow me, Hashi. Follow me, and we'll be runnin' half of downtown in a month!"

"I don't want to run half of downtown." I fell into step beside her. "I just want a safe place to sleep and food in my belly." I sniffed, cringing at the stench, but I couldn't tell if it was me, Maris, or the open sewage. "And maybe a bath."

"Huh. With what *you* can do, why not take more?"

"Because I've learned to have low aspirations. The more you want, the less you get in the end. There's always someone bigger who'll try to take it away."

"Ain't that the fuckin' truth." She walked on without another word.

Miras sounded sincere, and I hoped that she took my warning to heart. She didn't seem stupid, but then, neither had the princes in Mati. Miras, at least, knew what would happen to her if she betrayed me.

Chapter Seventeen
Supplication of Reason

From the journal of Hashi Severn –
Never argue with a fool, a zealot, or a necromancer. The first
two will make you look stupid, and the third will make you dead...or
worse.

Tori Blackbriar's estate lay outside the closely set buildings of
Haven proper. Not as far as Balshi's, but far enough to give it the
look of a country manor instead of a fortress. A high stone wall
topped with iron spikes surrounded the grounds, breached only by
an ornate wrought-iron gate defended by uniformed guards. Bromish
pulled the coach to a stop to announce us, and the guards opened
the portal. I glanced out the carriage window as we passed through.
No council meetings had ever been conducted here, so it was all new
to me.

Keep your wits about you here, Hashi.

No shit. For once, I acceded to Saraknyal's paranoia about Tori
Blackbriar. The man had been far too friendly lately, and it disturbed
me that I couldn't figure out why.

The manor house was surrounded by gardens and a narrow,
stone-lined moat sculpted to look like a meandering stream. A path
of stepping stones bordered the moat and led to stone benches
placed at random intervals beneath beautiful tropical trees entwined
with orchids in bloom. The grounds were well tended, but not
ostentatious. The place looked comfortable.

He gets points for aesthetics, at least.

The gravel drive curved to the manor house's front door, framed
by pillars and halberd-wielding guards. Two of the female guards
were as tall as me, but broad-shouldered and flaxen-haired, rare

around the Blood Sea. I wondered if they'd come with Tori from Fengotherond. A footman approached the carriage, but I opened the door and stepped down before he could assist.

"Lady Severn." He bowed with a smile. "Welcome to Blackbriar Estate." His eyes flicked right and left as my escort of four shades climbed down from the carriage and formed up behind me. "I'll see to your driver. Please," he waved a hand toward the open door where another uniformed figure stood, "Lord Blackbriar's butler will show you in."

"Thank you." I strode for the door.

"Welcome, Lady Severn." A feminine voice took me aback. Blackbriar's butler was a woman, tall and stately, middle-aged, with short but smartly styled salt-and-pepper hair. She didn't even look at my grim escort, but bowed from the waist. "Lord Blackbriar's in the sitting room, and breakfast awaits. This way, please."

"Thank you." I eyed her curiously. Most butlers were men. Hell, my *own* butler was a man. *Why have I never thought to appoint a woman as butler?* I wondered. Was I so steeped in tradition? My opinion of Tori Blackbriar climbed another notch.

Or maybe it's just because Blackbriar is overly fond of female company, Saraknyal snarked.

I followed her down a well-appointed hall to a comfortable sitting room. There, Tori sat sipping blackbrew with Vinchi Tinworthy and a beautiful woman in a pretty yellow dress with a plunging neckline.

"Lady Severn, milord," the butler said with another short bow.

"Ah, good morning, Hashi!" Tori stood with a smile. Though elegantly dressed, as usual, I noted his elf blade conspicuously absent from his hip. "This is Beatrice Galt, a local businesswoman who's deigned to join us for breakfast. You know Vinchi, of course."

"Hello, Vinchi." The young lord nodded, his eyes fixed on my shades. "Miss Galt." I nodded politely to the woman, but she strode right up to me and stuck out a hand.

"Lady Severn, *lovely* to meet you! I've heard *so* much about you." Her eyes flicked to my escort, but her smile didn't waver. "You've quite a reputation, and Tori tells me it's well-founded."

I shook her hand, surprised at her exuberance and firm grip. Most people have no desire to touch a necromancer, yet she didn't flinch. "That depends on what you've heard." *Who is she?* I asked Saraknyal.

Other than a lovely young woman, I've no idea. I'm not omniscient.

Nice to hear you finally admit that. "You're name's not familiar to me, Miss Galt. What business are you in?"

"Usually everyone else's, actually," she replied with a little laugh. "And please, call me Bea. Formalities get in the way, don't you agree?"

"Yes, I do. Please call me Hashi."

"Bea's one of my most valuable sources of information." Tori waved us toward a door where two white-coated servants stood. "She knows everyone who's anyone, and all their dirty little secrets."

The woman laughed as we followed Tori to the doors, which the servants opened to a formal dining room. After glancing at Vinchi, she leaned in and said in a quieter voice, "You'd be *astounded* what people let slip in the throes of passion."

Ahhh, Saraknyal chuckled, *she uses the kind of magic that we don't indulge in.*

Ahhh, indeed. "You're a...courtesan?" I glanced to see if Vinchi was listening, but the boy seemed totally absorbed in climbing onto his raised seat without help.

"Among other things, yes." She flashed me a lovely smile. "Remind me to give you my card."

I didn't respond, not knowing what to say without insulting her. I had no need of the services of a courtesan, and wasn't about to let an associate of Tori Blackbriar's—a spy, no less—that close to me. I took my seat, gesturing for two of my shades to take station a step behind my chair, and the other two to stand with their backs to the nearest wall. Just as a precaution. Too much friendliness made me nervous.

As servants brought out plated breakfasts, I changed the subject. I wasn't here to socialize. "So, Vinchi, do you have any idea how many of your people are under Jhavika's sway?"

"At least the top three foremen, and a number of the guard officers." He frowned. "I imagine you killed the ones in Jhavika's keep."

"The ones who wouldn't flee, yes, I'm afraid I did. I apologize for that."

"Don't." He began eating. "What else could you do? I thank you for getting me out of there. Jhavika's people are...strange."

"Strange how?" I sampled a delicate omelet, then a savory puff pastry. Both were delicious.

"They acted like nothing at all was amiss with abducting us, kept telling us we were honored guests, and how sorry they were that that the evil pirate, Longbright, had murdered our parents." He made a face. "I know they're under some kind of spell, but they seem completely delusional."

"They're ensorcelled," Tori corrected. "They absolutely *believe* whatever Jhavika ordered them to believe. She controls their every thought."

"I don't know about that." I washed down a bite with a sip of tea served exactly the way I liked it. Tori evidently paid attention to details, or had people watching me. Neither thought was reassuring. "The noncombatants seemed willing to talk about just about anything that didn't violate their orders."

"Well, *that's* a bonus," Tori said.

"But first things first." I turned to Vinchi. "You know the three foremen of the miners personally, right?"

"Yes, I've met them."

"And the miners, they know you by sight?"

"Yes." He nodded. "I know what you're going to suggest; I talk the miners into revolting against the foremen, right?"

"Exactly that. We can't know how many are really Jhavika's slaves, but I'm betting it's not more than a few key people. I looked through her notes and charts last night. She was very methodical about who she enslaved."

"You read her documents?" Tori cocked an eyebrow at me.

"Some of them. She had a lot of lists and charts, command hierarchies, I think. Confusing as hell. Once we deal with this crisis, I think we should talk to Jhavika's sage about them. But first things first." I pulled a piece of paper from my pocket and handed it to Vinchi. "These are some names I found in her lists that sounded gnomish. Do you recognize any of them?"

The little gnome perused the short list and nodded. "As we thought, she controls the foremen. Some of the guards listed here were at Jhavika's keep, so they're probably dead. The others may still be in Tinworthy Keep."

"Right. Now all we have to do is foster a little rebellion among the gnomes." Tori grinned. "Piece of cake!"

"It won't be *that* easy, but—"

"No, I mean...we *actually* have cake." Tori gestured to a plump woman in chef's garb entering the room with a luscious-looking pineapple cake topped with candied fruit. "Fostering rebellion is hungry work!"

"Oh, Tori, you're *so* droll." Bea laughed musically and dabbed her lips with a napkin. "Consorting with you is positively killing my figure!" She patted her flat stomach and sighed.

I refused to comment, rolling my eyes as I accepted a piece of cake. It felt a little crazy to be sitting here eating while some malevolent force smoldered in the Tinworthy mines, but...the cake was delicious.

We took separate coaches to Tinworthy Keep. Nobody wants to ride with a shade, even if they were only riding outside, and Saraknyal absolutely refused to ride with Tori. I considered our weak plan as I watched Haven pass outside the window. Convincing the gnomes to rebel against their foremen wouldn't be easy. Our success—and, apparently, the fate of Haven—rode on the narrow shoulders of a gnome boy ill-prepared to rule his house. Granted, Vinchi seemed mature for his age, but we were asking a lot from him.

But what do I know about children, I thought. Even when I was one, I didn't spend much time with others.

Worry less about Vinchi and more about Tori Blackbriar, Saraknyal reminded me. *He's got his blade on again.*

He'd been harping on about Tori from the moment he reappeared after excusing himself from breakfast, garbed in attire he considered appropriate for the coming mission: snug leather breeches with high boots, a white shirt over a layer of fine mail, a jaunty hat, kidskin gloves, and a bright lavender cape edged in gold. He cut a fine figure, the snug leather pants hugging him like a coat of paint. Bea looked as if she wanted to take a bite out of his codpiece, and I began to understand what women saw in him.

I'd always thought his suave persona an act, but I'd come to realize that it was just Tori. I envied him as he kissed Bea goodbye. I envied her a little, too. They both seemed so easy with others, so comfortable in their own skin.

Yes, there is Tori to consider...

Blackbriar's coach-and-four clattered along surrounded by a squad of light cavalry. I had only my four shades, but I'd take them any day over a score of soldiers. We didn't encounter anyone on the streets of Haven fool enough to impede our progress to Tinworthy Keep.

The keep, situated at the far eastern edge of the city, abutting a cliff of quarried stone, typified gnomish construction. Blocky and unimaginative, but functional, it obviously hadn't been modified to accommodate tall folk. The outer curtain wall, thirty feet of sheer stone as smooth as a baby's arse, was surrounded by a wide cobbled avenue, offering the gnomes atop the wall a fine killing field. I ordered Bromish to park down a side street with the back of the carriage facing the keep. Tori's carriage pulled up beside us. His team fidgeted and stamped, unaccustomed to my shades.

I got out the opposite side and told Bromish, "Hunker down out of sight, but be ready. We may need to get out of here quickly."

"Yes, mistress." He hunched down in the driver's seat, loaded crossbow in his lap.

My four shades formed up around me, and I lowered my voice to give them their orders. "You two, ward Tori Blackbriar from harm. You others, ward the gnome child."

"Yes, mistress," they all rumbled.

You're worried about Tori's safety and not your own? Saraknyal asked sarcastically. *How very selfless of you.*

With Soul Drinker strapped to my forearm, the energy of the souls Saraknyal had consumed in Jhavika's keep hummed through me. *Are you telling me I'm at risk for more than another shirt riddled full of holes?*

Well, no, not unless they're using enchanted or silver weaponry, which isn't likely. But why ward Blackbriar?

Because I don't want to explain why yet another *member of the Council is dead.*

You warned them you'd be better alone. If he dies, it's his own fault. They can't blame you.

Sure, they can. I rounded the back of my carriage and met Tori and Vinchi. Tori's escort remained mounted, and didn't look happy about letting their lord venture forth unguarded, but we'd decided the fewer soldiers the better. Besides, his guards could die, mine couldn't.

"Ready for this, Lord Tinworthy?" Vinchi looked very small and vulnerable.

"No, but we have little choice, do we?" He tugged his waistcoat straight.

"Just stay close to me, Vinchi," I said.

"Stay close to *both* of us," Tori corrected. He smoothed his immaculate moustache and wagged an eyebrow at me. "Into the breach, fair maid, we charge, steel in hand and courage in heart."

"Spare me." I drew Soul Drinker and balanced it point-first on a finger. "And I prefer *this* to steel."

"Fair *point.*" He laughed at his pun.

"Would you two stop sniping at each other?" Vinchi pleaded. "I'm nervous enough! And please, no weapons out. It'll only provoke them."

"Another fair point," Tori said.

I sheathed Soul Drinker. "Let's go."

We strode out of the side street and onto the wide avenue in front of the keep's main gate, Vinchi between Tori and me, two dark shades to either side of us. Tori seemed unfazed by the proximity of my shades, for which I gave him due credit. Vinchi seemed too nervous to notice.

The keep's battlements bristled with gnomes holding spears and crossbows, peering out at us from behind merlons. The doors themselves, barely tall enough for a mule-drawn wagon to pass through, were iron-reinforced wood set with chains geared to open them from within. Vinchi had told us that there was a portcullis behind that, and a pair of inner doors.

Our reception was about as warm as I'd estimated it would be.

"Stop there or we shoot you down!"

We stopped, barely halfway across the avenue.

"It's all you, Lord Tinworthy," Tori said with his usual aplomb.

"Right." Vinchi cleared his throat and took one tiny step forward. "By the power inherited from my father, Lord Blinth Tinworthy, and as your rightful lord, I command you all to stand down and open the gate!"

"Bugger off!" the same voice called out. "You take us for fools?"

"No, I take you for traitors if you don't follow my commands!" Vinchi took another small step, but still stood within my reach. "I'm Vinchi Tinworthy, rightful lord of House Tinworthy, and your master! Open the gates and stand down!"

"We don't believe you, little man!"

"Then summon your foremen. Senior Foreman Tipiri knows me!" He took another step, and I edged forward to keep him within reach. "Summon *all* of your foremen and subforemen to look upon me and know that I'm your rightful lord!"

Gnomish grumbling from atop the wall, but no one answered, and no one shot us.

"Well?" Tori asked.

"We wait," Vinchi said.

We waited. The sun went behind a cloud, easing the scorching heat, but the rumble of distant thunder announced yet another summer squall. I muttered under my breath, *No rain, no rain, no rain...*

Praying, Hashi? Saraknyal quipped.

Just pleading with the forces of the universe. Thunder boomed again, closer.

Good luck with that.

While we waited, the first few fat rain drops hit the cobbles to steam in the torrid air. From the street behind us, I heard the distinct sound of the approaching deluge, like a cloth being ripped asunder.

"Perfect," Tori said with a sardonic laugh, flipping up the collar of his cloak. "The gods must truly hate us."

"You've got a cloak and hat, at least." I gritted my teeth as the deluge struck, soaking me to the bone in seconds.

"On the upside, the rain should ruin their aim if they decide to shoot us," Tori added.

A great clank sounded from the gate.

"They're opening up!" Vinchi started to move forward, but I tugged him back.

"Wait. Not too close yet."

The outer gates groaned open, the chains clattering through huge gears. At the end of the tunnel we could see that the inner gates were opening, too, but the portcullis was still down. Ranks of gnomes filled the courtyard beyond, all of them armed and armored, crossbows leveled at us. In the fore stood three gnomes wearing red sashes, and several more wearing yellow ones.

"Those are the foremen and subforemen," Vinchi said.

"Progress," Tori said.

"Or a trap." I wondered how many of them were Jhavika's slaves.

We waited for the clatter of chains to subside, then Vinchi raised his shrill voice over the hiss of rain.

"Foreman Tipiri! As your rightful lord, I order you to stand down and raise the portcullis! You have put all of Haven in danger! Jhavika Keshmir is a traitor to this city. You do not follow *her* orders, but *mine*!"

"You said he was ensorcelled," I said low.

"Just setting the groundwork," the little gnome replied. "The others don't know about the enchantment."

"I don't recognize you as my lord!" Tipiri, one of the red-sashed gnomes, yelled. "You're either an imposter, or that witch beside you has put a spell on you! I won't open these gates to a necromancer!"

"Interesting that you should mention being under a spell, Tipiri, when it is *you* and the other foremen who are actually ensorcelled by

Jhavika Keshmir! I was rescued from her keep where I was being held by her magic-addled guards! She had my father and mother *murdered*, along with several other lords on the Council!"

"Lies! The pirate, Longbright, attacked Lord Balshi's celebration! Everyone knows this!"

"No, sir, he did not!" Tori called out, taking a step forward. "I'm Lord Tori Blackbriar, a member of the Council of Lords, and I was there along with Lady Severn, also a member of the Council. We were both attacked by Jhavika Keshmir's minions!" He gestured to me with a grin. "Lady Severn has since reduced Keshmir's forces to a few noncombatants."

"Gods and devils, Tori, exactly the *wrong* thing to say!" I whispered harshly.

Tipiri obviously felt the same. "More lies and now threats as well! Archers, make ready!"

"STOP!" Vinchi screamed. "I command you all to stand down! Foreman Tipiri is relieved of his post!" He screeched something in gnomish that I couldn't understand.

He's reminding them of the Death Stone, warning them of the unattended mines, Saraknyal said.

You speak gnomish?

*Of *course* I speak gnomish.*

Vinchi switched back to our language. "Why *else* would I be taken to Lady Keshmir's keep? Why send our soldiers away? Why close the mines, when you *know* what would happen? If you do not tend to your duties in the mines, we're all *dead*! Everyone! You *know* this!"

A murmur spread through the gnomes. Weapons wavered, and the miners chattered in their own language.

Saraknyal translated the gist. *They're questioning the foremen's actions and loyalty. It's working!*

"It's working," I whispered, just loud enough for the others to hear.

Then Tipiri shouted the others down in gnomish.

He's threatening to expel them, throw them out on the street if they don't follow his orders.

"Stand down!" Vinchi screeched. "This is a direct command from your rightful lord and heir of House Tinworthy!"

"He may only be two feet tall, but he's got the balls of an ogre," Blackbriar muttered.

I shot him a glare.

"Those who do not lay down arms are to be restrained!" Vinchi continued over the hiss of rain and the mutters of the gnomes. "Do this now or we are all doomed! You *know* this to be true!"

The tide turned in the courtyard, gnome miners dropping their crossbows and moving to restrain their foremen and the tight knot of guards surrounding them. Tipiri, however, was having none of it.

"Imposter! Lies! We will not open our gates to a necromancer! Shoot them down this instant!"

The knot of soldiers around the foremen aimed their weapons at us.

"Shit!" I reached out and grabbed Vinchi by the collar as crossbows twanged.

Vinchi yelped as I pulled him into a tight embrace and turned my back to the barrage. My shades interposed themselves between us and the hail of bolts. Several, however, found their marks. Rust and pulverized wood pattered against my back as the bolts harmlessly disintegrated. Beside me, steel sang and flashed as Tori wielded his sword.

Hashi!

Dread stabbed my heart, but Tori wasn't attacking me as Saraknyal had feared. In fact, he was defending himself. The elf blade left a trail of misted rain and shattered crossbow bolts.

Metal clashed on metal behind me. Through Saraknyal, I saw the miners mobbing the foremen and their guards, bearing them down to the flagstones and disarming them. Shouts rang out to raise the portcullis. The gnomes on the battlements lowered their weapons and hurried to the gate towers to comply.

"You can put me down now," Vinchi said calmly.

"Sorry for the rough treatment." I put him down and assessed the situation. Bolts bristled from my shades, but they stood firm. Unfortunately, at least one projectile had gotten through, and now stuck out from Tori Blackbriar's leg. "Tori! You're shot!"

"Yes, so it would seem." He sheathed his sword and scowled down at the bolt. "My best pair of fighting pants, too!"

Before I could offer to dissolve the bolt, Tori reached down and yanked it from his flesh. He didn't even flinch.

I gaped at him as he first raised the bloody head of the weapon to his eye, then cast it aside with a snort of disgust.

He's tougher than he looks, Saraknyal commented.

Indeed, I agreed, reassessing my opinion of the man once again. Tori came off as a dandy, but there was steel beneath his flippant manner. Below the wound, his pant leg ran with blood and rainwater.

"You're bleeding," I said.

"Yes, that *does* happen when one is shot." He drew a dagger, cut a swath of cloth from his cape, and bound his leg with quick, businesslike motions. "And the portcullis is opening."

"I think we're in," Vinchi looked up at us and smiled for the first time since I'd met him. "Thank you for saving my life, Lady Severn."

I grinned down at him. "My pleasure, Lord Tinworthy. Now let's see what's what, shall we?"

I ordered my shades back to the coach—the gnomes might react badly to them—and shouted for Bromish to park nearer the gate. Tori, Vinchi, and I strode under the rising portcullis to be met by the subforemen in yellow sashes. They knelt before Vinchi and bowed low, expounding their apologies in gnomish. He absolved them of guilt and instructed them to imprison the three foremen and those who had fired on us.

"Restrain them completely. Jhavika's spell won't allow them to surrender. They may hurt themselves trying to escape." Vinchi waved the prisoners away, and indeed some were still struggling, though several had been beaten senseless. "I want to inspect the mines," Vinchi said to the new senior foreman. "Take us there."

"Yes, milord!" An escort of gnomes formed up around us. "Unfortunately, you can only inspect them from the outside. The mine gates were sealed under orders from Foreman Tipiri, and now they're...um...frozen solid."

"Frozen? Ice in this heat?" Tori raised a questioning eyebrow.

*Void essence absorbs heat.*Saraknyal said. *It's apparently reached as far as the doors.*

198

I relayed Saraknyal's information, eliciting gnomish mutters and an honest-to-gods frown from Tori.

"Let's have a look anyway, shall we?"

The gnomes led us through the keep, the interior as bland and utilitarian as the exterior. The ceilings were barely six feet high, forcing Tori and me to stoop.

Numerous rotund gnomish women bustled about with bandages for the injured. The physical differences between male and female gnomes always mystified me. The men were thin and wiry, with hawkish features and large noses and eyes. The women were round, plump cheeked, and motherly, with tiny button noses and small bright eyes. One of them pushed a towel and a hot cup of tea into my hands. I accepted gladly, mopping the chill rain off my skin and sipping the tea as we walked. Tori kindly refused their ministrations, claiming that the injury wasn't serious. I knew it must be paining him, but he barely limped.

We followed our guides through a gate to a stone courtyard crowded with iron carts, picks, chisels, and shovels in orderly racks. Across the space two huge iron doors were built right into the mountainside, closed and barred. The rain that pattered against them had frozen into a sheen of ice.

"Those are...substantial," Tori said.

"Built to withstand a siege, but also to contain the Death Stone, at least for a time." The new foreman waved a hand at the doors. "I fear it's too late."

This doesn't bode well, Hashi.

Why? I asked silently.

For Void essence to have frosted the metal like that, it must have virtually filled the mine. Get me closer. I need to feel it.

"Do you mind if I inspect the doors, Lord Tinworthy?" Showing the boy formal deference earned me a look of appreciation from the gnomes.

"Not at all, Lady Severn." He gestured me forth.

I strode cautiously up to the doors. From a stride away, I could feel the cold emanating from them.

Place me against the metal, Hashi. There was something in Saraknyal's tone that I'd never heard before, and it chilled my blood. He was afraid.

I drew the blade and hesitated. *Just make sure you don't dissolve them.*

Ha! Trust me, I won't. They're the only thing keeping you alive right now, I think. In fact, even I can't withstand raw Void essence for long.

I placed the butt of the dagger gently against the doors.

Saraknyal muttered something in a language I didn't know, not his arcane tongue, but something old and dead.

What is it? I asked.

Death, he said. *There's death inside, more than I've ever felt before.*

Chapter Eighteen
Temptation

My first year in Haven was nothing short of miraculous, and I owed as much to Miras and her gang as I did to Saraknyal. Granted, they owed me, too, but they had far more than a dry place to sleep and full bellies. We'd carved out a sizable piece of real estate to the east of downtown. Within a two-block-wide square, every shop, brothel, pub, warehouse, and inn from the ground floor to just below the rooftop plazas paid us money for protection, and we provided it. Nobody messed with our businesses. If they did, they learned a painful lesson: don't mess with Severn's gang, or you'll end up worse than dead.

After we'd become well established, I let Miras run most of the protection business, only showing up when needed. My true joy was in prowling through the city's pawn and junk shops. Haven was a sanctuary for pirates, thieves, and smugglers, and they often didn't know the value of what they'd pillaged. I paid a few pennies for gnomish relics, Toki antiquities, and ancient Valakan artifacts, then sold them through a rather dodgy shop within our territory. The proprietor of *Priceless Treasures*, a young man named Bryce, could have sold anchors on a sinking ship. His cut from the items I provided—twenty-five percent—was making him quite rich. Of course, it was making me richer.

So, on the one-year anniversary of my arrival in Haven, Miras suggested a celebration of our success. At first, I balked. I didn't socialize and had no desire to. Then Miras explained.

"It ain't for you, Hashi. It's for your people. They deserve a celebration!"

I agreed, they *did* deserve a celebration, but I didn't know the first thing about throwing a party. I'd never even attended one—my mother never allowed me to—let alone hosted one. I also didn't want to seem like a dolt to my people. Saraknyal was no help, being almost as socially inept as I. There was only one person I dared ask for help.

"So, what do you think?" I'd asked the innkeeper of the *Naughty Nymph*, where I rented rooms that served both as my home and headquarters.

"Well, you'll want the common room for yourselves for the night." His eyes glinted as he started making a list of the charges. "Open bar, of course. And I'll hire a minstrel and some boys and girls from *Randy Rollie's*, for anyone who feels like...intimate company." He winked and grinned at me.

I hesitated, then threw fiscal caution to the wind. I owed Miras and the others more than I could repay, so why not go all out. It was only one night.

"And you'll want food, of course. I'll order a spread from the *Rooftop Grille*." He added another line to the bill, then asked, "How many guests you think?"

"Ahhh, twenty or so?"

"Don't worry," he said with a smile. "I'll take care of it."

That was how I ended up sitting at a corner table, my wraith standing behind me, Saraknyal on my belt, sipping strong ale and watching my associates carry on. Hardly the disheveled vagabonds I'd encountered on my first day in Haven, they were still a rough lot, but clean and clothed better. They also carried good steel at their hips and knew how to use it.

My gang, I thought with a silent, sardonic laugh. *How the hell did that happen?*

Your determination and knack for survival, my dear, Saraknyal reminded me.

Don't flatter me. It's cheap. Saraknyal and I had an arrangement. He kept my heart beating, and I fed him when the need arose, which was happening less and less as my reputation grew.

I'm just telling you the truth. You're a survivor, Hashi. A far better one than I was, and I respect you for it.

Well...thanks, I guess, though you're the one keeping me *alive.* And with every soul Saraknyal fed on, I obsessed about the evil that tainted my own soul. But that concern seemed far away right now. Right now, life was good.

I needn't have worried that the party would flop. Miras made up for my social ineptitude with a surplus of good-natured camaraderie. She had become my trusted lieutenant. My people respected her, but they also enjoyed her company. Miras was sly and witty, never vengeful or petty, and she was smart. In no time, the party was in full swing, and I caught myself smiling at their antics as they toasted, laughed, and swung the trollops from lap to lap.

When everyone had had a few drinks, but before they were utterly soused, I stood and banged my tankard on my table. "A word!" I shouted over the laughter and music. The players' strings fell silent, and every eye turned to me.

I cleared my throat, suddenly uncomfortable with their undivided attention.

"We've made amazing progress over the last year, and much of that is due to *your* efforts!" I raised my tankard to them. "Thank you all for your work and your loyalty."

The last, especially, I thought. The bosses of Haven gangs tended to be knifed in the back by their underlings, a disturbingly common method of ascending the hierarchy. That hadn't happened to me thanks to the ever-present reminder of my wraith, and the fact that I was making all of these people rich. "To our continued success!"

They roared and drank, laughing and joking.

"And to our fearless mistress, Hashi!" Miras leapt up onto a chair and thrust her tankard to the ceiling. "Baddest, blackest, most beautiful bitch in the burrows!"

My people cheered. I couldn't suppress a grin, but I was glad that my dark skin hid my blush. I toasted her and drank, then waved for quiet and cleared my throat.

"Thank *you*, Miras." I looked them all over, a bunch of thugs who had become the closest thing I had to a family. I swallowed the lump in my throat before continuing. "You're...invaluable, all of you. I couldn't have done this without you. *Thank* you. Now get drunk, get laid, and have a good time on me!"

They cheered, and the music struck up a lively tune. My lips twitched in a quick smile; my first party was a success. I headed for the stairs, my head buzzing from the ale, my wraith following. As I mounted the first step, a hand touched my arm. I turned to find Miras grinning up at me.

"Mind if I talk to you in private, Hashi?" She glanced over her shoulder at the party. "I want to...bring up somethin' that I think you might be interested in."

"No business tonight, Miras." I took her hand from my arm and gripped it hard in thanks. I owed her my thanks more than anyone. "Tonight's for you and the others. Enjoy it."

"Oh, I intend to, but this ain't business. It's...personal." She glanced nervously over her shoulder again.

She's acting strangely, Saraknyal said. *Something's brewing. Maybe some infighting in the ranks?*

That was all I needed. I hadn't noticed anything, but I relied on Miras to spot these things. "All right, come up."

"Thanks." She followed us up two flights to the suite I rented. It wasn't palatial, but it was comfortable, with a small sitting room I'd converted to an office, and a bedroom. Each room even had a window with a view. That was all I needed, more than I'd ever had.

My wraith turned aside and assumed his usual station outside my door. No one entered without his leave, and I slept better for it. I waved Miras in and closed the door behind her. Though already tipsy from the tankards I'd quaffed, I headed for my sideboard.

"Would you like a drink, or is this so important that it requires sobriety?" I picked up a bottle and poured brandy into a snifter. "If the latter, then maybe we'd best discuss this tomorrow."

"I don't need another drink for this, Hashi." Miras' suddenly serious tone caught my ear.

I turned to find her leaning back against my door, one leg cocked, her boot against the portal. "What is it, then? Serious, but not business? Personal, but so important that you're obviously up-tight about it?" I sipped my brandy and tried to analyze her, but I was more than a little drunk.

Careful, Hashi, Saraknyal warned *She's acting oddly. I can get rid of the alcohol if you wish.*

Get rid of the alcohol? What does that mean?

Touch me and I'll show you.

204

I flicked a fingertip against the dagger's hilt, and it felt as if a torrent of cool water flushed through my veins. My inebriation vanished. I stiffened. *What the hell was that?*

I've eliminated the toxins from your blood, Hashi. Now, pay attention. Something's afoot with Miras!

She was speaking, and I had to catch up.

"...must realize you're...something else." She regarded me like a cat scrutinizing a mouse.

"What?" I tried to focus, distracted by my sudden sobriety.

"You really *don't* know, do you?" Miras nudged forward off of the door to stroll around my sitting room, obviously not as drunk as she'd seemed downstairs. "Ain't much for people, are you?"

"No. I never have been." I sipped my brandy and tried to look relaxed, but her manner and Saraknyal's warning had me on edge. "Why is that important?"

She barked a laugh and stopped to lean against the edge of my desk. "It's *important* because you need to know how fucking *amazing* you are, woman!"

My mind stumbled on her words. "*What?*"

*Oh, so *that's* why she's acting strangely,* Saraknyal quipped.

Shut up! I fixed Miras with a steady stare. "What are you talking about?"

She barked another laugh. "*Fuck*, Hashi!" She lurched up off the edge of the desk and stalked toward me, her features intense, focused, fervent. "You're powerful, smart, and sexy as a brothel full of trollops! How the *hell* do you not know that?" She stopped a step away, hands on hips, a lascivious glint in her eye.

I gaped, taken utterly flat-footed. "I'm...what?"

"I *said*," she whispered huskily, stepping forward and raising a hand to my face, "you're sexy as all fuck, powerful, and smart. That's very...alluring." The backs of her fingers brushed my cheek, her thumb caressing over my lips, igniting my nerve endings. "How do you not *know?*"

"I've...never..." I choked on my words, leaning into her caress, one thing I'd never experienced. Her touch felt like lightning skittering across my skin.

"*Never?*" Miras looked shocked. "Oh, gods and devils, what a *horrible* waste."

I wasn't thinking clearly despite my sudden sobriety. "Waste? What do you—"

"Shhh." Her finger pressed against my lips. "Hashi, you are..." She stepped closer, so close I could smell her, feel the heat of her through the silk of my shirt. "I don't want to ruin what we've already got, but...we could be *sooo* fucking good together. No pressure here. If you tell me to go, I'll go, but I find you hot as a brothel on fire, and you really need to...*realize* what you're missing here." She trailed her fingers slowly across my chin, down my neck, and over my breast, caressing it through the slick material of my shirt. "Let me—"

I staggered back a step. "Miras, I don't think...this is..."

"Then don't *think*, Hashi!" She smiled at me. "You think too *much*, worry too much!" A step vanished the space between us. "Ever think you should just tell the world to fuck off and *live* for a change?" She reached up and caressed my neck, then pulled my face down to hers.

Saraknyal remained thankfully silent as my neck bent, like I had no control over my own muscles. Our lips met and parted, and our tongues caressed one another. Every nerve in my body flared at the sensation, my first kiss, so unique, so thrilling, so wonderful. My mind blanked as my body took over.

I knotted my fists in her hair and kissed her.

Miras moaned into my mouth, clutching me close, devouring me. Her fingers trundled down my neck, grasped my shirt, and yanked. Buttons flew, and I jerked my head back, wide-eyed as her hands caressed me, cupped my breasts, my nipples electrified between her thumbs and fingertips.

"See?" She grinned again, licking her lips, looking me over. "Let me show you what you've been missing."

Gods help me, I thought, pulling her to me.

Her lips and teeth and tongue set a fire in my flesh. For the first time in my life, I embraced human contact, lost myself in her touch, in being wanted. My breath caught in my throat, knees trembling as the experience overwhelmed me, blinding me to all else.

Which was exactly what Miras intended.

Hashi!

Saraknyal's warning came an instant too late.

Lost in sensation, I hadn't noticed Miras reaching for my belt. Barely had the necromancer's warning pierced my carnal fog before a lethal length of enchanted obsidian impaled me through the stomach. I felt the blade slide into my flesh, an odd sensation. Especially since there was no pain.

Miras grinned up at me, her teeth now bared and her eyes hard, the wolf preying on the lamb.

A surge of power suffused me, and I wondered if Saraknyal was consuming my soul. *Take it, Saraknyal. I'm already damned. Cheat the gods of their prize.*

Death's chill. Saraknyal's words flowed into me through the blade, and I awaited oblivion.

It didn't come.

Oh, dear Hashi, Saraknyal intoned. *I could never harm you.*

"What?" I looked down.

Soul Drinker was buried in my stomach, Miras' hand still trembling on the hilt. Her victorious grin—the triumph of stealing her mistress' power through seduction and assassination—melted to a terrified rictus as she strained to release the blade, to escape, to survive.

I'm holding her for you, my dear. She tried to take me from you. I couldn't let her do that.

I saw the horror mount in Miras' face. Through her contact with the blade, she heard Saraknyal's words.

How am I not dead? I asked him.

We're bonded, Hashi. I've tasted your soul. We are one.

Yes, I realized. I'd sacrificed part of my soul to him, and he'd accepted it. We were bonded more closely than lovers, than siblings, than father and daughter. We were one.

And I hated him for it.

"Let her go," I growled through clenched teeth, my hand closing atop Miras' on the blade.

Hashi, she tried to murder *you. This can't go unpunished. You need to make an example of her to the others, or they'll all be trying to fuck you to take me away!*

207

Chris A. Jackson

I gasped a wrenching sob. It had all been a lie, a deception, a seduction to murder me. Miras had offered something I'd never had: a lover's touch. I no longer craved companionship, love, or camaraderie, but she'd found the chink in my armor. The physical love I'd never experienced, never dared to pursue for fear of being hurt. Tears ran down my cheeks, burning tracks upon my soul.

But like embers igniting dry wood, the tears ignited my fury. Rage supplanted my anguish, my sorrow, the violation of what she'd done to me. *Yes*, I seethed. *She needs to be made an example of.*

Good. Satisfaction suffused me through Soul Drinker. *Now, let me show you how to make a shade.*

"A shade." I grinned Miras' wolf grin back at her and pulled the blade from my viscera. There was no blood, no pain, no damage. My skin closed up like black water behind a dipped oar. Vengeance swelled and filled me. "Show me how."

Fix her gaze and say, 'Look at me.' Then, breathe her in and think 'Shade.' I'll do the rest.

I glared into Miras' terror-filled eyes, eyes that only moments before had filled me with desire. I hadn't seen the betrayal, the greed, the thirst for power. "You tried to murder me." I said, and felt her tremble despite Saraknyal's hold on her. "Look at me."

She did. She had no choice. Saraknyal's arcane power surged, gripping her soul through the windows of her eyes. I inhaled her.

Miras' soul entered me like a flood of pearly light, beautiful and intoxicating, as sensuous as her touch, or the lie of it.

Shade.

Saraknyal's power tore through me, surrounding the gleaming soul of the woman who had tried to murder me. Arcane words I could never recall shot through me like shards of ice, piercing Miras' soul, changing it, twisting it into an abomination. Gradually the power ebbed, and within myself I felt the soul of a monster, a creature of hunger and rage.

Now, exhale the soul back into her body before it dies.

I did, expelling the putrid mass into the convulsing shell of Miras' body. The convulsions suddenly stopped. Wrenching the soul blade from her slack grip, I stepped back and watched her horrific transformation.

Miras' tawny skin deepened to ebony, her beautiful green eyes flushed crimson, and her red-gold hair writhed and darkened to the hue of a moonless night. Behind parted lips, her pearly teeth shattered, leaving jagged points suitable for rending flesh. My rage melted away as I stared, sickened by the transformation.

"Oh, gods, what have I done to her?"

Oh, quit whining! She got exactly what she deserved!

I've destroyed another soul...

Her soul's not destroyed, only...changed.

Not destroyed? I swallowed my nausea and walked slowly around the creature that had once been Miras. *Can you change her back, then?*

Um...no. The change is permanent, much like your wraith. If my soul ever perishes or passes from this world, their souls will revert, but you don't want to be there when that happens.

Why not?

You mean besides the fact that I would have been utterly destroyed? he said derisively. *But seriously, they tend to tear themselves apart. I've seen it happen before when necromancers die. It's not pretty.*

What happens to their souls when they revert? I raised a hand to touch Miras' cheek. The supple flesh I'd so recently kissed felt like hard leather.

I have no idea.

Saraknyal's utter lack of caring revolted me. "You're disgusting."

Sticks and stones might break my— Oh, right, I don't have bones anymore, do I? His mirth made me want to retch. *Now, take your new shade downstairs and show the rest of your people the consequences of betraying you. If you don't, another of them will try the same thing in a month or a year, and you're just gullible enough to fall for it.*

I glared down at the blade in my hand. "Gods and devils, I hate you."

Good for you. Now do your fucking job. You're the leader of this little band of reprobates. Lead them. Show them what betrayal means. Consuming the souls of your foes apparently wasn't enough of a deterrent. Maybe seeing Miras like this will convince them. It's the only way you can save their souls from me.

I hated him a little more for being right.

"Come with me, Miras." I strode for the door, dagger in hand, suddenly knowing what I had to do and how to do it.

"Yes, mistress," she growled, following on my heels.

My wraith fell in as well as I hurried down the stairs. Bursting into the common room, I took a deep breath and screamed, "*QUIET!*"

The party, my first—and last—celebration, died like a heart-shot dove. Laughter and music faded to gasps of horror and curses of shock as I strode to the center of the room. One trollop, a lovely young man, dropped his cup and stumbled back so blindly that he fell over a chair. The rest backed away, terror and revulsion in their eyes, for they recognized their charismatic comrade in the creature that strode at my heels.

"This party is *dead!*" I growled, thrusting the soul blade toward Miras. "*She* killed it by trying to murder me!"

More gasps and murmurs, whispers and curses.

"I don't know if any of you were in on this, and frankly I don't *care*. I warned you all. I warned Miras! And what do I get for bringing you out of the gutter? Seduction and a blade in my gut!" I held the soul blade high. "*This* blade! This blade that drinks *souls!*"

I plunged the soul blade into my stomach.

Someone screamed, but it died, too, as I pulled the blade out. My shirt was already open from Miras' lustful assault, baring the unmarred flesh of my torso. No blood. Not a scratch. More gasps and mutters, and they edged farther away.

"You've all profited by working for me. I thought that was enough to keep you happy, to keep you in line. But some people are just never fucking *satisfied!*" My rage built again as I stared at these people I'd considered family, watched them quail from me and avert their eyes. They might die in my service, for life in Haven was cheap, but none deserved the fate of this foul shade by my side. If it took terror to save their souls, then so be it. "Get this through your heads! I CAN'T...FUCKING...DIE!" With each word, I slammed the soul blade into my chest.

They stared at me in stunned silence.

Gods and devils, Hashi, I expected you to lay down the law, but holy shit!

Shut up! I seethed, gripping the blade that couldn't kill me until my knuckles popped.

"Now, you can continue to work for me." I sheathed the soul blade and swept the room with a cold stare. "And we'll all get rich together. Or you can betray me, and Soul Drinker will feed on you, or maybe you'll become like *this!*"

I turned, jerked the fine sword from Miras' hip, and plunged it through her stomach. The shade stood there without even flinching. I left the blade sticking through her and raked them all with my gaze.

"Miras, sheath your sword."

"Yes, mistress." She pulled the blade from her body, used her shirt to wipe the black ichor from it, and slipped it into its scabbard.

I surveyed the faces of my remaining people, mumbling a silent prayer that they would heed this final warning. "Go now, and never, *ever*, betray me."

The room emptied as if the building was on fire.

I whirled and climbed the stairs back to my rooms, shade and wraith as my silent—and only—companions. I stationed them both at the door, went inside, and closed it. Pressing my forehead to the cool wood, I heaved a breath.

Feel better?

"No. Now, shut up."

So you can sit here and cry and mope in your own self-pity? No. Talk to me. I'm here for you when all others will betray you, Hashi.

"Only because you *can't* betray me." I remembered now histories I'd read about soul blades, how, even if stolen, they could never be turned on their masters. Evidently, I was bonded to Saraknyal like that. A *necromancer*. As if I couldn't become more deeply damned.

True, but I also have a vested interest in your well-being. You're in a mood right now, though I can't honestly figure out why, and you need to talk it through.

"Not with you." Saraknyal wouldn't understand, couldn't, even if I explained it.

Fine, then, but I really need to give you some advice about the minion you just created.

Go ahead. It's not like I can stop you. I shoved myself away from the door and cast aside my riven shirt as I stalked to the bedroom.

*Shades are always ravenous, although, like wraiths, they don't really *need* much food. They follow orders, but you have to be careful about what you tell them to do. Given the opportunity, they'll gorge on any flesh they can get their teeth into.*

So, I'll tell her not to binge. I pulled on a robe and strode for the sideboard.

You should command it to never feed unless you give it leave to. Otherwise, you're likely to find it gnawing on one of the maids.

"Wonderful." I diverted to the door and opened it. Outside, my wraith and shade stood silently staring at one another. "Miras. Don't eat anyone, or any*thing* for that matter, unless I give you permission. Understand?"

"Yes, mistress."

I closed the door, locked it, went to my sideboard, and poured brandy. "Anything else?"

Yes, actually. You need to consider your own situation in the broader sense.

"I'm not talking to you about that tonight." *Not after I turned the first person ever to show me any kind of physical affection, the first person I ever kissed, into a cannibalistic monster.* I quaffed half my glass of brandy and savored the burn. If only it would burn away my sins.

Chapter Nineteen
In Defiance of Death

From the journal of Hashi Severn –

How in all Nine Hells do I get talked into things like this? I could simply leave Haven to its fate, but where would I go? There is no other port open to me, no place I can run. Haven is my only hope, and I seem to be the only one who can save it.

I sheathed Soul Drinker as I turned away from the frozen mine doors to face the others. "We are in deep, *deep* trouble."

"Deep, as in 'we need to evacuate the keep', or deep as in 'we need to evacuate *Haven*'?" For once, there was no jocularity in Tori's tone.

"The former for now, at least." I approached Vinchi and knelt down so we could talk without him cricking his neck. "Void essence has likely filled the mine. I'd suggest moving everyone not dealing with this to either Jhavika's keep or Lord Temuso's. I think the Council will agree and provide help."

"At once!" Vinchi looked up to Tori. "Can I ask you to get word to Lords Malchi and Brickhammer? We'll need wagons. There's a lot to move."

"Of course. I'll send riders. Meanwhile, I'd suggest calling your remaining foremen and advisors together to figure out what to do." He nodded to the frosted iron doors. "Those seem to be holding back the deluge, but I doubt they'll last forever."

He's right. Eventually, the iron will crystalize and shatter.

I relayed this to everyone, and added, "Time is of the essence."

"*Void* essence, to be precise!" Tori laughed, his unremitting humor apparently restored. "I'll be back with every wagon we can get our hands on!"

He's strange... I thought as I watched Tori striding away with barely a limp despite his recent wound. The more time I spent near him, the odder he seemed.

He is, and dangerous. The way he wielded that sword...

Vinchi's squeaky voice piped up. "We need to pull together everyone who knows anything about the first time the Death Stone was contained. My father's advisors, Loremaster Geoil, anyone you can think of!"

The new senior foreman looked suddenly stricken. "Foreman Tipiri had the loremaster imprisoned for speaking out against him. He's in the dungeon."

"Well, get him *out* of there and bring him and anyone else who might have a clue how to deal with this menace to the war room!" Vinchi screeched, his pitch threatening my eardrums. "The rest of you pack up everything and everyone! We're evacuating this keep!"

Gnomes scattered like leaves on the wind.

War room? They have a war room?

Evidently. I put a hand on the boy's shoulder. "Calm, Vinchi. They're not to blame."

*Why don't *we* have a war room?*

Because we've never gone to war, I reminded him.

"I know, Lady Severn, but it's just all so *frustrating*!" He heaved a sigh and put his little hand on mine. "Patience, I'm afraid, is something that comes to my people later in life."

The pit of my stomach lurched suddenly. Slowly I took my hand away, astonished by two observations: Vinchi hadn't quailed at my touch, as most people did. In fact, he'd seemed to find it reassuring. And, I was feeling oddly...maternal about the little gnome. Both bothered me for some reason. "Well, we'll work on patience later. Shall we go to the war room?"

"Yes! Follow me."

I ducked under the doorframe and followed, musing over a realization: Vinchi hadn't been the only one lately seemingly unaffected by my usually disconcerting nature. First Tori, then Beatrice Galt, and now Vinchi. I didn't know whether to be pleased or perturbed.

The gnomish war room looked like a banquet hall, save for the banners lining the walls like tapestries and statues of gnomish warriors or kings or whatever they were. There must have been a score of them, all rendered in inconceivably lifelike detail. They kind of gave me the creeps. At least the ceiling in this room was high enough to allow me to work the kinks out of my neck.

I sat in a low chair but couldn't even attempt to fit my long legs under the table. Gnomes trickled in, and round gnomish women brought tea, blackbrew, and mounded plates of cakes and sweetmeats. One of the little women even offered to mend and dry my shirt for me, but I declined. They wouldn't have anything my size that I could change into, and I didn't intend to sit in a council of war in a chemise. I did accept a cup of tea and a warm towel to dry my wet hair and wipe the pasty arrow dust from my neck.

Finally, a wizened gnome arrived, escorted by the new foreman.

Vinchi stood. "Loremaster Geoil, my apologies for your treatment."

"Vinchi, lad!" The old gnome leaned heavily on the shoulder of his escort, but his eyes were sharp. "Not your fault at all. I tried to talk sense into that twit, Tipiri. Closed the mines! I don't know what's got into him." He sat and accepted a cup from a gnomish maid, then his eyes shifted to linger on me, one eyebrow raising.

"He and several others were ensorcelled by Jhavika Keshmir," Vinchi explained, then gestured to me. "This is Lady Hashi Severn. She rescued me from Jhavika's keep along with the other heirs to the houses whose lords were murdered, and she's here to help us now. We need to figure out what to do about the mines! Lady Severn tells me it's full of Void essence!"

"Severn?" The old gnome blinked at me. "But isn't she..."

"I'm here to *help*, loremaster." I gave him a tight smile. "My methods might be unorthodox, but rest assured, I have as much to lose as anyone if Haven's consumed by this menace."

"Hmm, yes, well, maybe your...expertise might be of use here." He fixed Vinchi with a sharp look. "How much does she know?"

"I had to tell her and the other council members the truth, loremaster," Vinchi said, his tone defensive. "There was no other way. We need to figure out what to *do*!"

"Calm, lad." The old gnome sipped a cup and munched a cake. "The situation is dire, but we yet have time; the essence flows slowly. The answer, of course, is positive energy to cancel out the negative." He shrugged. "Just about any kind of energy will work. Fire is what we've been using for the past hundred fifty years or so."

"Fire?" I said incredulously. "You're telling me the mines are on fire?"

"Well, not *all* of them, but the shaft where the Death Stone was discovered, yes." Geoil's eyes took on a faraway look. "Rinkletwine was already an old city when the stone was unearthed and began to wreak its deathly havoc. My father told me stories of the mass exodus, of the gnomish exiles and their longing to return. Then a brave young gnome named Tinworthy—our young lord's father—figured out the answer: fire. Four ships full of coal he sailed into port. Block by block, they drove great iron wagons loaded with burning coal, the heat cancelling out the Void essence. On into the mines they pressed, risking their lives, until they had driven the essence back to the stone itself. Finally, we built a furnace around the damned thing. As long as we fed the fire, it remained contained."

"So, we do it again!" Vinchi chirped.

Geoil grimaced. "It's possible, but we probably don't have enough ready coal, and time is short, I gather."

"It is," I affirmed. "The doors to the mines are frozen and will eventually shatter. If they do, we'll be overwhelmed."

So light a fire and heat the doors! Saraknyal suggested.

I relayed the idea, and Geoil nodded. "A temporizing measure, but worth trying. It'll give us time to formulate a plan."

Vinchi ordered one of his new foreman to pile coal against the mine doors and light it, and the gnome ran off to comply.

"What other plan is there other than banishing the Void essence from the mines with tons of burning coal, then relighting the furnace?" Vinchi asked.

Geoil shook his head. "Even if we had the coal, we don't have the people. When we reclaimed the city, we had seven hundred laborers and twelve hundred tons of coal, and *still* we had casualties. The Void essence wafts around like a mist, and just a touch can maim or kill."

"Not just kill, utterly destroy," I said. "Void essence consumes soul essence as well as any other form of positive energy."

"*Really?*" Geoil blinked at me. "That's dire news."

What we need is something without a soul to delve the mine!

Ask Nahli. If fae really don't have souls, she'll be immune. If they do, we'd only be out one fae.

I ignored Saraknyal's suggestion. I was thinking along a different line. *Would zombies be affected by Void essence?* I asked him.

Well, no, but...

"Zombies," I announced, watching the horror spread across the assemblage of faces around me. "Zombies wouldn't be affected by Void essence. Unfortunately, only days ago, I sent more than a hundred of them into the sea." I rubbed my eyes and sighed. "I never thought I'd say this, but we're fresh out of corpses."

The gnomes looked a little ill at that. We all stared at each other for a long moment.

"Maybe Lady Twince can help somehow," Vinchi suggested. "She's got magic."

"We can certainly ask." But I doubted she could hold off pure Void essence.

"Send a messenger with details," Vinchi ordered, and a gnome scurried from the room.

"Pardon, me, milord," a matronly gnomish woman interjected with a curtsy. "But if it's dead bodies the lady needs, we've the catacombs. No shortage there, for certain."

*Catacombs? Why don't *we* have catacombs?*

Ash Keep's got enough dead without having more buried in the basement!

Consider it a stockpile of ready labor.

I tried to ignore Saraknyal's musing and concentrate on the problem at hand. While the rest of Haven had been burying their dead at sea—there was barely enough real estate for the living—Clan Tinworthy had apparently been interring their dead beneath their keep.

"Are they naturally mummified or do you embalm them?" I'd encountered enough desiccated corpses in my explorations to know that they crumbled with the slightest disturbance and would be no help to me.

"Oh, we embalm them," the matron said decisively. "It's not our way to let our dead decay to ruin."

Embalming's good. They won't have fallen apart.

"But we *honor* our dead!" a gruff gnome declared, shifting his glare between me and the helpful woman. "We don't despoil them or use them as slaves."

The gnomish matron put her hands on her plump hips and stared him down. "So, you intend to abandon the city again? Lose our home? They'd *want* to help if they could!"

I raised my hands in a calming motion. "If all they'll be doing is transporting coal, then they shouldn't be much damaged, and I can return them to their resting places when we're done."

Many of the gnomes grumbled at this news, but several looked thoughtful, and the matron looked downright vindicated.

I looked at Geoil. "What exactly needs to be done?"

"Well, if your walking dead can get to the furnace, they only need refill it with coal, then reignite it using one of the incendiary vessels that are kept there for emergency use." The old gnome actually looked hopeful.

Unfortunately, his words dashed my hopes. "Zombies aren't that smart. They need simple, direct, and explicit orders." A realization struck. "Unless..."

No! Saraknyal had figured out where I was going with this. *We are *not* going into that mine!*

Yes, we are, I told him. There was no way around it, not if Haven was to survive, and I was the only one with any chance of success. *You fed on Jhavika's soldiers and stored up quite a lot of soul essence. You can protect me.* Of course, if he couldn't, I'd be utterly destroyed. I considered that possibility for a moment and felt an odd lack of trepidation. After all the horrors I'd encountered just this week, oblivion seemed like a well-deserved respite. No more worries, no more fears, and especially no more destroying souls. No more...anything...forever.

I can protect you for a while, yes, but not long.

It shouldn't take long, and we can bolster your strength with the souls of the shades I brought along. I've more than enough extras. I'd already made up my mind, and didn't want to give Saraknyal a chance to deter my resolve. I nodded to Vinchi. "I'll have to go in with them."

The entire room looked at me in open-mouthed shock.

"That'll be dangerous in the *extreme*, Lady Severn," Geoil warned.

"You *think*? I don't *want* to do this, but what other choice do we have?" I snorted a bitter laugh and turned to the foreman. "How many laborers do you think I'll need?"

"Oh, best have a score, I guess. Ten carts, I'd say. Eight to block off the other tunnels and two to clear the path to the furnace. We've got that many spares in storage up here. Probably two...um...laborers apiece."

"And are there sufficient coal reserves for this?"

"Inside the mines there are great stockpiles. In the keep...*perhaps* enough to fill ten carts."

"Perhaps?" I didn't like the sound of that. "Well, scrape together all you can and let's do this. Waiting will only make it worse. I'll need a map of the mines and instructions on where to go and what to do."

They scrambled to comply. Maps of the mines were brought, a vast labyrinth that I thankfully wouldn't have to explore. The foremen indicated the coal stockpiles, additional tools and carts, and pointed to the tunnel that led to the Death Stone. Schematics of the furnace flue were produced; I need only shovel in coal and ignite it. Simple enough.

Encouraged, I turned to the rotund little gnome woman who'd suggested the catacombs. "Take me to your dead."

"Follow me!" She scurried off at a speed that belied her bulk and tested my ability to duck as we hustled through doors and down stairs.

The entire keep now resembled a kicked anthill. Gnomes scurried everywhere, carrying valuables, foodstuffs, clothing, children, and even pets. Like an ebbing tide carrying flotsam out to sea, they took everything with them. Against that tide we strode, my guide and I. Quikesi Tinkertwine was her name, and she served as senior keeper of keys for Tinworthy Keep. As proof, she pulled an enormous ring of keys from a pocket. Deeper and deeper we went, with Quikesi unlocking door after door. My neck and back ached, and I'd cracked my head half a dozen times when she finally stopped abruptly. Ahead stood an iron and stone door bedecked with gnomish script above and arcane wards engraved on the metal bindings.

"The catacombs," Quikesi announced, brandishing yet another key.

They lock up the dead with magic? Saraknyal gave a mental grunt. *They must have heard of me.*

Careful, old man, your ego's showing.

The wards flared, then faded as she turned the key. The doors swung wide, and I ducked inside. The chambers were low and vast, orderly rows of small niches lining the walls, each one the final resting place of a gnome. Male and female, old and young, armored or garbed in finery, they slept the endless sleep of death. I sneezed at the musty smell, but Saraknyal took in the dusty confines with a note of optimism.

*Now *this* I can work with.*

The foreman said a score. How much power will that cost you? I asked him silently.

More is better, I think, and the cost is minimal.

I looked around. *Maybe just raise the male corpses, the armored ones. I don't know how the gnomes would handle seeing their dearly departed women and children walking around.*

The dead are dead, their bodies are just shells.

I know that, but they don't, and gnomes have very different ideas of the roles of men and women. Just raise the men.

Very well. Do it. I'll direct the spell.

I gripped Soul Drinker and thought, *Arise!*

Dozens of dead gnomes stirred from their slumber, clawing and scrabbling out of their niches. They formed up into a ragged mob, faces blank, eyes sewn closed. That wouldn't matter; zombies didn't use flesh eyes to see anyway.

I turned to Quikesi, who looked remarkably calm despite the sudden rising of the dead. "I'm going to have them follow you. Please take them to the mine entrance and wait for me there. I need to get something from my coach."

"Very well, Lady Severn."

I ordered the zombies to follow her, and she bustled off. They shuffled after, jostling one another at the doorways, a tide of short, armored death. I sneezed again at the musty pall they raised.

At least they don't smell as bad as fresh ones.

I followed until we reached the ground floor, then worked my way toward the front of the keep, moving with the tide of fleeing gnomes. In the courtyard, I found that the promised wagons had arrived, but couldn't make it through the gate. Gnomish wagons were being filled inside, and everything that wouldn't fit was being carried out to the larger ones by hand and cart. At least the rain had stopped.

I found Tori Blackbriar directing the work at the gate, assisted by soldiers from his own, Malchi's, and Brickhammer's houses. He grinned when he saw me. "You look like you have a plan!"

I don't know what I looked like other than determined. "Sort of." I didn't have time to fill him in on the details, so I brushed by and wove my way through the confusion to my coach.

Bromish looked a little stunned by all the activity. "Mistress? What's afoot?"

I hate that phrase, Saraknyal quipped. *Tell him it's that thing attached to the bottom of his leg, but that's not important right now!*

I stifled a snort of laughter. *Humor from you? What's got into you lately?*

I'm giddy with the prospect of my pending annihilation in a pit of Void essence, he retorted sourly.

"I need my escort," I explained to Bromish. "Go head and help the gnomes with their loading. We're evacuating the keep." I had another thought. "Bromish, if things go poorly, you may need to get out of Haven. If I don't survive, get the household together, pack up all the valuables, then get aboard one of our ships. I'd suggest going to Valaka or Sariff, but it'll be up to you."

"If you don't *survive*?" He looked stunned. "But mistress..."

"No time right now. Just keep your wits about you, all right?"

"Yes, mistress." He didn't look comforted.

"Come with me," I ordered my shades, and we headed for the keep.

Tori met us at the gates again. "So, what's this *sort of* plan?"

"Someone's got to light a furnace in the mines that keeps the Death Stone contained." I stepped past him without pausing, working my way through the opposing crush of evacuees. "Fire cancels out the Void essence, but I've got to get to it."

"You're going into the mines?" Tori fell in a step behind me, actually jostling my shades out of his way. "Are you *mad*?"

"Stark raving," I shot back without looking at him.

"Hashi! You'll be destroyed!"

Hashi! He's going to—

Tori's hand closed on my arm. My four shades reacted with growls and bared teeth, but they'd been ordered to ward him only an hour ago, so they didn't attack, though he couldn't have known that.

I let him pull me to a stop and turned to face him. Clutching Soul Drinker, I looked down at Tori's hand, then into his eyes. There was no fear there, only concern.

"If you don't let go of me—"

"Wait!" He let go, raising his hands in supplication. "Just *talk* to me for a moment!"

"I don't *have* a moment." I resumed my way through the keep. "Someone's got to go in there, and I'm the only person who can direct my minions. I'll be protected for a time, long enough to get the furnace lit. That's the plan."

"Nothing personal, Hashi, but that's a *horrible* plan!"

"*Thanks*," I growled. "I'm the one who thought it up."

"Why can't you send in one of your shades? They follow complex commands, don't they?"

"Yes, but *they're* not protected." We ducked and dodged our way through to the back of the keep. "They've still got souls, so the first touch of Void essence would destroy them, and the zombies would just stop without direction."

"Zombies? What zombies?" he asked as we emerged into the back courtyard where the risen gnomes awaited me. "Oh, those zombies."

"From the gnomish catacombs. They'll be unaffected by the Void essence, but they need someone to tell them what to do. That someone is me." I rounded on him and added sarcastically, "Unless, of course, you're going to insist on accompanying me into the mines."

Tori grimaced and backed off a step. "Um...no."

Vinchi and the foremen stood nervously by. A mound of coal already blazed against the frozen door to the mines. The metal glowed dully at the base, but was still frosted white at the top, groaning as fire and Void essence waged a war of heat and cold. I wondered if the iron would shatter under the strain.

"So, this is the only plan we've got, and we don't have time to discuss it."

"Okay, not discussing, but what are *they* for, if they'd be destroyed by the Void essence?" Tori nodded to my four shades, which were still eyeing him as only shades could.

"To bolster my protection." I jammed Soul Drinker into my nearest shade. *Feed.*

Saraknyal consumed the creature's perverted soul. The shade's skin faded pale, and its eyes glazed over pearly white in death. *Arise.* Without pause, I fed the other three to Soul Drinker, animating their corpses before they could fall. Four more souls obliterated for power, but these weighed less heavily than most I'd destroyed; they were already twisted beyond redemption.

How do you feel now, old man? I asked Saraknyal silently. Power bristled every hair on my body.

Adequately sated. Unfortunately, there's no way to know if it'll be enough.

"You're going to use their soul essence as a shield?" Tori asked, his tone more curious than appalled at what I'd just done.

"Yes, an ablative shield against any Void essence not cancelled out by the flames." I gestured to the row of mining carts now mounded with coal and doused with oil. "My zombies will push those ahead of us to the coal reserves, which will hopefully fuel all the fire I need to clear out the Void essence to the furnace. I light the furnace, and we're done."

"You make it sound *simple.*" Tori still looked worried.

"All good plans are simple," I told him.

"Until they go wrong," he countered.

I shot him a dangerous smile. "Well, if this one goes wrong, you won't be able to tell me, 'I told you so,' so I'll consider that a win!"

He barked a laugh, then shook his head. "Be *careful*, Hashi. You're taking a horrible risk."

I sighed, exasperated by his continual and unsolicited concern for me. "Seriously, Lord Blackbriar, why do you *care*?"

He looked shocked, and I reveled for a moment at wiping the insufferable smile from his face. "Because you're an invaluable member of the Council of Lords, *Lady* Severn. And if you perish, who will stand against Jhavika's ensorcelled army?"

For some inexplicable reason, his pragmatic answer disappointed me.

He's lying, Saraknyal said.

I shook my head. It was time to go. "If this fails, you might look into getting the hell out of Haven."

Tori nodded and took a step back.

I turned to Vinchi and his foremen. "Lord Tinworthy, it's time to light the fires."

Chapter Twenty
Keeping Up Appearances

The incident with Miras put me in a dangerous frame of mind. Seeing her transformed by my own hand into this ravenous monster, this red-eyed creature of nightmares, sickened me. Anger and self-disgust drove me toward the brink. Everything I'd accused the necromancer of, I was now guilty of myself; destroying yet another soul for my own self-preservation. Consequently, the thought of dying now *terrified* me, facing an eternity of torment for my sins. With every soul, I damned myself deeper.

I couldn't discuss this with Saraknyal, and strove to keep my thoughts guarded. Thinking without forming discrete words—subvocalizing, as he called it—became my new normal, but I'd improved with practice, as evidenced by the decreasing frequency with which he chided me for moping.

For two days after the party, I barely left my rooms, my mood veering between anger and guilt. All I'd wanted was to live comfortably and indulge my passion for antiquities. Was that so selfish? And it wasn't just me who profited; the business had rescued my crew from the gutter, and Bryce was quickly becoming wealthy.

One question plagued me day and night, until I finally blurted it out. "Why did Maris do it?"

It's obvious. She wanted your power.

"Well, that clears things up!" I said sarcastically.

The necromancer mentally sighed. *If you really want the answer, then ask her!*

I shot up straight in my seat. Sometimes Saraknyal hit the issue right on the head when I'd been dancing all around it. Striding to the door, I opened it, ordered Maris inside, and got right to the point.

"Maris, why did you try to kill me?"

In a voice that scraped my nerves, she said, "Power."

I cringed. "But weren't you afraid of me? I warned you the day we met."

"Yes."

I clenched my fists in frustration. "Then why *risk* it?"

"With power, there is no fear."

Well, well! Saraknyal said admiringly. *She's more astute than I gave her credit for.*

"What?"

*Let me paraphrase little Maris; 'With power, there *should be* no fear,* he said. *You, however, avoid conflict. You rarely go out except to shop for antiques. You only flex your muscles when forced to. You look more like a victim than a predator.*

"I don't go out much because Haven is dangerous! People try to kill you for walking the streets, and when they do, I'm forced to take their souls. But that, obviously, doesn't keep the next attacks from happening." I waved Maris out the door and slammed it shut. "In fact, Maris attacked me *because* I'm powerful."

*Don't fear the power, Hashi. *Be* the power! Be the necromancer! Convince people that you're too dangerous to mess with. If you don't, they will, and you'll have no recourse but to create more shades or wraiths.*

"Being mistaken for a necromancer nearly got me killed in Mati and Sariff!" I protested.

That's why we're here; Haven has no laws against necromancy. No laws at all, in fact. And trust me, a formidable necromancer commands respect.

"At what cost?"

It's all about appearances, my dear, Saraknyal cajoled. *Look the part. Act the part. *Show* them. You have to get out of this room and be *bad*!*

"You just want me to attract trouble so you can feed."

*No, Hashi, though that's probably going to happen eventually anyway. This *is* Haven, after all. But you don't have to slaughter half the population to accomplish your goal; just a few will do. However, those few must be highly visible, not a random cutthroat or thug.*

"You make it sound easy."

Not easy, but if you want safety without laying waste to this entire city, that's the only path I can think of.

Like walking a tightrope over a pit of snakes... But what other alternative did I have?

The next morning I dressed in my best clothes, pulled on a dark maroon cloak, and swept out of the inn. One by one, I visited my people. Amazingly, none had bolted, though there were some sidelong glances toward my newest bodyguard. I accompanied them on their rounds, visiting every business that paid us protection money; speaking with every shopkeeper, bartender, manager, and bouncer; making myself the face of the business.

Under Saraknyal's guidance, I practiced a grim countenance, assured voice, and strong, nonchalant stance. My message was clear: *I* was in charge here, and I wasn't afraid of anything. I prayed to the gods that they wouldn't pierce the confident façade and spy the fearful imposter within, the young woman who saw only greedy eyes intent on doing her harm.

Look at them like they might be tasty, Hashi. As if you're considering what sauce to serve with their soul.

A revolting image, but I practiced that, for if anyone knew how to be a necromancer, it was Saraknyal.

It took three days to complete our circuit around my small territory. We suffered no attacks, probably because Maris was well known here. No one who saw her now could doubt my invulnerability. Of course, I still had to convince the rest of the city.

On the third day, I made a foray into enemy territory.

The bell over the shop door tinkled as I strode in. The shopkeeper stopped short when she saw me, her eyes flicking to my gruesome bodyguards just outside.

"I'd like to look at that vase you've got in the window," I said, pointing.

Swallowing hard, she fetched it. We proceeded to have an absolutely normal transaction, and she visibly relaxed.

"I'll take it," I said. While she wrapped it up, I looked about the shop. "You've got some nice things here. I hope you've got good security." At her suddenly fearful expression, I smiled. "No, I'm not in the business of stealing things. I *protect* them, and I just wondered if you might benefit from my services."

She looked warily about, then replied in a low voice. "I pay for it, but still I was robbed not a month ago, and two months before that."

"That's too bad. If anyone under *my* protection gets robbed, I make good on their loss and make sure the culprits will never rob anyone *ever* again." I accepted the proffered package, smiled, and strolled out.

She's watching you from the window, Saraknyal said.

Good!

The next few days passed similarly. I strolled the streets of a rival's territory, spoke with their businesspeople, and asked questions. Were they satisfied with their security? Did they feel safe? I applied no pressure—proposing a business deal while backed up by a couple of undead would be too threatening—but instructed several of my people to visit later and offer our services.

It took less than a week for one of my rivals to react. Pleased with my progress thus far, I was heading to a rooftop restaurant to treat myself to lunch.

Hashi! The big man in the green jerkin! He's holding a knife against his forearm, and his eyes are on you!

I froze in my tracks.

Of course, I was on a bridge.

Haven had bridges between buildings at several levels. While they afforded a safer path than the dangerous, shit-filled streets— "Keep your boots clean" wasn't just an adage here—bridges were inherently dangerous. High falls were one of Haven's preferred methods of assassination. The rope-and-wood kind swayed and rocked, but their hemp supports at least gave me something to hang on to. The stone bridges were worse: long, crowded, and without handrails.

And I stood smack in the middle of a stone span.

My gut tensed, and I dropped a hand to Soul Drinker's hilt.

Where?

Through Saraknyal's sight, I spotted the thug, a huge brute half a foot taller than me and twice my weight. He wasn't being subtle.

I drew a breath to alert my bodyguards, but the man was fast. He lunged past another passerby, thrust his knife into my wraith four times in quick succession, then shoved it out of his way. Unfortunately for him, he underestimated the undead. The wraith ignored the stab wounds, buried its claws in the assassin's shoulders, and dragged him over the side of the span.

The brute's eyes widened as he fell. His scream ended abruptly.

"Shit!" I had Soul Drinker out and stood back-to-back with Miras. Everyone else on the bridge backed away from us. Though I'd been expecting an eventual attack—in accordance with Saraknyal's plan—my heart still beat wildly.

No fear, Hashi! Don't show anyone that you're afraid!

I bit back my terror and forced a mildly annoyed expression. Stepping to the edge of the bridge, I looked over. The thug lay sprawled on the street below, his head splashed over the cobbles. My wraith had landed on top of him, and now stirred. Lurching up, it wobbled on a broken leg, the bone jutting out from its thigh. It straightened the fractured bone with a crack, then turned its eyes up toward me, waiting for direction.

"Bastard broke my wraith!" I swore.

Don't worry, Saraknyal assured me. *It's not badly damaged. They heal quickly.*

Really? I accepted Saraknyal's assurance; he was the expert. I embellished my act by declaring, "I'll have to make another one."

Witnesses to the attack were staring, muttering oaths, whispering to one another, avoiding my eyes.

They fear you. I heard someone say 'necromancer'. Good! Now, act like nothing's gone wrong, like you don't care.

Right. I sheathed Soul Drinker, sighed as if bored, and shouted down to the street. "Meet me at home."

My wraith nodded and marched off without even a limp. As it rounded the corner, street urchins swarmed the thug's corpse, fighting and tearing at the man's clothes, belt, weapons, and boots.

I strode off the bridge, struggling to keep my knees from trembling. But I had survived, and no souls had been consumed. This had been a clear assassination attempt, not some attempted

229

robbery. My faith in Saraknyal's plan grew a little bit, but I didn't know if my nerves would survive it to fruition.

I paused at a few more shops on the way home, keeping up my appearance as the invulnerable necromancer. When I arrived back at the *Naughty Nymph*, my wraith awaited me in the common room. The innkeeper wasn't happy.

"Not to complain, Miss Severn, but could you keep that...thing out of sight? Runs off payin' customers." He polished a mug with a dirty rag and looked despairingly around the empty room.

"Sorry." I tossed him a gold crown and waved my wraith to follow. Bone grated in its leg with every step.

I stationed my two bodyguards outside my door, slammed it shut, threw off my cloak, and sagged back against the portal. Here I was, inviting attacks, knowing that my soul was damned to an eternity of torment if I died. "I don't think I can do this."

*Whine, why don't you. I'm *sure* it'll help.*

"*Fuck* you, old man! I'm sick to *death* of your bullshit!" I plucked the dagger from my belt and threw it aside.

Or you could just throw a petulant fit, he chided.

I ignored him and stalked across the room to my sideboard. My hands shook as I poured brandy into a glass. I choked half the snifter down, slopping liquor down my chin and onto my shirt.

That stuff's better if taken internally, you know.

"Shut *up*!" I downed the rest and poured more.

No. You have to pull yourself together, Hashi. Just because... His voice trailed off.

"What?"

I think there's—

My bedroom door slammed open and a swarthy man in black lunged out at me. I flung my brandy in his face and dodged the dagger thrust. The assassin cursed, wiping at his eyes, and lashed out blindly with the blade.

Panic seized my hammering heart. Without Soul Drinker, I was vulnerable. Where the hell had I thrown the thing? *Saraknyal! Where are you?*

Here, against the far wall, near the chest!

I spotted the blade and lunged past the assassin, but he swept a kick at my legs. I sprawled flat, landing hard, but scrabbled forward.

"No, you don't!" A boot landed on my back. "This'll teach you to stick your nose where it don't belong!"

Hashi, move!

Envisioning the dagger coming down toward my back, I twisted and kicked blindly. I connected, but so did he. The blade pierced my back, grating against the bone of my shoulder blade before it tore free. My kick knocked his foot out from under him, and he went down.

Shock turned to agony as I scrabbled away toward Soul Drinker, pain lancing through my back with every move of my left arm. I lunged toward the weapon, but Saraknyal's warning came before my hand reached it.

He's up. Look out!

I rolled, kicking again, and the dagger that would have pierced my back only grazed my hip. I struggled to inch backward, one hand reaching out for Soul Drinker while fending off attacks with hysterical kicks. The assassin swore in a language I didn't know and knocked my legs aside.

Just a few inches more! Reach! Saraknyal screamed in my mind.

I reached, and my fingertips touched the blade.

"No, you don't!" The assassin leapt, smashing his foot down on my wrist. Planting his opposite knee on my chest, he raised his dagger for the last time.

I screamed as my wrist bones ground under his foot. An impact shattered the door, my minions coming to my rescue. But I needed no rescue, for his foot also pinned my hand against the haft of Soul Drinker.

The assassin's blade descended, and I raised my other hand reflexively. *Dust to dust.* The dagger dissolved, and I grabbed his clenched fist, screaming, "Death's chill!"

The magic coursed through me, and Saraknyal laughed in my mind. *Oh, well done, my dear!*

231

The assassin froze. Curling my fingers around Soul Drinker, I twisted the blade to stab his foot. Behind him loomed my bodyguards, blades also raised.

Don't kill him, Hashi! Saraknyal bellowed in my mind. *Make him a shade, and you'll learn who sent him!*

"Stop!" I commanded, and my guardians froze. Saraknyal was right. I needed to know who sent this assassin. I wrenched my wrist from beneath his paralyzed foot and glared up into his eyes. "Look at me!"

He couldn't resist, and I inhaled his soul in one wrenching breath. Saraknyal transformed the shining energy to the putrid, ravenous essence of a shade, and I exhaled it back into the dying shell before the flesh collapsed. The would-be assassin's skin faded black, and his eyes flushed red. The crackle of shattering teeth completed the transformation.

"Stand up," I commanded, and he did. I forced myself to my feet, clenching my jaw against the pain in my wrist, hip, and back. "Who sent you to kill me?"

"Tetsumo Hirachi," it replied in a gravelly voice.

I knew that name, a neighboring gang leader who worked protection and extortion rackets adjacent to my territory. I'd ventured into his domain only the day before. This was his retribution for trespass, but I had some retribution of my own.

"Go back to Tetsumo Hirachi and tell him that you failed in your mission. Tell him that you are now *my* creature, my undead minion, and that you've returned to not only report your failure, but to take his life. Then, I want you to kill him, cut out his heart, and eat it. If anyone tries to stop you, kill them, but otherwise, leave all witnesses alive. When you've finished with this task, return to me here."

"Yes, mistress." The shade turned to my bedroom and strode through the door. Presumably, he'd come in through the bedroom window, so that was the way he departed. "Use the front door when you return!" I called. I didn't relish him crawling through the window after I'd gone to bed.

Two assassins in one freaking day! I moaned.

We have no way to know who sent the first one. But taking out Harachi is perfect response, Hashi. You win!

Win? I didn't feel like I'd won anything.

You're bleeding.

Getting stabbed generally results in bleeding. I flopped into a chair and winced at the pain in my back and hip.

You're bleeding on the chair.

Fuck the chair. I could barely get my heart under control, let alone the bleeding. I glanced down at my hip. The dagger had slashed open my pants and cut a furrow in my flesh the width and length of my finger.

Your back is worse.

Wonderful.

You should have your wraith stitch you up.

I hadn't considered that, and looked at the former Jaguar Warrior. "Do you know how to tend wounds?"

"Yes, mistress."

"Good. Miras, step out into the hall and close the door as best you can. Guard it." The shade left without a word, wedging the shattered door into place. "Wraith, get my sewing kit from the chest there and bring it to me."

I sheathed Soul Drinker, struggled to my feet, and limped to the sideboard. There, I poured a snifter half full of brandy, drank a swallow, and turned back to find the wraith holding out my sewing kit. I picked out a spool of black thread and a needle, and dropped both into the snifter of brandy. My hands shook so badly I could barely undo the buttons of my shirt and pull it off. The back of it was covered in blood. I held Soul Drinker over my shoulder.

"How bad is it?"

Not life threatening, but it's bleeding steadily.

I wadded up my shirt and handed it to my wraith. "Use this to stop the bleeding."

"Yes, mistress." It pressed my shirt hard against the wound.

I bit my lip to keep from screaming. *I don't suppose you can magically heal wounds or take my pain away?* I asked silently.

Sorry.

I leaned against the sideboard and drank more brandy, careful not to swallow the needle. *Why didn't you see that bastard hiding in my bedroom?*

*I can't see through stone, and that door's really thick. I'd have to touch it to see through it."

Fine, then why didn't you hear him?

I was...distracted. You'd just thrown me across the room, remember?

You deserved it. I drank more brandy and pressed my hand against the wound on my hip. My wrist hurt, too, and it was swelling, but I didn't think anything was broken. I fished the needle and thread from my snifter and handed them to my pale guardian.

"Stitch me up as best you can."

"Yes mistress."

The following hour tested my ability not to scream in agony. I stuffed my bloody shirt between my teeth and cursed the alcohol for not blunting the pain.

My wraith was just tying the last stitch in my hip when the door fell open and my newest shade stepped in, covered in Tetsumo Hirachi's blood. There had been witnesses. They'd fled. Mission accomplished.

I didn't sleep well that night, even with both shades and my wraith guarding the windows and the shattered door.

Or maybe that was *why* I didn't sleep well.

The next day, exhausted but determined, I annexed Hirachi's territory. My people reported that rumors were flying, and I reinforced them, spreading the word that anyone messing with my businesses would be visited by my shades and receive similar treatment.

It never ceased to amaze me how utterly stupid people can be.

Even before my injuries were fully healed, two additional gang bosses tried to have me killed. That yielded three new shades and added two new neighborhoods to my territory. My income more than doubled over the next few months.

I made enough with the protection racket to expand my antiquities business, hiring a gap-toothed, black-bearded smuggler named Glosh Waymar, who ran three small ships nimble and fast enough to evade pirates and navies alike. He scoured the outer islands for old objects of dubious history and value, especially from Valaka, which had a wealth of undiscovered treasures gathering dust in junk shops. I cleaned them up, appraised them, and either sold them here or had Glosh smuggle them out to Sariff, Mati, and even Toki, where they'd earn higher prices.

I reorganized, assigning my best people to take charge of the day to day work. In another month, I'd quadrupled my income. Business was booming, but Saraknyal's plan demanded a much grander progression.

I've already got more than I can manage, and you want more? I sat at my desk going through the account books, looking for discrepancies. *I never studied as an accountant!*

*Not your territory, my dear, your *status*. Petty crime boss is beneath you.*

I blinked my burning eyes and regarded him. I still suspected him of engineering my rise to power for his own ends, but in this he was right. I had to show all of Haven that I was a major player, too dangerous to mess with.

The following day, my eight lieutenants gazed expectantly at me from around the big table in the *Naughty Nymph*'s back room, our usual locale for meetings. I didn't waste any time with pleasantries.

"I need a new place to live." I waved my hand to indicate our surroundings. "Someplace more secure than an inn. Someplace that tells people who and what I am."

"You need a keep." Dondi Ranse, a former pirate turned landside thug, picked his teeth with a dagger.

"Aye. You talk to the Tinworthy clan. They own a bunch of old estates and keeps that ain't been refurbished." Hyrem Wyze, my oldest boss, knew Haven better than anyone else on my crew.

"You'd sleep better for it." Mazie Twyne, a waifish young woman recruited from the late Tetsumo Hirachi's crew, looked me over critically. "And maybe drink less."

I narrowed my eyes at her, but didn't comment. "I'll draft a letter to the Tinworthy clan. Who's their lord?"

"Blinth Tinworthy. One seriously rich little fellow," Wyze said. "They control the mines, and owned about two thirds of Haven before the influx of exiles, pirates, and criminals."

I nodded. "I'll have it to you by noon. You can deliver it for me."

"Sure."

"And can someone recommend a skilled tailor? I need new clothes. Something that sends a message."

After all, Saraknyal said, *a necromancer should dress the part.*

Damn right they should. This part of his plan, I actually liked.

"What message?" Mazie asked.

"Something that says, 'Don't fuck with me,' but with style."

That earned me a chuckle, and they promised to ask around.

A few days later, I dressed in my best and met with a representative from House Tinworthy, a dour little gnome with a full squad of armed and armored bodyguards. He introduced himself as Glinth Tinworthy, brother to Lord Tinworthy and manager of the house's holdings. He wore a bright green waistcoat, a gold jacket, and a red ascot, and stood out like a high-priced doxy at a funeral amongst the drab furnishings of my office. We sat down, and I offered him a drink, which he declined. His guards eyed my shades nervously.

"Exactly what kind of home are you looking to purchase, Miss Severn?"

"Something that can be defended. I've recently been the target of several assassination attempts." I shrugged as if it were a mere annoyance.

His bushy eyebrows rose. "Well, fortified properties in Haven are rare, but we *do* own several that may serve your needs." He went on to describe them, two manor houses well outside the city, and two keeps in the city proper, the latter complete with outer walls and inner courtyards.

"I'd like to look at the keeps first, I think."

"Very well, but our carriage cannot accommodate your...escort, I'm afraid."

I sure as hell wasn't going without them. "Then I'll walk." I stood and retrieved my new ebony cloak from the hook beside my window.

The gnome frowned. "The nearest is some distance. Nearly a *mile*."

I smiled genuinely. *A mile...*

Careful, Hashi, you could get a blister, Saraknyal said with a chuckle.

"I've walked across entire *nations*, Master Tinworthy, through the ashes of dead civilizations. A mile across Haven isn't likely to stretch my endurance."

"Well..." He looked me up and down, his mouth pursing speculatively, "...you *do* have very long legs. Very well." He gave me directions to the nearest property, and we left my office.

With two shades and my wraith in tow, I stretched my legs, traversing Haven on the rooftops, enjoying the sun. I kept a thumb hooked over Soul Drinker's hilt and watched everything in my mind, especially while crossing the bridges.

I arrived at the first keep before the Tinworthy coach and escort, took a lift down to the street, and perused the high walls, unadorned gray granite with low crenellations. The front gate was too small for a human-sized coach. If the entire keep was similarly proportioned, it would require extensive renovation.

The Tinworthy carriage pulled up, six crossbowmen seated atop, sharp-eyed and ready. Glinth Tinworthy stepped out as the rest of his escort climbed down from their ponies. His bushy eyebrows arched above his hawk nose. "You *do* have long legs!"

They were, in fact, longer than he was tall, but I declined comment. "Is there a stable?"

"Yes, but not for horses, only ponies or mules." He pulled a chain beside the gate, and a bell sounded within. "The caretaker will show us around."

Metal clanked from the gate, and one huge door edged open. I could see no postern door, and the main entry had no portcullis. A sour-looking old gnome peered out at us, flinty eyes fixing on Tinworthy. "Yes, sir?"

"This is Miss Severn, a prospective buyer. You'll show us around the keep." Glinth turned to face me. "I must ask that you leave your escort here."

I considered protesting, but saw no reason to distrust the gnome; he wanted a deal. "If you insist."

The courtyard was small, the stable barely large enough to house a pack of hounds, and the keep itself squat and ugly with no towers. I had to stoop through the main entrance. Four floors of gnomish construction would mean only two for me when the remodeling was done. I could have more floors built, but that would be expensive. I might be making a good living, but I didn't want to blow all my profits on renovations.

Cramped and drab, isn't it?

I agreed. I didn't even ask the price. *Maybe buying one of the manor houses and building a wall around it would be a better answer.*

Finding one that's already been renovated and taking it would be the best answer, but you're too squeamish to do it.

I ignored the suggestion and turned to Tinworthy. "Let's have a look at the next, shall we?"

"Very well." He gave me directions and assured me that the next keep was roomier.

"I hope so." I strode off with my escort toward the nearest lift back to the rooftops.

Saraknyal remained blissfully silent as we traversed block after block, probably disappointed that nobody tried to kill me in transit. Our strategy of developing a dangerous reputation seemed to be working; people hurried past me, eyes averted. Word had spread.

Six blocks and five bridges later, I spotted a square tower of dark stone above the rooftops. *Think that's it?*

Maybe. I like the color.

Of course, you do. I edged closer to the brink of the rooftop for a better look. A peaked roof of black slate topped a tower pierced by small windows. Short crenellations jutted up from the outer wall like square, stubby teeth. I couldn't see over the wall, but there looked to be a good-sized courtyard within. The entire structure was crafted of jet-black granite, solid, strong, and the exact hue of my new cloak. I quirked a smile. *I like it.*

We descended to the street and met Tinworthy's entourage at the gate, an arched affair of black iron that might be tall enough for a small carriage.

"This was the keep of a renowned gnomish alchemist before the city of Rinkletwine was abandoned. It hasn't been lived in since Haven was reinhabited, and has no caretaker." The gate was secured with a massive padlock linking a thick iron chain between two ringbolts. Tinworthy produced an equally huge key and worked it in the lock. "I'm afraid the place is a bit dusty."

He waved his escort forward, and they pushed open the portal. The teeth of a portcullis peeked out from the stone archway above.

"Feel free to look around. Nothing's locked. I'm unfamiliar with the layout, but I *do* know that it has four floors in the main building, plus four more in the tower, and two floors below ground. The stable is larger than the last, but still only sized for ponies." He waved me through, but didn't venture forth himself.

"Why has no one lived in it for so long?"

"The...previous occupant murdered her husband and threw herself from the tower. The keep has a bad reputation."

He thinks it's haunted.

Is it?

I don't know, but that would be fun. I'd have someone else to talk to.

Can you really talk to ghosts?

Of course, I can. What part of 'necromancer' don't you understand?

Snarky bastard.

Since Tinworthy didn't tell me to leave my escort at the door, I brought them with me. I turned a slow circle in the courtyard. It would be big enough to turn a coach with room to spare once the stable was enlarged. The flagstones were gray, contrasting with the black walls, doors, and roofs. Climbing a dozen shallow steps to the lofty main entrance, I smiled to see that I wouldn't have to duck in the entry hall, at least.

I'm liking this.

It certainly is forbidding.

Unfortunately, only the front half of the ground floor was tall enough for me. A lot of serious refurbishing would be necessary. On the third floor, I found a disused laboratory and a large library bereft of books. The tower was slightly smaller than I would have liked, but would provide me with ample space for an office and bedroom.

At the top, I gazed out the window at the view. "I'd need a balcony."

Why?

"To glower down from on high and look menacing."

Right. Perfect.

"No ghosts?"

Alas, no, Saraknyal said with a forlorn sigh.

"Then I think it's perfect, too."

Good. Don't let Tinworthy hear you say that.

"No, *really?*" Sometimes Saraknyal stated the obvious.

I returned to the gate with a grim expression fixed upon my face. "It'll do, but it needs extensive work."

"That's understood." He named a price, less than I'd expected.

I glared and made a counteroffer.

We haggled and finally settled on a sum that I could pay without liquidating too much of my business.

"I'll have the funds delivered to Tinworthy Keep within a week," I told the gnome.

"Excellent!" He handed me the key to the gate. "Welcome to Ash Keep."

"*Ash* Keep?" I took the key and furrowed my brow. "Really?"

"Really. Of course, if you don't like the name, you can always change it."

I smiled. "No, I like it. It seems…apt."

After the gnomes left, I directed my shades to close the gates, then I locked them and looked up at the structure. Ash Keep for Ash Walker—it seemed almost prophetic. *Home sweet home...*

When can we move in?

As soon as I find someone to make the doorways tall enough. I twisted my neck to alleviate the crick in my spine and headed for the *Naughty Nymph. I'm already tired of ducking.*

Chapter Twenty One
To Delve the Depths

From the journal of Hashi Severn –

How ironic that death magic can protect me from elemental death itself. I wonder about the energy of Void essence. Historically, investigations of the elemental sphere of the Void have not gone well. I wonder if my own encounter will go any better. If I perish, at least my soul won't go to Demia for sorting of my sins.

"Light them!"

At Vinchi's command, gnomes lobbed lit torches onto the ore carts filled with oil-drenched coal. They ignited with a *whoosh*, and everyone but me stepped back. I took comfort in the searing heat, my first line of defense against the Void essence.

The gnomish zombies stood ready to push the carts into the mine, and my four former shades—now zombies—were poised at the iron portal itself. Tori and the small crowd of gnomes retreated to the keep's door to evade any Void essence that might spill forth when we opened the mine.

All was ready.

Except me.

My stomach clenched as I surveyed the preparations. The words I knew I had to say caught in my throat. Despite deliberately associating with death for decades, confronting the very essence of death itself was another matter entirely.

Are you sure you have enough energy to protect me?

Hell no, I'm not sure. How could I be?

Well, do your best, old man.

While I think this is foolish, I don't really have a choice, do I? If you perish, I perish.

For the first time, I was putting Saraknyal in as much danger as myself. The thought unnerved me, but I focused on my task. I waited until the iron carts began to glow a dull red, then took a deep, steadying breath. "Lift the bar!"

My former shades stepped into the smoldering coal fires at the base of the doors and lifted the bar.

"Pull open the gates! Push the carts forward slowly!" Undead flesh hissed as the gnomish zombies put their hands to the searing hot carts and pushed.

As the gates parted, ebony mist wafted from the dark maw of the cave. Where it touched the smoldering coals, the mists fizzled into nothing and the fires wavered.

Don't go out...don't go out. If the fires died, we'd have no choice but to close the mine back up and evacuate the city.

The burning carts rolled into the mists, and the glowing-hot metal dimmed to gray, but the fires kept burning. The black fog receded.

"It's working! Forward slowly!" My undead force advanced. I nervously tapped Soul Drinker, strapped against my forearm, and followed.

"Be careful, Hashi!"

I glanced back. Tori Blackbriar towered over the gnomes, his customary carefree expression absent. He actually looked worried. *For me or for Haven?* I wondered.

For Haven. Saraknyal said. *If you fail, his city will die.*

Saraknyal was probably right, not that it mattered. "Bar the doors behind me. I'll knock when the stone's contained."

He nodded.

I beckoned my former shades to follow, then strode into the mine, using Saraknyal's sight to penetrate the gloom. I've never been afraid of the dark or confined spaces, but this gave me chills. Trying to spot the wavering mists of Void essence in the dim flickering light of the coal fires strained even Saraknyal's enhanced senses. The iron doors to the mines boomed closed behind me, and I heard the bar drop back in place. We were locked in.

I followed close behind my undead entourage, Void essence wafting around us, receding before the flames. Cold radiated from the stone around me, so long exposed to raw Void essence that all the heat energy had been consumed. My breath puffed out in clouds of white, and frost rimed every surface.

About fifty yards in I found a large staging area, barely tall enough that I didn't have to duck, but wide and orderly with racks of tools and mining gear. Helmets set with glow-crystals were of no use, the crystals' magic consumed by the Void essence. Empty carts lined one wall. Numerous gates opened into vast storage chambers, some full of ore, but two full of coal.

"Stop here."

Several tunnels led away from the staging area. The second tunnel from the left would take me to the Death Stone. I directed eight burning carts to block off the tunnels I wouldn't need to delve, instructing zombies to keep feeding the fires. If the fires went out, the staging area would fill with Void mists, blocking my only exit. I tapped more zombies and assigned tasks.

"You, fill empty carts from there." I pointed to one coal stockpile, and they shambled off to comply. "You and you, follow me with full carts." I tapped the last of my entourage. "You four, push your carts down that tunnel." I pointed down the tunnel to the Death Stone.

*This is *really* stupid!*

Too late to back out now! The burning carts rumbled forward, mists of Void energy wafting around them. Snatching up and lighting a torch, I followed.

The heat of the burning coal kept the tendrils of Void essence at bay, but only just. The impenetrable mists swirled past us and closed in behind...a little too close behind. I split my escort into two, one cart in front of me, one behind. At a fork in the tunnel, I directed my procession left. We continued some distance, down a steady incline, and I silently thanked the gnomish miners for their fastidious tending of the tunnel. The floor was perfectly even, with shallow grooves carved into the stone for traction.

How are you doing, old man? I asked Saraknyal.

So far, fine. I've barely had to expend any energy at all. This actually seems to be working!

I gauged the blazing carts and cringed. The fires were consuming the coal quickly; I would need more coal soon.

Do you hear the next cart yet?

No. And the fires are burning low.

I know. Another hundred yards or so, I think. We slogged on through the murk, the wheels of the carts now squealing with cold. I couldn't feel it, thanks to Saraknyal, but frost had formed on my boots.

Finally, we reached the end of the tunnel, about a quarter mile into the mountain. A shaft opened in the floor ahead, an iron ladder plunging into its depths. Beside the ladder, a funnel-shaped flue had been bolted to the shaft wall. This flue led to the furnace—and the Death Stone—designed to be fed safely from here. Behind the flue, another pipe rose to the ceiling, mortared neatly into the living stone; a chimney. Along one wall stood racks of tools, iron barrels full of coal, and smaller casks of oil. Along the opposite wall stood a shelf of glass jars. So far, so good. It was all as the gnomes had described it.

Void mist flowed steadily from the shaft, and the coal fires wavered dangerously low.

"You!" I tapped two zombies. "Shovel coal from those barrels into your carts."

They followed my commands, and the fires steadied, dissolving the rising mists.

I took a closer look at the glass jars. Each contained lumps of some kind of substance floating in oil. Loremaster Geoil had told me they refined this compound from human waste—one abundant resource in Haven—and stored it in oil to prevent it from spontaneously combusting upon contact with air. They kept it to relight the furnace in emergencies.

Just what I needed.

I picked up a jar, cracked the lid, and poured the entire contents down the flue. The stuff in the jar should ignite and relight the furnace.

Black mists billowed from the flue, and I jerked back a moment too late. Power surged through me from Saraknyal, and the mist faded, but weakness now dragged at my limbs.

That cost me a lot! he warned.

"I felt it. But what went wrong? That stuff should ignite by itself." I backed away and waited, but nothing happened.

Not enough air, maybe?

"I'm still breathing," I pointed out.

For now...

Sarcastic bastard.

Maybe you shouldn't have poured the oil in with it. If it needs air to combust…

Now you tell me...

I opened another jar and used the end of an unlit torch to push the substance out and down the flue. Still nothing. I dropped a blazing torch down the flue, thinking that maybe the furnace needed a spark. The light of the flame immediately winked out, consumed by the Void essence or quenched for lack of air.

Shit! What the hell's wrong with this thing? I kicked the flume, but only managed to hurt my toe.

Well, standing here's not solving anything.

He was right. Experimentally, I dumped a shovel full of burning coal down the flue.

Nothing happened.

"What the hell's wrong?"

I don't know. A furnace isn't a complex piece of machinery. Fire only needs fuel, air, and a spark.

"It's got to be air, then. Would they have closed the damper on the thing?" I looked for a control, a lever or cable to pull, but found nothing.

*Gnomes *do* love their gadgets,* Saraknyal pointed out.

Two zombies arrived with a cart of coal. After sending them to get the next, I doused this one with oil and lit it with a torch. That solved the short-term problem of fending off the mists, but I still had to get the furnace lit.

"Something's not working at the furnace itself. I think I have to go down there."

I was afraid you'd say that. Saraknyal cursed in a language I didn't know. *Are you *trying* to get us utterly destroyed?*

"You've discovered my evil plan, old man. I brought you down here so we could both be consumed by Void essence!" I stepped closer to the shaft and peered over the edge, but even Saraknyal's keen perception couldn't pierce the gloom.

Tell me you're being sarcastic.

"I'm being sarcastic."

Thank you.

I glared down the shaft, but that didn't accomplish anything either.

"Oh, to hell with it!" I pointed to the nearest cartful of burning coal. "You and you! Dump that cart down the shaft."

They complied at once. Burning coal clattered down the shaft with a crash, and a red glow now lit the bottom of the pit of blackness.

What was that for? Saraknyal asked worriedly.

"To burn a path through the Void essence." I picked up another jar of the flammable stuff the gnomes refined and dropped it down the shaft, too. "And that's to add a little—"

The jar shattered and exploded with a *whoomp*, blowing smoke and bits of burning coal back up the shaft. The shockwave carried no Void essence with it, thank the gods.

"—kick." I leaned close to peer over the edge. The iron ladder had withstood the blast, and the fire was still burning. It would keep the mists a way for a little while at least. "Now or never!"

I'd really prefer never!

I grabbed the rails of the ladder and slid down into the shaft.

Suicidal bitch! Saraknyal howled as we descended.

Tendrils of Void essence brushed against me like chill fingers, and I felt the necromancer expending energy to keep it from devouring us. I might have thanked him, but I had bigger concerns.

I landed in the middle of the cartload of burning coal, though most of it had been blasted out to the edges of the chamber. I took some comfort from the blinding heat; it counteracted the Void essence. My boots were scorched, but I kicked away the live coals and stooped to examine the furnace.

Constructed of black iron, it was mortared and bricked right into the walls of the chamber, a door at the center currently frosted white. To one side of the door were three big levers. All three were in the down position, and nothing was labeled. I'm no engineer, but I thought I could figure this out. One must open the main door, since it had no handle, and another probably opened and closed the damper. Opening it would let air into the combustion chamber.

You know which lever to pull? I asked Saraknyal.

No, just don't open the door.

Trial and error, then. I pulled the lever on the right.

A small sliding door beneath the main door slid to the side. Oil and ash trickled out onto the floor.

That would be the error part, right?

Smart ass! I closed the ash door and pulled the next lever.

Iron clanged, then I heard the unmistakable sound of indrawn air, and something *whooshed* from within the furnace. I grinned.

"Well! I think that—"

The furnace exploded.

The shockwave blasted me off my feet. Flying bits of shattered iron shredded my clothes, but puffed into rust the instant it touched my skin. My back struck the far wall, and my head smacked against the stone hard enough to ring my skull like a bell. As I slumped to the floor, my backside landed on smoldering coals, and the pain staved off unconsciousness in a most unpleasant fashion. I laughed reflexively, and the coals beneath me died.

Hashi! Careful! Don't dampen the furnace!

Saraknyal had a good point, but my ass was literally on fire. I lurched up, brushing away charred leather. The burns stung something fierce, and my ears rang. I put a hand to my head.

Then I saw it.

The door and face plate of the furnace had been blown apart, giving me a clear view inside. The Death Stone sat suspended in the center of the furnace by six rods of white crystal, a dark sun within a halo of fire, an eternal battle between the flames of the coal fire and the Void essence.

*Now, *that* is something you don't see every day!*

"You have a gift for understatement, old man."

I stared in awe at the delicate balance of forces. *Not perfectly balanced*, I suddenly realized. With the door blasted open, a thin tendril of mist escaped the furnace to swirl around the room. It faded quickly in the heat from the coal I'd dumped down the shaft, but one brush from the ebony mist could kill me.

*Okay, we're done, right? Can we *go* now?*

"*Hell*, yes." I lurched for the ladder, but could barely make out the chamber above through the swirling black mists that still hung in the shaft overhead. "Shit!"

Void essence. It'll take a while to be consumed by the ambient heat.

We don't have a while! I peered through the mists and yelled up, "Throw down a torch!"

An unlit torch dropped down through the swirling Void essence. I managed not to let it smack me in the face, picked it up, and lit it from a lump of burning coal.

Better have them feed the furnace before the fire goes out.

Good point. "Shovel coal slowly into the flue!"

Coal rattled down the flue into the combustion chamber of the furnace, just below the Death Stone.

Holding the torch above my head, I started climbing one-handed. Aches and pains plagued me, but I had no time to rest. Void essence wafted around the ladder. I fought to intercept the swirling mists with my torch, but again felt the sapping touch of the deadly fog. Saraknyal's magic flared, then dimmed.

Hashi. Hurry... I'm almost... His voice faded to silence.

Saraknyal?

No answer. I was alone.

Cold infiltrated my flesh, chilling me to the bone, biting, numbing. I struggled to maintain my grip on the icy iron rungs. If I fell, I would perish. I managed another rung, waving my torch at the tendrils of dark mist. The flame faded, but didn't quite go out.

One more rung. My numb hand stuck to the icy metal, skin peeling away as I pulled free to grab the next. I gritted my teeth until I thought they might crack. Another rung, and my torch flickered and died. Midnight-hued mists brushed my face, burning like frostbite, weakness dragging at my muscles.

No no no no!

I dropped the useless torch and scrabbled up with all the haste I could muster. *Two more rungs! I can make it!* Another tendril of Void essence brushed my arm, and my grip failed. I frantically hooked my elbow over the rung and reached higher with my other hand. Ruddy light glowed above me: warmth, fire...life.

I clutched the top rung and heaved myself up, sprawling on the floor between two red-hot ore carts. I gasped in a breath and lay there for some time, breathing the torrid air and letting the heat infuse me. *Fire and ice,* I thought. *I'm caught between fire and ice. I'll either freeze or burn.*

Sensation crept back: pins and needles, then pain. My left forearm, withered to a husk, ached like a broken bone. I levered myself up onto my elbows and looked around the chamber. Corpses lay strewn about, inanimate. Saraknyal's magic had failed.

"Old man?" I wondered for a moment if the necromancer had perished utterly. I couldn't feel his presence, and the bone-chilling hum of Soul Drinker had fallen silent. If we were truly bonded soul to soul, wouldn't I feel if he'd been destroyed? If he'd perished, I'd be next. Even if I got out of the mine alive, my invulnerability would be over. All of my shades would tear themselves apart, leaving me defenseless. I'd fall victim to the next person willing to risk their soul to end me. As much as I hated to admit it, I needed him. And—I admitted to myself—I would miss him.

"Saraknyal, you need to speak to me." I tore the blade from my forearm sheath with bloody fingers and stared at it as if I could see the soul secreted inside. "I *need* you! Take a part of my soul. Take...my fear. I'm sick of being afraid anyway. Take it! I give you consent!"

Silence.

Please! I begged. *Save yourself! Take it!*

No. The single word fell as softly into my mind as a snowflake, but it hit me as hard as an avalanche.

I choked out a laugh. "Good to hear your voice, old man."

Yours...too.

"Come on." I heaved myself up, every muscle complaining, the soles of my feet stabbing me. My left arm hung limp, the flesh shriveled. "Let's get out of here."

Yes. Please.

I tucked Soul Drinker through my belt, since my forearm sheath flopped uselessly on my withered left arm. Without stone-to-flesh contact, I couldn't use any magic, but Saraknyal had nothing left anyway.

One-handed, I wrestled a few shovels full of coal down the flue. Hopefully, that would keep the stone contained long enough for the gnomes to fix their furnace. I lit two torches, tucking one in the crook of my shriveled arm and holding the other in my bloody right hand, and staggered up the tunnel. Making my way back to the staging area while fending off stray Void essence took longer than I'd expected. I arrived to the comfortable heat of the blazing coal carts. Thankfully, the smoke from the fires seemed to be flowing up a nearby shaft. More corpses lay scattered around, the zombies having dropped in place when Saraknyal's power waned.

I sat and rested there for a moment, my strength returning slowly. When I felt my legs would hold my weight without buckling, I dragged a shovel to the massive mine doors. Outside there was light and life, while here there was only death. I bashed the tool against the doors three times as hard as I could, which wasn't very hard.

Metal clanked, and the huge slabs of iron parted.

I squinted against the bright daylight, smiled at the massed gnomes staring up at me with wide eyes, and fell to my knees, my head suddenly spinning. As I toppled forward, I heard someone call my name. As if from very far away, concerned voices called for a healer. A face swam before my eyes: a gnome, Loremaster Geoil.

"Did you succeed, Lady Severn?"

"Yes," I mumbled. "Tend...the...fire. Be careful." I blinked, and the face had changed. Tori Blackbriar looked genuinely stricken. With a flourish, he settled his cloak over me, tucking the embroidered collar under my chin. It smelled good, like flowers and growing things. Like life.

"Here, Hashi." He cupped the back of my head with one hand and lifted, pressing the rim of a tiny crystal vial to my lips. "Swallow this."

Don't! Saraknyal's faint but urgent warning came as the cool liquid spilled into my mouth. *It could be poison! I can't...help...you.*

Don't be an idiot, old man. I swallowed, and warmth tingled down my throat to my stomach, then outward to my sinews, joints, and skin. I gasped with the sensation as strength perfused my every fiber, pulsing with every beat of my hammering heart.

"Gods and devils! What the *hell* was that?" I sat up, humming with sudden energy.

"A restorative." Tori smiled, though still looking concerned as he stood and held out a hand. "Can you stand?"

"I think so..." At the moment I felt like I could fly, or even spontaneously combust. I looked at my hands and gaped. The right was still smeared with blood, but the skin of my palm had been fully healed. The left, little more than a husk of shriveled flesh over bone mere moments before, was fully fleshed and flexed easily. "Some restorative!" I took his hand and allowed him to pull me up.

"Always happy to come to the aid of a lady in distress!" He grinned and bent to kiss my hand.

I jerked it away with a glare. "You're insufferable, Tori Blackbriar!" I threw his cloak at him, but he caught it and chuckled.

"Well, yes, but devilishly charming, and not a torture to look upon, you must admit." He draped his cloak over an arm and gave me a short bow, his usual lascivious smile present, but somewhat strained. "And you're welcome."

Tell...him...fuck...off, Saraknyal whispered.

"Yes, well, thank you for the potion." I brushed at my tattered clothes, every sinew of my body still humming with energy. I hadn't felt this good in years.

"I gather the stone's contained?" he asked as his eyes roved over me, lingering here and there, his brow furrowed. "You seem to be slightly worse for wear, or at least your clothes are. What happened?"

I pulled my tattered shirt closed where the rents exposed a little too much skin, repositioning Soul Drinker to its sheath, now snug against my healed forearm. Glancing at Tori, I found him staring not at me but at the obsidian dagger as if he'd never seen the thing before, though I never left home without it.

251

"The stone's contained, but it wasn't as simple a process as we'd thought. The gods-damned damper was closed on the furnace." I eyed the remaining gnomes, and found Loremaster Geoil. "Why didn't you tell me the damper was closed?"

"I'm sorry, milady, but we had no idea. The last to leave the chamber was Foreman Tipiri. He probably closed it to keep the fire burning low as long as possible. If Lady Keshmir ordered him to abandon the mines, and he couldn't disobey as you said, then closing the damper would have staved off the inevitable release of Void essence for a time. Until the fuel ran out, at least."

"Well, I'm afraid your furnace is damaged. The door blew off."

"Oh! Well, that'll be a delicate repair, but now that the fire's lit, we can manage." He bowed. "We owe you a great debt, Lady Severn."

"Indeed, we do!" Vinchi echoed with a bow. "For our very *lives*, in fact."

"You're welcome." I breathed the fresh air—hardly fresh, actually, laden with the stench of Haven, but better than coal smoke and Void essence—and nodded toward the door of the keep. "Now, I believe I'd like to go home."

"I'd be happy to escort you, since *your* escort seems to be...um...used up." Tori cocked an eyebrow, not leering, for once. He looked genuinely concerned again.

"Thank you. I accept." I followed him out through the keep. The invigorating energy of the elixir he'd given me began to subside, but my skin still tingled and I bounced with every step. I nearly cracked my head on the low ceiling.

He's an ass, Saraknyal whispered as Tori opened the door to my carriage, bowing like a footman as he handed me in.

True, I agreed, gritting my teeth to keep from smiling. I watched Tori as he closed the door and climbed up to ride with Bromish. *But it's a rather nice ass.*

And you're an idiot, the necromancer growled.

Well, maybe, but I'm alive. I flexed my formerly shriveled hand and sighed. *And I'm whole, thanks to that insufferable ass.* That Tori had been honestly concerned for me was obvious, but the persistent troubled look on his face confused me. What was he so worried about?

Fair point, but don't let it go to your head. Saraknyal seemed steadier, stronger. I wondered if he'd taken a bit of my soul to empower himself. I'd given him consent, but I didn't feel any different. *Now, let's talk about that stone. There's got to be some better way to contain it. Maybe even *harness* it!*

I shivered with remembered weakness and flexed my renewed left hand. "*Now* who's being an idiot?"

Despite washing off the coal dust, ash, rust, and soot from the gnomish mines, I still felt as if Void essence clung to my skin. I tried to put the experience behind me, but my obsessive nature wouldn't let one detail go.

"So, what did you take from me?" I finally asked Saraknyal. "What part of my soul?"

*What did I *take*? What do you mean? I didn't take anything from you.* He sounded incredulous.

"Then where did you get your energy? You could barely speak when we escaped the mines, but you perked up later like I'd fed you the souls of a hundred virgins!"

The soul of a virgin is no different than the soul of the most vile lecher, Hashi—for my purposes, anyway—and I didn't take anything from you.

"Why not? I told you to. I gave you consent." I stood at my balcony looking out over Haven, my home. A festering cesspool, yes, but my home nonetheless. "Why didn't you?"

Because I didn't want to.

A flicker of anger ignited in my gut. "You'd rather we both perish?"

We didn't. I knew we wouldn't.

"How could you know that?"

*Because I know *you*, Hashi. You're the most determined living creature I've ever known, and that includes a dragon or two. You're a survivor.*

I stared out at the city for a very long time, not knowing what to say or even think. Then I realized, "You never answered my question. Where did you get the energy after we escaped?"

Oh, that potion Blackbriar gave you. It really was a remarkable restorative, highly magical. I don't know who his alchemist is, but they know their business!

My mouth fell open. "I didn't know you could do that."

Neither did I until I did it. You were fully restored, and there was quite a lot of excess energy buzzing about, so I took some.

The implications struck me like a lightning bolt. "That means you don't need to consume *souls*, Saraknyal!"

I never thought of that, but I suppose so. He sounded uninspired by the news. *I don't think I could absorb the energy directly, but through you I could. Maybe ask that insufferable ass Blackbriar who concocted that potion for him.*

"I *will*." I whirled away from the window to pace my office, my mind a tornado of chaotic thoughts. All the souls I'd fed to Saraknyal over the decades...it had all been unnecessary. All the souls had perished for nothing. I felt like throwing up.

What's wrong, Hashi? You're distressed all of the sudden.

"Nothing." He wouldn't understand. Saraknyal didn't see human souls as anything but a resource. "What's done is done."

You should probably direct your energies to something more productive, like figuring out a way to harness the Death Stone!

"Saraknyal, seriously? Harness it? We were lucky to survive just *containing* it!"

But—

"No!" I glared at the dagger atop my desk. "We're *not* going to try to harness Void essence. If there's a better way to *contain* it than keeping it in a furnace, then I'm all ears."

Fine. Suck all the fun out of being a necromancer! Saraknyal fell silent for a long moment—either pouting or contemplating— then continued in a thoughtful tone. *Now that I think of it, a properly enchanted vessel *should* be able to contain the Death Stone. Consider, Hashi. For every negative, there is a positive. Balance in the universe. Necromantic magic transforms soul energy—a form of positive energy—into negative-energy effects: cold, terror, death, and paralysis. The proper incantation could do the reverse, transforming the negative energy of the Death Stone into a reflective surface and an impervious barrier. It would just take some research to see what's possible.*

I cocked my head. "Use the stone's own power to contain it?"

*Yes, and it'd be a *hell* of a lot safer than keeping a fire burning around the thing. This is intriguing, Hashi! A containment field energized by the very power source it's containing! Think of it!*

"Okay, see what you can come up with. I'll mention it to Vinchi at the next council meeting. The gnomes would probably welcome any effort to get the thing out of their mines." If it meant eliminating the chance of the stone destroying Haven, I was all for it. "We've got more important things to do in the short term. I need to send a letter to the other council members so we can all interview Jhavika's people."

You just want to see Tori Blackbriar again, don't you?

"What?" I narrowed my eyes at Soul Drinker. "Don't be a jerk."

He laughed. *Sorry, I couldn't resist teasing you a little after you ogled his ass like that.*

...not a torture to look upon. The memory made me smile. "You jealous?"

Don't be ridiculous. Just remember that he's dangerous, Hashi. I'm not saying you shouldn't...indulge yourself that way, as long as you're careful about it. Just not with him.

"No, not with him or anyone else. You know I can't trust anyone like that." I sighed, turned down the lamps, and headed for my bedroom. "I'm not worrying about anything else tonight." I hung my robe up, placed Soul Drinker on the nightstand, and crawled into bed.

Goodnight, Hashi, Saraknyal said.

"G'nite." I forced my mind to quiescence, safe and comfortable with the necromancer watching over me. Sleep descended like a warm blanket. Not that I needed much inducement; it had been one hell of a day, after all.

Chapter Twenty Two
Peace and Quiet

My brand new coach and four matching horses—black, of course—clattered through the open gate of Ash Keep. The big day had finally arrived; I was moving in.

I like what they've done with the place, Saraknyal said. *Even if they did take two years to finish.*

Never tell a dwarf to hurry. I'd been told exactly that when the renovations began. In fact, I'd been told in no uncertain terms to butt out.

Saraknyal yammered on, pointing out details, and, of course, criticizing everything. I amended my previous thought; *we* were moving in, and the necromancer just couldn't refrain from contributing his unsolicited opinion, as always.

My coach stopped before the line of my recently hired staff: three maids, three footmen, a stableman, a chef, and several scullery lads and lasses. I'd hand-picked them from all over Haven, talked to them all personally, and offered them good pay, as well as room and board for them and their families. I'd also assured them that, despite my grim reputation, I would keep them safe, secure, and healthy. All I wanted in return was solid work and loyalty. Disloyalty would earn dismissal. Betrayal meant far, far worse. By Haven standards, these arrangements were beyond generous.

I stepped down, and they all bowed and curtsied. "Welcome home, mistress," they said in perfect unison.

I couldn't help but smile; they must have rehearsed it. "Thank you." I turned to my driver, Bromish, who'd been with me for a year now. I'd found the young man breaking horses for a hostler, and he had a most amazing way with them. That was crucial, since horses instinctively shied from my ever-present ghoulish guards, and I went nowhere without them. "And thank you, Bromish. See to your girls, would you please?"

He grinned and tipped his hat. "Of course, mistress." He'd selected the four mares himself, and treated them like royalty.

"Miss Severn."

I turned to the deep yet feminine voice of Ingrid Brickhammer, the dwarvish woman I'd hired for the renovations. She stood about four feet tall and outweighed me by more than half, though I doubted there was an ounce of fat on her. I respected her both for her work and as the first female ruler of her clan, unheard-of in dwarven culture.

"You've been busy, I see." Ingrid narrowed her eyes as my undead entourage clambered down from the carriage. I now had six shades and two wraiths.

"If people would stop trying to assassinate me, I'd stop turning them into undead." I said blithely. "Some people just never learn."

Good for us, bad for them, Saraknyal quipped.

I ignored him. "Ready for our walk-through, Clan Mistress?"

"Aye. I don't expect any surprises."

Tell her if she expected something, it wouldn't be a surprise.

I ignored him, not about to insult this formidable woman. "I hope not."

Especially since you've already sold off almost everything else you own to pay for all this, Saraknyal groused.

He was exaggerating, but not by much. The remodeling costs—more than I'd paid for the keep itself—had forced me to reorganize my businesses in return for ready cash. I sold the majority interest in the protection rackets to my bosses, thereby cementing their loyalty while retaining a twenty percent cut of the profits. They handled the day-to-day work, while I stepped in as necessary to deal with hostile competitors. This move also freed up much of my time, allowing me to focus on my antiquities business, working with Bryce and Glosh Waymar to ensure a steady stream of income.

"One moment." I turned to my retainers. "Thank you all for turning out like this. See to your duties now. Dinner at sunset."

"Yes, mistress." As one, they bowed.

Ingrid shook her head as my staff hurried into the keep. "Dunno how you get *anyone* to work for you with them *things* lurkin' about." She jerked a thick thumb at my escort.

"*You* came to work for me, Clan Mistress." I gave her a wry look. "And my staff knows, as *your* people knew, that they're safer *with* my shades on guard than without them." I'd kept two of my shades stationed at the main gate throughout the work, allowing only workers and my own people to come and go.

She glowered, then nodded. "They're just...unnerving, if you get my drift."

Try living with a necromancer in your head, I thought.

Saraknyal chuckled, oblivious to the fact that I wasn't joking.

We began our tour of the keep, and I had to admit that Clan Brickhammer knew their business.

The renovations were spectacular and precise. From the cramped, blocky, gnomish architecture, they'd crafted high, elegant ceilings; arched doorways; and comfortable, spacious rooms. Decorating would be up to me, of course, and I had my work cut out if I hoped to match the work they'd done. My people had already moved in what little furniture I had. Aside from an antique banquet table in the main hall, and comfortable chairs and tables in my sitting room, the library, parlor, entry hall, and most of the tower rooms remained empty.

Ingrid hustled through the kitchen and pantries, pointing out her workers' renovations with pride. My staff bustled in and out, stocking the cellars with food, wine, and fine brandy. Maddie Catwaller, my rotund chef, smiled at me and patted his bulbous belly as we inspected his domain. Dinner already scented the lavishly equipped kitchen, and my mouth watered in anticipation at the luscious aromas; no more hand-to-mouth meals in a rented room for me.

An hour later, after we'd inspected each and every room, I paid Brickhammer the final installment of her fee and held out my hand. She ignored the gesture, handed the money to one of her people, nodded brusquely, and departed without another word. The brushoff piqued me, but I let it go. I'd worked for years fostering the mystique of a dreadful necromancer. Getting angry at someone for avoiding me would be the height of hypocrisy.

Alone at last, Saraknyal said as I climbed the tower stairs to my chambers.

Only if I throw you off a cliff into the sea, old man.

I get so little appreciation for my tireless hours of servitude and companionship.

I don't need companionship, and you'd serve me better if you'd shut up occasionally.

I rubbed my temples to score away the headache that seemed a permanent fixture these days.

Since the day I'd adopted Saraknyal's plan to foster my reputation as a necromancer, he'd appointed himself my constant critic and advisor. Granted, his plan worked—the frequency of assassination attempts had dropped precipitously—but I could only tolerate so many 'I told you so's.

I entered my chambers and closed the door behind me, taking a moment to soak up my own personal space. I'd found a nice desk and a couple of chairs for the office, and a bed and clothes press for the bedroom, but the walls were bare. I let my mind wander for a moment, mentally considering potential decorations.

Why so touchy this afternoon? Saraknyal interrupted, shattering my thoughts.

Please, Saraknyal, just leave me alone for a while. I went to the sideboard and poured myself a brandy.

Why? So you can mope and drink yourself into a stupor?

"Shut *up*, would you?" I unclipped Soul Drinker from my hip and dropped it on my desk on my way to the balcony.

No. You've got your base of operations. Now you need to start planning the next step.

"Not tonight." I stepped out onto the balcony and looked out at Haven. A rather dismal view, actually, looking out at a lot of rooftops and crowds of people bustling around. *Maybe I should have put my office on the harbor side.*

Don't start planning more remodeling before you've even got the place furnished! You need money, Hashi. Diddling in antiques isn't going to get you where you need to be. You should contract out your services. You'd earn gold and bolster your undead forces at the same time. And I don't mean helping out your racketeering friends when they run into a little competition. Making a gang leader piss their pants doesn't pay enough and doesn't enhance your reputation.

"Shut up." We'd had this discussion a thousand times. "They piss their pants *because* of my reputation. I'm *not* going to hire myself out as an assassin. End of discussion."

Fine. Sulk.

I gritted my teeth, which only intensified my headache. "I'm not sulking. I'm trying to relax and enjoy my new home for the very first time. Please let me do that, would you?"

Go ahead. I'm not stopping you. Drink yourself into oblivion and see if I care.

I quaffed my brandy just to be petulant and put the empty snifter on the balcony railing, cursing the irony of my new life. I dared not be parted from Soul Drinker, but Saraknyal plagued my every waking hour. If he didn't shut up, I felt I'd go mad.

Deep breaths, Hashi. I forced my death grip on the railing to relax. *Let it go...*

What's bothering you? he finally asked, breaking the five-minute silence.

"You are. Now please be quiet."

I'm just concerned for you, Hashi. Talk to me.

"No." I snatched up my snifter and stalked to the sideboard.

Fine, then listen. You need to diversify and strengthen your position. Six shades and two wraiths may have been plenty at the inn, but they aren't enough to keep this place secure.

I poured brandy and let him yammer on. I couldn't stop him; all I could do was ignore him. I needed him, and he knew it.

His diatribe continued through a delicious dinner in my sitting room, through hours of my attempts to read, right up until I retired for the night. Exhausted from the anticipation and efforts of moving in, not to mention several brandies and wine with dinner, I placed Soul Drinker on the nightstand and lay down to sleep.

Bedtime was the only time Saraknyal finally shut up, but even as sleep loomed at the edge of consciousness, I heard his thoughts as whispers in the back of my mind. Maybe this was my imagination, and maybe not. Sometimes I woke up in the night without knowing why or what had awoken me, and wondered if he spied on my dreams. I felt like a specimen in a glass case, always under scrutiny, always being watched.

Thumping my pillow, I turned on my side and forced myself to relax. Tonight I slept in my new keep. I was going to enjoy this. Tonight, I wasn't going to think about the future.

In the morning, I got to work.

"Glosh!" I strode into my smuggler's office. "I got your message! Let's see it!"

"Aye, mistress!" His teeth gleamed beneath his prodigious black moustache as he lurched up from his desk and beckoned me to follow him. We entered his vast storeroom and stopped beside a stack of lumber. Patting it with one hand, he said, "Here it is! Straight from Hyko. The finest money can buy!"

"Beautiful." I ran a hand over the rough-cut mahogany. It didn't look like much now, but crafted into furniture and polished, it would go a long way toward making Ash Keep feel more like home. "Is this all of it?"

Waymar shook his head. "I already sold the other half. Lumber's scarce in Haven. You'll turn a pretty profit even after my expenses. I'll forward this on to that master cabinetmaker so she can start in on your order."

"Excellent!" Without Glosh and his ships, my antiques business wouldn't be nearly as profitable, and goods from abroad would cost me a fortune to import. *Good employees are worth their weight in gold.*

Until they try to kill you, Saraknyal reminded me.

His jibe drew my gaze to the shade that used to be Maris. *Things are different now.*

Sure they are.

Done with Waymar, I headed toward the waterfront to check the junk shops I frequented for new inventory. Pirates tended to sell their goods in bulk to the highest bidder right on the quay, especially books, clothing, and bric-a-brac. Pirates weren't big readers or aficionados of luxury items, I supposed. The wharf-side merchants weren't much more discerning, selling booty by weight, rarely bothering to value it piece by piece. I often found my best deals here.

That afternoon, I found myself in a dilapidated pawn shop. The cantankerous old gnome who ran the place didn't like me, but I'd discovered good pieces lurking among the trash that filled the place to the ceiling. The heavy layer of dust on the oldest items brought back fond memories of my days digging through dead civilizations for antique bits and bobs, and I found myself missing those excursions: trekking across the wilderness, researching old maps, delving collapsed ruins... Sometimes I felt like a prisoner in Haven, unable to leave for fear of being hunted down and executed.

This day, I came upon a three-lock box made of cast iron, perhaps dwarven. It was about eighteen inches wide, a foot deep, and ten inches high, with no external hinges. The only features were three keyholes, one in each end and one on the front, oddly shaped to accept three-flanged keys. Unfamiliar engraved symbols decorated the face.

Magical runes? I asked Saraknyal.

None that I've ever seen, and I don't feel anything.

Intriguing...

"Closing time!" the gnome proprietor called out. "You buy something. Nobody come in with your monsters at my door! You owe me!"

"Do you have keys for this?" I tapped the box.

"No. Four gold crowns."

"How about four *silver* crowns." I scowled at him, but he scowled right back. He was better at it.

"Three gold. Dunno what inside," he said in his thick Chen accent, twirling the ends of his long, drooping moustache and wagging his bushy eyebrows. "Maybe *treasure.*"

Anything inside? I asked Saraknyal.

I don't know. I can't see inside. The metal's thick. It may be lined with lead.

What the hell good are you, then?

I keep blades from piercing your flesh, Hashi.

*Oh, yeah, I forgot *that bit.* I bit my lip. *Why would anyone line a lockbox with lead?*

Lead shields magic. Dwarves keep powerful trinkets in boxes like this. Prevents wizards from finding them.

So there actually might *be treasure inside?*

He snorted a laugh. *Not likely, and good luck finding a locksmith able to crack *those* locks.*

I mentioned this to the old gnome and countered his offer. "*One* gold crown."

The gnome scowled. "One and five. You find treasure inside, I get half."

I shook my head. "Only if *you* pay for the locksmith to crack it."

His face contorted into one big scowl, and he waved dismissively. "Fine. You keep whatever inside. One and five, final offer."

"Deal." I was probably paying too much, but my interest was piqued. Empty or not, I thought I might have a use for it, though I kept that notion to myself. I handed over the money and tried to lift the box. It barely moved. "Gods and devils, this weighs a long ton!"

"Not my problem. Yours now." The merchant waved a hand at the door. "Get your junk outta my shop! Closing time!"

Against the gnome's protestations, I called in one of my shades to lift the heavy box. The creature didn't show any strain, but I heard several joints pop as it hauled the box off the shelf. We trudged home only as fast as my minions could manage lugging the box. I instructed them to deposit it in my workshop, then dashed off a note to Bryce to find a locksmith to open it.

For the rest of the day I kept busy, reading, sorting through some new finds, and having Saraknyal translate a book in a language I didn't know. After a dinner of succulent lamb pie accompanied by a carafe of wine, I went to bed early, exhausted from guarding my thoughts. If Saraknyal learned the real reason I purchased the dwarven lockbox, I wouldn't get a wink of sleep.

It took a week for Bryce to find a gnomish locksmith capable of cracking the three-lock box. One might think a dwarf would have a better chance of dealing with a dwarven box, but while dwarves are unsurpassed at *smithing* locks, gnomes excel at cracking them. In a city like Haven, a knack for locks—and a little light burglary—would lead to a profitable career.

Nip Tinwhistle was a diminutive chap, even for a gnome, and he insisted that I bring the box to his workshop rather than coming to my keep. Unfortunately, Tinwhistle's workshop resided on the fourth floor of a gnomish tenement that hadn't been remodeled to accommodate humans. I slouched up the twisting stairway with two shades struggling up behind under the dead weight of the box.

At my knock, a viewing port clicked open at the height of my belt buckle. "Hashi Severn?"

"Yes. I brought the lockbox and your fee." I jingled my purse.

"Good." The viewing hatch snapped shut, and mechanical contrivances clattered for a full count of ten before the door opened. He looked me up and down, and nodded. "Well, bring it on in, Longlegs."

I considered calling him "Squirt" or something equally derisive, but refrained.

Tell him you'd consider making him a wraith if he was a little taller, Saraknyal suggested.

Smiling to myself, I ducked through the door and told my shades to bring in the box. The workshop looked like a museum for locks and other clockwork devices, everything laid out with meticulous care, from tools to glass cases of various whatnots. Tinwhistle closed the door behind us, shying away from my shades, and worked a crank that reset the locks and probably a number of traps as well.

Gnomes and their gadgets, Saraknyal muttered.

"Where do you want it?" I asked.

"Over here." The gnome bustled past me, his motions quick and ferret-like, and pointed to a low table sporting glow-crystal lamps with parabolic mirrors on articulating arms. He backed out of the way as my shades put the box down with a resounding thump. "Heavy, eh?"

"Very." I moved my shades back to make him more comfortable. "Either thick-walled, or maybe lined with lead? There are no keys."

"'Course there ain't no keys. Wouldn't need *me* if you had the keys, would ya?" He sat on a little stool and peered at the box. "Ain't seen a triple triple in years!"

"Triple triple?" I stepped close enough to look over the top of his head at the box, then realized what the term must mean. "Three locks with three sets of tumblers each, you mean?"

"Right ya are!" He looked up at me. "Yer a bright one, Longlegs."

"Can you open it?"

"'Course I can! Wouldn't of told you I could if I couldn't, would I?" He rubbed his tiny hands together, then opened a slim drawer. Inside lay about a hundred different picks, rods, and other tools. "Now, step back, if you please. I don't work for no audience, do I?"

I took a step back, but kept my eyes on him. If the box did have anything valuable inside, I gauged he might be quick enough to pocket something without my notice if I didn't pay attention. Even watching, I couldn't see how he managed to work three sets of picks at the same time, but the first lock clicked open after about five minutes of fiddling.

"Ha! One down!" He jammed a tool in the lock and moved to the next one. "Spring loaded, they are. Bloody dwarves and their contrivances. I shouldn't complain, thought, should I? Keeps me in business, it does."

I didn't comment, but watched him pick the other two locks and jam them open. He then grasped both sides firmly, braced himself, and lifted the lid of the box straight up about half an inch, then tilted it back on the internal hinges. The gnome chuckled and stepped aside, waving me forward with a grin.

"Afraid yer out of luck, Longlegs. Empty as the dwarf's head who built it! Ha!"

I peered down into the box. Empty as he'd said, but intriguing in its design. The hinges slid into recesses, and the locking mechanisms rotated hefty pins through the eyes of steel flanges that fit down into the frame. And, as Saraknyal had surmised, the interior was lined with half an inch of solid lead.

"Can you permanently jam the locks open without breaking them?" I asked.

"Oh, aye, easy enough. Just a wood peg in the pin slider there ought to do it. I could smith you new keys for it, but it'll cost ya."

"No, just jam the locks. I don't want to break them."

What are you going to use it for? Saraknyal asked as the gnome went to work.

For peace and quiet. The thought came into my mind before I could stop it.

What? What do you mean 'peace and quiet'? If you think for one moment I'm going to let you— He'd figured out my plan, as I knew he would eventually.

You can't stop me, old man, I told him.

Hashi! You don't need to do this! I promise, I'll be quiet whenever you say! You can't just...

He continued with his pleas all the way back to Ash Keep and up the stairs to my office. I tried to ignore him. When I instructed my shades to place the box on the corner of my desk and take station outside my door, he finally fell silent.

I lifted the lid to the box and pulled the soul blade from my belt. "I want you to know that I'm not angry with you, Saraknyal. I just need privacy every once in a while."

You don't have to do this. I'll be quiet.

"It's not about you being quiet, it's about me being able to think to myself without you in my head. I need privacy. If I don't have some time to myself, I'm going to go mad."

And what about me going mad? he asked, something new in his voice: desperation. *I can't see out of that box, Hashi. If you leave me in there, I'll go insane.*

"Oh, please!" I scoffed. "I'm not going to leave you in there for long, Saraknyal. Just a few hours. "You sat in a sarcophagus for *centuries* without going insane."

That's exactly why I'll go insane now, Hashi! I can't stand the sensory deprivation! Please!

I hesitated, but I couldn't stop now; my sanity depended on it. "Here." I picked a book from my bookshelf and lay it down inside the box. "You can do some light reading." I placed Soul Drinker on top of the book and reached for the lid.

Wait! Hashi, wait! You don't need to—

The lid slid into place, cutting off his voice. I stood there for a long time with my hands atop the box, listening.

Silence.

"Saraknyal?" I waited with bated breath. Nothing.

He couldn't hear me, couldn't see me, couldn't be in my mind, hear my thoughts, spy on my dreams... For the first time in five years, I was alone. Truly alone.

A desperate laugh choked me.

I looked around my office as if expecting someone to step out of nowhere, an apparition of Saraknyal, that face I'd seen so long ago in his hand mirror. Or perhaps an assassin, since I was completely defenseless. But nothing floated out of the ether to haunt me or sprang out of the shadows to murder me. There were no voices, no images, no eyes in my mind, and no assassins.

"Okay, Hashi," I said to myself with a sigh, "what do you do now?"

The answer came from the depths of my soul: I would revel in my solitude.

I strode to my sideboard, poured a healthy draught of brandy, then pulled the bell rope that summoned a footman. I paced my office in blissful quiet until a knock sounded at my door.

"Come in."

The young man entered and bowed. "Mistress?"

I remembered him, a boy I'd hired from a tavern because I liked the way he served, always graceful and precise. "I'd like a hot bath, please, Jareth. No attendants, just hot water and quiet."

"Yes, mistress." He bowed again and backed out.

The door closed, and I was alone again. I changed into a robe, a smile spreading across my mouth as my thoughts—my utterly *private* thoughts—swirled like a tornado in my head. *Alone...nobody watching me, nobody looking at me through my clothes.* I looked at myself in the full-length mirror, head to toe, nobody but me. I ran a hand down the smooth silk of my robe and my lips quirked into a smile. Five years of discipline—guarding my every thought—flew out the window.

The window... I whirled to my balcony and threw open the doors. Seventy feet of sheer granite wall separated me from the street below. An assassin would have to fly or climb like a spider to get at me, so I felt pretty safe without my dreadful Soul Drinker. The sultry sea breeze billowed my robe. I breathed it in and laughed. *Alone...* For so many years, being alone had tormented me with guilt, depression, and distress. Now, released from my desire for companionship, alone meant freedom.

I spent two hours alone that night, lounging in a hot bath, sipping brandy, and reading a book of fanciful tales, indulging in my solitude. Finally satisfied and a little sleepy, I finished my brandy, brushed my teeth, and opened the three-lock box.

"How are you, Saraknyal?"

Silence.

Worry tingled up my spine.

"Did you enjoy the book?" I reached in and lifted Soul Drinker from its bed.

Still no answer.

Anger flickered in my gut. "If you'd like to finish the chapter, I can put you back."

No...please.

He sounded contrite, but also angry. Considering that he would be watching over me for the next eight hours while I slept, I thought I'd better assuage his hurt feelings.

"I hope you understand my need for privacy, Saraknyal." I turned down the lamps and headed for my bedroom.

*No, I *don't* understand. What's so wonderful about being alone? I was alone my entire life, Hashi. It's...not all it's cracked up to be.*

"I know. You remember what I was like when we first met. Being alone tormented me. You changed all that, and I'm truly grateful." How odd that I'd consider the loss of a bit of my soul as a kindness. "You need me, and I need you, but every once in a while, I need solitude."

And you don't trust me to simply remain silent.

It's not just about quiet. I sighed, put the dagger on my night table, and sat down on my bed. *It's about privacy, not having you listen to my every thought.*

He didn't answer.

I doffed my robe and crawled under the sheet, the night air heavy and warm. "Goodnight, Saraknyal. Thank you for watching over me."

You're welcome.

I closed my eyes and listened to the sounds of Haven: the murmur of thousands of faint voices: fear, anger, love, hate, and hunger. But they were far away, no more intrusive than the susurration of the sea. I was safe here in my keep. I had everything I needed, everything I wanted. *I should be content...*

Contentment is dangerous, Saraknyal responded to my wandering thought.

See? That's what I'm talking about. Privacy.

Sorry.

I rolled over and tried to fall to sleep, wondering if he truly was.

Chapter Twenty Three
Curious Developments

From the journal of Hashi Severn –
The news of Jhavika's actions makes me wonder if the magic of the scourge has consumed her. I often wonder why the magic of Saraknyal hasn't consumed more of me.

"Seriously?" I flung the note onto my desk, not caring that it landed on my unfinished breakfast. "Reginald Malchi is *such* a dick!"

An established fact, Saraknyal agreed absently. He rarely paid attention to my morning correspondence. *What's he done now?*

"Read that." I stabbed a finger at the offending note and got up to pace, my appetite destroyed.

Lady Severn, Saraknyal read. *Now that we have successfully resolved the problem of the Tinworthy mines, I would request that you arrange immediate access to Jhavika Keshmir's keep for the Council to interview her surviving retainers. Your minions have denied us access. This is unacceptable. Please remedy this situation immediately.* He paused. *We? Really?*

"Exactly!" I ran my hands over my short-cropped hair in exasperation. "It's not like I didn't save all of *Haven*, nearly being *killed* in the process! He's been *inconvenienced*."

*Well, what does one expect from a *dick*, after all?* Saraknyal said snidely.

I strode to back my desk, pulled out several sheets of paper, then yanked on the bell rope that would summon Joss. I first dashed off a note to Nahli Twince, thanking her for her sincere congratulations on my survival, and assuring her that I would complete an inventory of the contents of Jhavika's keep today. She'd earned a portion of the spoils, after all. Next, I wrote a note to Vinchi Tinworthy, thanking him for his formal letter of appreciation for my efforts on his clan's behalf. Then a polite "No, thank you" to Tori Blackbriar in response to his invitation to a congratulatory dinner in my honor. Lastly, my anger now cooled, I drafted a short letter to Lord Malchi, telling him to inform the Council that any members wishing to interview Jhavika's surviving retainers could meet me at her keep *tomorrow* morning. Today I intended to go through the keep and choose my spoils; I'd earned them. As I finished the letter, a knock sounded at the door.

"Come in." Joss did, and I thrust out the papers. "Please have these written fair for my signature, and tell Bromish I'll need the carriage. Oh, and hire a wagon to be sent to Lady Keshmir's keep."

"Immediately, mistress."

*Only *one* wagon? Remember her library?* Saraknyal prompted.

"Make that two wagons, Joss!"

"Two wagons. I'll have the letters ready in a trice, mistress." He exited quickly, evidently picking up on my mood.

I took a deep breath and poured myself another cup of tea.

What else is bothering you?

"Tori. He's being...*persistently* friendly."

Oh?

"Invited me to a dinner."

*You're not *going*, are you?* He sounded panicked.

"Of *course* not." I forced myself to relax and finish my tea, dressed in comfortable clothes, strapped Soul Drinker to my forearm, and met Joss in the entry hall to sign the letters.

"Be careful, mistress," he said with a bow.

I choked back a laugh. I'd decimated an entire keep full of soldiers and delved a mine full of Void essence in just the last three days. Pillaging Jhavika's keep would be a peaceful respite. I boarded my carriage with two shades as escorts and sat back for the ride.

What a difference a couple of days made. Instead of blood and gore, the courtyard cobbles were so clean they gleamed in the sun. The retainers had been busy. I was met at the entrance to the keep by a liveried footman. He bowed to me with a neutral mien. "Lady Severn. Well met. Can we help you?"

"Yes, send for Lewin and Jhavika's alchemist. I'd like to talk to them both, but separately."

"At once, Lady Severn." He waved me toward a room off the main entry hall. "May I suggest the sitting room for your meetings?"

"That's fine." I strode past him. "I'm going to look around the keep when I'm done talking to them."

"I'll have a footman attend you."

"Thank you." I paced the comfortable sitting room.

He was very solicitous, Saraknyal mentioned.

I noticed. And they've scrubbed this place like they expect Jhavika to walk through the door any moment.

Maybe they do.

That was a discomforting thought.

A footman arrived and asked if I wanted anything for refreshment. I told him tea would be welcome.

"Hot or iced?" he asked.

"Iced?" I blinked at him. "Where do you get ice?"

The footman simply smiled and bowed. "One of Lady Keshmir's little secrets. May I suggest iced tea with mint? It's quite refreshing."

"Yes, please." He nodded and hurried off.

Jhavika likes her comforts.

She does. I surveyed the overstuffed settees set upon ornate rugs and the paintings that graced the walls. The footman returned in moments with a tall glass of iced tea, sprigs of fresh mint floating inside. I sipped it, and my eyebrows rose. It was very good.

Lewin arrived and bowed deeply. "Lady Severn. Very good to see you again. I trust all's well."

"Well enough. I'd like to ask you to look into a matter for me that has nothing to do with your mistress or her secrets."

"Of course. I'd be happy to."

"I'll be taking some things from this keep today, among them, the library."

His bushy eyebrows climbed his forehead. "The *entire* library?"

"Yes. Before I do, I'd like you to set aside any volumes pertaining to negative energy or necromantic magic. You know the library's contents, and I don't." This would save me days of sorting through the stacks looking for anything to help Saraknyal deal with the Death Stone.

"Very well, milady." Lewin didn't sound pleased, but I didn't care.

"Have it done by this afternoon, please."

"I'll be happy to help." He bowed and turned to go.

As he left, a small, dark-skinned woman with braided hair and scarred hands entered, her eyes cast steadfastly at the floor.

"I assume you're Jhavika's alchemist?"

"I am, milady. Eias Lavo." She curtsied, her eyes fixed on my feet and her hands clenched before her.

"Don't worry. I'm not going to hurt you." When she didn't respond, I said, "I'd like your opinion on a restorative potion I was recently given. It was quite remarkable, and even restored flesh that had been touched by negative energy." I flexed my left hand for her to see. "Yesterday, this was shriveled down to skin and bone."

Her eyes barely flicked up to my hand before returning to my feet. "My *opinion*, milady, is that such a potion is beyond my knowledge and skill to concoct."

She's terrified, Hashi.

I noticed, but then, she was just summoned by the woman who slaughtered the entire keep's guard.

True.

I continued, trying to make the woman feel more at ease. "Miss Lavo, as an alchemist, have you ever made a restorative potion?"

"Yes, but only to accelerate the body's natural healing. I can't restore destroyed tissue to its former state."

"Do you know any alchemist in Haven who might be able to craft such a potion?"

"No, milady, though there may be. Such magic is known to fae, elves, and some gnomes. Certain priests can also heal like that, but that's entirely different from the crafting of potions. You might buy one, but it would be powerfully expensive."

"Very well. Thank you, Miss Lavo. You've been helpful."

Her dark eyes flicked up for a moment, then back down. "You're welcome, milady. Will there be anything else?"

"No. You can go."

"Thank you, milady." She curtsied and hurried out.

Guess I'll have to look elsewhere for information on that potion.

Why not ask Blackbriar?

That would make me obligated to him, and that's a position I don't want to be in.

Probably wise. But I'd bet he's thinking of some intriguing positions he might want you in.

I scoffed. *I can't believe he wants the same thing from me that he wants from other women.*

Why not?

He has to know by now that I'm not interested. I couldn't have been more blunt about that.

True, but some men don't take the hint.

Tired of Saraknyal's insinuations, I finished my tea, pulled out paper and pencil, and began listing items of interest in the sitting room.

I worked my way through the entire keep. Jhavika didn't have many antiques, but did have some beautiful art, rugs, and sculptures. I put aside a few pieces that I liked and left the rest for Nahli to look over. What she didn't want, we'd sell and split the proceeds. I'd be damned if I let Malchi have a penny of it. I spent a few blissful hours in Jhavika's library, and another hour in her office, snooping more deeply than I had before. I didn't find anything of much use beyond what I'd discovered previously. All in all, it was a good haul. I took as much as would easily fit in two wagons, and conscribed half a dozen shades to load it.

Maybe you should ask Nahli about that potion, Saraknyal suggested as we rode back toward Ash Keep. The carriage rumbled along slowly ahead of the full wagons, six additional shades riding along as guards. The force guarding Jhavika's keep was larger than necessary.

"Maybe. Fae certainly are all about positive energy. Or do you think I could ask Tori to lend me his alchemist without telling him why?"

No! The man's a letch, but he's not stupid. You're not going to change your mind about accepting his invitation to dinner, are you?

"Hell, no."

Good. At least you're being careful.

"I'm always careful."

Tell me that the next time you leap down into a pit full of Void essence.

I couldn't suppress a smile. "Is that what's gotten into you, my reckless abandon for my own safety?"

Nothing's gotten into me. I'm just reminding you what happens when you have these sudden impulses of altruism. This one turned out okay, but that isn't always the case.

"I wasn't being altruistic. I was trying to keep Haven from being consumed by Void essence, you and me included."

We could have sailed away, you know.

"And gone where?"

Valaka comes to mind. A nice quiet castle on the shore with a view of the Serpent's Eye...maybe a visit by a dragon occasionally...

I snorted a laugh. "You're delusional, old man."

Says the woman who leapt down into a pit of Void essence.

The next day, Malchi, Ingrid Brickhammer, Que-Chen, Mah Hatsu, and Nahli arrived at Jhavika's keep to interview her people. Vinchi claimed he was busy, and Tori Blackbriar sent a note that he wouldn't be attending. His absence made me wonder if my refusing his invitation might have offended him. If so, it seemed I'd finally found a way to discourage his interest.

Every member of Jhavika's household, as well the twelve prisoners I'd freed from her dungeon, awaited us in the banquet hall. There were fifty-eight in all: cooks, gardeners, concubines, maids, footmen, a masseuse, scullery boys, a wine steward, a physician, and an armorer, in addition to the alchemist and sage with whom I'd already spoken. They all looked to be in good health and well-fed. One by one, they approached and stated their names and positions, which Malchi's scribe jotted down. Nahli placed a gentle hand on each person's shoulder, then nodded or shook her head to indicate whether she detected Jhavika's enchantment on them. The enchanted group comprised all of the staff, and questioning them proved as productive as interrogating a brick wall. None would admit that they were under any magical control or that Jhavika's scourge was the source of that control. The former prisoners, all unenchanted, were more forthcoming, but that amounted to little of consequence.

"And why did Jhavika go tearing off after Captain Longbright?" Malchi asked, clearly frustrated at the silence and blank looks.

Lewin seemed to have been elected their unofficial spokesman, and all eyes turned toward him. "We cannot surmise, though he did cut off her *hand*. Revenge seems a likely motive."

"This ain't gonna get us far," Ingrid grumbled. "I say we cut the prisoners loose and keep the rest here until the bitch is dead."

Most of the retainers looked stricken by that, and several were near tears.

Do you think the scourge's enchantment compels that much devotion? I wondered to Saraknyal.

They believe whatever she told them to believe. If she told them they loved her, they do.

That's disgusting.

And you claim that taking human souls is repugnant. At least I don't twist their minds to my will.

Because they have precious little mind left when you're done with them.

Aloud, I agreed with Ingrid, then added, "I'm going to consult with a few of the specialists for my own purposes."

"I don't see why you—" Malchi's protest faltered as a shade entered the room.

I recognized it as one assigned to the front gate. "Message, mistress." He held out a note wrapped in ribbon.

I spotted the Blackbriar crest impressed on the wax seal and cringed.

Probably a love sonnet, Saraknyal teased.

I opened it and knew instantly it wasn't anything of the kind.

"Tori says a ship's approaching the harbor." I looked up to the other council members. "One of Que-Chen's fleet that Jhavika commandeered. *Tiger Lily*. That was the ship she took herself!"

"She's back!" Ingrid growled, lurching up from her seat.

Malchi glared at me. "Why didn't we get warning from your smuggler?"

"I don't know. The ocean's a big place. Maybe they missed them."

Or they enslaved your people, interrogated them, and sank your ship, Saraknyal suggested.

That grim possibility gripped my gut in a vice. "Or Jhavika took them. If she did, and she has that blasted scourge, she knows everything we've been doing."

Ingrid swore, but Nahli shook her head. "Even so, we have her vastly outnumbered. She could have perhaps two hundred soldiers at most on that ship."

"Two hundred soldiers enchanted to fight to the death is no small force. We need to meet her with a united front!" Ingrid looked to Que-Chen. "The ship *technically* belongs to you, Que-Chen, so you need to be the voice of any action we take. Reginald, take him and as many soldiers as you can spare to the waterfront. I'll marshal my people at the shore batteries, though only one's workin' at the moment. I'll meet you at the quay!" She stalked out.

Nahli followed, promising to bring what allies she could.

"Hashi!" Malchi shot me a look as he headed for the door. "We'll need you there, too! And your…minions, of course."

*Oh, so *now* he wants your much maligned army of undead to protect him!*

"I'll be there." I turned to the shade. "You stay here. If anything untoward occurs, send word to me at the waterfront."

"Yes, mistress."

I strode out of the hall, considering strategies as I went. *If she's recovered her scourge, we're in trouble.*

*If she has, there's nothing to do but kill her. *Don't* let her lash you with it!*

On that, at least, we agree!

I ordered thirty shades to follow, boarded my carriage, and told Bromish to head for the waterfront at a pace they could match. The trip took longer than I wanted, the last few blocks clogged by onlookers who refused to get out of our way.

I leaned out the coach window. "Shades to the front! Move that crowd aside! Don't kill anyone!"

Spoilsport, Saraknyal sniped.

Finally we rolled onto the quay. I clambered out of the carriage and up to the driver's seat to survey the area. Nearby, Tori Blackbriar sat astride an impressive charger, surrounded by a score of mounted lancers and archers. To one side stood a motley force of fae, though I didn't spot Nahli among them. Farther to my right, I spotted Malchi's carriage surrounded by liveried soldiers, but I didn't see him. Ingrid was also nowhere in sight, though there were dwarves on the promontory manning the siege engines. Out on the harbor, several ships maneuvered—Malchi's armed merchantmen along with a few others mustered into action. And there, rounding the headland, sailed *Tiger Lily*.

"Tori!" I shouted as I leapt down. "What the hell's going—"

A resounding crack interrupted me as one of the shore catapults fired.

"Son of a..." I watched the granite ball arc high. "If they sink that ship..."

It would solve our problem quickly, wouldn't it? Saraknyal finished for me.

"Warning shot!" Tori shouted, and sure enough, the projectile splashed into the bay a ship's length ahead of *Tiger Lily*'s bowsprit. Tori kicked his mount nearer and vaulted from the saddle, his usual jaunty countenance intact. "Lady Severn! Well met!"

I guess he's recovered from you snubbing his invitation.

I approached him with my force of shades at my heels. Several horses in Blackbriar's contingent snorted and pawed nervously, shying away.

Tori handed his reins to another rider and stepped to the fore, sweeping a graceful bow, his crimson cape flowing in an arc. He wore a shirt of light mail under a blazing red tunic, snug breeches, and high boots. Of course, the elf blade rode at his hip. His soldiers were no less resplendent, clad in gleaming armor with Tori's coat of arms—a stylized tree capped with an arc of stars—emblazoned upon their gleaming breastplates.

"You seem to have already arranged a greeting for Jhavika," I said.

He has a coat of arms, Saraknyal commented. *We need a coat of arms.*

We have one, I countered. *I'm wearing it.* My shirt of midnight black silk, utterly featureless, was as deep and dark as death itself.

But you're... Oh, right. Well played.

"I was waiting for *you*, actually." Tori waved a hand toward *Tiger Lily*. "We received word from our lookout on the promontory that the ship appears to be lightly manned, which seems bizarre in the extreme. They're flying Jhavika's pennant, but she hasn't been seen on deck, and there are few soldiers."

"Or they're hiding below, waiting for us to do something stupid," I countered.

Well, since that's your specialty...

Smart ass, I growled inwardly.

Tori nodded. "Quite possible. The shore battery's poised to sink her, but so far they've shown no signs of hostility. That could be exactly the reason they're playing a ruse. Reginald and young Que-Chen are aboard one of the armed merchantmen. You and I are to join them in order to...negotiate *Tiger Lily's* surrender."

I narrowed my eyes at him. "You only want me along in case the ship's hold is full of soldiers."

"Well, yes, and to bring your own..." He waved a hand at my escort. "...minions along to deal with Jhavika. I doubt that her scourge would have much effect on a shade."

And how the hell does he know that?

"So, you're well versed in necromancy, Lord Blackbriar?"

"Not in the slightest." He shrugged. "By all means, give me your professional opinion. Do *you* think that Jhavika's scourge could ensorcel a shade?"

"No, but there's always a *chance*," I argued. "If it comes down to a fight with her, I suggest we simply shoot her full of arrows from a distance. We can't give her an opportunity to use that scourge on any of us."

Especially you, my dear. If Jhavika enslaves you, she controls your forces.

Right. The thought of that possibility made my skin crawl.

"A good suggestion. Nahli said she'd keep an eye on the ship from above and warn us if she spots anything untoward." He grinned and waved a hand to two waiting launches. "Shall we? I'm simply *dying* to find out what's afoot."

So am I. But since I'm already dead...

Ignoring Saraknyal's weak attempt at humor, I squinted at *Tiger Lily*, now turning into the wind with all her sails flapping. Sailors—too few of them, it seemed—fought to control the canvas as the anchor suddenly plunged into the bay. Soldiers aboard Malchi's ships began boarding launches.

"Let's go or we'll be late to the party."

"Excellent!" Tori boarded one launch with six of his lightly armored archers.

I split my force of shades, ordering half to guard Bromish and my carriage while the rest accompanied me aboard the second launch. It was crowded, and the sailors bent their oars with nervous glances at my minions.

"Don't worry," I told the rowers with a grim smile. "They only eat what I tell them to eat."

They muttered oaths, but kept rowing.

I looked to Tori, standing at the prow of his launch like some kind of nautical figurehead. I cupped my hands and called to him, "Why would only one of her ships come back?"

"I haven't the foggiest notion, but I'm sure we'll find out soon enough." Blackbriar cocked an eyebrow at me. "I must say, I'm sorry you couldn't attend my dinner party last night. Rest assured, I *regaled* my guests with tales of your heroism in the Tinworthy mines."

I stared at him coldly. "You *didn't!*"

"Oh, I did!" He laughed, his insufferable grin in place. "Several of the young ladies fairly swooned! A shame you weren't there. You could have had your pick!"

"Lord Blackbriar, I—" But he just waved me off and pointed to the other launches taking up position just out of bowshot of *Tiger Lily. Gods, he's an infuriating ass!*

I'm relieved to hear you say so, Saraknyal said.

As we approached the other launches holding station a safe distance from *Tiger Lily*, a young man's voice reached us over the swish of the oars. Que-Chen shouted into a speaking trumpet, but it didn't look like anyone aboard *Tiger Lily* was heeding his words.

"I am heir to House Chen of Haven, and that ship is *my* property!" Que-Chen howled, red-faced in impotent anger. "You will disembark and stand down to be interrogated by the Council, or we will board and cut you down!" He drew the katana at his waist and brandished it.

A memory of his father similarly armed and defiant struck me. I doubted Que-Chen would wade into battle, but he certainly put on a brave front. I shook my head and concentrated on the situation.

"Stand off!" a man called back. "We have orders from Lady Keshmir to take our prisoners to her keep! Stand in our way, and we'll shoot you down!"

"How go the negotiations, Lord Malchi?" Tori called out.

"Poorly," he replied. "They say Jhavika's not aboard, and they refuse to stand down."

I squinted into the blinding reflection of the sun on the water and used Soul Drinker to sharpen my view. The man aboard *Tiger Lily* looked like a soldier, not a sailor. He held a heavy crossbow braced on the railing, pointed at Que-Chen.

Look up.

A great white eagle flew high above the ship. *Nahli. I wish I could see with her eyes right now.*

So do I.

"I demand you stand down this instant! You have no authority here! We represent the Haven Council of Lords!" Que-Chen looked about ready to burst a blood vessel.

"We answer only to Lady Keshmir! Stand off!"

"I don't think he's going to be persuaded with diplomacy, Lord Que-Chen." Tori looked sidelong at me. "Any ideas?"

I stood, bracing myself with one hand on a shade so I wouldn't fall over the side. I'd be less intimidating soaking wet. "Jhavika Keshmir is no longer a member of the Council of Lords! Her keep has been seized and her forces defeated! She has no lands, no retainers, and no home here!" I laughed terror. Several of my rowers blanched and scrabbled away from me. I called out to the ship, "Give yourselves up or perish!"

Any bets which they'll choose?

They have no choice if they're enchanted, I thought. *I wish I knew how many*—

The high-pitched screech of an eagle sounded overhead, Nahli sounding the alarm. Before I could look up, a number of sailors leapt over *Tiger Lily*'s rail into the bay. Others struggled with the soldiers aboard.

As the sailors hit the water, the soldier who had called out earlier bellowed, "Shoot them!"

"Shit!" I swore, wondering if my fear spell had instigated this catastrophe.

As the sailors in the water thrashed toward the launches, soldiers rushed to *Tiger Lily*'s rail, leveled their weapons, and fired. Screams tore through the air, both from the water and the ship's deck.

Tori called out an order, and his archers stood and drew their longbows. Arrows flew, and soldiers screamed, a couple dropping their crossbows into the sea. The rest ducked back for cover. The men in the water swam clumsily, and one body floated face down, a bolt fixed in its torso.

"Oh, *hell*! Rowers, to the ship as fast as you can. My shades will shield you!" The sailors hesitated, but my shades didn't, each one taking up a stance between a rower and the ship. "Row, damn you, or I swear I'll take your souls!"

They rowed with a will.

Tori shouted again, this time to urge his own rowers forward.

I glanced at him. He still stood at the prow of his launch, now with the elf blade drawn, that insufferable grin intact. He looked like he was having the time of his life. "Tori! See to the sailors! I'll secure the ship!"

He saluted me with his sword and barked orders, pointing to the nearest sailor in the water.

You will? Saraknyal sounded skeptical. *Hashi, they could be lying. Jhavika could be hiding below with hundreds of soldiers!*

Well, if she is, this will be very interesting, won't it? I bared my teeth and scrambled to the bow of our launch.

You're crazy! Saraknyal swore. *What is it with you and taking unnecessary risks lately?*

Unnecessary? I grimaced as the soldiers aboard *Tiger Lily* stood to level their crossbows at the swimming sailors once more. *On that, we'll just have to disagree.* I laughed terror again, and may have foiled their aim a bit, for none of the shots struck true.

Tori's archers felled two more of Jhavika's soldiers, though how they fired accurately while standing in a pitching launch, I'll never know.

We rowed past the panicked sailors, some of them trailing blood in the water. The surviving soldiers aboard *Tiger Lily* rose again from cover to level their weapons, but this time they aimed at me.

Incoming!

"Protect the rowers!" I ordered my shades as the volley sang through the air at us. Two hit me and puffed into dust. Several others plunged into my shades, which didn't even flinch. Not one hit a rower. "Faster! Steer for that low part in the middle!"

"Mid-deck boarding hatch, lads!" The young woman at the tiller barked, hunkering low. "Pull like you *mean* it!"

They pulled, and white water curled from the bow of the launch. We passed the man who'd been shot in the back, floating face down. He wasn't moving.

So, what's the plan if Jhavika is aboard? Saraknyal asked, his tone curiously tense.

Haven't figured that out yet. I wondered at his trepidation. Every other time I'd faced armed soldiers, he'd egged me on, urging me to harvest their souls. *Murder, mayhem, hordes of new undead... You know, the usual.*

And if she lashes you with that scourge of hers?

I'd given this careful consideration; there was only one option. *In that instance, I want you to consume my soul completely, Saraknyal.*

Silence...if you didn't count the grunts of sailors, the hiss of water on the hull, and the zing of another flight of crossbow bolts.

Then, *I...don't know if I can do that, Hashi.*

What? The ship loomed ahead; there was no turning back now. *We've discussed this! I'm giving you consent!*

Just don't let it come to that, please! I've...bonded with you, Hashi. You know that! I...don't want to do that to you.

Either that or I writhe in agony for eternity, old man. I checked Soul Drinker, strapped as usual to my forearm, and tensed as the bow of the launch closed on the side of the ship. Crossbowmen leaned over the rail to aim down at us. They had too much cover for my winter spell to work well, and I didn't want to laugh and terrify my own rowers. *Careful, Hashi...*

They fired, and one of the rowers screamed in pain.

Promise me, Hashi! Don't let it come to that.

Shut up and get hungry, old man! The moment before the bow of the launch struck the side of the ship, I leapt.

It wasn't much of a leap, and my chest slammed into the hull hard enough to crush my breasts and knock the air from my lungs. Luckily, my fingers latched on to the railing.

Gods, that hurt! I thought as I clambered up into a throng of soldiers. Steel sang, but dissolved into rust at the touch of my flesh. I rolled and came up with Soul Drinker in hand. *How many soldiers?*

Eight of them up! Four down with arrow wounds! Strike now, while they're off balance.

I slashed a pair of legs, and soul essence coursed through my veins. A peal of laughter sent the soldiers staggering back. My shades scrabbled over the railing behind me, dark and feral.

A solder screamed and lunged at me, empty hands outstretched for my throat. I swept Soul Drinker through his arms, but he crashed into me hard enough to knock me flat, blood pulsing from his stumps even as his soul fed Saraknyal. I lurched up, spitting blood and wiping gore from my eyes. Two more were down, shades tearing at their throats with jagged teeth.

"Restrain them!" I commanded the rest of my forces.

Why, Hashi? They'll tear themselves to pieces trying to escape.

But if Jhavika's aboard and we manage to kill her, they'll be free.

That's incredibly optimistic, don't you think?

Indulge me, please.

My shades mobbed the four remaining soldiers, who thrashed and screamed, but couldn't break the iron grips of my minions.

I scanned the deck, but no other soldiers threatened. Several sailors lay dead, the source of the other screams I'd heard, I assumed. The main cargo hatch was closed, as were the doors forward and aft. I felt as if I'd stepped aboard a ghost ship. I took a second to check the sailors who'd risked their lives getting me here; only one of my rowers had a crossbow wound. The others maneuvered away from the boarding hatch to make room for the next launch. I strode to the main hatch cover and placed Soul Drinker against it. *What's below?*

Nothing in the main hold, but I hear something. Metal clanking around.

Metal?

Wings beat the air behind me, and I whirled to find Nahli Twince transforming from an eagle into herself, white gown rippling in the breeze. "Well done, Hashi. You saved many lives." She turned toward the restrained soldiers. "I have something that will help calm them, if you'll allow me." She produced a vial from her gown and raised it to show me.

"Why ask me?" I ordered my shades to help. "I'm not in charge of them."

"Thank you." With my shades forcing their clenched teeth open, Nahli tilted the crystal vial into each soldier's mouth, and they went instantly limp. "That should hold them for a time."

"Good." I ordered my shades to release them and stand ready. "The hold's empty. I'm going to—"

"Permission to come aboard?" Tori Blackbriar sprang through the boarding hatch with catlike grace. "Are you all right, Hashi?"

"I'm fine."

Several sailors and Tori's archers boarded behind him. The sailors lowered a boarding ladder, and some of Malchi's soldiers climbed up. Lastly, Malchi and Que-Chen stepped through the hatch.

"The main hold's empty, but I haven't searched the ship yet. We should be careful. There may be others still hiding."

"Agreed." Tori drew his blade, and his soldiers formed up with him. "We can't let you have *all* the fun, can we? I'll check aft, while you—"

"There are people below." Nahli stood with one hand on the main hatch cover, her brow furrowed. "They're in chains."

285

Her hearing's evidently better than mine, Saraknyal grumbled. *Or she's using magic.*

"One of the soldiers did mention prisoners," Malchi said.

"If there are prisoners, there may be guards." I turned back to the main hatch and Nahli stepped aside. "This could still be a trap. Let me have a look before we go off in three different directions, please!"

"Point taken." Tori stopped at the door to the sterncastle and gave me a nod.

The huge main hatch cover had a smaller man-sized hatch secured by a hasp with a wooden peg thrust through the hoop. I knocked the peg free and lifted the door to peer inside. Even with Saraknyal's keen sight, the contrast of daylight to darkness didn't let me discern much.

"Light!" called someone from below, their voice raspy and desperate. "Help us!"

Trap? Saraknyal suggested.

I don't think so. I didn't know why I thought that, maybe something in the voice. I still couldn't see. "Shades, lift the hatch cover off and move it aside."

"Yes, mistress." They stepped up, three on each side, and lifted the heavy hatch cover, then shuffled aside and dropped it onto the deck.

I leaned in, shading my eyes. The hold was empty save for a few crates fore and aft. In the center was a thick wooden grating that apparently could be lifted for access to the lower hold. Through the grating, I caught sight of movement, figures seated in the dark. Chains clattered as they shifted. "Prisoners. Quite a few of them."

I climbed over the hatch coaming and descended into the hold. Making my way to the grating, I lifted a section and peered down.

Grimy faces looked up at me, chains on their ankles clinking as they stirred. "Help us!"

"Anyone else down there?"

"The captain's chained below. Dunno if he's alive or not."

Still, suspicion plagued me. Could this really be a trap? If so, it was an elaborate one. I squinted up toward the hatch coaming.

"Nahli? I need you to tell me if these prisoners are under Jhavika's spell."

"A wise precaution." She swung over the coaming and dropped like a bit of down to the deck beside me, landing without a sound. A sphere of light blossomed in her palm, and she dropped it through the open grating. It floated down to illuminate the lower hold. The chained captives shielded their eyes, some muttering oaths. "Do you wish to go first?"

"*Wish* to?" I wrinkled my nose at the stench wafting up from below. "Not really, but I will."

*You're *so* brave...or just foolish.*

Shut up and keep watch. Warn me if you spot anything wrong. I descended one-handed, Soul Drinker ready in the other if this turned out to be a ruse.

*This whole *ship* is wrong. Why were there so few sailors? Why would Jhavika waste a whole ship just to send back some grimy prisoners?*

I don't know. Maybe we'll ask them. My feet touched the deck, and I looked around. At least two dozen people were chained down here. The stench wafted from a few buckets they'd been using as chamber pots. Some of the filth had spilled.

"They're ill," Nahli said from beside me. I hadn't heard her descend. "And some are injured."

I spotted the blood, filthy bandages, and the sheen of fever sweat on several faces. "Check them for enchantment, would you? They say the captain's below. I'll see."

"Of course."

As Nahli moved among the prisoners, touching each lightly, I called up to the others. "Only prisoners down here. No guards. Go ahead and search the rest of the ship!"

"Very good!" Tori waved and vanished.

I looked around for a way down.

"Hatch's over there." One filthy young woman pointed forward. "To port of the door there."

"Thank you." I wove my way through the prisoners. Thankfully none of them even tried to touch me; my nerves were still as tight as bow strings. Like Saraknyal had said, this just seemed so *wrong*. I found the hatch and lifted it up to peer down. The deck below was barely visible, and the reek wafting up made where I stood seem fresh in comparison. *Can you see down there, old man?*

Barely. One man in chains. Rats, too, and roaches.

I shivered at the thought of roaches. *Alive?* I asked him.

Well, the vermin are, but I can't tell about the man from here. He's not moving.

"Nahli?" I turned to find her squatting beside a prisoner, her hand on the man's abdomen. "There's one more below. He looks worse off than these."

"None of these people are enchanted." She stood, her fathomless eyes luminous in the glow of her light. "Some are very ill with wound poisoning. They've been in a battle, it seems."

"Bloody *right* we were," one of them grumbled. "That bitch, Keshmir, took our ship!"

I felt as if a cold hand had touched the back of my neck. "The *Scourge*? Are you Longbright's crew? Is he—"

"No, we ain't Longbright's," he said. "*Crimson Hawk* was our ship, and that's Captain Patak below, if he's still breathin'."

"We should release them," Nahli said.

"Let's see if the captain's alive first." I turned back to the hatch and descended, cringing when something skittered by my foot. *Keep the vermin off me, please, Saraknyal.*

Absolutely. A chill coursed through me, and the skittering mass fled.

Another light blossomed behind me as Nahli descended the ladder, gleaming off the eyes of rodents cowering in the shadows. I tried to stand straight, but my head bumped a timber. I looked around the fetid space. A few barrels were secured along the hull sides, and the prisoner lay chained to a support in the middle. His clothes were tattered, his flesh pocked with livid rat bites. His chest moved slightly with scant breathing.

"He's alive. Check him for enchantment, please."

Nahli hurried past and touched the man briefly. "He's in no condition to put up any kind of a fight, even if he *were* enchanted. Which he's not."

"En...chanted?" the man muttered, his filthy head turning slightly. "Who..."

"Never mind, captain." I reached down and touched the chains. *Dust to dust.* The heavy iron crumbled to rust, and he stirred weakly. "Don't worry. We're here to help."

The man lifted his head. Sweat sheened his flesh, his hair a wild mess, and his beard matted with blood. His legs were bound with grimy bandages.

Nahli put a hand on his forehead. "He's burning with fever."

I can purge that.

You can? I knew Saraknyal could kill infections in me, but not others. *You never told me you could do that.*

You never asked. Besides, we need him alive if we're going to get any information.

We certainly do. I knelt next to Patak. "I'm not going to hurt you. I can purge fever and wound poisoning. Will you let me do that?" He didn't look like he had the strength to resist, but some people distrusted magic, and alienating a potential ally wouldn't do.

"Who the...hell are you?" the captain grumbled.

"Hashi Severn. I'm a member of Haven's Council of Lords, as is Lady Nahli Twince here. One of your crew said that Jhavika Keshmir stole your ship. If you count Jhavika as an enemy, then we're on the same side. We need to hear your story, and you're deathly ill. So, will you allow me to purge your fever?"

"I..." He seemed about to protest, then shook his head wearily. "Go ahead."

I put a hand on his filthy head and thought, *Purge.* Energy coursed from Soul Drinker, through me, and into Patak. Saraknyal's death magic annihilated the infection and expunged the poisons from the captain's blood.

"Odea's sweet tits!" Patak gasped and coughed up a nasty gob of phlegm, his eyes wide. "Feels like you just wrung me out like a dirty swab!" Then, as if the shock of the purge was too much for his weakened body to handle, the captain's head fell back to the deck with a crack that made me cringe.

That's not a bad analogy, actually.

Nahli stooped over the barely conscious man. "We'll need help getting him out."

"Agreed."

Nahli led the way up one level, and I followed. I destroyed the chains restraining the rest of the crew, and purged those who were fevered. Several of the healthiest fetched Patak and heled him up the ladders. Back on deck, we found the other council members questioning a young officer dripping sea water. Several more soggy sailors stood with him.

"Who's this?" I asked.

"A fuckin' *dead* man, is who he is!" Patak staggered forward with balled fists, though he probably would have fallen if his mates hadn't held him up. The rest of the pirates—ill-treated but still strong—bristled aggressively behind their captain.

"Shades! Stop him, but don't hurt him!"

My shades—some still with crossbow bolts sticking out of them—interposed themselves between Patak and the officer.

The big man froze. "What the... What are *those* things?"

"They're shades. *My* shades, Captain. Now calm down. We have questions."

"Yes, we do, but first," Malchi waved a hand toward the young officer, "this is acting Captain Niland, commander of *Tiger Lily* by Jhavika's orders. And who is this?"

"Captain Patak, formerly of *Crimson Hawk*," Nahli said.

"Aye, Patak I am, and that whelp's gonna answer for keepin' me and my crew chained down with the rats!"

"I *had* to!" Niland protested, recoiling from Patak. "Jhavika commanded her solders to kill us if we didn't follow her orders to the letter!"

"Please, everyone just calm down." Tori stepped into the fray, hands raised. "What's important right now is to know when we might expect Jhavika to return. Captain Niland, was she following you back?"

"Before we begin, let me ensure that Captain Niland and his sailors are not under Jhavika's enchantment." Nahli stepped forward. "I've already confirmed that Captain Patak and his people aren't."

Patak turned to me as Nahli went from sailor to sailor, touching each lightly on the shoulder. "What enchantment?"

"Jhavika's. She had an enchanted scourge that she used to control people." I pointed to the soldiers lying on the deck, still comatose from Nahli's potion. "Like those."

"Bloody magic!" He spat.

Don't tell him you're a necromancer.

You don't think he's figured that one out?

"They're free from enchantment," Nahli pronounced.

"Good! Now, Captain Niland, what were your orders?" Malchi asked.

"Return to Haven with the prisoners," Niland cast an anxious glance toward the pirates, "and await her here. She intended to continue the search for Longbright aboard *Crimson Hawk*."

"Do you know where she went?"

"South of Twin Capes is all I know. She set up a relay of cutters to maintain communications among her ships, but no one had reported sighting Longbright yet."

"Still, it's only a matter of time until she returns," I said. "Can you give us any idea how much time we have?"

Niland and Patak involuntarily glanced at one another. Niland spoke first. "She's obsessed with Longbright. I'd say she won't return until she finds him."

"But *Scourge* won't be easy to track down," Patak put in. "Kevril's wily, a better seaman than Keshmir, and knows the Blood Sea like the back of his hand. Jhavika hasn't been to sea for years. If it's a game of cat and mouse, my odds are on him."

Tori looked thoughtful. "So, we might have time to develop our defensive strategy before Jhavika sails back to Haven. That's encouraging."

"We need to discuss options," Malchi looked over the pirates and wrinkled his nose. "And I daresay Captain Patak and his crew could use some attention before we make any decisions as to how best to employ their expertise."

Maybe ask him to bathe? Or is that not a pirate thing?

I stifled a smile at Saraknyal's comment. "Agreed."

"I'm fine!" Patak insisted, though he wavered on unsteady legs. "Gimmie a tot and a new set of togs, and I'll be right as rain."

"Both you and Captain Niland could use a good night's rest," Malchi insisted. "This isn't an inquisition. You both are our *allies*. I suggest I put up the captains tonight, and we all gather at my estate tomorrow evening for dinner and discussion."

"Another damned *party*?" I glared at Malchi. "*Really?*"

He glared right back at me. "Not a *party*, Hashi, nothing formal, just dinner. There's no reason we can't be *civilized*."

He's a Balshi-wannabe. Always the host so everyone has to kowtow.

And this gives him a full day to interrogate the captains on his own.

Nahli stepped up and smiled, a rare sight. "A kind offer, Lord Malchi, but since you already have one guest," she nodded to Que-Chen, "I propose that *I* host Captain Patak and his crew. I can tend to their injuries, and Captain Niland can accompany you. We can all meet tomorrow night for our discussion."

That's smart, Saraknyal commented. *We don't want all our eggs in Malchi's basket.*

Well done, Nahli, I thought.

Malchi opened his mouth, but Tori beat him to it. "That's a capital idea, Nahli! We can accommodate the rest of the sailors in Temuso's keep, since it's empty. Now that *that's* settled, what say we get off this ship and back onto dry land?"

"I second that!" I agreed. Even at anchor, the rocking of the ship was making me queasy.

"I'll meet you ashore, captain," Nahli said to Patak before clapping her hands over her head and morphing into the now-familiar white eagle.

"Bloody devils take me down," Patak muttered. "Dark sorceresses and now fae princesses! Haven ain't what I *thought* it would be!"

"Tomorrow evening then." As I strode for my launch, shades in tow, I stifled a smile. *Wait until he meets the denizens of Nahli's keep.*

Saraknyal chuckled in agreement. *He's in for one hell of a night!*

Chapter Twenty Four
Choose Your Enemies Wisely

Five years I lived in Ash Keep, expanding my antiquities business, supporting my trusted people, and nurturing my reputation as a dreadful necromancer. I had more than I ever wanted, until finally Saraknyal's dreadful prophecy came true.

Contentment is dangerous.

"We maybe got a problem brewin', mistress." Dondi Ranse, one of my former employees who now ran a small neighborhood racket of his own, had come to Ash Keep wringing his hands.

I sighed internally. "Another gang horning in on your territory?" It had happened before, and still people never learned.

"Not exactly, mistress. It's bigger than that." He wrung his hands again. "There's these...people, powerful people, and they've...banded together. They call themselves a Council. A Council of Lords."

Lords? Saraknyal sounded genuinely concerned. *That's bad, Hashi.*

I felt a chill up my spine. Lords meant an organized hierarchy. Something Haven had never had. "A *what?*"

Dondi cringed at my tone. "A Council. They're carvin' up the city into their own fiefdoms, pressuring smaller bosses to pay for protection from council members." He made a face. "It's a racket, and they've got the power to make it work."

"*Lords?* Seriously?"

He shrugged and frowned. "Fancy themselves royalty, I guess."

I matched Dondi's frown. "Sounds suspiciously like a fledgling form of *government.*" *And the first thing governments do is outlaw necromancy.*

We need to find out who these people are, Saraknyal suggested.

Why? So we can murder them?

Know your enemy.

I pushed a small pouch of money across my desk. "Thanks for the warning, Dondi."

He bobbed his head and pocketed the pouch. "I'll let you know if I hear any more."

Less than an hour later, I walked into *Priceless Treasures*. Bryce had expanded markedly, two floors now, with a pair of bruisers for security. They nodded to me without a word. I left my undead escort outside.

"Hoi, Miss Hashi!" Bryce smiled at me as he rounded a display. "Just shoppin' or is there somethin' specific you need?"

"I need some information." I heard a baby cry from the back of the shop, and Bryce's grin broadened. "And congratulations on fatherhood." I'd known his wife was expecting, but not that she'd delivered.

"Oh, my Tessa did all the work. Well...*most* of it anyways." He grinned until I thought his face might split. "Twins, you know! Boy and a girl!"

"Wonderful." I smiled at his obvious glee, but couldn't imagine living with that noise.

What's so wonderful about a couple of squalling babies? All they do for the first five years is eat, shit, and scream.

It's called procreation, Saraknyal. Everybody does it, or the race ceases to exist.

You don't.

No, I don't. Now be quiet and let me talk. I told Bryce what Dondi had told me. "What have you heard? Do you know who they are?"

"Just more successful criminals than the rest of us is what I hear," he replied. "You already know a couple of 'em. That dwarf woman who contracts out stonework. Another you bought your keep from, the head of the gnome clan that owns the mines. There's more. I'll get their names for you. Easy as pie."

"Be *careful*, Bryce. The last thing I want is their attention."

"Gotcha." He winked and nodded. "Discreet as a church mouse, me."

Are there any churches in Haven?

I ignored Saraknyal and thanked Bryce on my way out of the shop.

Two days later I had my list. There were seven in all. Several of them would be considered crime lords in any other city; in Haven, they were just successful business people. A woman named Ting Hatsu—exiled royalty from Toki—was a slaver, and never stepped out of her keep without her two komei bodyguards. Yirish Balshi, an older man originally from Tsing, now lived in the palace near the falls, immensely rich with his fingers in many illicit pies. A brash young man named Reginald Malchi specialized in trafficking controlled substances to Chen and Toki. Lo-Chen, a shipping magnate, had made a fortune transporting goods into and out of Haven. Two others—Blinth Tinworthy and Ingrid Brickhammer—I already knew controlled essential goods and services. Then there was Nahli Twince, a fae from the Jungles of Nin. I guessed they'd included her simply because it doesn't pay to piss off anyone who can wield that kind of magic.

The only ones who would give you trouble in a fight are Hatsu and Twince, Saraknyal surmised. *Komei use enchanted blades, and fae wield all sorts of magic. And what the hell's a fae doing in Haven?*

"Toki invaded the Jungles of Nin about twenty years ago."

So, Twince fled the war?

"I don't know about her specifically, but many fae fled rather than be captured."

Sounds familiar, he muttered.

"Unless they ban necromancy, I don't see that this Council's going to amount to much of an issue for us."

That's a big 'unless,' my dear.

"We've worked hard to build a reputation not to be fucked with. They should leave us alone out of simple self-preservation, if nothing else."

You hope.

A couple of months later, my hopes were shattered as my peaceful little world erupted in violence.

I was in my workshop, cleaning corrosion from a Valakan sculpture, when a resounding knock rattled the door.

"Yes?" I straightened and cracked my back.

Joss, my new butler, peered in. I hadn't really wanted a butler, but Joss had shown up at my gate one day, an escaped eunuch slave, crawling on bloody hands and knees, begging for sanctuary. Saraknyal chided me for taking him in, but I knew he'd never last the night on the streets of Haven. So far, he'd worked out well. "Mistress, there are some people here. They're injured, burned. They say they're Dunbar Flinn's crew. There's been...an incident."

"An incident?"

If Dunbar's not here himself, this is serious.

I dropped my tools. "Take me to them."

I followed Joss downstairs to the entry hall where a man stood shaking as two of my people tended his injuries. His shirt was off, and one arm and shoulder were blistered, his face covered in soot. Three others sat on the floor near the door, sooty and bloodied, breathing hard. They saw me and lurched to their feet, saluting in the nautical fashion.

"M-mistress Severn!" the injured man stuttered.

"What happened?"

"*Golden Gal* was attacked, mistress." He winced as the maid sponged soot from a burn. "Early this mornin' afore daylight. Thirty or so in two launches. Captain Flinn was killed, along with the rest. They looted and burned the ship."

I gripped Soul Drinker hard. "Who?"

"Dunno, but the bastard in charge had a crest on his tunic. A sword through a crown."

"Sword through a crown..." I knew that crest; it was hard not to have seen it all over Haven. "Balshi!"

*Why would *he* attack one of your ships?* Saraknyal wondered.

I don't know. But I'm going to find out. "Is Glosh in port?" I asked the sailor.

"No, ma'am. Hyko."

"Damn." I told my people to care for their injuries and assign them space, and resolved to check with Bryce.

I gathered up one shade and my Jaguar Warrior wraith, and took the most direct route to Bryce's shop. I walked with one hand on

Soul Drinker and a look on my face that sent people scurrying from my path.

When I descended from roof-level to Bryce's shop, however, I found the shop door stoved in.

"Shit!" I drew Soul Drinker and edged into the trashed shop. A man lay dead just inside the door, one of Bryce's guards. The other sprawled halfway to the main counter, an arrow fixed between his shoulder blades. Black and long, the arrow's notch was ivory banded with brass, the fletching white.

That's a komei arrow, Hashi, Saraknyal said nervously.

I froze, and a name sprang to mind. *Hatsu?*

One might be a fluke, but two is a conspiracy. Why would the Council want to screw with you?

I ignored him. "Bryce?" I called.

A baby cried a shrill note from the back of the shop.

"Tessa?" No answer, but the baby's cry stilled. I edged forward.

Stationing my shade at the door, I motioned for my wraith to accompany me. As we approached the counter, a door creaked open in the back of the shop. Tessa, Bryce's wife, peered out, her face tear-streaked and flushed.

"Oh, Mistress Severn!" She lowered the dagger in her hand and sniffed. "I thought..."

"Who did this? Are they still here?"

"No, they're gone. They...they beat Bryce something horrible. He's..." She looked over her shoulder into the back of the shop.

"Stay here," I told my wraith. "Nobody comes into the shop."

"Yes, mistress." He turned to face the entry, sword in hand.

"Take me to Bryce, Tessa."

I followed her into the living quarters behind the shop. It was homey, and not trashed like the shop had been. Tessa led me to a bedroom where Bryce lay in a bed, bloody bandages covering both arms, half his face, and one leg below the knee. The leg looked broken.

"Motherless son of a..." I bit off the curse and hurried to the bedside. "Bryce?"

His eye fluttered open. "Mistress Hashi..." He tried to grin, and I saw gaps where teeth had been knocked out.

"Who did this to you, Bryce?"

"Not just me. Dondi Ranse and Mazie Twine are dead." He lisped, either from the broken teeth or the cup of opium-laced wine at his bedside.

"They took out Flinn, *Golden Gal,* and most of her crew, too," I told him. "What the hell's going on?"

"They told me to tell you that I don't work for you anymore, Mistress Hashi. That they'll destroy your businesses, burn your ships, kill anyone who don't...pledge to them." He grimaced in pain and closed his eyes for a moment, then looked at me again. "Said to tell you just get out of Haven, never come back."

Get out of Haven? I looked at Bryce's battered body, recalled the few surviving sailors of *Golden Gal,* loyal Dondi and Mazie. How many more of my people would suffer just because they were associated with me?

Maybe we should *leave Haven.*

And go where? demanded Saraknyal. *We've had this discussion. Anywhere else, you'll be hunted down and burned as a necromancer.*

Get on a ship and just sail out into the Blood Sea? There are lots of islands out there.

And they might hate necromancers as much as anyone else. No, Hashi, you've got to fight this. We've got to fight this! You haven't built a life here just to have some council of lowlifes run you off.

Fight the whole Council? Seven of them, each with a keep and an army?

Balshi and Hatsu for a start. You can't show weakness, Hashi.

"Who's behind this?" I asked Bryce. "That Council of Lords?"

"They *said* it was, but that ain't so. Found out yesterday...that the Council wouldn't back a move against you. Three decided to do it on their own. I sent you word, but they got my messenger."

That explains why he was beaten, Saraknyal said.

"*Three?*" I seethed through clenched teeth. "Which three?"

"Lo-Chen, Hatsu, and Balshi. Balshi's the ringleader."

"Balshi..." My teeth chirped like crickets. "The one in the palace..."

"That's him." Bryce sighed and shook his head weakly. "Careful. Piece of work, he is."

"So am I." I turned to Tessa, fishing a heavy pouch from under my cloak. "Here. Pay for a healer and get the shop straightened up. Hire some help. Whatever you need, send word. I'm leaving my wraith here to stand guard. He won't hurt you."

She nodded, obviously scared, but holding up. "Thank you, Mistress Hashi."

"Don't thank me. It's my fault. I didn't think..."

Blaming yourself is pointless, Hashi! Blame the cowards who attacked your people instead of you.

Good point. I strode out of the shop, ordering my shade to follow, rage smoldering in my gut like a dormant volcano.

What are you going to do? Saraknyal asked.

They fucked with the wrong woman, Saraknyal. We're going to fuck back.

About gods-damned time.

But we have to be smart about this. They might try to hit Ash Keep directly if they know I'm not there. I have to keep my people safe.

So, button the place up tight and put your shades on guard.

Yes...that first, old man. Then we go to war.

At Ash Keep, I ordered everything sealed tight, stationed my dozen shades and second wraith on defense; hardly enough to man the walls, but they're hard to kill. I then told my people to prepare for a siege, but that if the walls were breached and my undead defenders destroyed, they were to surrender without a fight.

I ate dinner in my office without much appetite, watching the sun set over the mountains outside the window. When full darkness had settled onto the city, I prepared to go on the offensive. I dressed in all black, buckled a snug, sleeveless leather jerkin over my blousy shirt, and strapped Soul Drinker to my left forearm under the shirt sleeve, the cool obsidian against my flesh. Looking at myself in my mirror, I appeared unarmed. I was ready to go.

I know you don't like to, Hashi, Saraknyal said as I trundled downstairs, *but if you're going to take us into battle, I'll need energy.*

I know. I swept past Joss and out the front door.

"Please be careful, mistress," he said.

"Not today, Joss. Button up tight." I stopped suddenly and turned back. "Joss, if I don't return by morning, or if the shades suddenly go insane and start tearing themselves apart, take everything of value in the keep and get everyone out of here. There should be enough to get you all started somewhere else."

He stared at me blankly. "I...yes, mistress."

"Good man." I strode across the courtyard and out the postern door without looking back.

So, about my energy...

Don't worry, Saraknyal. I'll see you're fed before we get in too deep. That's why we're going to visit Lo-Chen first.

Not Balshi? He's the head of the snake.

He's also got the most resources. That makes him the most likely to have some kind of ugly surprise waiting for me.

Besides Hatsu's komei, you mean.

They're not really a surprise, are they? And that's why she's going to be the last of the three. I pondered a moment. *Will your magic affect the komei?* I asked hopefully.

Fear, probably not, but you could freeze them. Death's chill might hold them, but I wouldn't recommend letting one get that close. Saraknyal fell silent, never a good sign.

My long legs carried me through the dangerous streets of Haven. Lo-Chen's keep was only six blocks from mine, and I made it two blocks before being accosted. A laugh sent several poor wretches skittering into the darkness, but one desperate vagabond was crazy enough to attack me. I had counted on it.

I drew Soul Drinker and slashed the man's arm.

Feed.

The corpse fell in a heap, the wisps of his soul drawn into Soul Drinker like the inhalation of smoke. *Gone... Oblivion...*

He was insane, Hashi. He's better off gone than where his soul would have ended up.

I didn't respond until Lo-Chen's keep hove into sight. *Saraknyal, if this things go wrong tonight, I want you to consume my soul.*

A long moment passed before he replied. *You're sure?*

I'm sure. I'm damned, and oblivion beats the hell out of Hell. I took a deep breath and let it out slowly. *Ready?*

For anything, my dear. And don't worry. You'll survive. You're good at surviving.

Right now, I wish I was better at knife fighting. Despite some training with my Jaguar Warrior wraith, I didn't know if I could hold my own against hardened soldiers. Swallowing my feelings of inadequacy, I hurried across the street, then along the wall of the keep toward the gate. No shouts rang out from above; they either hadn't seen me or didn't think I was a threat.

I found a small postern door of solid oak and iron. *Here we go, Saraknyal. Tell me when you're low on energy. I'd rather not destroy souls unless I have to. The guards will just be following orders.*

I have enough now to make a shade or two, but not to cast the winter spell.

All right. I gripped Soul Drinker and placed my other hand on the door. *Dust to dust.*

The door crumbled to dust. The quiet hiss of destruction drew the attention of the two guards stationed inside. One immediately swung his halberd in a downward chop. The blade disintegrated instead of cleaving my skull.

I slashed the man's wrist with Soul Drinker and thought, *Feed!*

Saraknyal wrenched the soul out of the man's body, and energy thrilled through me. The second guard stumbled back a step and drew breath to scream.

"Look at me!" I hissed before he could speak.

His eyes met mine, and he gasped in terror.

I breathed in his soul—*Shade*—then exhaled it back into the body. "Follow me," I commanded him. "Defend me, and don't eat anything."

Well done, Saraknyal said. *Arrow slits in the wall ahead.*

I see them. The short corridor was a kill chamber, sporting six arrow slits spaced out along the thirty-foot right-hand wall. No shouts rang out as I traversed the length. The door at the other end was a copy of the one I'd just destroyed, and disintegrated just as easily to reveal two more stunned guards. I consumed one and pinned the other with my gaze. Seconds later I had another shade, and still no alarm had been raised. The new corridor turned right. I passed a door that probably opened into a guard house, but I wasn't here to slaughter guards. I was here for Lo-Chen.

"Do you know where Lo-Chen would be at this time of night?" I asked my shades.

"No, mistress," they both answered.

They must know where his chambers are.

But it's early. He might not be there yet.

We've got to start somewhere.

I clenched my jaw on a curse. "Take me to Lo-Chen's chambers."

"Yes, mistress," they answered.

The shades started down the curving corridor, making more noise in their armor than I would have liked. After passing several closed doors to my right, they turned left to a pair of double doors. They opened to the inner courtyard, two hundred feet of open space between us and the entrance into the keep itself. Lamps beside the portal illuminated four guards stationed there. The shades started across the open space, and I followed.

We're in it now, Saraknyal warned.

That we are. We made it almost halfway across before the door guards realized something wasn't right about the trio walking toward them.

One called out, "Stop there!"

We didn't.

"Stop!"

The command rang off the walls, and I saw through Saraknyal more guards on the battlements carrying torches. They were all looking at us. Still, we didn't stop.

The door guards leveled their halberds at us. "Who...*what* the *hell?*"

"Archers! Guards!" another bellowed. The wall guards charged toward the stairs down into the courtyard.

Thirty feet away, I called out, "Stand aside or perish. I'm here for Lo-Chen, not you."

"Stop or we'll fire!"

I glanced back at the guards aiming crossbows, and laughed fear.

Someone bellowed, "Fire!" and crossbows cracked in a ragged and ill-aimed volley. Bolts zipped past, three plunging into the backs of my shades, and one puffing into dust when it touched me. The rest clattered against the walls of the keep, some missing the guards there by mere feet.

The door guards backed up to the portal, halberds braced in trembling hands. Someone behind us bellowed for swords, and I glanced back to find the bowmen had dropped their weapons and were advancing in tight formation with swords and shields.

"Cut them down!" a burly man in the second rank commanded. "Charge!"

The formation charged.

"Kill the door guards," I commanded my shades as I turned to face the onslaught. "I've got this."

*You've got this? *Really?** Saraknyal sounded worried.

Well, we've *got this...*

When the formation was ten feet away, I screamed a blast of icy death in their faces. Four men perished, frozen solid in an instant. As they toppled forward to shatter on the flagstones, those behind stumbled and skidded, but others charged on, screaming in terror or defiance.

"Fools!" I stood my ground as they struck at me. Swords disintegrated. I slashed through one man's shield and the arm strapped behind it. His corpse fell as Saraknyal ripped away his soul. I fixed another with my gaze and turned him into a shade.

"Die, witch!" The commander of the troop lunged at me with a longsword, but the fine steel crumbled. He staggered and stared at me in horror.

"Not witch, *necromancer*." I leveled Soul Drinker at him. Frost had formed on the blade, chilling the air around it into a white fog. "Now stand aside, or I'll—"

He screamed and lunged again, dagger flashing. He was fast and skilled, but the blade vanished when the tip pierced my shirt. Unfortunately, momentum carried his blow into the pit of my stomach. Breath left my lungs in a *whoosh,* and I doubled over.

Hashi! Saraknyal bellowed in my mind.

I couldn't breathe, slashing blindly with Soul Drinker. The obsidian blade cut through the steel greave on the man's thigh, and he fell, his soul consumed. My knees hit the flagstones as I fought for air.

My vision blurred with tears, but I saw everything through Saraknyal. One of my shades was down, cut in half, but still struggled to grapple a panicked guard's legs. The other two flanked me, bloody weapons in hand. The remaining guards backed away, but I could see in their eyes that they'd seen that I wasn't invulnerable. I'd been hurt. More guards descended from the walls.

I finally managed a breath. "Fuck!"

"Mob her!" an officer still on the wall commanded. The soldiers edged forward uncertainly.

You need a meat shield, Hashi, Saraknyal suggested.

Right. I staggered to my feet and said, "Arise!"

All the dead rose. Well, most did; the thawing pieces of those I'd frozen only twitched. Confronted by their dead comrades, the resolve of the advancing soldiers wavered. They backed away, ignoring the hysterical commands of the officer.

"I'm here for Lo-Chen only," I growled through bared teeth. "Back off or perish."

The officer sputtered and spat curses, but his soldiers refused to advance. I whirled and strode for the doors.

Don't forget that dismembered shade, Hashi. Waste not.

Right. I fed him the soul of the bisected shade. The creature stopped twitching, and its black blood turned red. I swallowed the urge to vomit.

One touch reduced the keep's doors to ash and a heap of gold inlay, revealing turmoil within. The fight in the courtyard had alerted everyone to trouble, but hadn't prepared them for what walked through their front door.

As my undead mob tromped into the vast entry hall, a man dressed like a butler screamed and ran up the sweeping staircase. We left bloody footprints across the white marble floor. More guards poured into the room and fired a volley of crossbow bolts into me and my force, which had no effect whatsoever.

I laughed a peal of terror.

Crossbows clattered to the floor, and the guards staggered back. The oil lamps winked out, but the glow crystals in the chandeliers cast eerie shadows across the room. *Nice effect.*

Thank you.

"Where is Lo-Chen?" I growled. "He murdered my people and burned one of my ships! For that, he must answer!"

How melodramatic are you going to get here? Just slaughter them all!

Shut up! We do this my way!

Fine.

The soldiers drew swords, but didn't advance.

A richly dressed young man stepped into view at the top of the stairs, another contingent of soldiers behind him. "The Council of Lords will have your *head* for this, witch!"

I sighed. "I'm *not* a witch; I'm a necromancer! And who the hell are you?"

The young man's eyes widened, but he didn't falter. "I am Fa-Chen, son and heir to Lord Lo-Chen." He drew a katana with a flourish, settling into a practiced, two-handed grip.

Hashi, that's a komei blade. Have a care. I can't protect you from it.

My heart froze. I hadn't expected to face komei until Hatsu's keep. Fortunately, I'd become very good at hiding my fear. I had to think up a strategy quickly.

The young lord didn't give me time. "Kill her!" he screamed, and his troops advanced.

No shortage of idiots, Saraknyal quipped.

No shortage of expendable soldiers.

The thought of these pompous lords spending the lives and souls of their soldiers to preserve their own tender skins enraged me, but life in Haven was cheap.

The guardsmen charged. Swords puffed into dust, and Soul Drinker lashed out. Energy pulsed through me, filling me. Shades and zombies advanced with me, laying waste to the living. Every soldier who fell, I raised. Within the span of a few breaths, I stood at the base of the stairs with a roiling mass of undead at my back. But I still had a komei blade pointed at me.

Girding my nerves, I advanced slowly up the stairs. I looked a fright with my leather jerkin slashed to ribbons, but my flesh untouched, Soul Drinker trailing frost from the blade, and paced by a small army of undead minions.

I stopped well out of reach of the blade, ready to breathe winter if my ploy failed. "Now, Fa-Chen, where...is...your...father?"

"What in the Nine Hells *are* you?" Fa-Chen staggered back.

"What part of *'necromancer'* don't you understand?"

The young lord's face hung like a wet scarecrow in a downpour, the tip of his weapon drooping.

*He didn't *know*,* Saraknyal said in surprise. *His father must have, but...he sent his *son* to fight you.*

My lips pulled back from my teeth in disgust. Another sacrifice for the sake of the so-called nobility. "Listen to me, *Fa*-Chen. The *Council* has nothing to do with this! Lo-Chen and two others ordered my people beaten and murdered, my ship burned, and my businesses destroyed."

I locked my gaze with his, ready to freeze the young man solid if that komei blade moved an inch.

"And your *father* sent you here to stop me. Did he tell you that enchanted blade would keep you *safe*?" A twitch of Fa-Chen's eye told me that I had hit on the truth. "He *didn't* tell you I was a necromancer, did he? That to fall by my hand isn't just to die, but to be *consumed*, body and *soul*." I waved a hand toward the undead behind me and cocked an eyebrow. "*Think* on that, and tell me where he is, Fa-Chen, *heir* to Lo-Chen."

My words struck home, and realization flickered in the young man's eyes. His father had sent him to be destroyed. But if his father died, Fa-Chen would become lord of this house.

The young man's eyes hardened. "In his chambers, there's a bookcase. Pull the third book from the right on the second shelf from the top."

Not so stupid after all.

"*Thank* you!" I strode past him—my back itching with the proximity of the komei blade—and commanded my new shades, "Take me to Lo-Chen's chambers."

"Yes, mistress," they growled in unison.

The suite of gloriously appointed rooms dominated the third floor of the keep. Gods, these lords of the Council had money.

I went straight to the bookcase in the vast sitting room and pulled the designated tome. The entire shelf and the stone wall behind it popped out an inch. Grinning like a wolf, I pulled it open.

With a crack, a crossbow bolt struck me square in the chest. It puffed into splinters and rust, leaving a hole in my jerkin right over my heart.

*Lucky *that* wasn't enchanted,* Saraknyal said.

Thanks, smart ass!

I'm just saying, be more careful. I can't see through stone!

The room was small, a bolt hole. As Lo-Chen struggled to reload his useless crossbow, his trembling wife freed a wakizashi from the sash at her waist.

"Don't bother, Lo-Chen." I stepped into the room, shadowed by two shades. "You made your play and lost. You sent your *son* to confront me. What kind of father sacrifices his son's soul to save his own life? You should have *known* better than to fuck with a necromancer!"

"Fa-Chen?" The short sword trembled in the woman's hands as she stared at me wide-eyed. "My son... You murdered him?"

I opened my mouth to answer, but she cut me off.

"You!" The woman whirled to face Lo-Chen, her knuckles white on the dagger. "*You!* You *did* that?"

"Silence!" He glowered at me. "Fa-Chen bore our family blade! It would have cut her down if he'd had the courage to use it!"

The woman's lightning thrust pierced Lo-Chen's chest. His eyes widened in shock, then glazed over.

Oh, nicely done! Saraknyal crowed.

Lo-Chen fell to the floor, the blade still stuck in his heart.

His wife turned to me, her hands empty, tears streaking her face. "Take my soul if you wish, necromancer. It is empty."

"No." I took a step back. "And I didn't destroy your son. Teach him not to be a fool like his father." I turned away and strode for the exit.

On the stairs, Fa-Chen still stood, the komei sword in his limp grasp. "My father. Did you...kill him?"

"No, actually, your mother did."

The katana fell from nerveless fingers as he dashed past. For a moment I stared down at the blade that might have killed me.

Bonus! Saraknyal gloated.

I nodded and commanded one of my new shades to pick it up. "Balshi next."

My temper cooled during the long walk to Balshi's palace. My new minions kept the rabble from bothering me. I thought they might also make an impression on Balshi's guards.

They did.

I led my slashed and arrow-riddled undead force up to the high wrought-iron gate set in a spike-topped wall. Though not part of the keep itself, the fortification stretched from the lake to the north to the mountain cliffs to the south, a span of about half a mile. It wasn't built to withstand a siege, just keep out the riffraff.

Either Balshi's naturally paranoid or he's already heard about Lo-Chen.

I agreed, for about thirty soldiers glared through the gates, weapons at the ready. They eyed my undead entourage uncertainly.

"Halt or we'll fire!" The commander of the force sat on a leggy white charger well behind his troops.

"No." I stepped right up and gripped the gate's bars. "I'll warn you once. I'm here for Yirish Balshi. He ordered my people killed and my property destroyed. Your weapons are useless to stop me, so let me pass or I'll feast upon your souls."

The guard commander responded the way soldiers usually did. "Fire!"

In the midst of a swarm of bolts, I laughed fear, then reduced the lofty gate to a pile of rust. The soldiers' weapons drooped as I strode through, my undead mob at my heels. The commander bellowed commands as his horse reared in panic. Terrified pikemen charged, and I screamed an arc of icy death.

"Forward!" I commanded.

My shades crashed through the frozen corpses, zombies shuffling after. The soldiers broke, their commander helpless to stop the rout as his panicked mount bore him toward the palace.

I raised the fallen and followed, Soul Drinker smoldering cold in my hand. The outer court resembled a kicked anthill as dozens more soldiers streamed from barracks and stables to surround us before the keep's towering doors. I laughed, and their courage wilted.

I stopped and glared. "Stand aside or perish! I've come for Yirish Balshi!"

"You will not pass these gates!" a commander bellowed from somewhere behind his troops.

"Why do fools always hide behind the brave?" A rhetorical question, but apt. I turned to my mob of undead, now surrounded by pikes and blades. "Stay here."

What are you doing, Hashi? Saraknyal sounded worried.

Saving souls.

You always spoil my fun.

Live with it.

Oh, droll. If I wasn't dead, I'd be mortally wounded.

I strode up to the row of pikes and touched one with a fingertip. "Your weapons can't touch me." A thought reduced it to ash. The soldier gasped and stumbled back. "Stand aside, and let your master pay the price for his foolishness. Your very *souls* are forfeit if you try to prevent me from having my due."

The captain stood trembling behind his troops. I saw the dreadful decision in his eyes: obey orders and watch his men's souls destroyed, perhaps even his own, or survive to see the dawn. He opened his mouth, his lower lip quivering.

Please, I thought. *Don't...*

"Stand down!" he commanded.

The pikes dipped, and I released the breath I was holding.

"Stand aside! Let her pass!" The captain sheathed his sword, and he and his troops stepped out of my way.

"Thank you, captain. I hope your next master is more worthy of your bravery." I motioned my minions to follow and strode past the quaking soldiers to the high doors.

"They're sealed from the inside," the captain informed me.

I gave him an amused look. "Not for long." *Dust to dust.* The portal crumbled.

Beyond stretched a wide, lavishly decorated entry hall and a sweeping stair. Servants and a few more guards stumbled back as I entered.

This place is huge, Saraknyal said. *It'll take forever to find Balshi.*

No, it won't. I fixed my gaze on a black-uniformed servant with the house crest on his breast. "Are you the chief retainer of House Balshi?"

He struggled to recover his poise and performed a shaky bow. "I am." His voice broke, and he cleared his throat. "And you are?"

"I'm Hashi Severn. Tell Yirish Balshi that I'll speak to him right here in this hall, or I'll reduce his palace to dust."

Empty threat, Saraknyal chided.

He doesn't know that.

The butler glanced at the debris that used to be the front door, swallowed hard, then nodded jerkily. "I'll inform Lord Balshi of your...request."

"Good." I looked around. "I'll wait here."

I moved to the center of the entry hall as the man scurried off. The other servants found reasons to be elsewhere, but the house guard remained, stationing themselves around the periphery of the room. My shades grumbled and gnashed their teeth, some gnawing at the zombies.

"Be still and don't eat anything!" I hissed. The zombies were dripping various body fluids all over the polished floor, and the stench was getting thick.

Maybe I shouldn't have raised the zombies.

Nonsense. Gives these pompous asses a taste of the streets of Haven.

Good point.

In less time than I'd estimated, the master of the house and a surprisingly large entourage appeared at the top of the sweeping staircase. Yirish Balshi stood at the fore, looking disgusted, a gray-haired woman beside him, undoubtedly his wife. Behind stood a younger man, Balshi's son, and his beautiful young bride, who looked ready to faint. A girl, Balshi's daughter, perhaps ten years old, cowered behind her mother, staring wide-eyed at my undead mob.

"How *dare* you come here!" the elder Balshi seethed, contempt dripping from every word. "What do you want?"

"I want you to pay for killing my people, destroying my property, and terrorizing my businesses."

"Pay?" he sneered. "Fine! How much do you want for one rickety smuggling ship and a few menials? I'll offer you a thousand gold crowns!"

What a pretentious ass, Saraknyal growled. *He thinks he's untouchable.*

I smiled grimly and started slowly up the stairs. "Oh, I don't take payment in *gold*. The *menials* you killed were *my* people." I glanced significantly at his family. "What payment would *you* demand if I murdered *your* people?"

"I'll have your head on a pike, Severn!" he spat, trembling with rage.

I laughed, and the entire Balshi family staggered back as I mounted the last stair. "You're a pompous fool, Yirish Balshi. I hope your son makes a better lord than you."

"I'll see you *dead!*" He drew a sword then, a pretty weapon with a gilded crosspiece and hilts.

Do I need to worry about that, Saraknyal? I asked privately.

Not in the slightest, my dear.

I grinned and stepped forward, well within striking distance. "Death's too *kind* a fate for *you*."

He thrust the pretty blade at me, but his bravado crumbled with the weapon.

I snatched his wrist. "Look at me!"

We locked gazes, and Balshi drew a sharp breath as the chill necromantic magic seized his soul.

"Tell me, Yirish. Why did you do it? Why kill my people? Why attack my interests?"

"Because you're an upstart!" he hissed through spittle-flecked lips. "You needed to be nipped in the bud, like any encroaching *weed!*"

My smoldering rage finally ignited into a roaring inferno. I stepped close and inhaled his soul. *Shade.*

Saraknyal complied, transforming the shining essence into a putrid darkness of hunger and wrath. I exhaled the disgusting mess back into his dying body. Balshi's flesh darkened, his eyes flooded blood-red, and his teeth shattered into jagged points.

His wife screamed, while his son cursed and drew his own wife back. The younger daughter just stared up at her transformed father in wide-eyed shock.

"Yirish Balshi is no longer master of this house." Pointing to my troops, I gave him his first order. "Take your place with the rest of my minions!"

"Yes, mistress." The former patriarch of House Balshi descended the stairs to join his brethren.

"Now," I raked the others with a glare, "I *could* have destroyed your entire house. I could have ripped the souls from every last one of you and reduced this palace to ashes. I *didn't.* I hope you learned something from this."

I turned and walked away without looking back.

Damn, Hashi, Saraknyal muttered.

What's your problem now, old man? I gathered my mob and left the estate, lengthening my stride.

Oh, nothing. I'm just worried that you've made some serious enemies tonight.

You think so? I considered as we traversed the courtyard and passed through the disintegrated outer gate. *I don't think they'll give me any more trouble.*

Maybe not. What about Ting Hatsu and her komei? How are you going to handle her?

That'll depend on what kind of reception I get.

You're not going to kill her?

If she forces me to...and her komei don't get me first.

This should be interesting.

Yes... I considered my ragtag mob and ripped the spell away from the zombies. They crumpled, blocking the road to Balshi's Palace in a pile of putrefying flesh. Ten shades remained, Balshi at their fore. *Yes, it should be* very *interesting.*

Ting Hatsu surprised me, but also aroused my suspicions. When I walked up to her keep's gate, a red and gold-enameled affair that looked like something from a Toki temple, two guards stepped from the postern door to greet me. They bowed, hands on their katanas, their gleaming red and gold lamellar armor reflecting the torchlight from above. Luckily, they weren't komei—they didn't wear the gruesome masks that distinguished those elite warriors—but they looked proficient.

"May we help you, Miss Severn?" one asked as she straightened from her bow.

"You know who I am?"

"We were told you might be visiting and were instructed to pay you every possible courtesy. What is it you need from House Hatsu?"

Ting's head on a platter?

Hush! "I will speak with Ting Hatsu."

"Yes, of course. Please, come inside." She knocked a staccato sequence on the postern door, and it opened. Two more soldiers stood inside.

Careful, Saraknyal warned. *This could be a very courteous trap.*

You think? I frowned at the narrow corridor. "I'll enter through the main gate, if you please. To accommodate my escort."

"If you insist." She ordered the main gates opened.

After a few relayed orders, the beautifully lacquered doors swung inward to reveal a short tunnel lined with arrow slits and another open gate at the far end. Overhead, the tines of the raised portcullis peeked from the arched stone. Though tall enough to accommodate a carriage, and lit with wall-mounted sconces, the passage seemed ominously close and dark.

I don't like this, Hashi.

Neither do I, but I can't just slaughter everyone in Haven.

Why not?

Oh, shut up, for the gods' sakes! Steeling my nerves, I followed the two soldiers through the tunnel and into the courtyard beyond, one hand on Soul Drinker, and my shades at my back.

I found the place grandiose without being ostentatious, decorated in the Toki fashion with more red and gold accents, the Hatsu crest emblazoned in gold above the keep's doors. Soldiers stood atop the wall behind us, several others stationed at various doors. They all stood perfectly still, hands on the hilts of their katanas or the great black bows used by komei.

Those bows aren't enchanted, just to ease your mind.

Thanks. I breathed a little easier.

A pair of guards stationed at the main doors opened them as we approached and ushered us inside. More Toki architecture adorned the entry hall, the walls lined with potted shrubberies, each perfectly pruned and landscaped to resemble trees in natural settings. The floor was wood, glossy black and flawless. Lamps set with glow crystals shed golden light, and incense scented the air. Our escort stopped and bowed again.

"Please wait here. Lady Hatsu will arrive shortly."

"Very well." I crossed my arms, my hand resting lightly on Soul Drinker, and wished I wasn't wearing slashed and pierced clothing. I felt like a vagabond at the stoop of a rich lord, begging for food.

Courteous, but it's giving me the creeps.

Says the undead necromancer, I quipped, trying to convince my nerves that all was well. *Toki are all about formality. They invited me in. That means I'm a guest. A trap would be...rude, a breach of protocol.*

Ting Hatsu's a slave trader, you know, he said.

I never said she was a good person, but she's bound by the honor of her house.

Right...

Just keep a lookout for komei.

Duh!

In short order Ting Hatsu entered the hall, elegant in a beautiful kimono, her hands tucked into its draping sleeves, her hair bound up in an intricate coif by lacquered sticks. She wore pale makeup in the Toki fashion, creased at the corners of her eyes. Middle aged, I guessed, and a beautiful woman. A younger man and woman accompanied her, also dressed in formal Toki attire. Four komei clad in full armor and masks strode alongside, hands resting on the hilts of their enchanted swords.

Here we go, Saraknyal warned.

Just relax, I thought, girding my own trepidation. *She must know what's happened to her collaborators. She'd be a fool to start a fight.*

She attacked the interests of a necromancer. Isn't that fool enough for you?

Good point.

Ting Hatsu nodded politely. "Miss Severn. Welcome to my home. Can I offer you tea, or perhaps rice wine? I'm sorry that I don't have any brandy on hand."

She knows you drink brandy? That's creepy.

"No, thank you. This isn't a social call. I'm here to express my displeasure at your recent attacks on my people and businesses in collaboration with Lo-Chen and Yirish Balshi." I motioned my newest shade forward. "You may recognize Yirish."

One immaculate eyebrow rose, Hatsu's face otherwise impassive. "I do. I assume Lo-Chen met a similar fate?"

"He's dead, but not by my hand. I believe his wife and son are currently discussing the future of their house." I narrowed my eyes at her. "You don't deny your involvement in these attacks?"

Her red-painted lips twitched. "I wouldn't insult your intelligence so, Miss Severn. It was a *business* decision. Obviously a *bad* business decision. How can we reach a peaceful resolution to this situation?"

She's got more guts than a butcher shop.

"Lo-Chen paid with his life, and Lord Balshi with his soul. What currency do you offer?"

"I regret that I'm unwilling to pay with either my life *or* my soul, but let me assure you that I *have* learned from my mistake." She nodded politely, her features still impassive. "Let me apologize formally for my actions, and assure you that it will never happen again."

"You had my people killed."

"I have a lot of people killed." She shrugged minutely, withdrew an ornate fan from her sleeve, and opened it to fan her face.

"Business in Haven often requires killing. Our plan was to impede the growth of a powerful potential enemy, perhaps run you out of Haven. Lords Lo-Chen, Balshi, and I made a poor assessment of your...capabilities."

"Yes, you did." I constrained myself to a glower; insulting Hatsu in her own house would only be asking for trouble, and four komei were certainly troublesome. "I'm afraid an apology isn't sufficient."

"What, then, *would* be?"

I considered for a moment, glancing at her entourage. I thought about asking for one of her komei, but knew it would be futile; they were oath-sworn to their charges. Then I thought of something.

"A ship, ten crew, and a captain to replace the ones I lost."

Again that eyebrow arched. "A *small* ship, five crew, one captain."

"Seven crew, not slaves," I added.

"Seven, and not slaves," Ting agreed, nodding a fraction more deeply this time, almost a bow. "I'm glad we could come to a peaceful agreement."

"So am I." I smiled grimly. "Rest assured, *Lady* Hatsu, if you cross me again, we will *not* come to a peaceful resolution."

You're being deferential now?

She just gave me what I asked for, and I want to get out of here with my skin intact.

Just don't curtsy.

"I would *never* be so foolish *twice*, Miss Severn," Hatsu said with a polite smile.

I nodded, spun on my heel, and left, intensely aware of the four komei behind me. *Watch them for me, old man.*

Of course. They're eying you, but nobody's drawing weapons.

Thank the Gods of Light. My tense muscles relaxed once we reached the street. I turned toward to Ash Keep and lengthened my stride.

I must say that I'm impressed with you, Hashi, Saraknyal said.

"Don't flatter me, old man." I breathed in the sultry night, feeling lucky to be alive.

I'm dead serious. You did what you had to do, but showed remarkable restraint and forethought. More than I would have.

"I just hope it was enough. If the Council retaliates..."

*I don't believe they will. Leaving Ting Hatsu alive to tell them of your restraint, and the others' families as witnesses of what you can do, *should* be enough.*

"Unless they're fools," I said.

Well, there is that. He paused, then added, *But I don't think this will be the last you hear from the Council of Lords.*

His words made me queasy.

You may not want it, but you've attracted attention.

I don't want to think about it tonight. The souls I'd destroyed weighed heavily enough on my mind. *All I really want right now is a bath.*

And a brandy, probably.

Hell, yes, a brandy. I found myself smiling, and I didn't know why.

Chapter Twenty Five
Status Quo

From the journal of Hashi Severn –

Peace is harder than war. It requires constant work, convoluted maneuvering, investments of time and energy. Diplomacy is exhausting. I understand the allure of extreme necromancy: total annihilation of all opposition, foregoing all living contact... Easier, certainly, but that is, quite literally, a dead end.

I arrived at Malchi's estate at dusk and strode through the front door with two of my shades in escort. I wore a dress for the evening, and had even garbed my shades in proper attire; there was no sense in being rude. I also carried a long mahogany box under one arm. We were directed to a cavernous sitting room by Malchi's butler, where the other lords and ladies and their escorts were already assembled.

Why are we always the last to arrive at a party?

Blame all of my primping and preparations...

Saraknyal chuckled. Readying myself for the evening had taken all of five minutes; I'd strapped Soul Drinker to my thigh, donned a sleeveless black sheath slit just low enough to conceal the blade but high enough to allow me free movement, and slipped on a pair of comfortable flat sandals. I'd had the dress made several years ago on a whim because the material matched the hue of my skin perfectly. I'd honestly never thought I'd have the opportunity to wear it.

The room was a riot of colorful clothing, bustling footmen, and glowering guards. Captains Niland and Patak were present, looking much cleaner and healthier. Malchi's family—minus the grandchildren—were also in attendance, including the young man who had accompanied Ursilla Roque to Balshi's fateful ball. I wondered how he felt now about his dalliance with one of Jhavika's enslaved allies.

Into the breach...

Right. I stationed my shades near the door, swallowed my reticence, and strode into the fray.

Tori Blackbriar advanced on me with his usual grin. "Lady Severn, you look *lovely* tonight."

"Thank you." Frankly, so did he, dressed in a snug royal blue waistcoat and dinner jacket, an ivory shirt with a matching ascot and diamond pin, ivory breeches and shiny black boots with silver buckles. Of course, I didn't tell him so. Instead, I changed the subject. "I see Captain Patak survived Nahli's hospitality."

The pirate captain looked hale enough. He was certainly cleaner, but his hair remained wild and his beard untrimmed. With the filth gone, his part-islander heritage showed, though his beard was thicker than any islander's. A simple black coat and trousers, beige shirt, and soft boots replaced his ragged clothing from yesterday. He held a tumbler half full of amber liquid in his left hand, his right hovering at waist-height where a sword would have hung. He looked uneasy, but not fearful, as he chatted with Nahli.

"Yes, though he looked a little...*dazed* when he arrived." Tori leaned close. "Niland told me that Patak was sorely injured by Jhavika in her quest for information about Longbright."

"That doesn't surprise me in the slightest." *That also means he's probably itching for revenge.*

Good for us, bad for Jhavika. That man's seriously unhinged. Just look at his eyes.

I did, and found them wild and twitchy. *Well, he's been through hell.*

So have you, my dear, and you turned out beautifully.

I ignored the flattery and excused myself from Tori's company. "I have a little something for Que-Chen."

"Oh?" He glanced curiously at the mahogany box, but didn't ask.

I still think this is a bad idea. That thing's dangerous. Saraknyal didn't like my plan, but he knew as much about diplomacy as I knew about needlepoint. Of course, politics wasn't my strong point either, but Malchi's cozying up to Que-Chen made me wary, and I intended to remind the young lord that he had other allies on the Council.

I worked my way through the crowd to Que-Chen, who stood with Malchi.

"And what have you brought with you tonight, Hashi?" Malchi eyed the box curiously and reached out a hand. "A gift for hosting wasn't neces—"

"It's not for you." I held out the box to Que-Chen. "This once belonged to your father. Years ago, I had a disagreement with your grandfather, and this...fell into my possession. I thought I'd return it to its rightful owner."

The young man looked startled. "I... Um..." He lifted the box's lid and caught his breath.

So did Lord Malchi. "That's..."

"Your family blade, Lord Que-Chen."

You're literally putting a blade that can kill you into the hands of your enemy, Hashi.

No, I'm trying to turn a potential enemy into an ally. It's called diplomacy.
It's called stupidity.

"I..." Que-Chen tentatively lifted the beautiful weapon from the box, slipped it a few inches from the scabbard, and bent to examine the maker's mark. "Thank you, Lady Severn. This is..."

"The least I can do." I handed the empty box to a hovering footman and took a brandy from his tray. "May it serve you better than it did your grandfather." I raised my glass to him.

"Thank you." The young man slipped the katana through the sash he wore about his waist, then bowed to me. "I'll treasure this."

"My pleasure." A footman offered a tray of tidbits—tiny shrimp with crispy melted cheese on a thin toast of rosemary bread—and I sampled one. I had to restrain myself from grabbing the whole tray, raising an appreciative eyebrow to Malchi. "My compliments to your chef, Reginald."

"Yes, well, we do our best." He seemed disgruntled to only be receiving a compliment when his young guest had received an enchanted sword. "You're not wearing Soul Drinker tonight?"

I laughed, but without invoking Saraknyal's magic. "In *this* company? Oh, I'm *wearing* it, Lord Malchi, just some place where you can't see it."

Que-Chen glanced at me and blushed.

What does Malchi have up his sleeve, I wonder.

He's certainly buttering up Que-Chen. Excusing myself, I worked my way over to Nahli.

"Good evening Nahli. Captain, you're looking much better."

"Aye, Lady Twince's been right hospitable." He sipped his drink. "Gettin' my crew away from her's gonna be like pryin' an oyster from the shell, though."

"Oh, I'm sure they'll tire of fae hospitality soon enough, Captain." Nahli smiled and placed a hand on his arm. "Most mortals do...eventually."

"Well, I hope you're still eager to serve out some vengeance to Jhavika Keshmir," I said.

"Oh, aye. All the fae in the Jungles of Nin couldn't dampen that fire, Lady Severn."

"Good!"

Malchi tapped his belt dagger to a wineglass to still the scattered conversations. "Now that we're all here," he glanced pointedly at me, "I think we should hear the account of Captain Niland, who was pressed into service by Jhavika Keshmir at the point of a sword." He stepped aside and gestured to the young officer.

"Uh...it was a boarding pike, actually, that she wears in place of her right hand." Niland swallowed hard and clutched his hands together until his knuckles turned white. "I want to be clear about one thing; Jhavika Keshmir is insane."

Well, duh!

No commentary, please. Just pay attention.

Niland continued. "She stormed aboard *Tiger Lily* with a couple hundred soldiers, murdered my captain and the other senior officers, and told me I was in command, that I'd do her bidding or swing from a yardarm." He swallowed hard again. "In retrospect, I probably should have taken the latter option. I did...things, followed her orders out of fear for my own life. I should have died instead. I'll never go to sea again!"

"You *will* go to sea, you sniveling little whelp!" Patak's face flushed and tendons distended from his bull neck as he took a step toward Niland. Two of Malchi's house guards stepped between them. "You'll go to sea with *me* and help hunt down that murderous bilge cunt so I can cut her fucking *throat*! You *owe* that to me and my crew!"

Niland blanched and backed away.

Temper, temper! Saraknyal muttered.

"Captain Patak, please!" Malchi stepped forward. "Your anger is justified, but it should be directed at Jhavika Keshmir, *not* Captain Niland!"

"Aye, *maybe*," Patak seethed through clenched teeth. "There's one thing he said that I'll agree with: Jhavika's barking mad. She always was a grasper for power, but I never seen anyone so drunk on it as she is now. She snapped orders like a fuckin' queen, and her people hopped to without a twitch! I never seen the like. She had a gods-damned *komei* cut my..." His face flushed again, and he shook his head. "Gimmie a gods-damned ship, and I'll hunt the bitch down for you."

*No questioning *his* veracity,* Saraknyal said. I agreed; Patak was out for blood.

"How, exactly, *did* she manage to take your ship, Captain Patak?" asked Tori.

"Lured us in, pretendin' to be a merchant." He downed a swallow from his glass before continuing. "Thought we had a fat prize until soldiers came boilin' up from her hatches like rats and shot down my boarding party. She had maybe twice our numbers and surprise to boot. Tried to cut loose, but didn't have the chance."

"And *Crimson Hawk*, what type of ship is she?" Malchi asked.

Patak raised his chin proudly. "Three masted, barque-rigged, of about two-hundred tons. She's weatherly and can beat any galleon on the sea on any point of wind. No ship can touch her close-hauled."

What language is he speaking?

Nautical-ese, I think. What I knew of ships could fit in a thimble with room for a fingertip.

"And do you think she'll be able to catch the *Scourge* under Captain Longbright?" Malchi asked.

The pirate shrugged. "Depends. The ships are well-matched, though I'd wager Longbright's a better seaman. Jhavika's got more blades if they do come rail-to-rail." He eyed the lords. "Why does she want Longbright so bad?"

"That's a long list!" Tori laughed, counting off the points on his fingers. "Let's see, he tried to kill her, cut off her hand, stole her magical scourge, positively *ruined* her congratulatory ball, oh, and exposed her plot to enslave all of Haven and probably the entire Blood Sea!" He looked at me. "Did I miss anything?"

I clenched my teeth to keep from smiling. "I don't think so."

Patak's brow furrowed. "She did spout some hogwash about bein' Queen of Haven."

"Apparently she's been enslaving people for years toward that goal." Tori sighed. "We still don't know exactly how many she's lashed with that damned scourge."

"The only scourge she ever mentioned to me was the ship, *Scourge*, which she was adamant about catching," Niland said. "She also wanted Captain Longbright's head on a pike."

"No doubt." Malchi cleared his throat. "Her coup attempt failed, but if she retrieves that scourge, she'll be a grievous threat. Her ensorcelled army can't rebel and will fight to the death. We're doing all we can to bolster Haven's defenses, but if she should sail into the harbor with two *thousand* soldiers…"

Lambs to the slaughter, Saraknyal growled.

Even we can be overwhelmed by sheer numbers, I reminded him.

"Keshmir murdered my parents and commandeered six ships from my family's fleet." Que-Chen looked steadfastly at Patak. "I'm very much inclined to put you in command of *Tiger Lily* and send you after her, Captain Patak, but I don't have enough sailors to fight her entire fleet."

Patak blinked at the young man. "Well, she didn't have a *fleet* when I saw her."

"No, she didn't," Niland confirmed. "Three days out of Haven, *Scourge* vanished in the dark. Lady Keshmir ordered her armada to seven different destinations all across the Blood Sea, from Mati to Hyko. We sailed for Twin Capes; she thought Longbright might be there recruiting pirates to his flag. Instead, we found *Crimson Hawk*. She took the corsair because she wanted a faster ship."

"Aye, and I'd prefer somethin' faster than *Tiger Lily* to hunt *her* down with, but I'll take a fuckin' *canoe* if that's all I can get!" Patak downed his drink, glowing with bridled rage.

"Your enthusiasm does you credit, captain, but I think we need a more prudent approach." Malchi stepped away from Niland and over to Patak's side, grasped the man's arm genially. "Shall we eat while we talk over the details?"

Two wide panel doors opened at the end of the room, and white-coated footmen ushered us into the dining room.

Looks like Malchi's abandoned Niland and is trying to butter up Patak instead, Saraknyal observed.

I eyed the vast dining table, a stupendous display of porcelain and silver on a spread of white linen. A white-coated attendant stood behind every other chair, waiting to serve. *Looks like he's trying to butter everyone up.*

Well, he won't have any luck with me unless he serves up someone's soul for the main course.

Don't suggest it. He just might.

I could have gleefully murdered Malchi for seating me between his youngest son, Maurice, and Tori Blackbriar. I glanced up and down the table as servers ladled lobster bisque into our bowls and poured pale wine.

Keep your ears open. I can't listen to all the conversations at once.

Neither can I, but I'll keep my attention on Malchi. He placed Patak to his left and Que-Chen to his right, you'll notice. That's a lot of our sea power in one spot.

I noticed. He's maneuvering for control, and wants Balshi's place as unofficial head of the Council as well. I wondered how Brilla would handle that if she ever returned to Haven.

I'd barely sampled the delicious bisque when Maurice Malchi leaned close.

"I've never met a necromancer before." Maurice gave me a smoldering smile and an appreciative half-lidded gaze. "You're not at all what I expected."

Do you think Malchi seated me next to his son to distract me, or so the boy could seduce me?

Both, maybe. Perhaps he pimps him out to all the council members.

Good luck with that, I thought, though he was admittedly gorgeous and well mannered. *I'm old enough to be his grandmother.*

Nonsense, Saraknyal chided. *At least, you don't look it.*

Thanks to you.

You're welcome.

"Oh?" I replied casually to Maurice. "How so?"

"I expected someone less...warm. You seem too full of life to be so closely associated with death."

He has a point.

Shut up. "Outward appearances can be deceiving." I gazed at him sidelong and lowered a hand to the napkin in my lap. *Chill of fear, just a touch*, I thought, brushing his thigh with one finger.

You're deliciously evil, my dear. Saraknyal sent a shiver of terror through the poor boy.

The young lordling stiffened and paled. "I...see!" Maurice edged away, a light sweat sprouting on his smooth upper lip. He cleared his throat and emptied his wine glass, which a hovering footman promptly refilled. "You really are, then, aren't you? A necromancer, I mean."

"You doubted it?" I dabbed my mouth with my napkin and replaced it in my lap.

"No, but my father does." He leaned minutely closer and lowered his voice to a whisper. "He thinks it's that dagger you wear that gives you the magic."

The old bastard's more astute than I give him credit for.

Indeed.

We should murder him.

No. Not tonight, at least. I levied another smile at Maurice and chuckled. The candles near me fluttered, but didn't quite go out. "Your father sent you to find out, didn't he?"

"Yes." He edged a bit farther away. "You can't blame him, can you? You're..."

I cocked an eyebrow at him. "I'm *what?*" I had a fleeting desire to take him to my bed and return him to his father as a wraith.

"Imposing, I suppose. Powerful, certainly, which is why my father's scared of you. He's scared of losing what power he has, of course, as all powerful men are." Maurice sighed. "He makes me sick, if you want the truth. He's always after me to do this or do that to help his plots. I'd rather he just let me be. I don't want anything from him anyway."

I regarded the young lordling with a new understanding. *Youngest son, no hope of inheriting; he's his father's expendable weapon.*

A fair assessment, Saraknyal agreed.

"Then we have something in common," I told Maurice. "I, too, want only to be left *alone.*"

He looked a little shocked at my bluntness, but nodded and returned to his meal. His sister-in-law sat to his other side, and he turned to her for less-dangerous dinner conversation.

"Careful with that one, Hashi," Tori whispered in my other ear. "He's got a reputation with the ladies, you know."

I looked at him sidelong. "Worse than *yours?*"

"I'm mortally *wounded.*" Tori pressed a hand to his breast and gave me a patently false look of mortification. "How can you *say* such a thing?"

I narrowed my eyes at him. "You go through women like most men go through handkerchiefs, Tori Blackbriar. Everyone knows it. Your libido got you into trouble in Fengotherond, and you had to run away. That's why you're here, in Haven, where there aren't any laws and your *dick* can't get you into trouble."

He barked an incredulous laugh. "Oh, my dear Hashi, rest assured, it still *can* get me into *quite* a lot of trouble!" He laughed again, and, however I tried, I couldn't keep a smile from my lips.

"Not as much trouble as the women you seduce."

"And not as *deeply* into trouble as the young lord at your elbow, from what I hear." He smiled devilishly. "His father throws him at women to weaken their resolve. While their knees are still trembling, the senior lord moves in and makes them subtle offers of advancement. Then, of course, they're in his debt." He raised his glass to me. "That's how Captain Tan came to her current position, you know."

"Really?" I hadn't known, in fact, but didn't doubt Tori's claim. His spy network covered Haven like a skillfully thrown cast net. "Is that why he was on Ursilla's arm at Balshi's party?"

"From what I could learn, that was a mutual seduction. She made the first overture, and Lord Malchi told his son to...delve the depths of that well to its fullest." The mirth suddenly left Tori's face. "In light of our new knowledge, however, I'd wager Jhavika had something to do with that arrangement."

"Quite likely," I agreed. "If she got her hooks into young Maurice, then eliminated the older heirs..."

"Precisely." Tori arched an eyebrow at me. "You really are exquisite, you know."

Where the hell did that come from? I leaned away from him and glared. "And you really are an insufferable ass."

He grinned. "Guilty as charged."

You should just make a wraith of him and be done with it.
Don't tempt me.

The servers whisked away our bowls and replaced them with plates of artfully arranged greens and tropical fruit. As they refilled our wine glasses, Reginald Malchi tapped the side of his glass with a fork.

"I'd like to propose a toast to our captains." He raised his glass, and we all followed suit. "They epitomize a quality we all share: survival. Here's to our survival, ladies and gentlemen."

To that, I will drink.

Here, here! Saraknyal agreed.

"And in that vein, I'd like to discuss our current situation." Malchi ate a bite of mango and continued. "Now that Longbright's out of the picture, we need new blood for building our privateer navy, and we have here a most capable sea captain!" He clapped Patak on the shoulder.

Here we go. Was I right or was I right?

You were right. Maybe I should set you to telling fortunes.

"Your *what?*" Patak glared until Malchi removed his hand from the pirate's shoulder.

"Pirate's don't *like* navies, do they, captain?" Mah Hatsu asked, her big dark eyes fixed on him.

"No, we *don't!*" He stabbed the air with his fork for emphasis. "I'll have nothin' to do with *any* navy!"

"From the mouths o' babes," Ingrid chuckled.

"Let's just call it a fleet of privateers," Tori suggested. "*Navy* was Jhavika's word, and I say we forthwith ban all things Jhavika."

That earned a few chuckles

Malchi snatched back the floor. "Captain Longbright's assignment—before he tried to murder Jhavika and she countered with a coup attempt—was to recruit captains like yourself to join a privateer *fleet*." Malchi smiled in the face of Patak's glower. "I believe you would be an apt replacement."

Patak for Longbright? Hardly a fair comparison from what I've seen so far. He might be an able sea captain, but I doubt this brigand could rally others to our flag. If we had a flag.

I agree. And from the looks being cast around the table, so did many others.

Patak looked skeptical. "Recruit *how?*"

"By offering a safe harbor, a market to sell their plunder, and all the amenities of our city," Malchi continued.

"Amenities?" Patak's brow furrowed. "What's Haven got besides brothels and booze?"

Malchi smiled slyly. "Oh, you'd be surprised. In exchange for services, we'd provide low prices on supplies, provisions, and labor to repair ships under our flag, as well as—"

"And what would those *services* be?" Patak interrupted, downing his wine with a grimace.

Malchi motioned a footman over. "Get the captain something more to his liking to drink."

"Rum," Patak said.

"Let me summarize our situation, please." Tori interrupted before Malchi could continue. "Sea trade is Haven's lifeblood, and it would be far too easy for a foreign fleet to blockade the port. We're fortifying the city's coastal defenses and arming what ships we possess, but what we *really* need are fighting ships crewed by competent sailors. The presence of warships in the harbor should dissuade any attempted blockade. Hence, the idea is to amass a fleet of privateers, recruiting from Blood Sea pirates. Pirates have ships and expertise, we have the resources you need. A mutually beneficial arrangement!" He leaned back with a satisfied smile.

Ingrid took up the pitch. "We'd provide captains with letters of marque, changin' you from pirates into privateers."

Patak squinted. "And what's the catch?"

"Privateers would refrain from attacking ships under Haven interests, whether owned by council members or others here. *Other* merchantmen, however, would be fair game. Privateers would remit ten percent of the value of their plunder to the Council for defense expenses." Nahli's melodic voice made the terms sound more like a bonus than a cost. "You would also, of course, participate in Haven's defense should an attack occur."

The staff whisked away our salad plates and brought in platters of artfully arranged racks of lamb, vegetables, and potatoes, as well as pots of gravy, sauces, and jellies. While the aroma of the meat tortured me, they filled our glasses with a deep red wine. I requested the rarest bit on the platter. Bloody juice seeped into my potatoes as I sliced the meat. At the first bite, I nearly swooned. Reginald's chef was truly a gem. Not surprisingly, conversation lapsed as people ate.

Finally, Malchi broke the hiatus "Well, Captain Patak? What do you think of our offer?"

Patak regarded Malchi. "No offence, but Haven doesn't have the resources to support a fleet. You need lumber, tar, cordage, and shipwrights."

"We have *trade*, Captain," Malchi countered, "and a privateer fleet would enhance and protect that."

"And no shipyard." Patak added before popping a bite of lamb into his mouth, talking as he chewed and gesturing with his fork. "Build a shipyard and you'd have more privateers than you could handle. Only decent yards in the Blood Sea are at Sariff and Hyko. Hyko's too close to Toki for comfort, and Sariff don't tolerate corsairs in port."

Or necromancers.

"A shipyard?" Malchi frowned. "That would require a tract of waterfront, and real estate is *one* thing Haven doesn't have in excess. Not to mention the supplies required to build ships."

Patak shook his shaggy head. "I'm not talkin' about *buildin'* ships, just haulin' 'em out for maintenance. Right now we careen out on beaches at high tide to recaulk and replace rotten or damaged planks and timbers. That's dangerous, slow, and depends on tides. A proper cradle and trolley would make haulin' ships faster, easier, and safer." Patak reached across Malchi to spear another chop from the platter, dripping bloody juice on the white cloth as he brought it to his plate. "You build one and offer pirates the use of it at no cost, say once a year, and you'll have more privateers than you can put flags on."

I told you we needed a flag.

We do, and Patak's smarter than he looks.

But his table manners rival a shade's.

Silence settled over the gathering.

I wracked my brain and finally asked the question I knew everyone else was considering, too. "*Is* there any waterfront space where we could build a shipyard?"

"Ha!" Tori grinned devilishly. "I'm sure at least *one* warehouse on the waterfront is owned by Jhavika or one of her allies. I say we take it and deal with the repercussions later."

That sounds like his strategy with women, too.

I hid a smile with a sip of wine.

Malchi smiled broadly. "Excellent idea! And, may I say, Captain Patak, that I personally look forward to working with you as we build our privateer nav—um...fleet."

"About *that*." The captain emptied his glass once again and held it up for a footman to refill. "You get me a ship, *any* ship, and I'll hunt Jhavika Keshmir down for you, *and* sign your letter of marque, but I ain't your man for recruiting other captains." He drank deeply, shaking his head. "I'm a pirate, not a diplomat."

Everyone looked at one another

"Well, we need *someone*," Ingrid said.

"Captain Tan might do," Malchi offered, then cringed at his own suggestion. "*If* she returns."

"Nah." Patak shook his head. "You need a pirate to deal with pirates. You just send a messenger, they're more apt to take their ship than listen to them."

Nahli looked around the table. "Perhaps one of the Council of Lords could go?"

Everyone's eyes dropped; there'd be no volunteers for that job.

"Well," Tori said with a wry grin, "perhaps we'd better all pray for the return of Captain Longbright! And I think this subject is better dealt with at a regular council meeting, and not after copious glasses of Reginald's excellent wine." He raised his glass toward Patak. "But we can certainly celebrate our first fleet captain."

"What about Captain Niland?" I asked. "He *is* a seasoned commander."

"Not seasoned enough," Patak interjected, then grinned at the trembling young man. "Not until *I* get through with him, anyways."

Malchi nodded. "We can't afford to waste *any* nautical talent."

The young officer seemed to shrink into his seat as all eyes turned to him. "I...I'm only a merchant officer."

"Nonsense!" Patak waved a dismissive hand. The rum seemed to have mellowed his resentment for his fellow captain. "Just a matter of experience. All you need is some proper *instruction.*"

"Also," Nahli put in, "I'm sure Captain Niland could impart important intelligence about Jhavika's plans, her fleet's dispersal, and how well she's supplied."

The two captains exchanged a level stare, and finally Niland nodded.

"So, about this idea of a *shipyard*... " Tori interjected. "Shall we vote to procure property and start construction? All in favor?"

We all raised our hands.

"Excellent! We have a plan!" Tori raised his glass. "I so *love* mixing business with pleasure!"

"I suggest both captains get with Reginald and Tori tomorrow to discuss what kinda' supplies and such they'll need for this undertaking," Ingrid suggested. "We'll discuss the details later."

"Agreed!" Malchi crowed, clearly happy to have his fingers in the pie. "We wouldn't want to spoil *dessert* with too much talk."

A footman placed before me a plate with a wedge of dense chocolate cake drizzled with a raspberry sauce. My mouth watered as the aroma filled my head.

What do you think about—

Don't distract me. There's chocolate.

You're hopeless, Saraknyal chided as the first bite passed my lips.

And you're just jealous. I savored the bite and chased it down with a sip of wine. Bliss...

After dinner, we were ushered back into the sitting room and offered cordials and port. Fighting back a yawn after the copious food and wine, I paid my respects to Malchi, collected my shades, and bowed out.

Steps matched mine through the entry hall, and Tori Blackbriar caught up. "Calling it a night, Hashi?"

"Yes, I am." I stifled another yawn and descended the steps to the courtyard, my shades close behind. A rare westerly breeze blew from the mountains, raising gooseflesh on my bare arms.

"It's a chill evening. Can I offer you a warm beverage and polite conversation?"

"No, thank you." The carriages hadn't yet been brought around, so I strode for the stables, hoping he'd take the hint and go away.

"Don't you ever just like to *chat*, Hashi?"

What the hell is he getting at?

I don't know, but I don't like his prying. I shot him a cool stare. "What would we *chat* about?"

"Oh, anything. The weather, our favorite books, pastimes..." He remained undaunted.

"*Why?*" I let a chill edge my tone.

Tori barked a laugh. "Because I find you *interesting*, Hashi. You don't have to be so prickly. I'm not trying to *woo* you; I'd just like to know you better."

I stopped and stared at him. This had gone far enough. "I don't believe you. You want something from me. What is it?"

"To save you from dying of sheer *boredom*, if nothing else!" His mirthful expression faded to a concerned mien. "You affect this cold façade, Hashi, but I can see through it."

"Oh, *really*?" I suppressed the urge to reach for Soul Drinker. "See *this*, then: I have no desire for companionship, and I don't appreciate you prying into my private life, Lord Blackbriar!"

He looked suddenly sad. "I don't think you're as antisocial as you pretend, Hashi."

"I'm not *pretending*!" I took a step, our faces now only a handspan apart, and seethed through my teeth, "You don't *know* me, Tori Blackbriar. Don't presume to."

"Everyone needs social interaction." His voice had softened. "Everyone needs company now and then."

"Not *me*!" I whirled and stalked off toward my carriage, thoroughly enraged. *What the hell does he want from me?*

I don't know, but his persistence has turned into a full-on assault.

That was it; I felt like I was under siege. And no closer to knowing what Tori wanted from me.

Chapter Twenty Six
Entreaty

Well, Hatsu's made good on her word. I walked quickly up the gangplank from the small lug-sailed ship to the solid ground of the quay.

As long as she keeps her komei at bay, Saraknyal grudgingly agreed.

Barely a week had passed since my assaults on the keeps of Yirish Balshi and Lo-Chen, and I was taking possession of my new ship, *Dawn Wind*. I turned to her master, a Toki native named Wah Keto. "Thank you for the tour, captain. You have a beautiful, well-kept ship. I can tell you know your job."

"*Dawn Wind* is *your* ship, mistress, not mine," Keto said stiffly.

"I'm just the owner, captain. You're her master. She's *your* ship." Keto's expression softened slightly. So far, she'd been rigidly formal, probably scared to death of me, considering the rumors that were flying around Haven. "Do you know anything about antiques?" I asked, taking her off guard.

"Nothing, mistress," she admitted.

"Thank you for being honest with me. That'll be important to our relationship."

"You needn't worry about my loyalty, mistress."

I smiled. "I worry about *everyone's* loyalty, captain. But don't worry. If you're honest with me, I'll be honest with you."

"Of course, mistress!"

"However, since you're not familiar with antiques, which will be your primary cargo, I'll be putting four experienced sailors aboard your ship who *do* know about them. Is that a problem?"

"No, mistress."

"Good. I'll send them by and have cargo for you in two days."
She bowed, and I strode for my carriage, feeling good about how
things had turned out. Bryce was recovering, his shop was being
repaired and refurbished, and I had a new ship.

The only thing bothering me was the conspicuous inaction from
the Council of Lords. They seemed to be going about their business
of divvying up Haven, but hadn't touched any of my interests, or
even so much as sent a note. Saraknyal took this as a good sign,
while I worried like a condemned prisoner waiting for the axe to fall.

When I arrived home, it fell.

"This arrived while you were out, mistress." Joss proffered an
envelope of expensive vellum with a stylized 'HCoL' embossed on
the back.

I stared at it as if it coiled and hissed.

Just burn the thing, Hashi. Trust me.

Don't read my mail before I do! I snatched the letter and took the
steps three at a time up to my office. Closing the door behind me, I
drew Soul Drinker and slit open the envelope. The letter was short
and to the point.

Miss Severn,

We regret the recent unpleasantness between yourself and some
of the Council's members. We are, however, pleased that hostilities
did not escalate beyond the responsible parties, and respect your
restraint.

The Haven Council of Lords requests the honor of your
presence at a meeting two days hence at noon, at the keep of Lady
Ingrid Brickhammer. The Council will ensure your safety during the
interview, but you may bring an armed escort if you so desire. Rest
assured that the Council of Lords holds no rancor for your prior
actions. We desire only to peacefully resolve any remaining animosity
in the interest of future cooperation.

Sincerely,
Haven Council of Lords

And damned if it wasn't signed by every single one of them, including my two victims' heirs—Fa-Chen and Teris Balshi. I put the letter down and paced my office.

"What do you think?" I asked Saraknyal.

I think you should have burned that letter. It's a trap.

"You thought before that they wouldn't mess with me anymore, that they'd learned their lesson."

Yes, but I find it hard to believe that Fa-Chen and Teris Balshi would simply agree to move on after you murdered their fathers. The letter's too polite. They're baiting the hook.

"Good analogy."

Thanks. So heed it. You walk into that meeting, we're fucked.

"And if I snub their invitation and it's sincere?"

How could it be sincere? Three of these people tried to run you out of Haven. It didn't work, so now they'll try again, this time with the support of the whole crew. Surround you with komei, maybe have Nahli Twince cast some magic that nullifies mine, and we're done.

"You think she could do that?"

I don't know!

We both fell silent while I paced and bit my lip. Finally, I said, "I only see two options: ignore the invitation and look over my shoulder for the rest of my life, or accept the invitation and potentially walk into a trap."

Option three: wipe out the Council entirely.

I sighed and rubbed my eyes. "That's not an option."

Well, it is, but...

"Not one I'm willing to take until they deserve it."

Then I suggest you attend, but make it clear ahead of time that if this is a trap, you'll annihilate them. Maybe have a wraith deliver the message to Ingrid Brickhammer personally.

"Nice touch." I sat down at my desk and started working on my response. It took me three tries to craft a message that sounded cordial, mildly ominous, yet not outright threatening. I scrawled 'Lady Ingrid Brickhammer' on the front, then folded it and dripped a blob of black wax to seal it.

You need a signet ring. Maybe something with a skull?

"Now who's being melodramatic?" I pressed my thumb to the cooling wax and handed the envelope to one of my wraiths. "Deliver this to Ingrid Brickhammer personally. Tell her you'll wait for a reply."

"Yes, mistress." He grinned horribly and left.

Three hours later I had my answer, a single line scrawled at the bottom of my missive.

Miss Severn:

You have my personal assurance that you will be safe in my home as my guest.

Ingrid Brickhammer

A seal depicting a crossed hammer and axe was impressed into the lump of wax next to her name.

She's got a signet ring.

I dropped the note to my desk and heaved a deep breath. "So, what do I wear to a potential slaughter?"

For my meeting with the Council, I settled on black and silver. I don't generally wear jewelry, but I couldn't resist a pair of matching silver spiderweb bracelets that I discovered during one of my antique-buying expeditions.

A bit cliché, don't you think? My keep was meticulously clean.

Except for the bones.

Disposed of as soon as I was done with them. You didn't see any laying around, did you?

I refused to answer as I fit the bracelets over the cuffs of a black silk shirt, clipped Soul Drinker to my belt with a silver clasp, and pulled on a pair of knee-high leather boots with silver buckles up the sides. If it came to a fight, nothing I wore would hamper my movements, and I looked good to boot.

First impressions...

First impression? Do you think what you did last week somehow escaped their notice?*

Well, second impressions, then.

I took my Jaguar Warrior wraith and six shades, including the former Lord Balshi, because that was as many as I could fit on my coach. I just hoped it would be enough if things went badly.

Ingrid Brickhammer's home proved to be more of a cave than a keep, carved right into the face of the mountain. I shouldn't have been surprised, having delved more than one abandoned dwarven stronghold for relics. It sported no outer courtyard; the entry hall, stables, and everything else were all underground. Massive barbicans flanked double doors of dwarf-wrought granite three feet thick. I doubted anything short of a full-grown dragon would even chip them.

*Well, *that's* not intimidating at all,* Saraknyal said dourly.

Dwarves are paranoid.

*And *because* they're paranoid, they've survived for a very long time, far longer than humans. You could take some lessons from them.*

I called to Bromish to pull up outside. Stepping out of the carriage, I straightened my clothes as my escort formed up behind me. I'd given my Jaguar Warrior wraith, the most formidable of my minions, the sword I'd retrieved from Fa-Chen, with instructions to defend me specifically from komei. *I guess I'm paranoid, too.*

It's not paranoia if people really are out to kill you.

A squad of armored dwarves stood in formation beside the doors to Brickhammer Keep, each one clad in enough steel to render me incapable of movement if I'd tried to wear it. Their commanding officer—I assumed his status from his unique helmet with a horsehair crest—clanked forward and tapped the haft of his axe to the flagstones.

"Hashi Severn?" His flint-gray eyes darted to my left and right, inspecting my entourage.

"Yes." I suppressed a perverse impulse to transform his armor into a pile of rust just to see if I could break that legendary dwarven stoicism. "I was asked to attend a council meeting, and assured that my escort would be welcome."

"*Welcome?*" A deep rumble reverberated from the dwarf's chest. "Not *welcome*, but permitted. Follow me."

I wasn't offended by his dislike of my grim minions. I didn't particularly *like* them either, and they could take the slight personally. I followed.

I'd always found dwarven ruins cold, dusty, and eerily silent places. This was none of those things.

We entered a hive of bustling activity, life, and noise, from the distant ring of hammers to the thrum of low music, booming laughter, and murmuring voices. The noise ceased around me as dwarves stopped in their tracks and stared in awe, disgust, and open scorn.

At least you won't have to duck.

True enough. Dwarves, unlike gnomes, build to a grander scale than their diminutive statures required. Vaulted ceilings soared high overhead, and ornate tapestries adorned lofty walls. Furnishings were carved right into the living rock: seats crafted from solid blocks of stone, table bases jutting up from floors and spreading into foot-thick tops. Even divans and cupboards were hewn right into the stone. *I guess it saves on rearranging furniture.*

But makes redecorating difficult.

Despite my sightseeing, my nerves were as taut as bowstrings by the time we finally entered the meeting room. An enormous table stretched the length of the chamber. Ingrid Brickhammer, as host, sat at one end, with the other members of the Haven Council of Lords seated along the sides near her, each backed by their own bodyguards.

I recognized most of them. The Tinworthy lord, I'd never met, but he was the only gnome at the table. Likewise, the fae Nahli Twince was easily spotted. The only unknown member I assumed to be Reginald Malchi. He was younger than I'd expected—probably not even as old as me—and dressed in a brocade jacket more suited to a dinner party than a meeting of criminal minds.

My guide rapped the haft of his axe twice and announced, "Lords and ladies, Miss Hashi Severn."

The reaction to my arrival was immediate.

"How *dare* you!" Teris Balshi shot up from his seat, one trembling finger pointing just beyond me. "You *murder* my father and make a mockery of his death by parading his defiled corpse in *here*?"

*Well, *this* meeting is getting off to a ripe start!* Saraknyal said sourly.

I glanced back at the shade of Yirish Balshi, then shrugged. "First, I didn't murder him. He's not dead. He's a shade. Second, he tried to run me through. I consider his punishment just."

Balshi's face flushed red with anger. "I demand—"

Ingrid Brickhammer slapped one broad hand on the tabletop with a report like a thunderclap. "Young Balshi, you may have the richest and most powerful house, but you're *new* to the Council. You can have your say once you've grown into your station, but you're in no position to *demand* anything at this time. Now *sit down*!"

Okay, I'm starting to like Brickhammer.

I'd known bringing his father's shade would get a rise out of the young Balshi, and intended it to throw them off their game. *First impressions...*

Balshi dropped into his seat, fuming.

"Miss, Severn, thank you for comin'." Ingrid Brickhammer gestured to the empty chair. "Please have a seat and let me introduce everyone."

Not too close to the fae, Saraknyal warned. *They sense magic and see things that mortals don't.*

Could she recognize you for what you are?

If she touched me, certainly. From a distance, I don't know.

Better safe than sorry. "I'll stand, thank you. And I know who everyone is." I crossed my arms and rested one hand on Soul Drinker. "What do you want?"

Don't piss them off, Hashi. It's a long way to the front door.

Ingrid Brickhammer cleared her throat. "The Council has recognized you as an up-and-coming power in Haven, and—"

"What *I* want," Reginald Malchi interrupted, "is to know what your intentions are for the future."

I cocked an eyebrow at him. "Why should I have to declare my intentions to anyone? There are no laws in Haven, and I don't answer to you. Or is your *Council* setting itself up as a nascent government?"

Ting Hatsu looked annoyed. "We are *not* a government, and we have no plans to try to govern Haven. The Council was established for other reasons entirely."

"*What* reasons?" I asked.

"Primarily, as non-aggression and non-competition pacts between our houses." Blinth Tinworthy's voice was high-pitched, but firm and hard. "All business interests in Haven are intertwined in some way, shape, or form, a natural result of our isolation and lack of real estate. Inter-house competition became an unsustainable drain on profits. As Council members, we agree to not directly interfere with or murder each other."

"So instead of fighting one another, you decided to attack *my* businesses, kill *my* people."

Ingrid Brickhammer shook her head. "Now, that's not how it was. We've been watchin' you, but *most* of us didn't want to...confront you." She cast a glance at Teris Balshi. "The houses who went after you feared for their livelihoods. They learned a painful lesson."

I rolled my eyes. "I deal in antiquities and help out a few *small* protection businesses. How can that threaten anyone's livelihood?"

"Perhaps not now," said Hatsu primly, "but you have particular...skills that could present unbeatable competition. Consider, for example, if you engaged in the slave trade. *Your* type of slaves," she flicked long-nailed fingers toward my undead minions, "are readily available from the streets of Haven, require no housing or nourishment, don't try to escape, and never die. How am I to compete with that?"

"Oh, come on!" I protested. "*This* is what keeps you up at night? That I might *outcompete* you?"

She's right, you know. Saraknyal said. *Tinaros' economy was—*

Shut up!

"Not all threats are economic." Nahli Twince's voice, though musical, was tempered with steel and a hint of disgust. "Necromancy is a perversion of the natural order and inherently expansionist.

What's to stop you from raising an army of undead and seizing Haven? You have shown yourself to be formidable, but so are *we*. Make no mistake, we will *not* stand by and allow you to take over Haven with your necromantic powers, Miss Severn."

How the hell do they expect to stop you? Saraknyal quipped, but I was beyond considering any of this amusing.

I raked them all with my gaze and clenched my fists in rage. "This is *bullshit*!"

"Now, listen here, Miss Sev—"

"No, *you* listen!" I snapped, pointing a finger at Brickhammer to cut her off. "I've done *nothing* to deserve this! You have a preconceived and unsubstantiated fear of me that has absolutely *no* basis! Inherently expansionist? *Wrong!* The Empire of Tinaros existed for centuries under strict laws governing the use of necromancy, until a race of *peaceful* herbivores exterminated every man, woman, and child within their borders! I came to Haven because it's the only place where I can live in *peace*, and that's just what I've done. Ten years, and I haven't raised an undead army to seize this city. I haven't even tried to *kill* anyone who didn't try to kill me first! Can any of *you* say the same? I will *not* be lectured to and threatened by the likes of you!"

I thought you didn't approve of the Tinaran system, Saraknyal reminded me.

Shut up!

After a long, smoldering silence, Ingrid once again slapped a meaty palm to the table. "Now that everyone's had their say, let's get to the reason for this little confab. Miss Severn, we didn't invite you here to condemn or threaten you." Her eyes shifted around the table to her fellow council members. "In fact, we'd like to offer you a seat on the Council."

"You wha...?" I admit, she caught me utterly flat-footed.

Close your mouth, dear.

"I *said*, we'd like to offer you a seat on Haven's Council." Ingrid shrugged. "Consider our positions, please. We may not *like* you, what you do or represent—frankly, we don't like each *other* much either—but this is about survival. If you join us, the Council will ensure that no other members bother you, and that *you* won't bother *us*."

Join them or slaughter them. Those are your only two choices now.

I didn't really want to do either. "And if I *don't* join the Council?"

Nahli Twince shrugged. "Then we cannot ensure that one or more of us will not, in the future, interfere with you or your holdings."

Damned if you do, damned if you don't

I'm already damned. The Council had me between a rock and a hard place, and they knew it, but I wouldn't kowtow to them. "I'll think it over."

"Please do," Brickhammer said. "We'll meet here tomorrow at midday and expect your answer."

"All right." I nodded to them—I'd dance naked in hell before I thanked them—turned on my heel, and walked out.

Chapter Twenty Seven
A Sudden Change

From the journal of Hashi Severn –

It's nice to know that sometimes good things happen without my intervention.

"Gods and devils, I've got to take a break!" I dropped my pen and stood to stretch, stiff from bending over my lab bench.

Oh, come on! It's only been…what, seven hours?

If Saraknyal had had a neck, I would have wrung it. Since our encounter with the Death Stone, he'd been working constantly on designing a receptacle to contain it. Not having to sleep helped his progress. Unfortunately, he barely allowed me any sleep either.

In an effort to delay the inevitable return to work, I tapped the diagram we'd drafted last week. "Let me go over this again and see if I've got it straight, okay?"

Fine. Go ahead.

"We'll inscribe three layers of enchantments, each into a different metal layered on the inside of the casing."

Correct. Transformative, reflective, and containment enchantments, each layer annealed to the previous, within an outer iron shell.

"But won't coating the interior with molten metal destroy the previously inscribed layer?"

That's why we use three different metals, my dear, each one with a different melting point.

"Right. First gold, then silver, then lead."

Yes. Let's just hope that dwarf's up to the challenge.

I'd commandeered Jhavika's armorer, a dwarf named Hipshill, for the metalwork, transferring his entire workshop from Jhavika's keep to a newly constructed forge in my own courtyard. I'd brought Lewin and Lavo over, too. The former because he knew Jhavika's library—now mine—like the back of his hand, and the latter simply because I'd never had an alchemist, and thought I might get lucky and find someone with a recipe for Tori's miraculous elixir. I kept shades watching over them constantly. They were still ensorcelled, after all.

I tapped the notes beside the diagram. "But I still don't understand how you can transform negative energy into positive. It seems impossible."

Magic is the impossible made real, my dear, Saraknyal assured me. *If I can transform soul essence into a blast of winter, I can puzzle out how to transform Void essence into other magical effects.*

"If you say so." This project both intrigued and worried me, primarily because I had to trust Saraknyal not to create some kind of dreadful weapon.

Now, back to work! I estimate we can transcribe the rest of these runes today, if you just buckle down.

"Easy for you to say." I picked up the pen again. "You have no hand to cramp."

Whiner, he said without rancor. *Now, draw a line at a forty-five degree angle from left to right...*

I followed Saraknyal's instructions exactly to scribe the next rune. As soon as I completed the last line, the symbol blurred, unreadable except to those with arcane talent. I waved the page to dry the ink, then put it atop the pile of already completed pages, grabbed a blank page, and dipped my pen.

Isn't this fun? You and me working together on magic! It's been so long since I've crafted any spells.

Saraknyal's enthusiasm had worn thin on me, but I couldn't make myself tell him to tone it down. I'd never seen him so happy.

Now, vertical line from center down two— Saraknyal's instruction was cut short by a loud knock my laboratory door.

Tell them to go away! he snapped. *Our work's too important.*

Desperate for a break, I called, "Come in!"

Joss burst in. "Mistress! You must come. Something's happened!"

"Shit!" I lurched to my feet, dread twisting my guts. "Jhavika?"

It had been blissfully peaceful since the dinner at Malchi's estate, but we'd all been poised for trouble. The shore defenses had been completed and manned, we'd assigned Patak command of *Tiger Lily* until we could procure a proper warship, and put him on harbor watch with Niland under his command. We were as ready for an attack as we could be, but no one could guess at what forces Jhavika might return with.

"Oh, *no,* mistress! Sorry." Joss cringed. "It's Lewin, Lavo, and Hipshill. They wish to speak with you immediately. They say it's *very* important. I put them in your office."

All three of them? I wondered what had happened.

Tell them to wait. We're busy!

No. This could be important. "Thank you, Joss. I'll deal with this."

I climbed the stairs slowly, my legs stiff from hours perched on a stool. I entered to find Lewin, Lavo, and Hipshill pacing and chattering incessantly, their shade guards looming nearby. This alone startled me, for Lavo and Hipshill barely spoke when I addressed them directly. They immediately approached me, all three grinning like children released from school early.

"Lady Severn!" Lewin stepped to the fore, positively ebullient. "The enchantment's broken!"

"The..." It took me a moment to understand. "*Jhavika's* enchantment?"

*Holy shit! This really *is* more important than our work!*

"Well, the enchantment of the scourge, but yes!" He shared grins with the other two. "We're free! We can talk to you about absolutely anything!"

"Aye, and I want ta thank you proper for gettin' us outta there!" Hipshill bustled forward, his strong hands clenched before him as he took a knee before me. "I'd be honored ta work for you regular like, if you'll have me! I got the form for that castin' almost done! Ingenious design, by the way, but a right bugger to git right. A dodecahedron's a hard shape, you know. No straight circumference ta—"

My mind reeled. I raised my hands to calm him down. "Of course, you can continue to work for me, Hipshill. And you both as well, if you wish. We'll work out the details later. Now, tell me how you know the enchantment is broken."

"Well, I can bloody *speak*, fer one thing!" Hipshill grinned through his beard and laughed a booming peal. "That bloody handed bitch ordered me to only speak when spoken to, and then as little as possible. She's a right shrew, she is! Why, I'd like ta—"

"Milady, we were all commanded to *always* act, speak, and even *think* with Jhavika's best interest in mind," Lewin explained. "Abolishing that compulsion allowed us not only to *act* as we wish and *say* whatever we like, but also freed our minds. We're free to *think* for ourselves!"

"Lady Severn, you must understand." Eias Lavo stepped forward, her features at once intense and overjoyed. "Jhavika was a tyrant and paranoid in the extreme! She controlled our very minds!"

"A right maniac is what she is!" Hipshill added.

"And the enchantment's suddenly broken? Just gone?"

"Yes, Lady Severn. Completely and utterly," Lewin confirmed.

This can mean only one of two things, Hashi: either Jhavika's dead or the scourge has been destroyed.

My mind spun. *But if she was killed and someone else took up the scourge, wouldn't they gain control over her slaves?*

No. Magic doesn't work that way. The scourge connected each subject to their master's will. One link in that chain was broken. If either the scourge or the master are gone...

Then the magic dies, and its effects cease.

Precisely!

But if someone else picked it up... "Lewin, you were Jhavika's sage. Now that the enchantment's gone, what more can you tell me about the scourge?"

He shook his head slowly. "Very little, unfortunately. I researched it in depth at her behest, to no avail. I couldn't find anything about it in the literature at my disposal, which was extensive. She never allowed me to examine it directly."

Something else nagged at me. "Where did Jhavika *get* the scourge?"

The sage shrugged. "I have no idea. She already had it when she approached me nearly four years ago. She lashed me with it, and that was the end of my free will."

"The rest of the Council needs to hear this!" I pulled the bell rope for Joss, and he arrived moments later. "Send messages to all the council members. Tell them Jhavika's spell of compulsion is broken. I'm convening a meeting at Jhavika's keep to interview her retainers."

"At once, mistress! Your carriage?"

"Yes, and an escort. Thanks!" Joss nodded and hurried off.

I turned to the others. "You'll come with me. The Council will have a lot of questions, but once this is finished, you'll be free to do as you wish. *All* of you will be. I'll insist upon it." They'd been through hell for who knew how long.

"Thank you, milady!" Eias Lavo fell to her knees, tears in her eyes. "You have no idea what this means to us!"

"It's the least I can do."

*The *least* would be nothing, or better yet, telling them they owe you for releasing them.*

But I didn't release them, Saraknyal.

True. Someone else did that, and I can only think of one likely culprit.

My mind clicked on the most probable answer: *Captain Longbright.*

Exactly. He either found a way to destroy the scourge or killed Jhavika.

An icy hand gripped the back of my neck. *Gods and devils preserve us if he killed Jhavika and took the scourge for his own.*

I swear, if I have to listen to anyone else babble on about Jhavika's gods-damned enchantment, I'll suck their soul right out through their eyeballs!

I'll let you. I boarded my carriage and left Jhavika's keep, hopefully for the last time.

For days the Council had interviewed the victims of Jhavika's enchantment in an effort to uncover her plots. Multitudes came forth pleading to be heard and exonerated. Most told similar tales, though we suspected some of telling only half-truths, unwilling to reveal their most heinous actions under Jhavika's spell. The most pitiful were those forced to satisfy her carnal desires.

Nahli assumed responsibility for the formerly enchanted concubines. Scarred in both body and mind, she took them to her keep for healing. "They're in a state of utter emotional breakdown," she'd explained. "They were commanded to love her, to think of nothing but how to please her. Now, I'm afraid, they don't know *what* to feel."

I finally bowed out and headed for home. I had urgent business of my own.

I went straight to my laboratory, eager to get back to work. Atop the bench rested the Death Stone containment vessel. Hipshill had cast the outer casing—two inches thick—from black iron in two halves. Fitted together, they formed a perfect dodecahedron about one foot across. The inside of the casing was spherical and plated with a layer of gold. Already, I'd engraved about a third of the precious metal with runes. I'd started slow, taking several minutes to etch each rune, fearful of making a mistake, but I soon increased in both proficiency and speed.

I adjusted the multi-lens magnifier, picked up a fine engraving stylus, and poised my hand above the gold. Beside me lay a page depicting a single rune, blurred, since I lacked the arcane talent to read it. I placed atop it a notched card that covered three quarters of the rune. The visible portion snapped into clarity. Etching that quarter-rune onto the gold, I then shifted the card to uncover a second quarter of the rune. Continuing this way, I quickly completed the rune, waited for Saraknyal's approval, and started the next, then the next...

Hours later, as my stylus approached the gold, Saraknyal said, *Hashi, someone's at the door. Don't be—*

Joss burst into the lab. "Mistress!"

—startled.

Saraknyal's warning had saved me from an error that would have cost us hours. I dropped the engraving tool and turned to glare at my butler. "Joss, this better be important."

"Yes, mistress, it is." He held out a note. "Jhavika's ships have been spotted."

"All of them?" I snatched the note with aching fingers and tore it open.

"No, mistress, only two, but the city's buzzing like a hornet's nest!"

I scanned the message. *Bluebonnet* and *Peony* had been sighted in Snomish Bay. Both commanded significant forces of soldiers on deck, but flew flags of truce.

Real surrender or a ruse?

Better safe than sorry. "Joss, ready my carriage. I'll be taking a force of shades to the waterfront."

"At once, mistress!" He whirled to go.

"And Joss?"

"Yes, mistress?" He turned back.

"I'm doing *delicate* work here." I gestured to the casing on the bench. "One mistake could be catastrophic. Next time, knock quietly before you come in."

"Oh! *Yes*, mistress!" He looked duly horrified. "Sorry, mistress."

"It's all right." I waved him out.

It's not *all right! If one rune is incorrect, this entire thing could—*

I know. Don't lecture me. I stood and stretched. Sitting stooped over my work for hours cramped every muscle in my neck and back, and even a cushioned stool left my backside numb.

By the time I arrived at the waterfront with a contingent of shades, *Bluebonnet* and *Peony* had just dropped anchor, and the rest of the Council had already assembled their forces. I directed Bromish to pull up as far from the Blackbriar contingent as possible. I had no desire to speak to him. Ingrid informed me that Captain Patak had sailed out to meet the two ships, and hadn't encountered any resistance. One of *Tiger Lily*'s cutters now sailed briskly toward us, hopefully with more information.

We waited tensely as the cutter pulled alongside the quay and furled sails.

"Lords and ladies!" One of the former pirates clambered up a ladder from the boat and knuckled his forehead in salute. "Capt'n Patak's compliments. He's taken charge o' *Bluebonnet* and *Peony* with no trouble at all. He sends in these here fer questioning."

With considerable help from the sailors, two forlorn figures struggled up onto the quay. I barely recognized Ursilla Roque and Tambris Matesh.

I'd always found Tambris exotically handsome, with his perfectly trimmed beard and Marathian garb. Now, half of his face bore healing burns, one eye covered in a black eyepatch. His remaining eye smoldered deep in its sunken socket, vacant and haunted. His left arm, swathed in bandages, hung in a sling.

Ursilla looked like death warmed over, no longer the exuberant woman I'd last seen at Balshi's ill-fated party. She'd lost weight, her cheeks sunken and her clothes hanging as if from a skeleton. Vacant eyes gazed uneasily at her peers, then she looked away.

"So," Malchi began, breaking our shocked silence, "you're both back alive, I see."

"It was closer than you might think." Tambris' words came out slurred and hoarse. I suspected he was either inebriated or taking something for the pain.

"We know you have questions." Ursilla's voice trembled. "We... Our actions... *Jhavika...*" She spat the name like a curse, her face twisting into a grimace. "...enchanted us."

"We know all about the enchantment," Tori assured her. "*And* about Jhavika's scourge."

Ingrid Brickhammer pulled a flask from a pocket and offered it to the two. "May the gods preserve us and the devils torment Jhavika Keshmir to the depths of the Nine Hells."

"By the tree..." Nahli stepped closer to peer at Matesh's weeping wounds and scabbed face. "Tambris, come to me after we finish here. I'll see to your injuries."

"I..." He took a slug from the flask, then cleared his throat. "I'll heal, Nahli, but thank you."

What's that about? Marathian pride?

351

Maybe he doesn't trust any kind of magic after being ensorcelled. "How did Jhavika get to you?" I asked, overwhelmed by curiosity. "Did you *know* you were enchanted?"

"I did," Matesh volunteered bitterly. "She…lashed me some years ago, commanded me never to mention anything to anyone."

Ursilla looked aimlessly about, her gaze dull, her voice listless. "I didn't know until that damned ball. Jhavika was fighting with Kevril, then she ordered her *friends* to protect her, and my body just *moved*. I…couldn't stop myself!" Her eyes glistened now, and she turned to me. "I wanted to warn you, Hashi, after you killed Vakna. I was afraid she'd command us to attack you." Her gaze fell upon Soul Drinker. "I didn't want to die like that."

"Gods, I wish you'd have killed that maniacal *bitch*, Hashi," Matesh growled.

"So do I, but I would have had to go through you and half of Balshi's guards. And I wasn't about to give her an opportunity to take this." I unsheathed Soul Drinker and spun it in my palm. "If she had, we'd be in much *deeper* trouble."

"Put that away!" Tori snapped, one hand on his elf blade.

I stared at Tori in surprise and sheathed the dagger. I'd never seen him so intense, so serious. "Don't get your knickers in a twist."

"Yes, well…" Malchi cleared his throat and looked to Ursilla and Tambris. "We know you've gone through hell, but we need a little information. When did you last see Jhavika?"

"I haven't seen her since we sailed," Matesh said. "She sent me to Ton Chi looking for Longbright, and I ran afoul of a pirate. We survived, but barely." He nodded to Que-Chen. "*Bluebonnet* was badly damaged, but we repaired what we could."

"I hold Jhavika responsible for the damage, Lord Matesh," the young man assured him.

"I last saw Jhavika at Dunnhaven Rock. She ordered me aboard *Crimson Hawk* for a conference." Ursilla drained the last of Ingrid's flask. "She's a fucking maniac. I've never been…so helpless, so terrified. Her steward overheard us speaking about the scourge, and she had him executed. She… Her last command to me was to search the city of Valaka for any sign of Longbright. She was going to scour the windward coast, then come up the leeward side to meet me there. I did as she ordered and waited for her, but she never arrived. Eight days after we parted ways, the enchantment vanished. I couldn't deal..." She shook her head. "I very nearly took my own life."

"Well, you're back here now and safe," Tori said in an upbeat tone. "We think Jhavika must be dead or the scourge destroyed."

Both of them nodded.

"I don't suppose either of you spotted Captain Longbright's ship, did you?" Malchi asked.

They shook their heads, but Ursilla spoke up. "Tan was ordered to search Valaka, but never reported in. We don't know what happened to her or *Golden Harlot*. The others, the ships commanded by Jhavika's slaves, are probably on their way back here, like us, unless they chose to go pirate or just sail away."

"We can only hope they return," Que-Chen said. "Frankly, we need the ships. This whole episode has interrupted trade."

Matesh looked at us and asked bluntly, "Can we *go* now?"

"Of course," Ingrid said. "I brung carriages for you both. Just to warn you, there's some hard feelin's around the city, so I'd suggest you take your soldiers home and lay low for a bit. Anythin' you need?"

"A proper bath, anything to eat besides salt pork and ship's biscuit, and something better than grog." Ursilla handed the flask back to Ingrid and shuffled away. Matesh followed.

"I'll have Patak ferry Tambris and Ursilla's soldiers ashore," Malchi said.

If we're done here…

Let's go.

I caught sight of Tori Blackbriar as I turned to leave. He stared at me with a look on his face I'd never seen on him before: no mirth, not worry, but…horror? Revulsion?

What's his problem?

I opened my mouth to ask, but Tori beat me to it. "You should learn a lesson from what happened to Jhavika, Hashi."

"What are you talking about?" My hand drifted to Soul Drinker.

"That!" He stabbed a finger at the dagger. "Do you recall what Nahli said to Jhavika on the occasion of her joining the Council? She warned her: *Have a care, lest it consume you.* Jhavika was *consumed* by the magic of her scourge. If you're not careful, that...*thing* will do the same to you."

Thing? Tell him to fuck off, Hashi!

"I don't—" But Tori whirled and strode away, his warning clear in my mind. I *did* remember Nahli's words, but since when did Tori Blackbriar spout dire prophecies? *What the hell was that about?*

*He's scared of you, that's all."

He never has been before. I boarded my carriage for home, trying to sort out Tori's string of curious behavior. *First he's overly friendly, then he saves my life with that elixir, and now he's foretelling my doom?*

Forget about it. We've got work to do.

Right...work. Work on a magical construction designed by a necromancer, engraving spells that I could neither read nor understand, with the goal of containing the very essence of death. Tori's warning haunted me all the way back to Ash Keep. I wondered if he wasn't right, or if his warning was simply half a century too late.

Two more of Jhavika's former armada surrendered in the following days. *Summer Violet* was commanded by Jhavika's senior man at arms, Yorish. He and seventy or so of Jhavika's former soldiers threw themselves on the mercy of the Council. Yorish seemed astonished when we declined to administer punishment. As a military man, he expected consequences for his actions, even if he'd been following orders he couldn't refuse, but we decided that his enchantment by Jhavika had been punishment enough.

The beamy junk, *Jasmine*, was more of a mystery. By the time Patak boarded, Jhavika's commander and his cadre had disappeared. The remaining officers told him that the commander's name was Busashi, and that he and his five companions knew nothing of seamanship, but enforced Jhavika's orders with the edge of a sword so adroitly that none argued. Once the enchantment lapsed, they'd sequestered themselves in the captain's cabin. Upon arriving in Haven, they disappeared before anyone knew they were gone.

After the ships were thoroughly searched and everyone aboard interrogated, those soldiers formerly under Jhavika's enchantment were put to work on the new shipyard or assigned to patrol the waterfront. Those from other houses were dispersed to their respective keeps.

Just when we all thought this appalling saga would come to a close without serious conflict, all Nine Hells broke loose.

Chapter Twenty Eight
The Long Game

One day.

One day to make a decision that would affect the rest of my life.

I obsessed all the way home, and Saraknyal remained blissfully silent. I think he was worried I'd lock him in his box if he harangued me.

Back at Ash Keep, Joss met me at the door, his brow furrowed with worry. "All's well, I trust, mistress?" His tone told me he thought otherwise.

My people knew I'd been summoned before the Council. I'd successfully fought back against three council members individually, but I'd never survive a consolidated attack. Of course they were worried.

They're afraid I can't protect them any longer.

Well, you'd better allay those fears if you don't want them to abandon you.

"Not to worry." I told Joss, forcing a smile. "The Council had some questions, that's all. I'll be meeting with them again tomorrow." All true, but I'd omitted the dreadful details.

"Very good, mistress."

After dinner, which I could barely eat for my singing nerves, I stood on my balcony, brandy in hand, staring out over the city and considering my situation. I hated the idea of being manipulated by these so-called lords, but I had little doubt that they could make my life a living hell. Being on the Council sounded like a royal pain in the ass, but I didn't have a lot of options: Join and deal with them, decline and end up fighting them, or leave Haven. Unfortunately, if I declined and stayed, I wasn't the only one at risk. I thought of

Bryce's beating, the look in his wife's eyes, the sailors burned on *Golden Gal*.

"I don't know what to do, Saraknyal," I finally admitted. "The Council's afraid of me, but can't get rid of me. Since they can't get rid of me, they want me to join. What kind of fucked up logic is that?"

*The 'keep your friends close and your enemies closer' kind of logic. It's exactly the logic you should be using, too."

"I don't want anyone close to me." I quaffed brandy and gritted my teeth.

What are you most afraid of if you join the Council?

His question took me off guard. "I'm not afraid, but I don't *trust* them. The fae despises me, and Fa-Chen and Balshi are out for revenge. That won't go away."

*So, you don't trust them. Good. You shouldn't. But that's the 'keep your enemies closer' part. Now, what are you afraid of if you *don't* join?*

"That they'll hurt or kill my people."

*Think closer to home. What might the Council do that would affect you *personally*?*

"Outlaw necromancy," I answered immediately. "That was the reason I was run out of Mati and Sariff. I'm running out of places to go. And Haven is my home…"

*Exactly! And what's the best way to prevent that from happening? By sitting at the table where those decisions are made. By using your influence to affect those decisions. By making Haven's future *your* future.*

"Make Haven's future *my* future? What does that even mean?"

You're a student of history, Hashi. Who do you read about in the history books?

"That's easy: the winners. They're the ones who write history."

Correct. Now, you can't win a fight against the entire Council using violence, so how do you fight them?

The answer was simple. "Sit at the table."

I silently sipped my brandy and considered his words. I didn't want to be a part of this Council, didn't like being manipulated, but if I refused, I would lose my voice to oppose them. Decisions… Life is doing a lot of things you don't want to do. Minutes passed before Saraknyal spoke again.

Hashi, where do you see yourself in fifty or sixty years?

I snorted a laugh and choked on my brandy. "Fifty or sixty *years*? I'll be *dead* by then!"

Not unless someone manages to murder you.

His statement took me aback. "What?"

How old are you?

"Thirty-five. Why?"

Look in the mirror.

"Why? What are you getting at?"

*Just look in the gods-damned *mirror*, Hashi. I want to show you something.*

I sighed and strode for my bedroom and the full-length mirror in the corner. A woman stared back at me, a beautiful woman, tall and dark-skinned, with short cropped hair and a sensual mouth. I still wore the clothes and jewelry from the Council meeting: a shirt of finest black silk, snug leather pants, and silver at my wrists, belt, and boots.

"Okay, now *what* am I looking at?"

Look very closely and tell me if you look thirty-five years old.

A chill crept up my spine. I placed my snifter on the dresser and stepped up to the mirror, peering at my face. I turned my head this way and that, scrutinized myself as I'd rarely done. Then I realized what I *wasn't* seeing. Not a line marred my smooth skin, not a wrinkle or blemish. Not even the fine crow's feet that crinkled the corners of the eyes of most middle-aged people. My lips were full and smooth, my teeth white, my eyes clear and sharp. *Necromancy...* The chill invaded my gut, and I shivered.

"No!"

*Yes, Hashi. The moment you allowed me into your soul, we bonded. My magic works through you, and it works *on* you. The years aren't touching you. You're unique, my dear, not a necromancer but sustained by one. I don't know how long you'll have, but it'll be a hell of a lot longer than seventy years.*

I staggered back from my reflection, my ageless, undying, immortal self. "I don't want it!"

Then lay me aside and walk through the streets of Haven until somebody murders you for those fancy boots and pretty bracelets.

He was right; I could escape life that way, or simply take a step off my balcony. But my soul... I was damned to the Nine Hells. Mortas, the Deathless One, awaited me, and I had no doubt that he would devise an imaginatively horrible eternity for me, the unwilling necromancer. I shuddered and hugged myself.

Or... Saraknyal continued, *...you could stop screwing around and look at the *long* game.*

"The long game..." I thought of the future, the *real* future, for the first time. Not the next year, two years, or even ten, but fifty, a hundred, five hundred. What would Haven be? What would *I* be?

Heaving a deep breath, I faced myself in the mirror. The only one way to influence the future was to be part of it. If I remained sequestered, acting only within my own sphere, others would decide it for me. I plucked my snifter off of the dresser and drained it.

"Yes," I stared into my own dark eyes and saw the future. "The long game..."

The following morning, I rose late, broke my fast, dressed, and summoned my carriage. I took only two escorts, my Jaguar Warrior wraith and the former Lord Balshi. Bromish delivered me to the gates of Brickhammer Keep without incident.

The same armored dwarf met me with a grunt and a nod. "This way, if you please."

The meeting room was the same, except today a fire roared in the hearth, the air thick and warm. The Council members all sat exactly where they had been before, all unsmiling, all looking at me. Teris Balshi's eyes still shot daggers, and Nahli Twince's expression remained utterly unreadable.

"Miss Severn," Ingrid Brickhammer gestured to an empty chair, "would you sit with us this time? Perhaps take some refreshment?"

Before each council member sat a wine glass, tumbler, or tankard, and a sideboard was laden with decanters and bottles. I pulled out the chair and sat, never taking my gaze from the members. "Brandy, please."

An attendant poured brandy, but in a glass, not a snifter. I swirled it under my nose and sipped. *Disappointing...*

They're obviously barbarians, Saraknyal quipped.

"I'd like to thank you for comin', and ask what you've decided." Brickhammer's face remained set in stone.

"I've decided to take you up on your offer to join the Council, but I have two conditions. *Nonnegotiable* conditions."

Two? Saraknyal sounded worried, but I ignored him.

"Conditions?" Malchi snorted indignantly. "You can't come in here and start *dictating* to us!" He glanced around at his fellow council members as if to gauge their support.

They all stared at me, their expressions even more grave than before, if that was possible.

Blinth Tinworthy broke the uneasy silence. "*What* conditions?"

I hope you're not overplaying this, Hashi.

This is what you wanted, I reminded Saraknyal. *I'm playing the long game.*

Well, let's hope that this game's long enough for you to get out of here alive.

"My *first* condition," I continued, raking my gaze around the table, "is that necromancy will *never* be outlawed in Haven."

Several members murmured urgently to each other, but Ingrid Brickhammer looked me in the eye. "We're a *Council*, not a government, Miss Severn. None of us particularly *like* laws, which is why we're in Haven, and we don't expect to be passin' any."

Says every fledgling government.

I put my hands up, palms out. "I just want to make that point up front so there are no mistaken expectations in the future. Take it or leave it."

They all exchanged glances and nods, then Brickhammer looked back at me, eyes narrowed, tone wary. "We'll concede that point. And your *second* condition?"

I frowned, and the air seemed suddenly thicker, harder to breathe, the tension palpable. They stared at me expectantly, and their guards shifted, hands drifting toward weapons.

Hashi…? Saraknyal warned.

"My second condition…" I sipped my brandy and leveled a hard stare around the table. "Is that you invest in a higher quality of brandy. This stuff is *really* vile!" With an exaggerated grimace, I nudged the glass away.

"Ha!" Ingrid's laugh popped the tension like a soap bubble.

Several council members smiled—save for Balshi, who sneered—and even Nahli Twince's expressionless mien seemed to relax.

Well played, my dear.

"All in favor of admittin' Hashi Severn to the Council, say aye," Ingrid said. After a unanimous response—albeit hesitant in Balshi's case—she announced, "Welcome to the Haven Council of Lords, *Lady* Severn."

I picked up my glass and raised it to the rest of the Council. "To the future of Haven, and the survival of all."

We all drank. Or, at least, I pretended to. The brandy really was hideous.

Minutes later, I walked out of Brickhammer Keep and boarded my carriage.

That couldn't have gone much better, though you might have warned me about that second condition.

Spur of the moment. I thumped on the roof and called out, "To the quay, Bromish. I want to pick something up."

Why the quay? Saraknyal asked warily. *No more lead-lined boxes!*

Don't worry. This has nothing to do with you.

We pulled up and I took a lift to my favorite bookseller's shop. Five minutes and ten silver crowns later, I climbed back into the carriage and set my purchase reverently upon my lap.

And what's this *for?*

I ran my fingers over the tooled black leather cover, opened it up and sniffed the fine parchment, beautifully blank and ready for writing.

As you said, Saraknyal, I'm in this for the long game. I'm a historian. I've got to make sure it gets recorded accurately.

Accuracy can be overrated. What would have happened if you'd read that Tawkh Keep belonged to a necromancer? We might never have met.

I shrugged. *What's done is done. I've got to look toward my future now.* "Bromish!" I called. "Take me home!"

Take us home.

Yes, I agreed. *Take us home.*

Chapter Twenty Nine
Confrontations

From the journal of Hashi Severn –

I don't need anyone. I don't want anyone. Life is simpler alone, safer, quieter... I've been telling myself this for fifty-five years. I still feel no need for companionship, for love, for all of the things I've never had yet wanted so badly as a young woman. Now, I don't know if I made the right choice in allowing Saraknyal to consume that part of me. Perhaps, if I'd perished in the flames, I would have found peace.

Darkness still struggled against dawn's light as I stood in the courtyard of Ash Keep, near the open doors of the forge, watching Hipshill at work. He'd heated one half of the Death Stone containment vessel to a precise temperature, then clamped it concave-side up onto a spinning cradle that resembled a potter's wheel. As it spun, he poured pure molten silver, cooled to barely above its melting point, into the vessel's center. Centripetal force spread the metal outward, coating the interior in a thin layer, covering the rune-inscribed gold, before solidifying.

The table spun down and stopped. Hipshill peered at the interior with a magnifying lens, then looked up at me with a grin. "That should do, mistress. Just a little dressin' up 'round the edges."

He's really a master, Hashi, Saraknyal said in honest appreciation.

I released my held breath and smiled. "Hipshill, I—"

Hashi! Saraknyal broke in. *There's a disturbance at the postern door.*

What? I forced my gaze away from the forge. My single remaining wraith and several shades stood at the open door, facing down an armed man in dark leathers. *What's it about?*

If I knew, I'd tell you. A visitor. He keeps saying it's urgent.

"Bother!" I tore myself away and strode across the courtyard.

The unfamiliar man saw me, shouted out, "Lady Severn!" and tried to step past my guards.

Instantly, three lengths of cold steel hovered at his throat.

"Stop!" My minions froze, and so did the incautious visitor.

He's either stupid or new in town.

The man eyed the blades, then looked back to me. "Lady Severn, I bear an urgent message from Lord Blackbriar!" He flipped up a patch on the breast of his jerkin to show Tori's coat of arms. "He had no time to draft a note!"

"Sheathe your weapons," I said, and my undead servants complied. "What's so urgent that he couldn't pen a note?"

"A ship's sailing into the harbor! She's *Hyacinth*! Brilla Balshi's in command."

I rolled my eyes. "What's the problem? Captain Patak should be able to deal with them."

"They aren't flying a white flag. Only the banner of House Balshi. And soldiers from Balshi Keep are marching to the quay. Lord Blackbriar's requested that the Council meet at the city quay immediately!"

"Shit! How many soldiers are marching?"

"Some two hundred, milady!"

How did she call her soldiers down?

I have no idea, but she's got another hundred at least aboard Hyacinth.

At least! Saraknyal sounded hopeful, as if his appetite had been whetted.

"What the hell is Brilla *doing*?" I growled in frustration.

"My Lord Blackbriar doesn't know. He only requests that you come with all haste."

My thoughts raced. Moving a force of shades to the waterfront would take more than an hour. Even readying the coach and racing down with as many as I could cram aboard might take nearly that long. Then I noticed the messenger's riding clothes. "You have a mount?"

"Yes, milady, but..."

Hashi, what are you—

Shut up! I turned to my wraith captain. "Assemble forty shades and come to the waterfront with all haste. Don't kill anyone on the way unless they attack you directly."

"Yes, mistress."

As he whirled away to follow my commands, I turned to the messenger. "I'm taking your horse."

The fuck you are! Saraknyal bellowed in my head. *Riding alone through the streets of Haven? Are you *trying* to get killed?*

The messenger made it here alive.

"Um...yes, milady. He's right here at the gate. I'll warn you, though, he's a right bastard."

"Then we'll get along famously." I slipped past him through the postern door to the street outside. A leggy stallion stood with his reins tied to the gate ring. He glared at me.

Hashi, you shouldn't go alone! What if this is some sly trap by Blackbriar? He almost drew his blade on you last time you saw him.

Then I'll just have to murder him, won't I? I approached the stallion and he stamped a foot at me, his shoe knocking chips from the cobbles.

"Here! Stop that!" The messenger stepped past me and grabbed the horse's reins, giving them a sharp jerk. "You be civil!" He turned to me. "Watch out, he's headstrong. Best give him his head through Haven; it's the only way to make it through the bad areas in one piece. Oh, and he bites."

"Wonderful." I had brief second thoughts—my previous mounts had all been well-mannered—but forged ahead. If Brilla Balshi intended some kind of attack or, gods-forbid, had somehow recovered Jhavika's scourge, every minute counted, and I could help even without my shades.

"He'll fight you some, but use a firm hand. Get him pointed in the right direction and kick him hard."

"Thank you!" I let the horse smell me, keeping my hand at a safe distance. When he didn't try to take my fingers off, I found a stirrup and lurched into the saddle. They were a hand too short for me, but I didn't have time to adjust them. "You can shelter in Ash Keep until I return."

"Thank you, milady." The messenger released the reins and stepped back.

The stallion kicked and pawed, thrashing his head. I hauled him around and kicked him in the flanks. He bolted in the general direction of the waterfront. I kept a firm grip on the reins, rose up from the saddle, and gave him his head.

If you die doing this, I'm never going to forgive you!

I was too busy hanging on to tell him to shut up.

The stallion raced through the streets, skidding around corners, but didn't fall and didn't throw me. The riffraff of Haven didn't have time to accost us in passing, though they threw epithets and refuse. By the time the harbor hove into view, my thighs ached from the too-short stirrups and keeping my ass off the saddle. When we burst onto the wide quay, the stallion and I were both lathered. I hauled back on the reins to keep him from plunging into the bay, and we skidded to a halt. I didn't see any Balshi soldiers, so I assumed I'd beaten them here. Out on the bay, a beamy galleon approached the quay under reduced sail, trailed by *Tiger Lily* and another of Que-Chen's armed merchantmen.

"Hashi!" I recognized Tori's call and spotted his red cape amidst a throng of milling lancers and a few of our new shore patrol. There were maybe fifty in all. The stallion was tired enough not to fight me much, so I coaxed him forward, reining him in to stand nose to nose with Tori's charger.

"Is that my *messenger's* horse?" Tori asked, his eyes narrowed.

"Yes," I replied tersely. "And your messenger's safe and sound at Ash Keep. You said all *haste*!"

He looked mollified and nodded toward the stallion. "I'm surprised he let you mount him. He's a—"

"A right bastard, as your messenger said, but he didn't throw me, so I guess we got along. Here." I slipped off and handed the reins to one of Tori's lancers. "I'd rather be on foot if this goes badly." I scanned the sparsely populated quay. "Where are the others?"

Tori shot me a sour look. "They *apparently* didn't commandeer my messengers' horses to get here as quickly as you did. I imagine most of them weren't even awake yet. Hopefully they're on the way."

"Why didn't we get more warning?"

"An offshore squall concealed *Hyacinth* until a lookout spotted her only a league off the harbor mouth."

I raised a questioning eyebrow. "How did *you* get here so quickly?"

"I was up early, or rather, *still* up. I'd been...out late."

The belle of the ball, snarked Saraknyal.

I craned my neck to peer through the phalanx of lancers, and spotted *Hyacinth*'s sails still full. "Why aren't they anchoring?"

"They haven't said." Tori's brow creased. "Patak asked their intentions, and they told him to stand off or they'd respond with force. He sent a cutter in for instructions, and I told him to let *Hyacinth* proceed. I didn't want to start a war with the most powerful House in Haven." He looked to me and nodded once. "Especially since, at the time, I was here alone!"

"And the Balshi forces?"

"About four blocks away, by my latest report." He gazed out toward *Hyacinth*. "And you can see she's got more aboard, though I haven't seen Brilla yet."

I worked my way through the lancers to stand at the quay's edge and shaded my eyes. *Hyacinth* tacked closer, barely fifty yards away now, her deck crowded with soldiers wearing House Balshi colors. No Brilla.

"If they arrive before any of our allies..." Tori had maneuvered his horse up beside me. "We could use a little help here if things turn sour."

His worried tone seemed uncharacteristic. "Is this the same Tori Blackbriar who faced down a keep full of armed gnomes with me?"

He eyed me sidelong, his gaze dropping to Soul Drinker. "I don't like our position. We could end up with water on one side and enemies on the other. You may be immune to blades, Hashi, but I doubt that dagger will keep you from drowning."

He's right there. Saraknyal admitted. *And I don't relish spending eternity at the bottom of Haven's harbor.*

Tori was right, but it bothered me more that he seemed to know that my invulnerability stemmed from Soul Drinker.

Shouts from sailors aboard *Hyacinth* interrupted us. Sails furled and heaving lines were thrown, thicker hawsers passed and secured to the great iron bollards along the quay wall. Huge hemp bumpers cushioned the ship's hull as she was drawn in. The sailors secured a wide gangplank to the quay. No one disembarked, but the ship's deck bristled with heavily armed soldiers at the ready.

As if choreographed, the sound of marching soldiers rumbled through the streets behind us, echoing on the walls of the warehouses as they took up position on the quay. The troops from House Balshi had arrived, and our own reinforcements were nowhere in sight.

"Now we're between the hammer and the anvil," I whispered to Tori.

"Indeed," Tori responded quietly. "This could go catastrophically bad, Hashi." At his gesture, the lancers of House Blackbriar shifted to block access from the gangplank to the quay. Then he called out to the ship, "Where is your captain? Who speaks for you?"

"Lady Balshi will speak to you momentarily," an officer said flatly.

"Well, she's alive, at least," I said.

*You say that like it's a *good* thing.*

I craned my neck to assess the Balshi forces behind us. Their weapons weren't drawn, but we were now boxed in and badly outnumbered. I wondered how long until my shades arrived.

If this goes wrong, Hashi, don't hesitate.

No shit! Do you have enough energy for a winter spell?

No.

Double shit. I clenched my fist on Soul Drinker's hilt and waited.

Finally, a figure emerged from *Hyacinth*'s sterncastle. Brilla Balshi hobbled to the rail on the arm of a soldier, but not the lovely, vibrant Brilla who had attended the ball for Jhavika only a month ago. White streaked her formerly dark hair, her skin the hue of dirty chalk. Hands like claws clutched her escort's arm, her whole body trembling. Her eyes were the worst: sunken and dark, lifeless and cold. If Ursilla Roque had looked like death warmed over, Brilla Balshi seemed a stone-cold corpse.

Tell me she's not undead, I thought.

She's not undead, Saraknyal deadpanned back. *No, really.*

"I am Lady Brilla Balshi of House Balshi." Her voice grated out through quaking pale lips. "Get out of my way or I'll order my soldiers to attack."

"In light of recent events, Lady Balshi," Tori called to her, "I'm sure you understand that we must take certain precautions for the protection of Haven. I must request that you answer a few questions. Is Jhavika Keshmir aboard with you?"

"*Jhavika?*" Her voice broke on the word, and she barked a shrill, hysterical laugh. "Jhavika Keshmir is not with me. She is lost to me...lost to the world. Can't you *feel* it? She's...lost..." Her voice dwindled into unintelligible mutters.

"Uh..." For once, Tori Blackbriar seemed speechless.

What the fu—

The ball! I recalled, and said quietly to Tori, "At the ball, after you'd left, Brilla called Jhavika 'my love'. If the emotional state of Jhavika's concubines is any indication, then Brilla's having similar...issues."

Tori shot me a wide-eyed glance. "That's *bad.*"

*Great! So she's powerful *and* barking mad.*

"Necromancer!" Brilla's screech rent the air, her soulless eyes pinning me. "Can you return Jhavika to me?"

Every eye on the quay turned my way, and murmurs of "Necromancer" wafted through the crowd.

Don't piss her off, Hashi, Saraknyal warned.

I shook my head and held my hands out palm up in a gesture of helplessness. "I'm sorry, Brilla. There's nothing I can do." I glanced at Tori, found him staring intently at me. Shrugging, I said, "It's up to you."

With a nod, he turned back toward *Hyacinth.*

"Just a few more questions, Lady Balshi. What are your intentions here?"

"My *intentions?*" Brilla's eyes rolled wildly as she surveyed the crowd upon the quay. "I intend to go to my home and try to forget the last year of my life! If you, *any* of you, try to stop me, I will strike you *down*!" Her tone elevated to a shriek at the end. At her raised hand, her troops readied arms—crossbows raised, swords unsheathed—and stood alert for their lady's command.

She's very close to the edge, Hashi. Tell Blackbriar to let her go now, before she snaps!

I agreed whole heartedly. "Let her go, Tori. Pull your lancers back. I don't want to wade through *another* sea of blood."

He glanced sharply at me, then nodded, and motioned for the lancers to make a path for those aboard the ship. "The Council will not hold you responsible for your actions under the enchantment of Jhavika Keshmir's scourge, Lady Balshi." His words were so smooth, his voice so reassuring, I felt suddenly calmer myself. "If you will go to your keep in peace, we won't impede you. When you feel able, the Council would meet with you, but we understand you're distraught from your trials."

"*Distraught?*" Another shrill laugh escaped Brilla's trembling lips, but she nodded.

A carriage bearing the colors of House Balshi emerged from one of the side streets, and Tori motioned his lancers to make room. The soldiers aboard *Hyacinth* crossed the gangplank and took station along the path to the waiting coach. Then Brilla tottered down, her steps short and tremulous, her knuckles white on her escort's arm. She stared straight ahead, looking at nothing, no one, and boarded her carriage in silence.

I can't imagine what she's gone through...

Sympathy from the necromancer?

Sympathy? No, I was just stating a fact.

I dismissed his hedging and concentrated on the Balshi troops. As Brilla's carriage lurched into motion, her soldiers spun on their heels and followed. We stood in silence, watching, until we were the only ones left.

"Well, *that* was close!" Tori heaved a sigh and regarded me sidelong. "We make a good pair, eh, necromancer?"

I squinted at him, surprised by the comment. "When it comes to facing down armies, I suppose we do."

He opened his mouth, but a sailor from Hyacinth trundled down the gangplank to grasp his arm, rattling off questions about what had happened.

I turned away. It was too early in the day for this shit. I considered heading home, but decided to wait for my shades to arrive. If I wasn't here to instruct them to return to Ash Keep, they'd just stand here and scare people. I sat atop one of the quay bollards and closed my eyes to enjoy the morning sun and sea breeze until they arrived.

*What does *he* want?* Saraknyal's complaint came just before the sound of approaching footsteps. I opened my eyes.

"Hashi!" Tori strode over, the reins of his horse in hand, and stopped several strides away. In the distance, his lancers trotted away in perfect formation. He quirked a smile. "I wanted to thank you, both for your timely arrival and your suggestion that we let Brilla go."

I stood to keep from looking up at him. "I'm sure the rest of the Council will be devastated to have missed it."

We stared at one another in silence for a long moment before I asked, exasperated, "Tori, what do you want?"

"What I *want*," he said slowly, with no bluster, no humor, no suave repartee, "is to know why a necromancer would hesitate to harvest souls? Why *you*, time and again, refrain from doing what comes as innately to most necromancers as breathing."

I remained silent, staring him down.

"I'll *tell* you why; you're *not* a necromancer." His words were quiet, but they hit me with the force of a slap.

"What are you *prattling* about, Tori Blackbriar?" I sneered at him. "Of *course* I'm a necromancer. Or maybe you think I hired those," I pointed to my wraith and shades as they jogged onto the quay, "from a brothel?"

Take him out, Hashi! Saraknyal demanded.

Not yet. My hand crept to Soul Drinker's hilt. *I have to know what he knows.*

"*That*," Tori nodded toward Soul Drinker, his eyes narrowed, "is the true necromancer. A soul blade."

"Did Nahli tell you?" I demanded to know.

Fucking fae!

Tori's eyebrows raised. "No, she *didn't* tell me. I did what I do best; I gathered information and put two and two together. It's rumored in…certain quarters that you draw your power from that dagger. You're never without it. The necromancer directs their spells *through* you."

I laughed, but it sounded hollow even to my ears. "Really, Lord Blackbriar, you believe all the rumors whispered around town?"

Tori dropped his mount's reins and held up his hands in a calming gesture. "Please let me explain."

Yes, please do, Saraknyal snarled, *before we consume your soul!*

"I've long wondered," Tori began, "about your reticence to kill, to take souls, so different from other necromancers."

I scoffed. "*Other* necromancers? Since necromancy has been banned everywhere except Haven for centuries, I guess you've been reading fanciful tales, Tori!"

Waving a dismissive hand, he continued. "I deal in facts. At the gnomish mines, when I touched you to help you drink the restorative, I felt the truth; you have no inherent magical talent. Not a whiff of arcane ability."

"You *felt* it?" That took me aback. "*How?*"

I've never detected him casting a spell.

Tori's smile became pained, almost a grimace. "I *also* felt…a void in your soul. Hashi, that…that *thing* is consuming you bit by bit. Feeding on your soul!"

That's not true! I only took what you told me to take, Hashi! Only that one time! I swear it! Saraknyal sounded more hysterical than I'd ever heard him, and I didn't doubt his word for a moment.

"You're *wrong*, Lord Blackbriar." I seethed. "Soul Drinker *is* a soul blade, but I *consented* to him taking a portion of my soul. In fact, I *begged* him to take it!" It was the literal truth, despite lack of context, but I'd be damned if I'd explain to him.

"Why would you *do* such a thing?" A tear slipped from Tori's eye and tracked down his cheek.

"Don't you *dare* pity me, Tori Blackbriar! I did it to *survive!*" Drawing Soul Drinker, I eyed his enchanted sword. One on one, he outmatched me, but with my shades…

Tori moved his hands away from his sword. "Hashi, I mean you no harm. And I'd like to apologize."

I narrowed my eyes at him. "For what? Being a nosy *ass?*"

"Well, yes, that, but also for misunderstanding. For making assumptions. For not coming to you straightaway when I had questions. Although…" he quirked a smile "…I *did* try, but you're a hard woman to pin down."

I eyed him warily, still suspecting some ploy. "All right. Apology accepted."

"Don't worry, Hashi. I'll keep your secret. And I'd also like to apologize about not telling you the truth…about myself."

"What, so you're a wizard or something?"

"No. Not a wizard." He reached out tentatively, the other hand carefully away from his sword hilt. "May I?"

Don't, Hashi! Saraknyal warned.

My curiosity got the better of me, and I nodded shortly, but I raised Soul Drinker until the point lay lightly against his arm. I wasn't stupid, after all. "If you're lying…"

"I'm not lying." Tori laid his hand on my shoulder, and suddenly changed before my eyes.

I drew a shocked breath, staring in awe. He was taller and slimmer, with sharper features and long, graceful ears. His large, almond-shaped eyes sat below curved brows, their pupils shifting in rainbow hues. His skin fairly glowed the hue of white gold.

"I am not a part-elven duelist in ill favor with the Fengotherond Court, Lady Severn, but a high elf of the House of Tree and Star." His voice chimed like sweet bells, beautiful and otherworldly.

Shocked beyond reason, I fought to maintain a neutral mien. I looked down at Tori's hand, then back into his eyes. *Chill of fear.*

Magic coursed through me…and nothing happened.

"Don't bother with that, Hashi," he said, leaving his hand on my shoulder. "The necromancer's magic can't touch me."

The fuck? Saraknyal cursed.

Tori chuckled, and it rang through me like music. "I heard that, necromancer. I don't fear your tricks, for my soul is my own. You have no power over me."

"You can *hear* him?" I blurted.

Holy shit! Saraknyal hissed.

I looked around at the bustling crowds along the quay, but none seemed to be paying us more than casual attention. "Why don't they—"

"They see only what I wish them to see, as always, Hashi." He withdrew his hand and was suddenly Tori Blackbriar again, the suave, arrogant duelist. "And I see that this...relationship of yours with Saraknyal isn't what I assumed."

"Yes, well..." I cleared my throat and put Soul Drinker back in its sheath. "We have a mutual understanding."

"So, I see." He arched an eyebrow. "This is unique in my experience. Might we come to a similar understanding?"

"What *kind* of understanding?" Elf or no, I still didn't trust him.

"I'd like to talk with you, Hashi," Tori said, then raised his hands to forestall the protest that rose to my lips. "*Just* talk. It can be on your terms, at a time and place of your choosing."

This again? Tori's desire for conversation wore on my nerves. "And what would we talk about?"

"Hashi, I've spent my entire *life* in pursuit of knowledge and the unraveling of puzzles, and you pose the greatest contradiction that I've encountered in...well...many, *many* years."

"Contradiction?" I asked, confused. "What contradiction?"

Tori shook his head as if in wonderment at my ignorance. "You are...*extraordinary*, Hashi Severn. Your soul has been riven, and yet, even so injured, you resist the evil."

His intensity took me aback. "What the hell are you talking about?"

Um, I think he's talking about me, Hashi. And he's right, you know.

"What?" I realized I'd spoken aloud, and cringed. *What do you mean he's right?*

*I'm a necromancer, Hashi. I consumed souls for centuries to further my own power, to extend my life, to *rule*. I've goaded you for almost fifty years to follow that same path, and you've resisted. Others wouldn't have. You are *most* extraordinary."

"He speaks to you even now," Tori said, "telling you to use that blade, to have your shades slay me."

I shook my head with a rueful smile. "No, he's actually *agreeing* with you!"

Tori blinked and reeled back. "What?"

"He's telling me you're right. I've...resisted the temptation, but..." I looked away. "It doesn't matter. My soul is damned anyway. I might as well—"

"No!" Tori stepped right up to me and put both hands on my shoulders, ignoring the menacing growls from my shades. "You are *not* damned, Hashi! You still feel compassion, you *care* for people, you're not wholly corrupted. I *see* that in you!"

I stared into Tori's eyes, saw no deception there, but then, I'd also seen how well he concealed his true self. If he spoke the truth, this changed everything, but could I trust him? There was only one way to find out, but I'd do it on my own terms. Not Tori's, not Saraknyal's, but mine.

"What's in it for me, if I agree to talk with you?" I asked.

You're not thinking of actually doing this, are you? Saraknyal sounded panicked.

Tori smiled and lowered his hands from my shoulders. "You, too, are a seeker of knowledge, a historian, yes? Well, I am two thousand forty-two years old, Hashi. I've seen empires rise and fall; dragons hatch, grow, and wither of their own greed and loneliness; trees sprout from seed, grow sky high, and die of old age. Surely we can find *something* of interest to discuss."

My mind stumbled at the thought: two millennia of history, not in books, not written by the winners, but experienced first-hand.

Not a good idea, Hashi. He's an elf! He'll put a spell on you, if he hasn't already!

You'd know if he put a spell on me.

Well, yes, but...

He's two thousand years old, Saraknyal! Think of all the history...

*He's *seducing* you, Hashi, with the one thing you can't resist: the promise of knowledge!*

Probably true, but in this case, I don't see the harm in being seduced.

Tori's smile faltered. "You're discussing it with him?"

"Yes." I cleared my throat and licked my lips. "He's not exactly *comfortable* with you."

"Then we're even," he admitted. "I'm not interested in *him*, Hashi, but *you*."

That's what worries me, Saraknyal warned.

I looked into Tori's eyes and took a leap of faith. "All right. Tonight, at Ash Keep. We'll talk, but I have one stipulation."

Tori sketched a graceful bow. "Name it."

"You leave the elf blade at the door." I pointed at the sword at his hip.

"Of course." He flashed that damned gorgeous smile of his one last time. "I'll bring the wine."

About the Author

Born and raised in Oregon, Chris meet his wife and soulmate, Anne, while attending graduate school in Texas. Since then they have been nigh inseparable: gaming together since 1985, sailing together since 1988, married since 1989, and writing together off and on throughout their relationship. Most astonishingly, they have not killed each other during the creation or editing of any of their stories…although it was close a few times. Since 2009, the couple has been sailing and writing full-time aboard their beloved sailboat, *Mr Mac*. They return to the US every summer for conventions, always happy to sign copies of their books and talk with fans.

Preview Chris' books and get updates on upcoming events at jaxbooks.com. Follow Chris and Anne's cruising adventures at www.sailmrmac.blogspot.com.

Novels by Chris A. Jackson

From Jaxbooks
A Soul for Tsing
Deathmask

Blood Sea Tales
The Pirate's Scourge
The Pirate's Truth
The Pirate's Bane
Ash Walker
Blood Walker (2022)
Death Walker (2023)

Weapon of Flesh Series
Weapon of Flesh
Weapon of Blood
Weapon of Vengeance
Weapon of Fear *
Weapon of Pain *
Weapon of Mercy *
(* with Anne L. McMillen-Jackson)

The Cornerstones Trilogy
(with Anne L. McMillen-Jackson)
Zellohar
Nekdukarr
Jundag

The Cheese Runners Trilogy
(novellas – also on Audible)
Cheese Runners
Cheese Rustlers
Cheese Lords

Check out these and more at
JAXBOOKS.COM
Want to get an email about my next book release?
Sign up at http://eepurl.com/xnrUL

www.ingramcontent.com/pod-product-compliance
Lightning Source LLC
Chambersburg PA
CBHW071201250626
47159CB00001B/159

* 9 7 8 1 9 3 9 8 3 7 2 8 8 *